GROTTO OF THE DANCING DEER

GROTTO OF THE DANCING DEER

AND OTHER STORIES

The Complete Short Fiction
of Clifford D. Simak,
Volume Four

Introduction by David W. Wixon

OPEN ROAD

INTEGRATED MEDIA
NEW YORK

"Over the River and Through the Woods" © 1965 by Ziff-Davis Publishing Company. © 1993 by the Estate of Clifford D. Simak. Originally published in *Amazing Stories*, v. 39, no. 5, May, 1965.

"Grotto of the Dancing Deer" © 1980 by The Conde Nast Publications, Inc. Originally published in *Analog*, v. 100, no. 4, April, 1980.

"The Reformation of Hangman's Gulch" © 1944 by Popular Publications, Inc. © 1972 by Clifford D. Simak. Originally published in *Big-Book Western Magazine*, v. 14, no. 4, Dec., 1944.

"The Civilization Game" © 1958 by Galaxy Publishing Corporation. © 1986 by Clifford D. Simak. Originally published in *Galaxy Magazine*, v. 17, no. 1, November, 1958.

"Crying Jag" © 1959 by Galaxy Publishing Corp. © 1987 by Clifford D. Simak. Originally published in *Galaxy Magazine*, v. 18, no. 3, Feb., 1960.

"Hunger Death" © 1938 by Street & Smith Publications, Inc. © 1966 by Clifford D. Simak. Originally published in *Astounding Science Fiction*, v. 22, no. 2, Oct., 1938.

"Mutiny on Mercury" © 1931 by Gernsback Publications, Inc. © 1959 by Clifford D. Simak. Originally published in *Wonder Stories*, v. 3, no. 10, March, 1932.

"Jackpot" © 1956 by Galaxy Publishing Corp. © 1984 by Clifford D. Simak. Originally published in *Galaxy Science Fiction*, v. 12, no. 6, October, 1956.

"Day of Truce" © 1962 by Galaxy Publishing Corp. © 1990 by the Estate of Clifford D. Simak. Originally published in *Galaxy Magazine*, v. 21, no. 3, Feb., 1963.

"Unsilent Spring" © 1976 by Random House, Inc. © 2004 by Richard S. Simak and the Estate of Clifford D. Simak. First appeared in *STELLAR NO. 2 SCIENCE FICTION STORIES*, ed. by Judy-Lynn del Rey, Ballantine Books. Reprinted by permission of the Estates of Clifford D. Simak and Richard S. Simak.

Introduction copyright © 2015 by David W. Wixon

Cover design by Jason Gabbert

978-1-5040-6034-9

Published in 2020 by Open Road Integrated Media, Inc.
180 Maiden Lane
New York, NY 10038
www.openroadmedia.com

CONTENTS

Introduction: The Language of Clifford D. Simak   vii

Over the River and Through the Woods   1
Grotto of the Dancing Deer   13
The Reformation of Hangman's Gulch   35
The Civilization Game   87
Crying Jag   117
Hunger Death   143
Mutiny on Mercury   179
Jackpot   207
Day of Truce   253
Unsilent Spring   279

INTRODUCTION: THE LANGUAGE OF CLIFFORD D. SIMAK

"The day the barn caved in, Pa was ready to admit flat out that there was something to what Butch's Pa had said. It was all Ma could do to keep him from going up the road to see Andy Carter and talk to him by hand."

—*Clifford D. Simak, in "No Life of Their Own"*

One of the most notable features of the works, and particularly the earliest short stories, of Clifford D. Simak was his frequent use of colloquial language; in fact, sometimes his characters became so "colloquial" as to suggest parody. And such usages were particularly jarring when they came from the mouths of people working in a highly technological environment like outer space (see "Mr. Meek Plays Polo" for one example). To modern ears and eyes, such language appears completely unrealistic. Who would believe that future people would be so primitive, so uneducated?

Some of these usages, I would suggest, were deliberate, exaggerations intended to remind us that the future would still have a place for people with simple lives reflecting simple mores, even if they had to handle complicated technologies. How better to show that the character typically found in down-home, unsophisticated country dwellers would continue to be around in the future?

It should not be thought that such language represented how Simak himself spoke. Keep in mind that he was a teacher for several years before he went into journalism, that he worked in journalism at a high level for more than 45 years, and that he wrote and sold both fiction and nonfiction. (The nonfiction books, as well as the long-running series he created for his newspaper, were of a scientific nature.) And I will attest, from personal experience, that neither Cliff nor his brother spoke in such fashion.

It seems likely that Cliff, during his youth in a rural area of the early twentieth century, knew people who spoke in a rough fashion, and that when portraying similar types he exaggerated their distinctive speech for effect. But that's all it was: a tool used to make a point in the stories. Clifford Simak had learned not to let an apparent lack of polish, the veneer of a "civilized" lifestyle, mislead him into rejecting the value of those people, their abilities, and their humanity.

So when Bat Ears Brady says (in "Junkyard") that "'there's been planets . . . I wouldn't of minded so much being marooned on, but this ain't one of them. This here place is the tail end of creation'"—don't let it blind you to the man's common sense and inherent dignity.

To modern readers, Simak's use of a variety of now-dated phrases—phrases that might once have been familiar to midwestern Americans, but that have now passed out of common usage—may seem strange.

For example, the expression *tin shinny* appears in several of Cliff's early stories. It refers to a hockey-like game boys used to play in the streets using tree branches and a flattened tin can. And although one theory states that the word *shinny* comes from an old Scottish game, the spirit of the American game—and of Cliff's use of the phrase—can best be understood if you think of what a sharply struck flattened tin can might do to one's shins. If you played tin shinny, you knew how to take your lumps and give some back; you could play rough.

The Internet aids modern readers (I count myself one) who find themselves puzzled, even taken aback, when they first run across some of the language Cliff used in his fiction. And although I called myself a "modern reader" a moment ago, I don't have to resort to my computer to understand the meaning underlying the title of "Party Line." I'm old enough to have experienced a party line, and to understand that Cliff, in using the phrase, was making an analogy between the situation in the story and the era when rural telephone subscribers often had to share a single (hard-wired, as they say now) telephone line strung out from the nearest small town into the countryside. The consequence: Everyone on that line could, if they wished (and they often did), listen in on the conversations of their neighbors.

And when Cliff refers to "an old whippoorwill chunking up the hollow" (seen in other iterations as "chugging") in his novel *Why Call Them Back from Heaven?*, he is simply using now-dated rural speech to describe the sound made by that species of bird calling in the night from somewhere up in the farther reaches of a small valley. (He also utilizes a word that mimics the sound, a literary device occurring in many of his stories.)

Better known, perhaps, is the phrase *Dadburn the kid*, which Gramp Stevens mutters on the first page of the short story "City." Cliff specifically pointed at that expression when pulling "City" and its related stories into book form (*City*), painting with some amusement the puzzlement it brought to the doggy historians of the far future, who clearly did not inherit humankind's extensive stock of mild expletives.

The phrases *By Lord!*, *Thank Lord!*, and *I be damned!* appeared frequently in his earlier stories, but were eventually laid aside. My first, widely separated, readings of those phrases in Cliff's stories made me think that some typesetter had omitted the words *the* or *will*, but once I began to reread a lot of that older fiction over a short span of time, I realized that the same wording came up too many times to be mere mistakes: The phrases popped up the way Cliff wrote them, and perhaps that was the way they were said in the time and place of Cliff's youth. (I myself grew up with the phrase *used to*, as in *We used to go to the lake,* Cliff's variation of that phrase in "Earth for Inspiration, *They never use to come back,* irritated me more than I would expect because of that missing *D.*

Other expressions include *Indian sign,* which once meant calling down a curse or hex on someone; *tying a tin can* to someone, which meant firing them from their job; and the frequent references to the word *radium* in Cliff's early stories seem to be pre-Atomic Age references to atomic power.

Clifford D. Simak was already a professional newspaperman when he began to write fiction, and that fact explains much of the dialogue found in his earliest stories. For instance, he tended not to use contractions—they were not often used by journalists—which makes his earliest attempts at dialogue seem stilted, at least at some times.

Another reason Cliff's dialogue was bad in those early days was that he simply had no practice at writing dialogue—you don't do that in newspapers, usually. So he learned to do dialogue by reading other people's stories. And back in the 1930s, much of that was dreadful.

But Cliff learned.

David W. Wixon

OVER THE RIVER
AND THROUGH THE WOODS

The great message in the stories of Clifford D. Simak is that simple country people—and equally simple nonhuman beings—can be more understanding, and less afraid, in the face of the strange and the alien than many would think or expect; that the lessons learned in their apparently humdrum lives are as good as most to help them deal with something new. In other words, the value system we know as "common sense" retains its worth in a changing world.

"Over the River and Through the Woods" originally appeared in the May 1965 issue of Amazing Stories, *and it's a sweet reflection of Cliff Simak's love for his maternal grandmother, Ellen Parker.*

—dww

I

The two children came trudging down the lane in apple-canning time, when the first goldenrods were blooming and the wild asters large in bud. They looked, when she first saw them, out the kitchen window, like children who were coming home from school, for each of them was carrying a bag in which might have been their books. Like Charles and James, she thought, like Alice and Maggie—but the time when those four had trudged the lane on their daily trips to school was in the distant past. Now they had children of their own who made their way to school.

She turned back to the stove to stir the cooking apples, for which the wide-mouthed jars stood waiting on the table, then once more looked out the kitchen window. The two of them were closer now and she could see that the boy was the older of the two—ten, perhaps, and the girl no more than eight.

They might be going past, she thought, although that did not seem too likely, for the lane led to this farm and to nowhere else.

They turned off the lane before they reached the barn and came sturdily trudging up the path that led to the house. There was no hesitation in them; they knew where they were going.

She stepped to the screen door of the kitchen as they came onto the porch and they stopped before the door and stood looking up at her.

The boy said: "You are our grandma. Papa said we were to say at once that you were our grandma."

"But that's not . . ." she said, and stopped. She had been about to say that it was impossible, that she was not their grandma. And, looking down into the sober, childish faces, she was glad that she had not said the words.

"I am Ellen," said the girl, in a piping voice.

"Why, that is strange," the woman said. "That is my name, too."

The boy said, "My name is Paul."

She pushed open the door for them and they came in, standing silently in the kitchen, looking all about them as if they'd never seen a kitchen.

"It's just like Papa said," said Ellen. "There's the stove and the churn and . . ."

The boy interrupted her. "Our name is Forbes," he said.

This time the woman couldn't stop herself. "Why, that's impossible," she said. "That is our name, too."

The boy nodded solemnly. "Yes, we knew it was."

"Perhaps," the woman said, "you'd like some milk and cookies."

"Cookies!" Ellen squealed, delighted.

"We don't want to be any trouble," said the boy. "Papa said we were to be no trouble."

"He said we should be good," piped Ellen.

"I am sure you will be," said the woman, "and you are no trouble."

In a little while, she thought, she'd get it straightened out.

She went to the stove and set the kettle with the cooking apples to one side, where they would simmer slowly.

"Sit down at the table," she said. "I'll get the milk and cookies."

She glanced at the clock, ticking on the shelf. Four o'clock, almost. In just a little while the men would come in from the fields. Jackson Forbes would know what to do about this; he had always known.

They climbed up on two chairs and sat there solemnly, staring all about them, at the ticking clock, at the wood stove with the fire glow showing through its draft, at the wood piled in the wood box, at the butter churn standing in the corner.

They set their bags on the floor beside them, and they were strange bags, she noticed. They were made of heavy cloth or canvas, but there were no drawstrings or straps to fasten them. But they were closed, she saw, despite no straps or strings.

"Do you have some stamps?" asked Ellen.

"Stamps?" asked Mrs. Forbes.

"You must pay no attention to her," said Paul. "She should not have asked you. She asks everyone and Mama told her not to."

"But stamps?"

"She collects them. She goes around snitching letters that other people have. For the stamps on them, you know."

"Well now," said Mrs. Forbes, "there may be some old letters. We'll look for them later on."

She went into the pantry and got the earthen jug of milk and filled a plate with cookies from the jar. When she came back they were sitting there sedately, waiting for the cookies.

"We are here just for a little while," said Paul. "Just a short vacation. Then our folks will come and get us and take us back again."

Ellen nodded her head vigorously. "That's what they told us when we went. When I was afraid to go."

"You were afraid to go?"

"Yes. It was all so strange."

"There was so little time," said Paul. "Almost none at all. We had to leave so fast."

"And where are you from?" asked Mrs. Forbes.

"Why," said the boy, "just a little ways from here. We walked just a little ways and of course we had the map. Papa gave it to us and he went over it carefully with us . . ."

"You're sure your name is Forbes?"

Ellen bobbed her head. "Of course it is," she said.

"Strange," said Mrs. Forbes. And it was more than strange, for there were no other Forbes in the neighborhood except her children and her grandchildren and these two, no matter what they said, were strangers.

They were busy with the milk and cookies and she went back to the stove and set the kettle with the apples back on the front again, stirring the cooking fruit with a wooden spoon.

"Where is Grandpa?" Ellen asked.

"Grandpa's in the field. He'll be coming in soon. Are you finished with your cookies?"

"All finished," said the girl.

"Then we'll have to set the table and get the supper cooking. Perhaps you'd like to help me."

Ellen hopped down off the chair. "I'll help," she said.

"And I," said Paul, "will carry in some wood. Papa said I should be helpful. He said I could carry in the wood and feed the chickens and hunt the eggs and . . ."

"Paul," said Mrs. Forbes, "it might help if you'd tell me what your father does."

"Papa," said the boy, "is a temporal engineer."

II

The two hired men sat at the kitchen table with the checkerboard between them. The two older people were in the living room.

"You never saw the likes of it," said Mrs. Forbes. "There was this piece of metal and you pulled it and it ran along another metal strip and the bag came open. And you pulled it the other way and the bag was closed."

"Something new," said Jackson Forbes. "There may be many new things we haven't heard about, back here in the sticks. There are inventors turning out all sorts of things."

"And the boy," she said, "has the same thing on his trousers. I picked them up from where he threw them on the floor when he went to bed and I folded them and put them on the chair. And I saw this strip of metal, the edges jagged-like. And the clothes they wear. That boy's trousers are cut off above his knees and the dress that the girl was wearing was so short . . ."

"They talked of plains," mused Jackson Forbes, "but not the plains we know. Something that is used, apparently, for folks to travel in. And rockets—as if there were rockets every day and not just on the Earth."

"We couldn't question them, of course," said Mrs. Forbes. "There was something about them, something I sensed."

Her husband nodded. "They were frightened, too."

"You are frightened, Jackson?"

"I don't know," he said, "but there are no other Forbes. Not close, that is. Charlie is the closest and he's five miles away. And they said they walked just a little piece."

"What are you going to do?" she asked. "What can we do?"

"I don't rightly know," he said. "Drive in to the county seat and talk with the sheriff, maybe. These children must be lost. There must be someone looking for them."

"But they don't act as if they're lost," she told him. "They knew they were coming here. They knew we would be here. They told me I was their grandma and they asked after you and they called you Grandpa. And they are so sure. They don't act as if we're strangers. They've been told about us. They said they'd stay just a little while and that's the way they act. As if they'd just come for a visit."

"I think," said Jackson Forbes, "that I'll hitch up Nellie after breakfast and drive around the neighborhood and ask some questions. Maybe there'll be someone who can tell me something."

"The boy said his father was a temporal engineer. That just don't make sense. Temporal means the worldly power and authority and . . ."

"It might be some joke," her husband said. "Something that the father said in jest and the son picked up as truth."

"I think," said Mrs. Forbes, "I'll go upstairs and see if they're asleep. I left their lamps turned low. They are so little and the house is strange to them. If they are asleep, I'll blow out the lamps."

Jackson Forbes grunted his approval. "Dangerous," he said, "to keep lights burning of the night. Too much chance of fire."

III

The boy was asleep, flat upon his back—the deep and healthy sleep of youngsters. He had thrown his clothes upon the floor when he had undressed to go to bed, but now they were folded neatly on the chair, where she had placed them when she had gone into the room to say goodnight.

The bag stood beside the chair and it was open, the two rows of jagged metal gleaming dully in the dim glow of the lamp. Within its shadowed interior lay the dark forms of jumbled possessions, disorderly, and helter-skelter, no way for a bag to be.

She stooped and picked up the bag and set it on the chair and reached for the little metal tab to close it. At least, she told herself, it should be closed and not left standing open. She grasped the tab and it slid smoothly along the metal tracks and then stopped, its course obstructed by an object that stuck out.

She saw it was a book and reached down to rearrange it so she could close the bag. And as she did so, she saw the title in its faint gold lettering across the leather backstrap—*Holy Bible.*

With her fingers grasping the book, she hesitated for a moment, then slowly drew it out. It was bound in an expensive black leather that was dulled with age. The edges were cracked and split and the leather worn from long usage. The gold edging of the leaves was faded.

Hesitantly, she opened it and there, upon the flyleaf, in old and faded ink, was the inscription:

> *To Sister Ellen*
> *From Amelia*
> *Oct. 30, 1896*
>
> *Many Happy Returns of the Day*

She felt her knees grow weak and she let herself carefully to the floor and there, crouched beside the chair, read the flyleaf once again.

Oct. 30 1896—that was her birthday, certainly, but it had not come as yet, for this was only the beginning of September, 1896.

And the Bible—how old was this Bible she held within her hands? A hundred years, perhaps, more than a hundred years.

A Bible, she thought—exactly the kind of gift Amelia would give her. But a gift that had not been given yet, one that could not be given, for that day upon the flyleaf was a month into the future.

It couldn't be, of course. It was some kind of stupid joke. Or some mistake. Or a coincidence, perhaps. Somewhere else someone else was named Ellen and also had a sister who was named Amelia and the date was a mistake—someone had written the wrong year. It would be an easy thing to do.

But she was not convinced. They had said the name was Forbes and they had come straight here and Paul had spoken of a map so they could find the way.

Perhaps there were other things inside the bag. She looked at it and shook her head. She shouldn't pry. It was been wrong to take the Bible out.

On Oct. 30 she would be fifty-nine—an old farm-wife with married sons and daughters and grandchildren who came to visit her on weekends and on holidays. And a sister Amelia who, in this year of 1896, would give her a Bible as a birthday gift.

Her hands shook as she lifted the Bible and put it back into the bag. She'd talk to Jackson when she went down stairs. He might have some thought upon the matter and he'd know what to do.

She tucked the book back into the bag and pulled the tab and the bag was closed. She set it on the floor again and looked at the boy upon the bed. He still was fast asleep, so she blew out the light.

In the adjoining room little Ellen slept, baby-like, upon her stomach. The low flame of the turned-down lamp flickered gustily in the breeze that came through an open window.

Ellen's bag was closed and stood squared against the chair with a sense of neatness. The woman looked at it and hesitated for a moment, then moved on around the bed to where the lamp stood on a bedside table.

The children were asleep and everything was well and she'd blow out the light and go downstairs and talk with Jackson, and perhaps there'd be no need for him to hitch up Nellie in the morning and drive around to ask questions of the neighbors.

As she leaned to blow out the lamp, she saw the envelope upon the table, with the two large stamps of many colors affixed to the upper right-hand corner.

Such pretty stamps, she thought—I never saw so pretty. She leaned closer to take a look at them and saw the country name upon them. Israel. But there was no such actual place as Israel. It was a Bible name, but there was no country. And if there were no country, how could there be stamps?

She picked up the envelope and studied the stamp, making sure that she had seen right. Such a pretty stamp!

She collects them, Paul had said. She's always snitching letters that belong to other people.

The envelope bore a postmark, and presumably a date, but it was blurred and distorted by a hasty, sloppy cancellation and she could not make it out.

The edge of a letter sheet stuck a quarter inch out of the ragged edges where the envelope had been torn open and she pulled it out, gasping in her haste to see it while an icy fist of fear was clutching at her heart.

It was, she saw, only the end of a letter, the last page of a letter, and it was in type rather than in longhand—type like one saw in a newspaper or a book.

Maybe one of those new-fangled things they had in big city offices, she thought, the ones she'd read about. Typewriters—was that what they were called?

Do not believe, the one page read, *your plan is feasible. There is no time. The aliens are closing in and they will not give us time.*

And there is the further consideration of the ethics of it, even if it could be done. We can not, in all conscience, scurry back into the past and visit our problems upon the people of a century ago. Think of the problems it would create for them, the economic confusion and the psychological effect.

If you feel that you must, at least, send the children back, think a moment of the wrench it will give those two good souls when they realize the truth. Theirs is a smug and solid world—sure and safe and sound. The concepts of this mad century would destroy all they have, all that they believe in.

But I suppose I cannot presume to counsel you. I have done what you asked. I have written you all I know of our old ancestors back on that Wisconsin farm. As historian of the family, I am sure my facts are right. Use them as you see fit and God have mercy on us all.

Your loving brother,

Jackson

P.S. A suggestion. If you do send the children back, you might send along with them a generous supply of the new cancer-inhibitor drug. Great-great-grandmother Forbes died in 1904 of a condition that I suspect was cancer. Given those pills, she might survive another ten or twenty years. And what, I ask you, brother, would that mean to this tangled future? I don't pretend to know. It might save us. It might kill us quicker. It might have no effect at all. I leave the puzzle to you.

If I can finish up work here and get away, I'll be with you at the end.

Mechanically she slid the letter back into the envelope and laid it upon the table beside the flaring lamp.

Slowly she moved to the window that looked out on the empty lane.

They will come and get us, Paul had said. But would they ever come? Could they ever come?

She found herself wishing they would come. Those poor people, those poor frightened children caught so far in time.

Blood of my blood, she thought, flesh of my flesh, so many years away. But still her flesh and blood, no matter how removed. Not only these two beneath this roof tonight, but all those others who had not come to her.

The letter had said 1904 and cancer and that was eight years away—she'd be an old, old woman then. And the signature had been Jackson—an old family name, she wondered, carried on and on, a long chain of people who bore the name of Jackson Forbes?

She was stiff and numb, she knew. Later she'd be frightened. Later she would wish she had not read the letter, did not know.

But now she must go back downstairs and tell Jackson the best way that she could.

She moved across the room and blew out the light and went out into the hallway.

A voice came from the open door beyond.

"Grandma, is that you?"

"Yes, Paul," she answered. "What can I do for you?"

In the doorway she saw him crouched beside the chair, in the shaft of moonlight pouring through the window, fumbling at the bag.

"I forgot," he said. "There was something papa said I was to give you right away."

GROTTO OF
THE DANCING DEER

Winner of both the Hugo and the Nebula Awards, "Grotto of the Dancing Deer" originally appeared in the April 1980 issue of Analog Science Fiction and Fact. *The story demonstrates yet again Cliffora Simak's perennial interests in immortality, prehistoric man, and cave paintings—but it also explores his recurring theme of loneliness.*

—*dww*

1

Luis was playing his pipe when Boyd climbed the steep path that led up to the cave. There was no need to visit the cave again; all the work was done, mapping, measuring, photographing, extracting all possible information from the site. Not only the paintings, although the paintings were the important part of it. Also there had been the animal bones, charred, and the still remaining charcoal of the fire in which they had been charred; the small store of natural earths from which the pigments used by the painters had been compounded—a cache of valuable components, perhaps hidden by an artist who, for some reason that could not now be guessed, had been unable to use them; the atrophied human hand, severed at the wrist (why had it been severed and, once

severed, left there to be found by men thirty millennia removed?);
the lamp formed out of a chunk of sandstone, hollowed to accommodate a wad of moss, the hollow filled with fat, the moss serving
as a wick to give light to those who painted. All these and many
other things, Boyd thought with some satisfaction; Gavarnie had
turned out to be, possibly because of the sophisticated scientific
methods of investigation that had been brought to bear, the most
significant cave painting site ever studied—perhaps not as spec-
tacular, in some ways, as Lascaux, but far more productive in the
data obtained.

No need to visit the cave again, and yet there was a reason—
the nagging feeling that he had passed something up, that in the
rush and his concentration on the other work, he had forgotten
something. It had made small impression on him at the time,
but now, thinking back on it, he was becoming more and more
inclined to believe it might have importance. The whole thing
probably was a product of his imagination, he told himself. Once
he saw it again (if, indeed, he could find it again, if it were not a
product of retrospective worry), it might prove to be nothing at
all, simply an impression that had popped up to nag him.

So here he was again, climbing the steep path, geologist's
hammer swinging at his belt, large flashlight clutched in hand,
listening to the piping of Luis who perched on a small terrace,
just below the mouth of the cave, a post he had occupied through
all the time the work was going on. Luis had camped there in his
tent through all kinds of weather, cooking on a camper's stove,
serving as self-appointed watchdog, on alert against intruders,
although there had been few intruders other than the occasional
curious tourist who had heard of the project and tramped miles
out of the way to see it. The villagers in the valley below had been
no trouble; they couldn't have cared less about what was happening on the slope above them.

Luis was no stranger to Boyd; ten years before, he had shown
up at the rock shelter project some fifty miles distant and there

had stayed through two seasons of digging. The rock shelter had not proved as productive as Boyd initially had hoped, although it had shed some new light on the Azilian culture, the tag-end of the great Western European prehistoric groups. Taken on as a common laborer, Luis had proved an apt pupil and as the work went on had been given greater responsibility. A week after the work had started at Gavarnie, he had shown up again.

"I heard you were here," he'd said. "What do you have for me?"

As he came around a sharp bend in the trail, Boyd saw him, sitting cross-legged in front of the weather-beaten tent, holding the primitive pipe to his lips, piping away.

That was exactly what it was—piping. Whatever music came out of the pipe was primitive and elemental. Scarcely music, although Boyd would admit that he knew nothing of music. Four notes—would it be four notes? he wondered. A hollow bone with an elongated slot as a mouthpiece, two drilled holes for stops.

Once he had asked Luis about it. "I've never seen anything like it," he had said. Luis had told him, "You don't see many of them. In remote villages here and there, hidden away in the mountains "

Boyd left the path and walked across the grassy terrace, sat down beside Luis, who took down the pipe and laid it in his lap.

"I thought you were gone," Luis said. "The others left a couple of days ago."

"Back for one last look," said Boyd.

"You are reluctant to leave it?"

"Yes, I suppose I am."

Below them the valley spread out in autumn browns and tans, the small river a silver ribbon in the sunlight, the red roofs of the village a splash of color beside the river.

"It's nice up here," said Boyd. "Time and time again, I catch myself trying to imagine what it might have been like at the time the paintings were done. Not much different than it is now, perhaps. The mountains would be unchanged. There'd have been no fields in the valley, but it probably would have been natural pasture. A few trees here and there, but not too many of them. Good hunting. There'd have been grass for the grazing animals. I have even tried to figure out where the people would've camped. My guess would be where the village is now."

He looked around at Luis. The man still sat upon the grass, the pipe resting in his lap. He was smiling quietly, as if he might be smiling to himself. The small black beret sat squarely on his head, his tanned face was round and smooth, the black hair close-clipped, the blue shirt open at the throat. A young man, strong, not a wrinkle on his face.

"You love your work," said Luis.

"I'm devoted to it. So are you, Luis," Boyd said.

"It's not my work."

"Your work or not," said Boyd, "you do it well. Would you like to go with me? One last look around."

"I need to run an errand in the village."

"I thought I'd find you gone," said Boyd. "I was surprised to hear your pipe."

"I'll go soon," said Luis. "Another day or two. No reason to stay but, like you, I like this place. I have no place to go, no one needing me. Nothing's lost by staying a few more days."

"As long as you like," said Boyd. "The place is yours. Before too long, the government will be setting up a caretaker arrangement, but the government moves with due deliberation."

"Then I may not see you again," said Luis.

"I took a couple of days to drive to Roncesvalles," said Boyd. "That's the place where the Gascons slaughtered Charlemagne's rearguard in 778."

"I've heard of the place," said Luis.

"I'd always wanted to see it. Never had the time. The Char-lemagne chapel is in ruins, but I am told masses are still said in the village chapel for the dead paladins. When I returned from the trip, I couldn't resist the urge to see the cave again."

"I am glad of that," said Luis. "May I be impertinent?"

"You're never impertinent," said Boyd.

"Before you go, could we break bread once more together? Tonight, perhaps. I'll prepare an omelet."

Boyd hesitated, gagging down a suggestion that Luis dine with him. Then he said, "I'd be delighted, Luis. I'll bring a bottle of good wine."

2

Holding the flashlight centered on the rock wall, Boyd bent to examine the rock more closely. He had not imagined it; he had been right. Here, in this particular spot, the rock was not solid. It was broken into several pieces, but with the several pieces flush with the rest of the wall. Only by chance could the break have been spotted. Had he not been looking directly at it, watching for it as he swept the light across the wall, he would have missed it. It was strange, he thought, that someone else, during the time they had been working in the cave, had not found it. There'd not been much that they'd missed.

He held his breath, feeling a little foolish at the holding of it, for, after all, it might mean nothing. Frost cracks, perhaps, although he knew that he was wrong. It would be unusual to find frost cracks here.

He took the hammer out of his belt and, holding the flashlight in one hand, trained on the spot, he forced the chisel end of the hammer into one of the cracks. The edge went in easily. He pried gently and the crack widened. Under more pressure, the piece of rock moved out. He laid down the hammer and flash, seized the slab of rock and pulled it free. Beneath it were two other slabs and they both came free as easily as the first. There were others as well and he also took them out. Kneeling on the floor of the cave, he directed the light into the fissure that he had uncovered.

Big enough for a man to crawl into, but at the prospect he remained for the moment undecided. Alone, he'd be taking a chance to do it. If something happened, if he should get stuck, if a fragment of rock should shift and pin him or fall upon him, there'd be no rescue. Or probably no rescue in time to save him. Luis would come back to the camp and wait for him, but should he fail to make an appearance, Luis more than likely would take it as a rebuke for impertinence or an American's callous disregard of him. It would never occur to him that Boyd might be trapped in the cave.

Still, it was his last chance. Tomorrow he'd have to drive to Paris to catch his plane. And this whole thing was intriguing; it was not something to be ignored. The fissure must have some significance; otherwise, why should it have been walled up so carefully? Who, he wondered, would have walled it up? No one, certainly, in recent times. Anyone, finding the hidden entrance to the cave, almost immediately would have seen the paintings and would have spread the word. So the entrance to the fissure must have been blocked by one who would have been unfamiliar with the significance of the paintings or by one to whom they would have been commonplace.

It was something, he decided, that could not be passed up; he would have to go in. He secured the hammer to his belt, picked up the flashlight and began the crawl.

The fissure ran straight and easy for a hundred feet or more. It offered barely room enough for crawling, but, other than that, no great difficulties. Then, without warning, it came to an end. Boyd lay in it, directing the flash beam ahead of him, staring in consternation at the smooth wall of rock that came down to cut the fissure off.

It made no sense. Why should someone go to the trouble of walling off an empty fissure? He could have missed something on the way, but thinking of it, he was fairly sure he hadn't. His progress had been slow and he had kept the flash directed ahead of him every inch of the way. Certainly if there had been anything out of the ordinary, he would have seen it.

Then a thought came to him and slowly, with some effort, he began to turn himself around, so that his back rather than his front, lay on the fissure floor. Directing the beam upward, he had his answer. In the roof of the fissure gaped a hole.

Cautiously, he raised himself into a sitting position. Reaching up, he found handholds on the projecting rock and pulled himself erect. Swinging the flash around, he saw that the hole opened, not into another fissure, but into a bubblelike cavity, small, no more than six feet in any dimension. The walls and ceiling of the cavity were smooth, as if a bubble of plastic rock had existed here for a moment at some time in the distant geologic past when the mountains had been heaving upward leaving behind it as it drained away a bubble forever frozen into smooth and solid stone.

As he swung the flash across the bubble, he gasped in astonishment. Colorful animals capered around the entire expanse of stone. Bison played leapfrog. Horses cantered in a chorus line. Mammoths turned somersaults. All around the bottom perimeter, just above the floor, dancing deer, standing on their hind legs, joined hands and jigged, antlers swaying gracefully.

"For the love of Christ!" said Boyd.

Here was Stone Age Disney.

If it was the Stone Age. Could some jokester have crawled into the area in fairly recent times to paint the animals in this grotto? Thinking it over, he rejected the idea. So far as he had been able to ascertain, no one in the valley, nor in the entire region, for that matter, had known of the cave until a shepherd had found it several years before when a lamb had blundered into it. The entrance was small and apparently for centuries had been masked by a heavy growth of brush and bracken.

Too, the execution of the paintings had a prehistoric touch to them. Perspective played but a small part. The paintings had that curious flat look that distinguished most prehistoric art.

There was no background—no horizon line, no trees, no grass or flowers, no clouds, no sense of sky. Although, he reminded himself, anyone who had any knowledge of cave painting probably would have been aware of all these factors and worked to duplicate them.

Yet, despite the noncharacteristic antics of the painted animals, the pictures did have the feeling of cave art. What ancient man, Boyd asked himself, what kind of ancient man, would have painted gamboling bison and tumbling mammoths? While the situation did not hold in all cave art, all the paintings in this particular cave were deadly serious—conservative as to form and with a forthright, honest attempt to portray the animals as the artists had seen them. There was no frivolity, not even the imprint of paint-smeared human hands as so often happened in other caves. The men who had worked in this cave had not as yet been corrupted by the symbolism that had crept in, apparently rather late in the prehistoric painting cycle.

So who had been this clown who had crept off by himself in this hidden cavern to paint his comic animals? That he had been an accomplished painter there could be no doubt. This artist's techniques and executions were without flaw.

Boyd hauled himself up through the hole, slid out onto the two-foot ledge that ran all around the hole, crouching, for there was no room to stand. Much of the painting, he realized, must have been done with the artist lying flat upon his back, reaching up to the work on the curving ceiling.

He swept the beam of the flashlight along the ledge. Halfway around, he halted the light and jiggled it back and forth to focus upon something that was placed upon the ledge, something that undoubtedly had been left by the artist when he had finished his work and gone away.

Leaning forward, Boyd squinted to make out what it was. It looked like the shoulder blade of a deer; beside the shoulder blade lay a lump of stone.

Cautiously, he edged his way around the ledge. He had been right. It was the shoulder blade of a deer. Upon the flat surface of it lay a lumpy substance. Paint? he wondered, the mixture of animal fat and mineral earths the prehistoric artists used as paints? He focused the flash closer and there was no doubt. It was paint, spread over the surface of the bone which had served as a palette, with some of the paint lying in thicker lumps ready for use, but never used, paint dried and mummified and bearing imprints of some sort. He leaned close, bringing his face down to within a few inches of the paint, shining the light upon the surface. The imprints, he saw, were fingerprints, some of them sunk deep— the signature of that ancient, long-dead man who had worked here, crouching even as Boyd now crouched, shoulders hunched against the curving stone. He put out his hand to touch the palette, then pulled it back. Symbolic, yes, this move to touch, this reaching out to touch the man who painted—but symbolic only; a gesture with too many centuries between.

He shifted the flashlight beam to the small block of stone that lay beside the shoulder blade. A lamp—hollowed-out sandstone, a hollow to hold the fat and the chunk of moss that served as a wick. The fat and wick were long since gone, but a thin film of soot still remained around the rim of the hollow that had held them.

Finishing his work, the artist had left his tools behind him, had even left the lamp, perhaps still guttering, with the fat almost finished—had left it here and let himself down into the fissure, crawling it in darkness. To him, perhaps, there was no need of light. He could crawl the tunnel by touch and familiarity. He must have crawled the route many times, for the work upon these walls had taken long, perhaps many days.

So he had left, crawling through the fissure, using the blocks of stone to close the opening to the fissure, then had walked away, scrambling down the slope to the valley where grazing herds had lifted their heads to watch him, then had gone back to grazing.

But when had this all happened? Probably, Boyd told himself, after the cave itself had been painted, perhaps even after the paintings in the cave had lost much of whatever significance they originally would have held—one lone man coming back to paint his secret animals in his secret place. Painting them as a mockery of the pompous, magical importance of the main cave paintings? Or as a protest against the stuffy conservatism of the original paintings? Or simply as a bubbling chuckle, an exuberance of life, perhaps even a joyous rebellion against the grimness and the simplemindedness of the hunting magic? A rebel, he thought, a prehistoric rebel—an intellectual rebel? Or, perhaps, simply a man with a viewpoint slightly skewed from the philosophy of his time?

But this was that other man, that ancient man. Now how about himself? Having found the grotto, what did he do next? What would be the best way to handle it? Certainly he could not turn his back upon it and walk away, as the artist, leaving his palette and his lamp behind him, had walked away. For this was an important discovery. There could be no question of that. Here was a new and unsuspected approach to the prehistoric mind, a facet of ancient thinking that never had been guessed.

Leave everything as it lay, close up the fissure and make a phone call to Washington and another one to Paris, unpack his bags and settle down for a few more weeks of work. Get back the photographers and other members of the crew—do a job of it. Yes, he told himself, that was the way to do it.

Something lying behind the lamp, almost hidden by the sandstone lamp, glinted in the light. Something white and small.

Still crouched over, Boyd shuffled forward to get a better look.

It was a piece of bone, probably a leg bone from a small grazing animal. He reached out and picked it up and, having seen what it was, hunched unmoving over it, not quite sure what to make of it.

It was a pipe, a brother to the pipe that Luis carried in his jacket pocket, had carried in his pocket since that first day he'd met him, years ago. There was the mouthpiece slot, there the two round stops. In that long-gone day when the paintings had been done the artist had hunched here, in the flickering of the lamp, and had played softly to himself, those simple piping airs that Luis had played almost every evening, after work was done.

"Merciful Jesus," Boyd said, almost prayerfully, "it simply cannot be!"

He stayed there, frozen in his crouch, the thoughts hammering in his mind while he tried to push the thoughts away. They would not go away. He'd drive them away for just a little distance, then they'd come surging back to overwhelm him.

Finally, grimly, he broke the trance in which the thoughts had held him. He worked deliberately, forcing himself to do what he knew must be done.

He took off his windbreaker and carefully wrapped the shoulder blade palette and the pipe inside, leaving the lamp. He let himself down into the fissure and crawled, carefully protecting the bundle that he carried. In the cave again, he meticulously fitted the blocks of stone together to block the fissure mouth, scraped together handfuls of soil from the cave floor and smeared it on the face of the blocks, wiping it away, but leaving a small clinging film to mask the opening to all but the most inquiring eye.

Luis was not at his camp on the terrace below the cave mouth; he was still on his errand into the village.

When he reached his hotel, Boyd made his telephone call to Washington. He skipped the call to Paris.

3

The last leaves of October were blowing in the autumn wind and a weak sun, not entirely obscured by the floating clouds, shone down on Washington

John Roberts was waiting for him on the park bench. They nodded at one another, without speaking, and Boyd sat down beside his friend.

"You took a big chance," said Roberts. "What would have happened if the customs people . . ."

"I wasn't too worried," Boyd said. "I knew this man in Paris. For years he's been smuggling stuff into America. He's good at it and he owed me one. What have you got?"

"Maybe more than you want to hear."

"Try me."

"The fingerprints match," said Roberts.

"You were able to get a reading on the paint impressions?"

"Loud and clear."

"The FBI?"

"Yes, the FBI. It wasn't easy, but I have a friend or two."

"And the dating?"

"No problem. The bad part of the job was convincing my man this was top secret. He's still not sure it is."

"Will he keep his mouth shut?"

"I think so. Without evidence no one would believe him. It would sound like a fairy story."

"Tell me."

"Twenty-two thousand. Plus or minus three hundred years."

"And the prints do match. The bottle prints and . . ."

"I told you they match. Now will you tell me how in hell a man who lived twenty-two thousand years ago could leave his prints on a wine bottle that was manufactured last year."

"It's a long story," said Boyd. "I don't know if I should. First, where do you have the shoulder blade?"

"Hidden," said Roberts. "Well hidden. You can have it back, and the bottle, any time you wish."

Boyd shrugged. "Not yet. Not for a while. Perhaps never."

"Never?"

"Look, John, I have to think it out."

"What a hell of a mess," said Roberts. "No one wants the stuff. No one would dare to have it. Smithsonian wouldn't touch it with a ten-foot pole. I haven't asked. They don't even know about it. But I know they wouldn't want it. There's something, isn't there, about sneaking artifacts out of a country . . ."

"Yes, there is," said Boyd.

"And now you don't want it."

"I didn't say that. I just said let it stay where it is for a time. It's safe, isn't it?"

"It's safe. And now . . ."

"I told you it is a long story. I'll try to make it short. There's this man—a Basque. He came to me ten years ago when I was doing the rock shelter . . ."

Roberts nodded. "I remember that one."

"He wanted work and I gave him work. He broke in fast, caught onto the techniques immediately. Became a valuable man. That often happens with native laborers. They seem to have the feel for their own antiquity. And then when we started work on the cave he showed up again. I was glad to see him. The two of us, as a matter of fact, are fairly good friends. On my last night at the cave he cooked a marvelous omelet—eggs, tomato, green pimentos, onions, sausages and home-cured ham. I brought a bottle of wine."

"*The* bottle?"

"Yes, *the* bottle."

"So go ahead."

"He played a pipe. A bone pipe. A squeaky sort of thing. Not too much music in it . . ."

"There was a pipe . . ."

"Not that pipe. Another pipe. The same kind of pipe, but not the one our man has. Two pipes the same. One in a living man's pocket, the other beside the shoulder blade. There were things about this man I'm telling you of. Nothing that hit you between the eyes. Just little things. You would notice something and then, some time later, maybe quite a bit later, there'd be something else, but by the time that happened, you'd have forgotten the first incident and not tie the two together. Mostly it was that he knew too much. Little things a man like him would not be expected to know. Even things that no one knew. Bits and pieces of knowledge that slipped out of him, maybe without his realizing it. And his eyes. I didn't realize that until later, not until I'd found the second pipe and began to think about the other things. But I was talking about his eyes. In appearance he is a young man, a never-aging man, but his eyes are old . . ."

"Tom, you said he is a Basque."

"That's right."

"Isn't there some belief that the Basques may have descended from the Cro-Magnons?"

"There is such a theory. I have thought of it."

"Could this man of yours be a Cro-Magnon?"

"I'm beginning to think he is."

"But think of it—twenty thousand years!"

"Yes, I know," said Boyd.

4

Boyd heard the piping when he reached the bottom of the trail that led up to the cave. The notes were ragged, torn by the wind. The Pyrenees stood up against the high blue sky.

Tucking the bottle of wine more securely underneath his arm, Boyd began the climb. Below him lay the redness of the village rooftops and the sere brown of autumn that spread across the valley. The piping continued, lifting and falling as the wind tugged at it playfully.

Luis sat cross-legged in front of the tattered tent. When he saw Boyd, he put the pipe in his lap and sat waiting.

Boyd sat down beside him, handing him the bottle. Luis took it and began working on the cork.

"I heard you were back," he said. "How went the trip?"

"It went well," said Boyd.

"So now you know," said Luis.

Boyd nodded. "I think you wanted me to know. Why should you have wanted that?"

"The years grow long," said Luis. "The burden heavy. It is lonely, all alone."

"You are not alone."

"It's lonely when no one knows you. You now are the first who has really known me."

"But the knowing will be short. A few years more and again no one will know you."

"This lifts the burden for a time," said Luis. "Once you are gone, I will be able to take it up again. And there is something . . ."

"Yes, what is it, Luis?"

"You say when you are gone there'll be no one again. Does that mean . . ."

"If what you're getting at is whether I will spread the word, no, I won't. Not unless you wish it. I have thought on what would happen to you if the world were told."

"I have certain defenses. You can't live as long as I have if you fail in your defenses."

"What kind of defenses?"

"Defenses. That is all."

"I'm sorry if I pried. There's one other thing. If you wanted me to know, you took a long chance. Why, if something had gone wrong, if I had failed to find the grotto . . ."

"I had hoped, at first, that the grotto would not be necessary. I had thought you might have guessed, on your own."

"I knew there was something wrong. But this is so outrageous I couldn't have trusted myself even had I guessed. You know it's outrageous, Luis. And if I'd not found the grotto . . . Its finding was pure chance, you know."

"If you hadn't, I would have waited. Some other time, some other year, there would have been someone else. Some other way to betray myself."

"You could have told me."

"Cold, you mean?"

"That's what I mean. I would not have believed you, of course. Not at first."

"Don't you understand? I could not have told you. The concealment now is second nature. One of the defenses I talked about. I simply could not have brought myself to tell you, or anyone."

"Why me? Why wait all these years until I came along?"

"I did not wait, Boyd. There were others, at different times. None of them worked out. I had to find, you must understand, someone who had the strength to face it. Not one who would run screaming madly. I knew you would not run screaming."

"I've had time to think it through," Boyd said. "I've come to terms with it. I can accept the fact, but not too well, only barely. Luis, do you have some explanation? How come you are so different from the rest of us?"

"No idea at all. No inkling. At one time, I thought there must be others like me and I sought for them. I found none. I no longer seek."

The cork came free and he handed the bottle of wine to Boyd. "You go first," he said steadily.

Boyd lifted the bottle and drank. He handed it to Luis. He watched him as he drank. Wondering, as he watched, how he could be sitting here, talking calmly with a man who had lived, who had stayed young through twenty thousand years. His gorge rose once again against acceptance of the fact—but it had to be a fact. The shoulder blade, the small amount of organic matter still remaining in the pigment, had measured out to 22,000 years.

There was no question that the prints in the paint had matched the prints upon the bottle. He had raised one question back in Washington, hoping there might be evidence of hoax. Would it have been possible, he had asked, that the ancient pigment, the paint used by the prehistoric artist, could have been reconstituted, the fingerprints impressed upon it, and then replaced in the grotto? Impossible was the answer. Any reconstitution of the pigment, had it been possible, would have shown up in the analysis. There had been nothing of the sort—the pigment dated to 20,000 years ago. There was no question of that.

"All right, Cro-Magnon," said Boyd, "tell me how you did it. How does a man survive as long as you have? You do not age, of course. Your body will not accept disease. But I take it you are not immune to violence or to accident. You've lived in a violent world. How does a man sidestep accident and violence for two hundred centuries?"

"There were times early," Luis said, "when I came close to not surviving. For a long time, I did not realize the kind of thing I was. Sure, I lived longer, stayed younger than all the others—I would guess, however, that I didn't begin to notice this until I began to realize that all the people I had known in my early life were dead—dead for a long, long time. I knew then that I was different from the rest. About the same time others began to notice I was different. They became suspicious of me. Some of them resented me. Others thought I was some sort of evil spirit. Finally I had to flee the tribe. I became a skulking outcast. That was when I began to learn the principles of survival."

"And those principles?"

"You keep a low profile. You don't stand out. You attract no attention to yourself. You cultivate a cowardly attitude. You are never brave. You take no risks. You let others do the dirty work. You never volunteer. You skulk and run and hide. You grow a skin that's thick; you don't give a damn what others think of you. You shed all your noble attributes, your social consciousness. You shuck your loyalty to tribe or folk or country. You're not a patriot. You live for yourself alone. You're an observer, never a participant. You scuttle around the edges of things. And you become so self-centered that you come to believe that no blame should attach to you, that you are living in the only logical way a man can live. You went to Roncesvalles the other day, remember?"

"Yes. I mentioned I'd been there. You said you'd heard of it."

"Heard of it. Hell, I was there the day it happened—August 15, 778. An observer, not a participant. A cowardly little bastard who tagged along behind the noble band of Gascons who did in Charlemagne. Gascons, hell. That's the fancy name for them. They were Basques, pure and simple. The meanest crew of men who ever drew the breath of life. Some Basques may be noble, but not this band. Not the kind of warriors who'd stand up face to face with the Franks. They hid up in the pass and rolled rocks down on all those puissant knights. But it wasn't the knights who held their interest. It was the wagon train. They weren't out to fight a war or to avenge a wrong. They were out for loot. Although little good it did them."

"Why do you say that?"

"It was this way," said Luis. "They knew the rest of the Frankish army would return when the rearguard didn't come up and they had not the stomach for that. They stripped the dead knights of their golden spurs, their armor and fancy clothes, the money bags they carried and loaded all of it on the wagons and got out of there. A few miles further on, deep in the mountains, they holed up and hid. In a deep canyon where they thought they would be safe. But if they should be found, they had what amounted to a fort. A half mile or so below the place they camped, the canyon narrowed and twisted sharply. A lot of boulders had fallen down at that point, forming a barricade that could have been held by a handful of men against any assault that could be launched against it. By this time, I was a long way off. I smelled something wrong,

I knew something most unpleasant was about to happen. That's another thing about this survival business. You develop special senses. You get so you can smell out trouble, well ahead of time. I heard what happened later."

He lifted the bottle and had another drink. He handed it to Boyd.

"Don't leave me hanging," said Boyd. Tell me what did happen."

"In the night," said Luis, "a storm came up. One of those sudden, brutal summer thunderstorms. This time it was a cloudburst. My brave fellow Gascons died to the man. That's the price of bravery."

Boyd took a drink, lowered the bottle, held it to his chest, cuddling it.

"You know about this," he said. "No one else does. Perhaps no one had ever wondered what happened to those Gascons who gave Charlemagne the bloody nose. You must know of other things. Christ, man, you've lived history. You didn't stick to this area."

"No. At times I wandered. I had an itching foot. There were things to see. I had to keep moving along. I couldn't stay in one place any length of time or it would be noticed that I wasn't aging."

"You lived through the Black Death," said Boyd. "You watched the Roman legions. You heard first hand of Attila. You skulked along on Crusades. You walked the streets of ancient Athens."

"Not Athens," said Luis. "Somehow Athens was never to my taste. I spent some time in Sparta. Sparta, I tell you—that was really something."

"You're an educated man," said Boyd. "Where did you go to school?"

"Paris, for a time, in the fourteenth century. Later on at Oxford. After that at other places. Under different names. Don't try tracing me through the schools that I attended."

"You could write a book," said Boyd. "It would set new sales records. You'd be a millionaire. One book and you'd be a millionaire."

"I can't afford to be a millionaire. I can't be noticed and millionaires are noticed. I'm not in want. I've never been in want. There's always treasure for a skulker to pick up. I have caches here and there. I get along all right."

Luis was right, Boyd told himself. He couldn't be a millionaire. He couldn't write a book. In no way could he be famous, stand out in any way. In all things, he must remain, unremarkable, always anonymous.

The principles of survival, he had said. And this part of it, although not all of it. He had mentioned the art of smelling trouble, the hunch ability. There would be, as well, the wisdom, the street savvy, the cynicism that a man would pick up along the way, the expertise, the ability to judge character, an insight into human reaction, some knowledge concerning the use of power, power of every sort, economic power, political power, religious power.

Was the man still human, he wondered, or had he, in 20,000 years, become something more than human? Had he advanced that one vital step that would place him beyond humankind, the kind of being that would come after man?

"One thing more," said Boyd. "Why the Disney paintings?"

"They were painted some time later than the others," Luis told him. "I painted some of the earlier stuff in the cave. The fishing bear is mine. I knew about the grotto. I found it and said nothing. No reason I should have kept it secret. Just one of those little items one hugs to himself to make himself important. I know something you don't know—silly stuff like that. Later I came back to paint the grotto. The cave art was so deadly serious. Such terribly silly magic. I told myself painting should be fun. So I came back, after the tribe had moved and painted simply for the fun of it. How did it strike you, Boyd?"

"Damn good art," said Boyd.

"I was afraid you wouldn't find the grotto and I couldn't help you. I knew you had seen the cracks in the wall; I watched you one day looking at them. I counted on your remembering them. And I counted on you seeing the fingerprints and finding the pipe. All pure serendipity, of course. I had nothing in mind when I left the paint with the fingerprints and the pipe. The pipe, of course was the tip-off and I was confident you'd at least be curious. But I couldn't be sure. When we ate that night, here by the campfire, you didn't mention the grotto and I was afraid you'd blown it. But when you made off with the bottle, sneaking it away, I knew I had it made. And now the big question. Will you let the world in on the grotto paintings?"

"I don't know. I'll have to think about it. What are your thoughts on the matter?"

"I'd just as soon you didn't."

"Okay," said Boyd. "Not for the time at least. Is there anything else I can do for you? Anything you want?"

"You've done the best thing possible," said Luis. "You know who I am, what I am. I don't know why that's so important to me, but it is. A matter of identity, I suppose. When you die, which I hope will be a long time from now, then, once again, there'll be no one who knows. But the knowledge that one man did know, and what is more important, understood, will sustain me through the centuries. A minute—I have something for you."

He rose and went into the tent, came back with a sheet of paper, handing it to Boyd. It was a topographical survey of some sort.

"I've put a cross on it," said Luis. "To mark the spot."

"What spot?"

"Where you'll find the Charlemagne treasure of Roncesvalles. The wagons and the treasure would have been carried down the canyon in the flood. The turn in the canyon and the boulder barricade I spoke of would have blocked them. You'll find them there, probably under a deep layer of gravel and debris."

Boyd looked up questioningly from the map.

"It's worth going after," said Luis. "Also it provides another check against the validity of my story."

"I believe you," said Boyd. "I need no further evidence."

"Ah, well," said Luis, "it wouldn't hurt. And now, it's time to go."

"Time to go! We have a lot to talk about."

"Later, perhaps," said Luis. "We'll bump into one another from time to time. I'll make a point we do. But now it's time to go."

He started down the path and Boyd sat watching him.

After a few steps, Luis halted and half-turned back to Boyd.

"It seems to me," he said in explanation, "it's always time to go."

Boyd stood and watched him move down the trail toward the village. There was about the moving figure a deep sense of loneliness—the most lonely man in all the world.

THE REFORMATION
OF HANGMAN'S GULCH

Described by an unnamed editor as a "smashing owlhoot novel," "The Reformation of Hangman's Gulch" was originally published in the December 1944 issue of Big-Book Western Magazine, *which, at that time, bore a cover price of fifteen cents. In this and perhaps a couple other westerns, Clifford Simak displays his apparent fascination with the way smoke from a burning cigarette can rise up into the eyes of the smoker.*

—dww

Chapter I
Six-Gun Invitation

A gust of wind swept up the canyon and set the thing that hung in the cottonwood to swaying. Stanley Packard's horse shied, skittish, as the rope creaked against the limb. Packard spoke softly to the animal and reached out to pat its neck.

The horse quieted and Packard spurred closer, staring up at the man who hung there. Something familiar in that grotesque shape, something that struck a chord of memory in him.

A cloud sailed clear of the moon and light struck down through the autumn-thinned leaves of the mighty tree . . . light that for a moment revealed the face bent at an awkward angle against the hangman's knot.

The eyes were open in terror and the pressure of the rope pressed the jaws tighter than they should have been, but there was no mistaking the face. Too many times had Packard seen that face, leering eyes squinted against the smoke that drooled from a cigarette hanging from its lips. Hanging could not change the tiny, well-cared-for mustache nor death wipe away the old knife scar that ran along the cheek.

The body swayed slowly, like a pendulum, and the dead eyes stared at the moon. The boots dangled pitifully, toes hanging down, as if the man were reaching for the earth. The hands were tied behind the back and a tiny stream of blood had drooled from one corner of the mouth, leaving a dark stain meandering down the chin.

A sudden chill struck into Packard, a chill that was not of the autumn night. Swiftly he looked around, panic rising in him.

But there was no sign of life except the twinkle of the few lights far down the canyon, lights that marked the outskirts of the town of Hangman's Gulch. Otherwise there was only rock and scrub, and here and there a tree, bare limbs lifted against the night.

Packard's hand went up to his coat, fingers pressing against the letter in the inside pocket. A rustle of paper told him it still was there.

He let his hand fall back again and shuddered. If that letter had caught up with him a little quicker, if he'd come a little sooner, there might have been two men on that limb instead of one.

Cardway, of course, hadn't written exactly what he had in mind. But it wasn't hard to guess, wasn't hard to read between the lines. Not too hard when Packard remembered the straight thin lips with the dangling cigarette that poured smoke into those leering, squinting eyes.

But now, he told himself, he'd never know for sure what Cardway had in mind. Men who decorate a cottonwood don't make explanations.

Carefully Packard backed his horse away from the cottonwood, back into the trail, headed once again for Hangman's Gulch.

The trail broadened out into a street as the canyon flared to make a pocket, with the shacks and tents that were Hangman's Gulch clambering up the two slopes.

Packard made note of places as the horse clopped down the street. A stagecoach stood, horseless, in front of the express office. The place blazed with light and two men armed with rifles sat just inside the door.

Sounds of revelry came from the Crystal Palace, the tinny tinkle of an out-of-tune piano, the shrill laughter of a woman, the drunken shout of some miner in to drink his dust.

In an empty restaurant a Chinese sprawled across a table, fast asleep. A barber next door trimmed industriously while a long row of men waited for the shears. Two men sat, hiked back in tilted chairs, in front of the livery stable. Just beyond stood a two-story structure, the word "Hotel" painted in a sprawl across one lighted window.

Packard pulled up at the stable, swung himself from the saddle. One of the men thumped down on his chair, clumped forward, picking his teeth with a stem of hay.

"Do somethin' for you, stranger?"

"Got any grain for the horse?" asked Packard. "He's been on the go all day."

The man shook his head. "Nothin' but hay. Good stuff, though. Can't get no grain freighted in. Costs too much."

Packard nodded, remembering the trail that he had covered. Freight would be costly along a road like that.

"If you come all the way from Devil's Slide," said the man, "you know what I mean."

Packard smiled tightly. He recognized the words as a way to ask a question in a country where questions were something one simply did not ask.

"No harm in saying I came from Devil's Slide, is there?" asked Packard.

The man scratched his chin with dirty fingernails. "Can't say as there is, stranger. Didn't happen to see anyone along the way, did you?"

"Aw, hell, Clint," said the man still tilted against the stable, "he wouldn't see anyone. The Canyon gang don't bother with nothin' except stagecoaches plumb weighed down with dust."

"Only man I saw," Packard told them, "was hanging in that old cottonwood just outside of town."

"Oh, him," said Clint. "He was a hombre who wandered in a couple weeks ago. The vigilantes got him."

"Vigilantes?"

"Damn tootin'," declared Clint. "This here town is plumb going to get civilized or bust a lung tryin'. Been too much hell-raisin' to suit the citizens."

"Shoot someone?" asked Packard.

The man tilted against the stable supplied the answer. "Yeah, he killed someone all right. One of the guards down at the express office."

Packard nodded. "I see. Trying to stick up the place."

"Hell no," said the man. "Just met him on the street in broad daylight and let him have it. Never gave no reason."

"Funny thing," said Packard.

"Ain't it," the man agreed.

"Must of knowed him somewhere else," Clint opined. "Maybe been followin' him."

The stable man moved away, leading the horse inside the barn.

"If you want to wash up," said the other man, "the horse trough is out in back."

Packard smiled. "Maybe I will," he said.

"Crystal Palace is the only bar in town," said the man, "and that place next door is the only hotel. If you don't go for hotels, Clint can fix you up a place where you can spread your blanket."

"Thanks," said Packard.

A man shuffled off the board sidewalk and moved through the darkness toward them. He was a small man, Packard saw, and he wore a checkered suit of black and white. A gold watch chain glittered across his vest.

His cheeks were puffed out like a gopher's scurrying home with a load of grain and his lips were puffed out, too, in what seemed an eternal pout. A jaunty mustache rode his upper lip and struck a grotesque note.

"Good evening, gentlemen," said the little man.

"Good evening," said the man in the chair.

"I'm looking for my eye," said the man. "You haven't seen it, have you?"

The chair crashed forward and the man in it was aghast.

"You're looking for your what!"

"My eye," explained the little man. "It fell out and I lost it."

He pointed toward the left side of his face, out of which stared an empty socket.

"It was a glass eye, you see," he said. "It would look something like a marble."

The man in the chair wheezed in bewilderment.

"No, I haven't seen it. What makes you think you lost it here?"

"Don't know where I lost it," explained the little man. "Got drunk, you see, and when I sobered up it wasn't there."

"Oh, I see."

"It might be most anywhere," said the little man.

"I'll keep a watch for it," the man in the chair promised.

"I wish you would," the other told him. "I feel undressed without it." He turned and shuffled off, head bent, as if looking for the eye.

The man in the chair looked up at Packard.

"We get the damndest people here," he apologized.

Packard stood with his elbows on the bar, nursing his drink and staring in the mirror.

The Crystal Palace roared with life. Through the buzz of voices came the clink of glasses, the whir of gambling wheels, occasionally the soft snick of chips from the poker tables in the back. In one corner an old man with a violin and a younger one with an accordion teamed with the out-of-tune piano, fought a losing battle with the throaty rumble that ran through the place.

So Preston Cardway had shot an express company guard and been hung by the vigilantes, his body left dangling in the tree as a sort of grim warning for any who might come riding down the trail!

Well, it was something anyhow, Packard told himself, staring at the bottle-stacked mirror, to have that kind of warning. Even if Cardway had to die to give it. Cardway, the damn fool, going off half-cocked and shooting down a man. Although he hardly could be blamed for thinking he could get away with it. In his day, Cardway had shot down many men in the main streets of many towns in broad daylight and gotten away with it. What reason could he have had to think it would be any different here?

Only there was something wrong. Something that didn't click somehow. Hangman's Gulch didn't seem the kind of town that was cleaning up, not the kind of place where vigilantes rode to bring law and order.

For one thing, Hangman's Gulch wasn't old enough. It still was new and raw, a boom town scarcely dry behind the ears. There was too much yip and ki-yi in it. Towns don't get civic conscious, Packard told himself, until the shiny newness is worn off of them.

A man elbowed his way through the throng, thrust himself alongside Packard. In the mirror, Packard studied him. A man with a white collar and a black cravat in which a diamond stickpin gleamed, the tie bunched above a fawn-colored vest that sported a slender chain with a dangling golden toothpick.

The man's mouth moved. "A stranger, aren't you?"

"That's right," said Packard, talking to the reflection in the mirror rather than the man himself. "Just rolled in tonight."

"My name," said the man, "is Jason Randall. Owner of this place. Saw you here. Wanted to tell you that you're welcome."

"Mine is Packard," Packard told him. "Stanley Packard. Just riding through."

"Thought maybe you might stick around," said Randall. "Lots of people do. Hangman's Gulch is a good town. Won't find none better between here and the coast."

Packard studied the man with open interest. A slick customer, he figured. Ruthless and mean. Glossy and soft like a spider squatting in his web.

Randall's eyes shifted away from Packard's, stared beyond his shoulder. Packard swung around. A man stood just inside the swinging doors. A tall, straight man who didn't wear a gun, a man whose silver hair was brushed back from his forehead like a gleaming crown of light, shining in the crystal lamps swaying from the ceiling. His head was high and he looked at the smoke-dimmed crowd with something that was close to pity on his face.

Someone on the floor saw the man standing by the door and shouted at him: "Hey, here's Preacher. Come on, Preacher, belly up. I'll stand you to a drink."

The man did not move, eyes still searching the crowd. A woman tittered, a shrill, high sound that cut across the wheezing music, the rumble of many voices, the clatter of the wheels.

The man saw Randall now, stood staring at him for a moment, Randall staring back. Then, slowly, the man paced forward. The crowd parted to let him pass. Faces turned after him.

He halted in front of Randall. His voice was low: "Mr. Randall, could I see you for a moment?"

"Reverend," boomed Randall, "anything you got to say to me, you can say right here."

"It is scarcely—" began the man, but Randall cut him short.

"You want me to close up."

The man nodded. "Sunday is the Lord's day," he said. "It is scarcely right that a place like this—"

"All that's the matter with you, Reverend," yelled Randall, "is that you're sore because I have a crowd and you don't have one. Because your two-bit sermons can't compete with what I offer here."

"It would only be for Sunday," said the minister. "Say, from Saturday midnight until Monday morning. I have no quarrel with what is done on other days of the week, but on Sunday, certainly, there should be some peace and decorum. Drunken men should not be sprawled on the street so that ladies who come to my church have to walk out in the street to get around them."

Randall spat on the floor. "Look, Reverend, you're sticking in your nose where you have no call. I'm attending to my business and you attend to yours. If both of us do that, we'll get along—"

Packard's hand reached out, closed on Randall's shoulder, spun him around with a vicious tug that pulled and twisted his coat tight against his body. With another savage tug, he drew the man close to him, so that their faces were no more than scant inches apart.

"Look," said Packard, "where I come from we hold some respect for men who wear the cloth. Maybe we don't agree with them, but at least we treat them decent."

"Why, you dirty . . ." Randall's hand was flashing toward his belt.

The minister moved swiftly, closing in on Randall, knocking his hand aside even as its fingers reached the gun. Deftly, the silver-haired man spun Randall's gun from out the holster, caught it in mid-air.

"Take it easy, Reverend," said Packard softly. "No use of you getting mixed up in this."

He shoved Randall backward, sent him crashing against the bar.

"I had my left fist filled all the time," said Packard. "If he'd ever got that gun I'd tore a hole dead center through his belly." He stared at Randall. "I don't like people who push other folks around," he said. "If you make a move or any of your men make a move, you'll be eating sawdust."

A deathly silence had fallen on the place, a brilliant silence that glittered in the lamplight.

"I don't care whether you close up or not," said Packard. "It ain't no skin off my nose either way around. But the next time you speak to the Reverend, be sure you are polite."

The silence held, a tense and breathless silence.

"Reverend," said Packard, "maybe you better get out of here. Seventeen different kinds of hell are apt to bust loose almost any—"

Packard's head exploded with a mighty roar. Roman candles speared across the darkness and burst with a screaming sound that spewed whirling stars . . . stars that grew in size and brilliance as they whirled until they were eye-searing balls of light. He was falling into a foaming sea of brilliant light and he hit it and went under and the light was dark.

Chapter II
Glass Balls—Glass Eyes

Slowly, Packard became aware of himself. Aware of pain that lanced across his head with throbbing, knife-like strokes. He raised his hands to his throbbing head.

"There, lad," said a gentle voice. "Just lie back again."

He groped for his belt, found the holster empty.

"Your guns are over on the table," said the voice.

Packard opened his eyes and light tortured them. He shut them again, but he knew that he was not on the floor of the Crystal Palace nor sprawling in the street nor heaved in some back alley as something that had died.

"The bartender," said the voice, "hit you with a bottle."

Carefully Packard opened his eyes again, saw the face of the silver-haired man bending over him.

"Hi, Reverend," he said.

"I wish you wouldn't call me that," the man told him. "My name is Page and they call me Preacher Page. Mostly just Preacher."

Packard hitched himself erect, saw that he had been lying on an old and battered sofa. Ponderously, he swung his feet to the floor, sat hunched on the sofa's edge.

"How did I get here?" he asked.

"I carried you," said Preacher Page. He chuckled. "It was the least I could do for you after what had happened."

Packard glanced about the room. It was furnished shabbily, but it had a certain touch . . . a touch of home. A rickety rocking chair stood in the corner and there was an old oblong table with a lamp placed upon an embroidered scarf. There were pictures on the wall and some books on shelves.

His guns, he saw, were on the table beside the lamp.

"So the bartender hit me," said Packard. "Then what happened?"

"Then one of Randall's gunmen jerked out his weapon and was pointing it at you and I shouted at him and waved the gun I'd taken from Randall. I told them: 'Gentlemen, I should regret to shoot you, but if you harm that young man, I shall have to do it.'"

"Would you have shot?" asked Packard.

The minister's face twisted in a grimace. "Fortunately, I didn't have to make that decision."

Shakily, Packard got to his feet, crossed to the table, picked up the guns. Expertly he broke them one by one, spun the cylinders to check the cartridges, slid them into his belt again.

"Thanks, Preacher," he said. "Thanks for all you did for me."

"But you aren't leaving?"

"Sure, I am. I got a date with Randall."

Preacher gasped. "But you can't. They'll be waiting for you. They'll—"

"If he wants to go, Father, let him go," said a voice from the doorway.

Packard swung around.

A girl stood there. A girl one would have known anywhere as Preacher Page's daughter. The same quiet face, the same level eyes. Plain, thought Packard. Plain, but pretty.

"Father," said the girl, speaking to Packard, "always is bringing home broken-down saddle tramps or young brawlers who happen to get hurt."

"But, Alice," protested the old man, "this gentleman stood up for me. He's the first man since I've come here who stood up for me—"

Thunderous knocking hammered at the outside door, and Packard spun around, right fist jerking clear a gun.

Preacher's voice snapped at him, a voice with the edge of steel. "Put that away. In this house there'll be no—"

"Preacher," snarled Packard. "Open up that door. And be sure you stand to one side when you do it."

"There'll be no shooting," said Preacher. "This is my house and there'll be—"

Packard took a step toward him. "You heard me! Open up that door . . . quick and fast!"

The gun came up and Preacher moved swiftly, lithely toward the door, swung it open with a jerk. In the fan of light that streamed out into the earth-packed yard stood a tall man, a man with hair graying at the temples, with cheeks that looked like tanned and wrinkled leather, a handle-bar mustache that drooped affectionately over the corners of his mouth.

"Howdy, Preacher," said the man.

"Hello, Hurley," said Preacher gravely.

Hurley's eyes fastened on Packard. "If you're Packard," he said, "I got to talk to you."

"Talk away," said Packard.

Swiftly the man stepped into the room, slammed the door behind him, stood with his back against it.

"You'd better hit the trail," said Hurley. "Stover's on the prod."

"Who's Stover?"

"Stover," explained Preacher Page, "is Randall's top-notch gun-hand. Deadly shot, I'm told."

"So am I," snapped Packard.

Hurley studied Packard quietly. "Just how good a shot?" he asked.

"Good enough for Stover," Packard told him. "Good enough for any of the two-bit gunmen who hanker for my blood. Learned it in a circus. Fellow rode ahead of me and threw up glass balls, fast. I shot them in the air."

"You should have stayed with the circus."

"I was agreeable," said Packard. "But they didn't keep me."

Hurley chewed at the corner of his mustache. "Found out who you were, huh?"

"That's right," said Packard. He stared at the man, a tight, grim-lipped stare. "How come you know?" he asked.

"I rode with your daddy," said Hurley. "Was with him when he died. Would know you anywhere. At that time he looked just like you do now."

Hurley looked at Page. "One word of this, Preacher," he warned, "and I personally will plumb tie you into knots."

"Gentlemen," said Page, "I haven't heard a thing."

Hurley opened the door, asked: "How about it, kid?"

Packard holstered his gun. "Just point out this Stover to me."

—

The board walks were frosty beneath their boots as Packard and Hurley climbed the steps that led to the porch of the Crystal Palace. Inside the lights still burned and a dawdling swamper wielded a broom. Back of the bar the bartender was yawning and cleaning up the glassware. A drunk was sleeping it off at a table in the corner.

Hurley led the way across the room toward a door that led into the back. The swamper went on sweeping and the bartender took no notice of them. The drunk snored and sputtered in his sleep, thrashing his arms on the table top.

Packard felt the hair stir at the base of his neck. There was something wrong, he knew. Nothing he could put his finger on, but something that was wrong. The way the swamper went on sweeping, the way the barkeeper yawned and went on polishing his glasses. Paying no attention to them. Almost as if they might have been expecting them.

"Hurley," said Packard. "Hurley, there's something . . ."

A faint sound warned him, the whispery creak of the swinging doors up front. Like a cat, he whirled, guns already coming out.

In the doorway stood a man, a man whose pistoning arms were a blur of motion, whose eyes were gimlets of steel shining in the light. Steel, like the gleam of light on glass balls spinning in the sunshine.

The man's guns were clear of leather and were swinging up and, behind him, the batwing doors swung gently to and fro, almost robbed of motion, but still swinging.

Flame exploded in Packard's hands, the blasting flame of jumping guns that bucked and hammered, filled the room to bursting with their roar.

The man in front of the batwing doors was slammed through them, hurled backward through them as if someone had grasped and hurled him with tremendous force. One of his guns was still in his hand, but the other spun from his fingers and skidded through the sawdust.

And then the doors were swinging violently, flapping to and fro and from under them protruded two boots, toes pointing toward the ceiling.

The barkeep stood with both hands spread upon the bar, amazement on his face. "I be damned," he said. "I be double-damned."

The swamper leaned upon his broom and stared. The drunk had come alive and was trying to burrow into the sawdust underneath his table.

The door in the back flung open and Randall stroke out. He stopped, staring at the boots, at the flapping doors.

Then, slowly, his gaze switched to Packard and Packard raised his guns.

"You next?" asked Packard.

Randall simply stared.

"By rights," said Hurley, coldly, "he'd ought to give it to you. You went and double-crossed us. It was supposed to be a fair fight."

Randall shrugged. "What difference does it make? Packard, here, won out."

"Four shots," said the bartender. "Four shots and every one dead center. Four shots before Stover hit the floor."

"What's going on here?" asked Packard coldly. "You gentlemen better start to talk."

Randall laughed shortly. "Hell," he said, "no use of getting riled. Packard, you just killed yourself a job."

"A job?"

"Sure, Stover's job. I'll need a man to take his place."

"I told you the kid had the right stuff in him. Just like his old man," Hurley told Randall.

"I don't want the stinking job," said Packard.

Packard turned on his heel and walked away. Through the silence of the room he heard the rasp of the swamper's broom, the still frightened gulping of the drunken man. At the door, he pushed the batwings wide and walked around the body of the man who'd tried to shoot him in the back.

Outside the air was crisp and new with the coming of the day. The stars were paling and Packard suddenly realized that he was sleepy and hungry.

The frost crunched crisply underfoot as he strode down the walk toward the hotel and suddenly his head felt light and giddy and the throb took up again . . . the throb of his scalp where the bottle had landed.

He walked slowly past the livery stable, where a smoky lantern burned redly in the office window. Out of the shadows of the alleyway between the stable and hotel a voice hissed at him.

Startled, Packard's right hand plunged for his gun, but the voice said: "Take it easy, Packard. I'm a friend of yours."

Hand still on the gunbutt, Packard stepped into the dim alleyway, saw the face of the man before him. A moonlike face, puffy and dissolute, with blubbery lips.

"Craig is the name," said moonface. "Cardway said you would be coming."

"Cardway's dead," snapped Packard. "I saw him, hanging in a tree. What was Cardway to you?"

Craig stepped closer. "We can get along without him, Packard. Just the two of us to split."

Packard frowned. "What about this man that Cardway killed?"

"Name of Jett," said Craig. "One of the express office guards. Same as I am."

"But why did Cardway kill him?"

The flabby face twisted impatiently in the shadow. "Jett was in with the Randall crowd. He heard us talking."

Packard's hand shot out, grasped the man's vest, twisted it tight and drew him close. "Talk sense," he snarled. "What has Randall got to do with it?"

Craig wriggled. "Didn't Cardway tell you?"

"Not a word," said Packard. "Just wrote to me and said that I should come. Said there was a good thing here."

"It's the gold," wheezed Craig. "Ready for shipment. Randall's gang holds up the stages. Easier and safer than holding up the office."

"This Jett was Randall's man, you say. Tipped him off when a big shipment was on hand."

Craig nodded vigorously. "You catch on quick. Cardway said you would. Said your dad . . ."

Packard jerked the man even closer.

"You say that Randall's gang holds up the stages. Who else knows this? Everyone in town?"

Craig gulped unhappily. "No sir, they don't. Just me now. You see, Cardway found it out and told me and now—"

"And Cardway figured on beating Randall to the draw. Figured on robbing the office before the stage ever started out."

Craig gulped again and nodded.

"And how much were you to get?"

"A quarter, Cardway said. Said I'd get a quarter and you and he would get the rest. But now that he's dead, I figured maybe you could do some better by me."

"Want me to tell you how much Cardway really would have given you?"

"He said a quarter."

"Not a damn ounce," said Packard coldly. "He'd use you and he'd shoot you down. You see, I knew Preston Cardway."

"But he said—"

"You shouldn't have stopped me here," snarled Packard. "Don't do a thing like this again. Don't speak to me again. Don't act like you've ever seen me. I'll look you up when it's safe to talk."

He released his hold upon the vest.

"Make tracks," he told Craig curtly.

A grim smile on his lips, he watched the man scuttle down the alleyway to be swallowed in the shadow.

Back on the street again, Packard sat down on the hotel steps and built himself a smoke.

So it had been gold that Cardway had been after. An inside job, fixed up with the office guards. Probably could have pulled it off, too, if it hadn't been for Randall. Randall, naturally, wouldn't have wanted anyone horning in and so Randall had fixed up a vigilante deal.

Packard's head hurt and it was hard to think and even through the pain of the throbbing head, he was so sleepy that his eyes drooped shut as he nodded over the cigarette.

Steps sounded on the boards and he snapped awake. Before him stood a little man with a checkered suit.

"Oh, it's you," said Packard.

The man squinted at him with his one good eye.

"Haven't seen an eye?" he asked. "A glass eye. I lost it and I've looked everywhere . . ."

"Oh, hell," exploded Packard. "I'm going up to bed."

He rose and climbed the stairs to the porch. The little man in the checkered suit stood and watched him go.

Chapter III
Like Father, Like Son

Jason Randall was sitting in the chair beside the window, smoking a cheroot and with a whisky bottle on the table at his elbow, when Packard awoke. 'You sleep innocent," said Randall.

Packard swung himself off the bed, located his boots, stomped his feet into them. "What the hell," he asked, "are you doing here?"

"Wanted to talk with you," said Randall, smoothly.

"I haven't got a thing to talk with you about," snarled Packard.

Randall did not press the point. "Weren't taking any chances, were you?" he asked. "Sleeping like that with your clothes on."

"I was too tired to take them off."

"Wouldn't want to be set for a quick getaway?"

Packard shucked his gunbelt to a more comfortable position.

"Look, Randall," he said, "I'm not making any quick getaway. When I leave this town I ride out, on my own horse, in broad daylight."

"I hope so," said Randall. "I most sincerely hope so." But he sounded as if it was just too much to expect. He reached out for the bottle, tipped it toward one of the two tumblers setting on the table. "Drink?" he asked.

Packard nodded. Watching Randall pour, he saw that the sun was slanting through the window before which Randall sat. It must be late afternoon, he told himself. An hour or so to sundown.

He crossed the room and took the tumbler, sat down on the edge of the table. "Let's have it, Randall," he demanded. "What's on your mind?"

"It's the job," said Randall. "The one that you turned down."

"I'm still turning it down," said Packard.

Randall clucked sympathetically. "And with jobs so hard to get . . . and keep."

"I'll find one," said Packard.

"Look," Randall told him, "there's no use of running a bluff on me. You can't keep a job and you know it. Your old man was an owlhooter and pretty well known at that. When whoever you're working for finds that out, you're hunting another job. You tried to change your name and it didn't work. Too many people knew your old man."

"Hurley's been talking to you," Packard said.

"Sure, why not? Hurley works for me."

"I didn't know, though I should have. So that deal with Stover was all cut and dried. Except maybe that you figured it would work out the other way."

"Don't go blaming Hurley," Randall warned. "If it hadn't been for him, you'd be buzzard meat right now. I was pretty sore, you see, the way you acted, and I told Stover to go out and finish you. But Hurley told me who you was, and said you should have a chance."

"A chance! With Stover sneaking in the door behind my back?"

"It wasn't planned that way," Randall told him. "It was to be fair and square. But Stover, the dog, double-crossed us all! Well, he got what was coming to him. It probably seemed pretty raw to you, but it wasn't meant to be. And a man who handles guns like you do is too good a man to let get away."

Packard shook his head. "I got other things to do."

"Like holding up the express office?" asked Randall.

The liquor in Packard's tumbler jerked and slopped, but he held his face steady. "Something like that," he admitted.

If Randall knew, there was no use denying it. "You saw Cardway out on the trail?" asked Randall. And when Packard nodded:

"Hell of a way to die," Randall said.

"Never aim to die that way," said Packard.

"Neither did Cardway," Randall told him.

He emptied his glass and set it down. "If it's gold you want, why not come in with me. It's safe. I run the town."

He drummed his fingers on the table. "Leastwise, I'm still running it. But I been sort of lax. One man I have to tighten up on."

"Preacher Page," said Packard, casually.

Randall nodded. "Threatening to ask for martial law," he said. "But it's not going to happen. I'll take care of Page.

"Let's put down our cards. You came here to hold up the express office. Probably you'd never done anything like that before, but more than likely you figured since you couldn't keep a job, you might as well be what people thought you were. You figured what the hell."

Packard nodded soberly.

"Well," continued Randall, "you can't hold up the express office, for I've got the gold staked out. Anyone that lifts a finger toward it is signing his death warrant."

He stared hard at Packard. "Agreed?" he asked.

"Agreed," said Packard.

"All right, then," said Randall, "let's get together. You can't hold any other sort of job than the one I'm offering you, for people always will find out just who you are and then out you go. And I need a man like you."

"I suppose," guessed Packard, "that if I refuse you'll try to fix it up so I don't leave town alive."

"Your reasoning," Randall told him, "is downright uncanny. Of course, if you have some ideas of your own . . . ?"

"Not a one," Packard told him.

"O.K.," said Randall, "you're on the payroll. Five hundred a month and splits."

"And my duties?"

"Act as if you aren't one of us. Build up the idea that you are out to get my pelt. I'll help the idea along a bit."

"Outside man," said Packard.

Randall nodded. "Exactly, except—except you're going to be on one hold-up. A big shipment is going out tomorrow. You'll ride out tonight."

"Just so I'm in deep," said Packard. "So I'm one of you."

"In this business," Randall told him, "we can't have any pure and holy hombres. Your neck's got to be nominated for the noose just like the rest of us."

"You," said Packard, "don't leave a single thing to chance, do you, Randall?"

"Not a thing," said Randall.

"And how will I know what I'm to do? Where I'm to go?"

"You'll be told," said Randall, shortly.

He pushed himself from the chair, walked across the room. At the door he turned back. "And you'll be watched," he added.

"I figured," said Packard, "that I would."

Listening to Randall's footsteps going down the hall, Packard reached out for the bottle, poured himself a drink and gulped it, set the tumbler back on the table again.

It was the only way that he could play it, he told himself, staring at the door. To have refused Randall's offer would have meant that he'd be dead before the hour had passed.

Getting up, he shucked his gunbelt, shaped his lips into a twisted grin. First he'd get some food. He jingled the few dollars left in his pocket and grinned. He could use some of that money Randall was paying him. Maybe he'd ought to go and hit him for something in advance.

At the Chinaman's, Packard hung his hat on a nail, sat down and gave his order.

The Chinaman prattled as he ran with knife and fork and plates. "You new man in town, maybe?"

"Maybe," agreed Packard.

"Maybe man who shot Stover?"

"Might be," said Packard.

"Good shooting," said the Chinaman.

He scuttled into the kitchen and out again.

"Preacher Page, he in to find out if you been in. Ask you go his place soon as you show up."

"Thanks," said Packard. He ate hurriedly, gulping his food and thinking.

He was glad that Page wanted to see him, glad that the man had inquired about him. It would be taking a chance with Randall to go and see the minister, but he had to take some chances. If Randall climbed him about it, he could say that in seeing Page he was merely out to create the impression he was not on Randall's side.

Dusk had fallen on the street outside and the first faint stars were beginning to glitter in the east. Packard leaned against the front of the restaurant and fashioned himself a cigarette, strolled leisurely away.

He recognized the twisting path down which he and Hurley had come the night before and took it, following its windings up the mountain side.

Halfway up, he stopped and rested. The climb was steep and he was not used to walking. Below him were the lights of Hangman's Gulch, a cluster of sparks in the gathering dark.

Steps came up the path and drew closer. A man stood outlined in the gloom. A hunched, bow-legged man who shambled in the deepening dusk. Five feet away he stopped. "What are you doing here?" he asked.

"Walking," said Packard.

The man moved closer. "If you're goin' where I think you're goin', you better change your mind."

"Why?" asked Packard, flatly.

"The boss wouldn't like you goin' to see Page."

Packard took a quick step forward and the man went for his gun. But Packard's fist beat the gun, smacked against the jaw.

The man snapped backward, straight and stiff, rocking on his heels, hit the ground with a thump that bounced him.

Bending over the fallen man, Packard yanked the gun out of his belt, heaved it into the brush. Still squatting, he rolled another cigarette, used the match that he struck to light it to study the man's face. But it rang no bells. If he'd seen him in the Crystal Palace, he did not remember it.

The man groaned and struggled to a sitting position, rubbed his hand tenderly against his jaw. His eyes found Packard, stared at him. His lips twisted. "The boss will get you for this," he mumbled.

"He set you to tail me?" asked Packard.

The man nodded.

"He didn't tell you to stop me from going anywhere or doing anything?"

"No, he didn't, but—"

"But he wouldn't want me to see Page."

"That's it," said the man. "He'll be sore as hell. Sore at both of us."

"How do you know he didn't send me to see Page?"

The man gaped. "Did he? Did the boss . . ."

"That," said Packard, "is none of your damn business."

Packard rose. "I'm going on," he said. "If you want to come, I don't mind. But see you stay behind . . . a long ways behind."

Page opened the door at Packard's knock, reached out a hand and dragged him in, thumped him on the back. "So you came," he said. "You saw the Chinaman."

Packard frowned. "Don't get your hopes up, Preacher. I know what you have in mind, and I can't do it."

The old man's silver hair was shining in the lamplight and the pictures were on the wall and the books still on the shelves. From the kitchen came the smell of frying meat and the quick, swift tap of a woman's feet.

"But you killed Stover," Page protested. "You gunned the fastest gunman this town has ever known. You got him even when he was sneaking up behind you, with his guns half out."

"What's your proposition?" Packard asked, flatly.

"A marshal's badge," said Page. "A marshal's badge and other men to back you up."

"Marshal's badges," said Packard, "can't be picked up anywhere."

"I can get you one," Page told him.

"And while you're talking the authorities into giving me one, what am I to do?"

"You'll leave town tonight. There's a trail over the mountain and I have a horse. You can get your men."

"I haven't any men," said Packard.

"But . . . but . . ."

"Sure," said Packard, "you're just like the rest of them. You've got me pegged for an owlhoot rider. You figure that maybe I kill a man every day for breakfast. You figure that I have a band of curly wolves hidden out somewhere and that if you could get me to bring them in, we'd wipe out Randall's gang in one grand blaze of gunfire."

"But," protested Page, "there would be compensations. Blanket pardons and—"

"I haven't done a thing," said Packard, "to be pardoned for, except maybe shooting Stover and that was self-defense. And I haven't any men. So forget your dream of using me to clean up the town for you."

The old man slumped into a chair, face suddenly haggard. "It was wrong of me," he said, almost as if he were speaking to someone who wasn't in the room. "It was not my way of doing, nor my church's way of doing, but sometimes a man's vision can be clouded. Force is wrong . . . as wrong for me to use as it is for Randall. But I was tempted. I saw a way to make this a decent town . . ."

"I'm sorry, Preacher," Packard said.

"Don't," said a voice from the doorway, "waste any sorrow on us."

Packard jerked his head around and saw the girl. He took off his hat. "Good evenin', miss," he said.

"I wish you wouldn't come here," she said, tartly. "It's bad enough with Hurley seeing father all the time. I've told him that he ought to go away where he wouldn't meet men like that. There isn't any reason that he should stay out here when he could go somewhere else, some place that's civilized."

"Don't pay any attention to her," begged Page. "She's angry. Angry because I'm sending her east to school. This isn't any place for a woman to stay."

But Packard scarcely heard the old man. He was looking at the girl. "Miss," he said, "just to get the record straight, I want to tell you something. You maybe won't believe me, but it really doesn't matter. Until I killed Stover I never killed a man. But I am getting tired of two-bit gunmen wanting to add me to their kills so they can brag they killed Steve Packard's kid. I don't hanker to become a notch on someone's gunbutt, miss, and I figure maybe the only way to keep from it is to collect some notches of my own."

She did not speak, but from where he stood Packard could see the blood beating in her throat, could see her lips half open to reply, then close again.

"You've had bitter disappointment, son," said Page. "And you are too impatient. There is good in the world—"

"I haven't seen any of it," snapped Packard.

"You came here," said Page, "with something in your mind. I don't know what it is, but you best get rid of it. It will bring you nothing but everlasting sorrow."

"Save your preaching," Packard told him, "for someone who wants to listen to it. It's people like you who shove a man along a path he doesn't want to travel and then use him as a horrible example when he up and follows it."

He turned to the door and opened it. Then turned back. "You were right, Preacher," he said. "I did come here for something and I'm going through with it."

Out on the path he strode rapidly down the hill. Night had fallen and Hangman's Gulch was a blur of darkness speared with blinking lights, filled with the hum of a fevered humanity.

It was all, Packard told himself, how you happened to be born. It your father killed men and held up stages and robbed banks, you killed men and held up stages and robbed banks. You might try hard not to do it. You might try to live another kind of life, but it would catch up with you in the end. As it finally had caught up with him. A man, after all, had to make a living somehow.

At the bottom of the hill, just before the path broke out on the street, a man stepped from behind a tree. Packard stopped, hands lifted to his guns.

"The horses," said the man, "are up this way."

Packard moved toward him, walking softly. Close at last, he asked: "You're riding with me?"

"That's right," said the man. "Blade is the name. John Blade. Put her there, pardner. I'm proud to be ridin' with you."

By impulse, Packard put out his hand, found the other's in the darkness. The man's handclasp was swift and sure. Swift and sure and warm . . . a warmth that sent a thrill through Packard, a feeling of comradeship.

"Blade," he said, "I'm proud to be riding with you, too."

Chapter IV
Death For A Pinch Of Dust

The moon was late in rising and the night was dark, dark and chill, with an autumn wind whining along the ridges and whipping down the canyons. Blade seemed to know the way almost by feel and although they went slowly, there seemed no hesitation at the choosing of the path. Packard rode behind him.

Apparently the man who had been set to tail him had not reported back to Randall. For if Randall had known of his visit to Page, he at least would have been called upon the carpet, asked for an explanation.

Randall, undoubtedly, thought that he had him trapped, that he had no choice but to play Randall's game. Packard smiled grimly in the darkness. Something would happen tomorrow, he felt certain, something that would give him the chance that he was waiting.

Grimly he speculated upon his chance of having defied Randall, knew almost as soon as he posed the question that it would have been no use. There actually had been no choice. Randall had had him dead to rights. Had known who he was and why he came to town. Had known his connection with Cardway. Randall, he knew, would never have let him get out of town alive.

Actually, he told himself, this satisfied him better than the Cardway deal. Even with the connivance of the guard, robbery of the express office under Randall's nose would have been the height of madness.

Although it wasn't only the matter of saving his own skin. It was something else as well. A certain bitter hatred that a man like Randall could hold and rule a town, could set up no matter how temporary an empire with the use of six-gun power. That a man like Preacher Page could be placed in danger because he dared oppose such a six-gun empire. That a man could say that if gold were stolen, he was the one to steal it, that he had the right of thievery staked out.

He had not been anxious to tie up with Cardway, he remembered. Only the bitterness of desperation had driven him to fall in with the schemes Cardway vaguely hinted at. Cardway had been all right, of course, but he was a shifty character. Packard found himself remembering the cigarette that drooped from his lips and poured smoke into the squinting eyes.

Cardway, without a doubt, had been ready to use him. Had sat and watched him shooting at those glass balls and sensed the advantage such marksmanship might have. Had found out who he was and worked on that.

"Hell, kid, you haven't got a chance. No one will ever give you a break, see. The world ain't built that way. Always looking for someone to kick. And your old man gives them a chance to kick you. Quit being a sucker, kid. With a knack with guns that you live, there's money to be made . . ."

There was some truth in what he said. A hell of a lot of truth, in fact. There was the job with the circus and the one before that with the feed store down in Kansas and the two weeks Packard worked as bank guard until the trembling, horrified directors found out who he was.

The moon came up, bulging over the eastern horizon, a huge red ball bisected at the moment by a straggly pine that grew atop a ridge.

Blade drew his horse to a stop and Packard rode alongside and pulled up.

Blade had his makings out and was building a cigarette. Packard sat his horse and stared over the wild and tumbled land, half lighted by the reddish moon-glow, half-buried deep in shadow.

Blade handed over the sack and papers.

"Have one on me," he said.

"Thanks," said Packard.

Blade thumbed a matchhead into flame, lit his smoke, tossed the match away.

"So you went to see Page," he said.

Raising his cigarette to his lips to lick the paper shut, Packard stared across at the other man. Deliberately he tongued the cylinder, put it in his mouth. "Maybe," he finally said. "that ain't a question you should ask."

"Perhaps it isn't, Packard. But I figured that you would. Randall's one slick operator."

Packard nodded, seeking for the meaning in the other's words. Apparently the man believed that Randall had sent him to Page.

Smoke drooled out of Blade's nose and suddenly the smoke turned into a bloody spray. Blade opened his mouth to scream, but the scream did not come out and his mouth stayed open, with the cigarette still sticking to his lower lip.

A sound ripped through the night and Blade was falling from his horse, tipping in the saddle and going over and the horse was rearing as if to spill him off.

Packard's fist drove for a six-gun, whipped it clear of leather, fighting his plunging mount with the other hand.

"Put away the gun, kid," said a voice.

Packard swung around. A man was standing just outside the shadow of a clump of pines, rifle in his arms. "Hurley!" yelled Packard.

"That's right," said Hurley. "I've just dealt myself a hand." He stepped out into the trail, seized the reins of Blade's frightened horse, talked to the animal in a soft, soothing tone.

"Can't have you runnin' home, feller," he said. "Can't have you going back and tippin' Randall off."

"I thought," said Packard, coldly, "that you ran with Randall's pack."

"Sure," admitted Hurley. "Sure I do. Or did. Now I'm switching back to the Packard gang. Don't know anyone I'd rather ride with than a Packard bunch."

"There isn't any Packard bunch," said Packard.

Hurley gulped. "Don't mean to say, kid, that you are on your own?"

"That's right."

"Well, I be damned," said Hurley. "The nerve of it . . . the blessed nerve of it."

He chuckled. "Just like your old man," he said. "Never had a big bunch. Said they got in one another's way. Just you and me and Jim and Charley and the four of us could have given Randall aces and beat him at the laydown."

Warning bells rang in Packard's head. "You're barking up the wrong tree, Hurley," he declared. "I'm riding Randall's trail. None of the lone wolf stuff for me. Randall made a deal and it sounded good to me."

Hurley shambled forward until he stood close to Packard's horse, looked up at the younger man, the full light of the moon shining on his face.

"You're lying, youngster," he declared. "No Packard would mean a thing like that. You're figuring on taking over once the gold is where you want it. You'll be using Randall's gang to help hold up the coach, but Randall won't see an ounce of the stuff."

"And you're figuring on dealing in with me?"

Hurley spat. "Damn right. I rode with your old man . . . Say, is Charley coming in?"

"Charley?"

"Sure, Page. Me and Charley Page and Jim Davis, we were the ones who made up the Packard gang. Now Jim is dead and Charley's got religion and . . ."

Packard drew in a deep breath, let it out slowly. "So Page knew who I was all the time. The low down hypocrite!"

"Charley ain't no hypocrite," snapped Hurley. "He's really got religion. Only, I thought maybe Charley might be getting a bit discouraged and he's only human—"

"But," said Packard, "Page knew who you were."

"Sure, but he never said a word about me and I never give him away. Randall knew who I was, of course, but none of the other boys. We never got well known, the way your old man did. He was the front, you see—"

"Yes, yes, I know," said Packard, impatiently.

Hurley sighed. "So I guess Charley won't be coming in. It's just the two of us."

"Look," snapped Packard, "you're the only one who's been talking about double-crossing Randall. You're the one that's all steamed up about it. I haven't said a word."

"Ah, hell," protested Hurley, "you can talk to me. I was your old man's pal."

"I suppose," said Packard, "that you'll have to ride along with me. I don't know the way, you see."

He pivoted in his saddle, looked at the huddled heap lying in the trail.

"I hope," he said, "you got a good one figured out to explain why it's you instead of Blade with me."

"Shucks," declared Hurley, "that won't be hard to do. The boys won't know who Randall sent along. We'll not mention Blade at all. They'll think that it was me who was with you all the time."

"Somehow," said Packard, "I don't like what you done to Blade. He was an O.K. hombre."

"Tell you the truth," confessed Hurley, "I'd just as soon it had been someone else. Can think of a couple I would rather it had been. Blade was the one . . . But you ain't told me your plans."

"I haven't any plans."

"Look, kid, you can't fool me. You can't—"

Packard leaned over from his horse. "Are you riding along or not?" he snapped.

"Oh, sure. Sure, I'm riding along."

Hurley tied Blade's mount to one of the pines, got up on his own, trotted up the trail. Packard urged his horse to follow.

Packard's stomach was a leaden knot of disgust as he watched Hurley's swaying form.

So this was the way it was, he told himself. You gunned down your own friends, you broke faith with your own gang, you did anything that put your groping fingers into a sack of gold. You had no honor and you walked with your back hunched against a bullet that might come from a man that you called a friend, because in this business there were no such things as friends . . . just other men that you watched, wondering if the day would come when they killed you or you killed them for an ounce or two of gold, a roll of bills, for anything at all.

Even Preacher Page!

The moon climbed higher and from some far ledge a wolf howled lonesomely. An owl swooped down over Packard's head, a bulleting soundlessness that floated through the night. Little things scuttered and scampered along the rocky trail.

Their horses turned a sharp bend in the trail and in a pocketed valley a tiny fire was burning.

Hurley turned his head. "That's the camp," he said.

Packard nodded.

"How about it, kid?" asked Hurley. "Got anything to tell me?"

"Not a thing," said Packard.

And his mind thought: *I can't trust you, Hurley. How do I know you're on the up and up? How can I be sure that Randall didn't plan it all just to sound me out? If I talked to you, really told you what I had in mind, you might pay me off with a bullet in the head.*

But Hurley had played square with Page, hadn't peeped to Randall about who the Preacher was. And it would have been worth a lot to Randall to have known that, with Page threatening to bring in martial law. It would have given Randall a club that would have either silenced Page or sent him scuttling out of town.

That was the hell of it, Packard told himself. You never could be sure.

The men were waiting around the fire when they arrived. Hard-faced men who stared at them for a long moment without speaking.

Finally one of them strode forward.

"Howdy," he said. "New man?"

Hurley chuckled. "That's right, Pinky. A new one that Randall wants us to break in. Name of Packard. Steve Packard's kid."

A smile split Pinky's face.

"Ought to be all right," he said, "if he's anything like his old man."

He walked toward Packard, hand held out. "Name is Traynor, Packard. But the boys all call me Pinky."

Packard shook his hand.

"Meet the boys," said Pinky. "This old hombre is Pop Allen. And the one over there is Marks. The fellow by the fire is Sylvester. Hell of a name, ain't it?"

For a single instant Sylvester's left eye flashed, picking up and reflecting the flare of the campfire . . . and there was something about the man's face that rang bells of recognition in Packard's brain . . . a haunting recollection that sent his thoughts scurrying back along the last few days.

The cheeks were flat and the lips were tight, but there was an angle to the chin and the way the hair swept back from his forehead that seemed to fit in with some other face back in Hangman's Gulch.

Then Sylvester was saying: "Howdy, Packard," and stepping forward with his hand held out, a chubby hand that did not seem to be made to fit a six-gun grip.

And Packard, gripping Sylvester's hand, stared at the left eye which no longer glinted.

Suddenly he knew Sylvester, his mind filling in the face as he had seen it before . . . a face with some sort of plastic material worked into the cheeks and in front of the gums to puff out the cheeks and lips, to distort the face so that once the silly little mustache had been pasted on no one would ever recognize the man.

He spoke low, lips scarcely moving, so that no one else might hear.

"I see," he told Sylvester, "that you found your eye."

Chapter V
We Don't Waste Lead!

From far down the canyon came the faint clatter of wheels, the muffled clop of horses' hoofs.

Crouched in the clump of juniper beside the trail, Packard stared out across the rock-ribbed cleft that climbed, twisting deep into the mountain range.

Again came the far-off squeal of wheels and Packard, straining his ears, tensed, then relaxed again. Eyes narrowed against the morning sun, he took stock of the situation.

Pinky was across the trail, almost opposite where Packard crouched in the juniper. Marks was farther up. Sylvester and Hur-

ley were between himself and Marks, each on their own side of
the trail. Pop Allen was back in the little side canyon, a quarter
mile away, holding the horses.

The four of them, Pinky had told them, were to let the stagecoach pass, were to remain out of sight until Marks stepped out
and fired a shot, the first one over the driver's head, the second
one in his head if he made a hostile move.

Sylvester was to cover the shotgun messenger up on the seat
beside the driver, with Hurley to back him up. Packard and Pinky
were to take care of other guards, if there should happen to be
any. There probably would be, Pinky had said . . . up on the roof.

Packard felt perspiration trickling down his face behind the
blue handkerchief which served him for a mask.

He was nervous, he told himself, somewhat surprised. And
he shouldn't be nervous. Never had there been a time when he
needed the rock-hard sureness of hand and eye that he might
need in the next few minutes.

The chance he waited, he knew would come in that first
moment of swift action when Marks stepped out into the trail
and flung up his gun.

Cautiously, Packard squinted up the trail, trying to make out
the positions of the others. He knew where they should be but
there was nothing to betray them. No single flutter of a wind-
blown handkerchief, no hint of color in the tangled shrubs, no
stirring bush.

Hurley would be up there somewhere. Hurley, who had shot
down Blade when the man wasn't even looking and thus dealt
himself a hand. Hurley, he knew, would be watching him, waiting for the sign that would send him into action. Hurley was no
fool. Hurley knew there was something in the wind, probably was
more than a little nettled that the son of his old friend and trail
partner hadn't let him in on it.

And yet, Packard told himself, he couldn't have let him in on
it, for there wasn't really anything . . . no well-defined plan, no

thought-out course of action. Just a hunch that a chance would come, waiting for the break that would give him the upper hand. And when it came there'd be no time for thinking, no time for planning . . . he'd have to act by what would amount to instinct.

And there was Sylvester. Just where did Sylvester fit? The man had a glass eye, but one that was so perfect his companions of the owlhoot trail had never found it out. If they had he would bear a nickname that would have marked him as a man of certain distinction. That eye would have furnished more than one jibe, more than one good-natured joke, more than one tall tale.

If Sylvester was a *bona-fide* member of the Canyon gang, why should he have been in Hangman's Gulch, tricked out with facial disguise and checkered suit? And even if he did want to promenade around without anyone knowing who he was, why all that ridiculous hoorah about losing his glass eye? A thing like that wouldn't accomplish a single thing except attract attention to him.

The rattling wheels were closer now and the clop of the horses' hoofs were distinct sounds in the dust. Around the bend a filmy cloud arose, the slowly drifting dust disturbed by the coach's passing.

Packard hunkered lower in the juniper, carefully slipped the six-guns from his belt, clasped them with sure, deft hands.

The stage swung around the bend, the horses surging into the uphill pull, harness creaking with the effort. The driver slouched forward easily, reins loose in his hands, but his head darted from side to side, watching the bushes along the trail. Beside him the shotgun messenger sat bolt upright, the butt of the gun planted against his knee, muzzle pointing toward the sky, left hand grasping the barrel. Another man knelt one-kneed on top of the lurching coach, rifle at ready.

The coach lumbered past, one wheel squealing, blobs of dust dropping from the slowly moving tires and spatting in the tracks that still smoked from the passing of the iron-shod wheels.

Breath still caught in his throat, Packard watched it pass. His fingers shifted slightly, taking a new grasp on the six-gun grips.

Carefully, he raised his head a bit, stared after the coach, heard the seconds beating in his head as time slowed to an agonizing crawl.

A man rose out of the bushes, like a jack-in-the-box popping up when someone snapped the catch. A man who yelled and raised a gun and fired.

The driver rose in his seat, hauling on the reins while the horses reared, a tangled mass of leather and striking forefeet and flying manes.

The shotgun messenger half raised his gun, jerked forward as a six-gun bellowed, bending in the middle as if he were on a hinge. For a moment he hung there, etched against the morning sun, a bent over man with the gun tumbling from his hands. Then slowly he pitched forward like a diver slanting off a board, pitched forward between the horses, fell beneath their feet.

The guard on top of the coach had leaped to his feet, his rifle coming to his shoulder in one swift blur of fluid motion. A gun spatted angrily behind him, like a snarling cat, and the guard stiffened and staggered, fell and rolled, slid halfway off the coach and hung there, knee caught beneath the low iron railing that ran along the top. His hands hung down limply and swung slowly to and fro, like unsteady pendulums, while blood dripped from his mouth and spattered in the dust.

Then there was no sound except that of the driver talking to the horses, talking in a soothing tone that trilled with hidden terror, trying to quiet the animals that reared and plunged and fought the bits and kicked and shied at the bloody thing that rolled beneath their hoofs.

Packard had risen from the juniper, but had not moved, had not even raised his gun. The action had been too swift, the deadly six-gun execution too well planned.

He looked across the trail at Pinky and above his red hand-kerchief mask, Pinky's eyes glittered with excitement. Smoke still trickled from the gun he held in his hairy hand.

"That's the way we do it, kid," said Pinky. "Fast and neat. No time or bullets wasted."

And what he said was true, Packard realized. Only a few seconds had ticked away since Marks had risen from the bushes, only three shots had been fired and two men were dead.

Marks had stepped to the head of the horses, was fighting them to a standstill while Hurley still held his gun on the struggling driver.

Sylvester was talking to someone inside the coach, talking in a voice that was conversational, almost as if he might be chatting with a next door neighbor.

"There ain't no cause to be alarmed, ma'am," he was saying. "The boys don't aim to harm a hair of your head. Just you step out and sit down in the shade while we get the dust. That's all we want. We'll just take the dust and be gallopin' along."

But he still kept a gun in his hand and he kept it in position as he moved closer, grasped the handle and jerked the coach door wide open.

"Please ma'am," he said. "Be sensible. Yelling and screamin' won't help you none at all."

"I don't intend," the woman told him, "to do any yelling or screaming. And I'm not coming out. I'm staying here."

The voice sent a chill of fear through Packard—an icy chill that gripped and held him like a mighty hand. For he knew that voice, had heard it only the night before . . .

"She says," Sylvester told Pinky, "that she ain't a-comin' out."

"The hell she ain't," snarled Pinky.

Swiftly he strode forward, lunged for the door of the coach, reached in. The woman screamed and Pinky yanked, hauling her out of the door, leaping back to escape her clawing hands. She stumbled and fell in the dust.

"Get them up," yelled Packard. "Get them up and keep them there. I'm taking over."

Sylvester and Pinky swung around, stared at the gun-mouths that scowled at them from Packard's fists. "You're loco!" yelled Pinky. "You can't—"

One of Packard's guns drooled flame and smoke and Pinky's hat lifted in the air, skidded downward in a rapid glide and plopped onto the ground.

"The next one," said Packard, "will be right between the eyes."

Wide-eyed, the two of them lifted their hands, high above their heads.

"Get out of the way, Miss Page," said Packard quietly. "There might be some shooting if these gents should get uneasy."

"You're too considerate," the girl told him. "Why don't you shoot them down?"

"Get out of the way," snapped Packard. "Around here people do what I say for them to do."

He raised his voice. "Marks, you walk down this way. Hurley, climb up and throw down the gold. Both you hombres shuck your guns."

A sledge hammer slammed into his shoulder, spun him around, and he was falling forward, the ground rushing up at him with express train speed. Through the roaring in his ears came the sullen clap of a high-powered rifle.

Pop, he thought. Pop Allen. I forgot all about the damn old fool. What did he mean by horning in, anyway? He had no business to. He was supposed to be off in the gully holding them horses.

He hit the ground and exploded, sailing off into space, part of him going one way and part of him another . . . but finally the pieces came back together and he was whole again and he wallowed in a bed of pain and thirst.

A voice said: "He's coming to." Another voice snapped: "Quit champin' at the bit, Marks. Be a damn shame to string him up and him not know about it."

"Ought to lug him back and hang him alongside Cardway," someone else suggested.

The voice that had snapped, protested. "Too far. And anyhow, Randall ain't anxious to give Hangman's Gulch no bad name. Hangings right in town got to be legal-like . . . vigilantes and all the fixin's."

The words seeped into Packard's brain, seeped and simmered, thoughts clawing at their meaning.

Packard's left shoulder ached with a dull, monotonous thud that beat and beat, as if someone were hitting it with a padded hammer. His throat ached, too and when he put his right hand up to feel it, there was something there. Something that was hard and scratchy and was pressing just a bit too tight.

Feebly he clawed at the thing around his neck, trying to loosen it so he could breathe more easily. He was sitting on the ground, with his legs stretched out in front of him and his back against the hard, rough trunk of a good-sized tree. He pressed his back harder against the tree and felt the scaly bark bite into his flesh.

Sitting against a tree, with a rope around his neck. And probably the other end of that rope went over a limb somewhere above his head. One yank . . . one good, stout yank by a couple or three men and he would be swinging free. He would be a thing like Cardway was . . . swinging the way that Cardway swung in the breeze that had swooped up the canyon bed.

"Give me that pail of water," said a voice. "Damn it, he's playing possum, that's what."

Water sloshed into Packard's face with stinging force, ran in ice-cold rivulets off his hair and down his neck, sopping his shirt.

Packard shook his head, opened his eyes, stared at the man before him.

Chapter VI
A Deal In Hot Lead

Pinky held the bucket in his hand and Hurley stood beside him, one hand on his gun-butt. Marks leaned against a tree, holding the free end of the rope which angled down from the limb above Packard's head. Sylvester squatted on his heels a few feet from where Hurley stood. Pop Allen was putting wood on a small, newly-kindled fire.

And beyond Pop, hands tied behind her and with the rope lashed loosely around another tree, was Alice Page. There was a streak of dirt across her face and she had lost her hat and her hair had fallen down over one shoulder. Her dress was dusty and bedraggled.

"How do you feel?" asked Pinky.

"Better," said Packard, "than you're going to feel when I get through with you."

"We're going to hang you," Pinky told him. "We're going to string you up and leave you hangin' here for the crows to eat."

Marks laughed, showing his teeth through his heavy beard. "You forgot, Pinky. We ain't going to leave him hangin'. This here is my rope and I ain't going to lose it. Too good a rope to go away and leave it."

Alice Page's face was twisted with horror and across the few yards that separated them, Packard's eyes caught hers, held them for a moment.

"What you going to do with her?" he asked.

Marks laughed again, a high-keyed, nasty laugh. Pinky said: "We're holding her until her old man comes to terms. He's been raisin' too much hell to suit the boss."

Packard stared at the girl. Her head still was high, high with that bewitching tilt that he remembered from the other times he'd seen her.

"Don't pay any attention to her," Preacher Page had told him. *"She's just angry because I'm sending her away."*

But Preacher Page hadn't said she was leaving the next morning and he hadn't asked. He should have warned the old man. Should have told him not to send her on the next coach. But there had been other things to think of, other things to say.

Randall had known, of course. Somehow Randall had found out. Hurley, perhaps. Hurley and Page still were friends and Hurley might have known. And Hurley would do anything that would help himself.

It wasn't only gold that Randall had wanted off the coach. It had been the girl as well . . . the girl to hold as a whip over Preacher Page's head. A way to make Preacher knuckle down, make him forget all about martial law, silence his demands for law and order.

Marks twitched on the rope and it tightened on Packard's throat with a strangling jerk.

"What the hell are we waiting for?" asked Marks. "We might as well string up this saddle stiff and be on our way."

"Wait a second," said Packard.

Slowly he rose to his feet, stood leaning against the tree, his head light and giddy with the effort of standing on his own.

"You're wasting your time," snarled Pinky. "You can't talk yourself out of that rope. We got you dead to rights and if you talked a million years we still would run you up."

Packard looked at Hurley and the man's eyes moved away, unwilling to meet the stare. Sylvester still squatted on his heels, scratching at the ground with a stick he had picked up, his broad-brimmed hat shading his face.

"If you got anything to say," said Pinky, "go ahead and spit it out. We ain't ones to deny a man a last word. Last smoke, too, if you want it. Hurley will roll you a smoke."

"The hell with it," snapped Hurley. His hand plunged for his gun-butt and the gun was coming out, a glare of steel in the brilliant sunlight. Packard, startled, crouched back against the tree, his stomach muscles tightening as if by contracting them they might be armor against the coming bullet.

Sylvester went into action from the ground. Like a compressed spring, he rose and hurled himself at Hurley's arm. The gun coughed sharply and a bullet chunked with a vicious clap into the tree trunk inches from Packard's head.

The gun flew from Hurley's hand and Hurley dropped back a pace, caressing his twisted wrist.

"Damn you," he snarled. "I'll—"

"Come ahead," Sylvester invited him. "Come ahead and do it." His hand hovered like a waiting hawk above his six-gun butt.

Hurley did not move. "Go ahead and haul him up," he yelled. "What are you waiting for? What—"

"You seem too anxious to have him hauled up," Marks said. "Maybe there's a reason for it. Come to think of it, you're the one he told to climb up and throw down the gold. Seems like maybe he was pretty sure that you would do it without making any trouble. Seems like maybe we ought to have a talk—"

"Talk!" yelled Hurley. "That's all you hombres do. You sit around and shoot off your yaps and never get nothing done."

"Shut up!" snapped Pinky.

Hurley glared at him.

Crouched against the tree, Packard closed his eyes, felt the throb of his wounded shoulder shaking his whole body. He had held hopes that Hurley might step in and help. But that was out now. Hurley had dropped him like a hot potato at the moment when his string had been played out. Hurley was not a man who would back lost causes.

"What Marks says is right," declared Pinky. "What do you know about Packard, Hurley?"

"Not a thing," said Hurley. "He's just a new man, that's all."

"I can tell you something about him," said a new voice.

Packard opened his eyes. "You keep out of this," he warned.

But Alice Page paid him no attention. She was looking at Pinky and there was a challenging defiance burning in her eyes.

"Mr. Packard," she said, "is a United States marshal."

A bombshell of quietness broke upon the group, a bombshell of chill and quietness.

Alice Page's words dripped through the quietness. "If you kill him," she said, "you'll be hunted down like mad dogs. The government never forgets a thing like that. It isn't just like killing anyone, you see."

Pinky moved slowly toward the girl.

"You lie," he snarled. "You know damn well that he's no marshal. He didn't act like no marshal back there at the stage. He told Hurley to climb up and throw down the bags of dust and no marshal would do that. And he didn't say a thing about arresting us. A marshal always shoots off his face about arresting someone."

He halted and stood squarely in front of the girl, but Alice Page stood unmoved, her chin up.

"Go ahead, then," she challenged. "Go ahead and hang him and see what happens to you. That's the surest thing that you can do to break up your rotten gang."

Pinky hauled back his arm. "I have a notion to slap you down," he snarled. "You dirty little—"

"Pinky!" yelled Packard.

Pinky whirled around.

"Leave the girl alone," warned Packard. "She's not mixed up in this. She's only doing what she can to help me."

Pinky sneered. "Sweet on you, eh?"

"Damn you, Pinky," roared Packard. He dug in his heel and thrust himself out from the tree, but Marks hauled smartly on the rope and he was jerked back, heels dragging, noose tighter around his throat. With his one good hand, he clawed erect against the tree, stood gasping.

Across the space that separated them, he looked at Alice Page.

"It was a good try, miss," he whispered, "and thanks a lot, but it just won't hold water."

Deliberately, Pinky whirled around, arm swinging with him. His palm smacked open-handed across Alice Page's mouth and drove her back, staggering against the tree. Her body slammed hard into the tree, knees buckling beneath her. She fell forward and the rope jerked up her hands and held her in a kneeling position.

From where he stood Packard could see the white imprint of Pinky's hand across her face and he moved one foot forward, then brought it back. By sheer power of will, he held himself against the tree, willed his body rigid while the flame of hatred and rage ate through him like a fire.

It wouldn't do him any good, he knew, to try another lunge. Marks was waiting, watching him, with a grin behind his beard. Marks would like to have him try to reach Pinky or the girl.

"Next time," said Pinky, savagely, "I'll break your neck."

He swung on his heel and looked at Hurley, a scowl twisting at his face.

"Hurley," Pinky said, "you better talk. And make it fast and straight."

Hurley didn't talk. He moved. One second he was facing Pinky, hands dangling at his side and the next he was plunging for the gun that Sylvester had twisted from his grasp. In a single leap he was beside it, stooping over, scooping it up in a lightning motion.

Pinky's arms pistoned and his guns struck fire in the noonday sun as they came whispering from leather.

At point blank range the guns roared fire and smoke, the three reports blending into one. The handkerchief around Pinky's throat whipped suddenly as if struck by a tiny gale and out in the sunlight Hurley was tipping over, twisting awkwardly to keep his feet.

His gun slipped from his fingers and feebly he clawed at it, trying to pick it off the ground while his hand was far above it. Then, gently, almost as if he meant to do it, he toppled over and lay huddled on the grass.

Pinky stood on spraddled legs, watching Hurley fall, then calmly tucked the smoking guns back into his belt and turned his back on Hurley's body.

His face was almost pleasant as he spoke to Packard. "I guess," he said, "you won't have time for that smoke, after all."

He nodded to Marks. "Haul away."

"Cripes," protested Marks, "you don't expect me to do it all alone. Packard there weighs close to a couple of hundred!"

"Pop," ordered Pinky, "go lend Marks a hand."

Pop rose slowly to his feet, ambled forward.

Packard straightened, tense against the tree, thoughts racing in his brain. He was going to be hanged. Run up by a brawny bearded man and a shriveled oldster while a man called Pinky stood to one side and watched.

And there wasn't a thing he could do about it . . . not a thing.

Pop was grumbling. "Hell, why don't you shoot him, Pinky. This here is too much work."

"Just a minute," said a voice and Packard twisted his neck, saw Sylvester standing almost at his elbow. Sylvester had pushed his hat on the back of his head and both his guns were out.

Pinky stared. "Now what?" he demanded. "Can't a fellow hang a man without all the hoorah that's been going on here?"

"Possibly," said Sylvester, conversationally. "But you aren't going to do it, Pinky. Right now, you aren't hanging anyone at all."

Pinky's face twisted with sudden, violent rage and his hand twitched up. The gun in Sylvester's left hand leaped and spat and Pinky screeched as the bullet smashed his wrist.

Out of the corner of his eye, Packard saw Pop and Marks going for their guns, Sylvester twisting on his heel to meet them. Marks, he saw, had dropped the rope. This was his chance.

Packard lowered his head, hunched his one good shoulder, drove with all the power that was in his legs. Above him he heard the soft hiss of the rope running across the limb.

He felt his shoulder and lowered head crash into yielding flesh, felt the lance of pain that knifed through his shattered arm and other shoulder. Then Pinky was going over, backwards, and Packard was staggering, spread-legged above the outlaw leader floundering on the ground.

A spurred boot lashed up at him and Packard danced out of the way, drove in again, hurling himself upon the outstretched body of the man, his right hand spread wide, aimed at the naked throat.

He felt the softness of the throat beneath his fingers and his fingers closed with a vise-like viciousness while a dull and spreading anger glowed within his brain.

Beneath him, Packard sensed that Pinky was clawing for a gun, blindly groping with his uninjured left hand for a weapon in his belt. Savagely he hauled upward on the throat within his grasp as if he meant to tear it out and then crashed it back to earth again with all the power that was in his driving muscles. Pinky's head sounded like a breaking egg and it bounced and rolled sidewise sickeningly as it hit the ground.

But still Packard's fingers held their grip, dug deeper as he remembered the marks of a hand across Alice Page's face.

Behind him he heard the roar and crash of six-guns, but there was a thunder in his brain that drowned out all other sound. He felt himself tipping forward, felt a cloud of red mist move in through his eyes and swirl within his head.

His fingers loosened and his hand fell off the throat and he was crawling blindly, like a dog on hands and knees.

"Get up, man!" a voice screamed at him and he staggered to his feet, stood swaying while his vision cleared. He shook his head and saw Sylvester standing before him, while behind

Sylvester loomed a white and misty face that he knew was Alice Page's.

Sylvester dabbed at his face with a hand and Packard saw that the hair and one side of his face was thick with blood where a bullet had barked him.

Marks lay upon the ground, arms outspread above his head, a red streak soaking through his coal-black beard. Pop Allen sat with his back against a tree and held both hands to his side. Like a kid, thought Packard. Like a kid that's eaten green apples and has the belly ache.

Sylvester's face came into sharper focus and Packard spoke to it.

"Mister," he said, "I'm still wondering what it's all about."

"I thought you guessed," Sylvester told him. "I thought that you knew when you found out about my eye."

"I knew there was something wrong," confessed Packard, "but I couldn't figure it."

"I'm an insurance dick."

"Come again?" said Packard.

"An insurance detective. Randall, you see, was working it both ways. He was insuring gold that he shipped out on the stage. Then he'd hold up the stage and get the gold. Then he'd soak us for insurance money."

Sylvester mopped at his face again, left finger-streaks of red across his cheek.

"We better be getting out of here," he said. "Get that rope off your neck. Miss Page will fix your shoulder while I catch up some horses."

"Would you mind," asked a voice, "staying just a while?"

They whirled, the three of them, stared at the man who sat the big bay horse just at the tiny clearing's edge. A man in black broadcloth and a fawn-colored vest above which was bunched a white silk cravat. A diamond flashed in the sunlight as the man held the six-gun on them.

"It would seem," said Randall, "that I have the drop on

you. Better shuck those guns, Sylvester, and walk away from them."

Slowly, Sylvester unbuckled his belt, let it drop to the ground. With his gun, Randall motioned them away.

He chuckled, watching them. "Too bad," he said. "You almost got away with it."

"Maybe they didn't get away with it this time," said Alice Page. "Maybe these two men may never get away with it. But sometime someone will. You can't go on forever."

Randall tipped his hat, but his gun still was unwavering in his hand. "How right you are, Miss Page," he said. "And now if you'll just walk away and turn your back . . ."

"Always a gentleman," said Packard, bitterly. "You wouldn't for the world shoot a man in front of a woman's eyes."

"Of course not," said Randall. "There are certain social graces that cannot be ignored."

He nudged his horse around, lifted the six-gun. "Miss Page, if you please will—"

"No!" screamed Alice Page. "You can't—you can't—"

She was running toward him, arms flung up as if to ward off the bullet that the gun was set to throw.

"Alice!"

The bellow was bull-throated and it stopped the girl in midstride, swung her around.

"Father!" she cried.

Preacher Page stood beneath the tree where Pinky lay sprawled with a lolling neck and he held a heavy rifle at the ready.

"Get away, child," he bellowed.

Randall jerked the six-gun up and then stiffened. The rifle muzzle in the old man's hand was pointing at his midriff. If that gun went off . . .

"Throw away the gun, Randall," said Preacher. "Throw it away and get down off that horse."

Randall hesitated.

Preacher squinted his eyes. "I am not a man," he said, "who wishes to shed blood, but if you don't heave that gun away, I'll let you have it right through your dirty guts."

Randall heaved the gun away, scrambled off the horse. Sylvester stepped out and picked up the gun.

Slowly Preacher moved toward Randall. "See if he had any other guns," Page told Sylvester.

Swiftly, Sylvester ran his hands up and down Randall's coat.

"Not a one," he said.

Preacher heaved his rifle to one side.

"Get up your dukes," he told Randall. "I'm going to give you the worst beating that a man has ever taken."

Randall sprang forward, one fist lashing out, the other cocked for a killing blow. Preacher ducked, slid under the swishing fist, uncorked a punch that skidded Randall on his heels.

Then the two were together, slugging toe to toe, boring in, absorbing punishment, deadly silent. Their feet beat a stolid measure on the grass and there came the sound of flesh on bone, the rasp of heavy breathing, the muffled grunt and panting breath of earnest men fighting with a deadly hatred.

Randall was weakening. Under the sledge-hammer blows of the minister, he was falling back. Once he tried to break away and run, but Preacher chased him, closed in and forced the fight.

The end came swiftly. A blow staggered Randall and Preacher moved in slugging, right to the jaw, left to the heart, another right to the jaw that lifted Randall off his feet and slammed him to the ground.

For a long moment the old man stood in the sunlight above the fallen man, his white hair shining and stirring in the breeze, his chest rising and falling as he gasped for breath.

Then he turned away, walked to the three, brushing off his coat, straightening his shirt cuffs.

"Either of you want that man?" he asked.

"I do," Sylvester told him.

Preacher looked at Packard sternly. "I was hoping it might be you."

Packard shook his head. "Not me. I guess I'll be riding again. No use of going back to Hangman's Gulch."

Preacher reached out his arm and drew Alice to his side. "Got to worrying about you, child," he said. "Thought what a foolish thing it was for me to send you off on that stage. So I got a horse and rode. Thought that I might catch up and sort of ride as guard. See you safely through. But I was too late. I heard shooting . . ."

He brushed at his eyes with a gnarled hand.

Packard reached up to his throat, was surprised to find the rope still dangling there. Savagely he ripped the noose open, tossed it over his head, turned and walked away.

There was a horse tied up in the timber. It would be an easy matter to get there by just ambling along. Then he'd jump into the saddle and no one, he was sure, would try very hard to catch him.

For after all he was almost as bad as Pinky or any of the others. Not in as deep, perhaps, but not because he hadn't tried. There was no use trying to fool anyone. He'd tried to get that gold, tried just as hard as any of the others.

"Packard!"

He heard the thump of feet behind him, stopped and waited. Slowly he turned to face the old man.

"Yes, what is it?"

"You're going back with us," said Page.

Packard shook his head. "No, Preacher. Hangman's Gulch is going to be a respectable town now, with Randall and his gang mopped up. And I don't belong . . ."

"Look, Packard," said Preacher. "I want you to listen to me. Next Sunday I'm going to get up in the pulpit and I'm going to tell the people who I am. And I want to make a deal with you—"

Packard gasped. "But you can't do that. You're sitting pretty. There's no reason for doing it."

"But there is a reason. I've got to be square with myself. I can't go on living a lie."

"All right," agreed Packard. "Have it your own way. But I can't see where it has anything to do with me."

"I told you I had a deal," said Preacher. "If the people throw me out, all three of us will leave, you and I and Alice. But if they let me stay, all three of us will stay."

Packard looked beyond Preacher at Alice and her eyes, he saw, were smiling.

"Is it a deal?" asked Preacher.

"It's a deal," answered Packard, not even looking at him.

THE CIVILIZATION GAME

One of Clifford Simak's journals notes that he sold a story entitled "Apron Strings" to Horace Gold on May 1, 1958. Given its publication date, the November 1958 issue of Galaxy Magazine, and its subject, playtime for humanity, I think that the timing is about right for "Apron Strings" to reappear.

This story is also another example of Cliff Simak's proclivity for featuring cavemen in his science fiction.

—dww

I

For some time, Stanley Paxton had been hearing the sound of muffled explosions from the west. But he had kept on, for there might be a man behind him, trailing him, and he could not change his course. For if he was not befuddled, the homestead of Nelson Moore lay somewhere in the hills ahead. There he would find shelter for the night and perhaps even transportation. Communication, he knew, must be ruled out for the moment; the Hunter people would be monitoring, alert for any news of him.

One Easter vacation, many years ago, he had spent a few days at the Moore homestead, and all through this afternoon he had been haunted by a sense of recognition for certain landmarks he had sighted. But his visit to these hills had been so long ago that his memory hazed and there was no certainty.

As the afternoon had lengthened toward an early evening, his fear of the trailing man began to taper off. Perhaps, he told himself, there was no one, after all. Once, atop a hill, he had crouched in a thicket for almost half an hour and had seen no sign of any follower.

Long since, of course, they would have found the wreckage of his flier, but they might have arrived too late and so, consequently, have no idea in which direction he had gone.

Through the day, he'd kept close watch of the cloudy sky and was satisfied that no scouting flier had passed overhead to spot him.

Now, with the setting of the sun behind an angry cloud bank, he felt momentarily safe.

He came out of a meadow valley and began to climb a wooded hill. The strange boomings and concussions seemed fairly close at hand and he could see the flashes of explosions lighting up the sky.

He reached the hilltop and stopped short, crouching down against the ground. Below him, over a square mile or more of ground, spread the rippling flashes, and in the pauses between the louder noises, he heard faint chatterings that sent shivers up his spine.

He crouched, watching the flashes ripple back and forth in zigzag patterning and occasionally a small holocaust of explosions would suddenly break out and then subside as quickly.

Slowly he stood up and wrapped his cloak about him and raised the hood to protect his neck and ears.

On the near side of the flashing area, at the bottom of the hill, was some sort of foursquare structure looming darkly in the dusk. And it seemed as well that a massive hazy bowl lay inverted above the entire area, although it was too dark to make out what it was.

Paxton grunted softly to himself and went quickly down the

hill until he reached the building. It was, he saw, a sort of observation platform, solidly constructed and raised well above the ground, with the top half of it made of heavy glass that ran all the way around. A ladder went up one side to the glassed-in platform.

"What's going on up there?" he shouted, but his voice could be scarcely heard above the crashing and thundering that came from out in front.

So he climbed the ladder.

When his head reached the level of the glassed-in platform area, he halted. A boy, not more than fourteen years of age, stood at the front of the platform, staring out into a noisy sea of fire. A pair of binoculars was slung about his neck and to one side of him stood a massive bank of instruments.

Paxton clambered up the rest of the way and stepped inside the platform.

"Hello, young man!" he shouted.

The youngster turned around. He seemed an engaging fellow, with a cowlick down his forehead.

"I'm sorry, sir," he said. "I'm afraid I didn't hear you."

"What is going on here?"

"A war," said the boy. "Pertwee just launched his big attack. I'm hard-pressed to hold him off."

Paxton gasped a little. "But this is most unusual!" he protested.

The boy wrinkled up his forehead. "I don't understand."

"You are Nelson Moore's son?"

"Yes, sir, I am Graham Moore."

"I knew your father many years ago. We went to school together."

"He will be glad to see you, sir," the boy said brightly, sensing an opportunity to rid himself of this uninvited kibitzer. "You take the path just north of west. It will lead you to the house."

"Perhaps," suggested Paxton, "you could come along and show me."

"I can't leave just yet," said Graham. "I must blunt Pertwee's attack. He caught me off my balance and has been saving up his firepower and there were some maneuvres that escaped me until it was too late. Believe me, sir, I'm in an unenviable position."

"This Pertwee?"

"He's the enemy. We've fought for two years now."

"I see," said Paxton solemnly and retreated down the ladder.

He found the path and followed it and found the house, set in a swale between two hillocks. It was an old and rambling affair among great clumps of trees.

The path ended on a patio and a woman's voice asked: "Is that you, Nels?"

She sat in a rocking chair on the smooth stone flags and was little more than a blur of whiteness—a white face haloed by white hair.

"Not Nels," he said. "An old friend of your son's."

From here, he noticed, through some trick of acoustics in the hills, one could barely hear the sound of battle, although the sky to the east was lighted by an occasional flash of heavy rockets or artillery fire.

"We are glad to have you, sir," the old lady said, still rocking gently back and forth. "Although I do wish Nelson would come home. I don't like him wandering around after it gets dark."

"My name is Stanley Paxton. I'm with Politics."

"Why, yes," she said, "I remember now. You spent an Easter with us, twenty years ago. I'm Cornelia Moore, but you may call me Grandma, like all the rest of them."

"I remember you quite well," said Paxton. "I hope I'm not intruding."

"Heavens, no. We have few visitors. We're always glad to see one. Theodore especially will be pleased. You'd better call him Granther."

"Granther?"

"Grandfather. That's the way Graham said it when he was a tyke."

"I met Graham. He seemed to be quite busy. He said Pertwee had caught him off his balance."

"That Pertwee plays too rough," said Grandma, a little angrily.

A robot catfooted out onto the patio. "Dinner is ready, madam," it said.

"We'll wait for Nelson," Grandma told it.

"Yes, madam. He should be in quite soon. We shouldn't wait too long. Granther has already started on his second brandy."

"We have a guest, Elijah. Please show him to his room. He is a friend of Nelson's."

"Good evening, sir," Elijah said. "If you will follow me. And your luggage. Perhaps I can carry it."

"Oh, course you can," said Grandma drily. "I wish, Elijah, you'd stop putting on airs when there's company."

"I have no luggage," Paxton said, embarrassed.

He followed the robot across the patio and into the house, going down the central hall and up the very handsome winding staircase.

The room was large and filled with old-fashioned furniture. A sedate fireplace stood against one wall.

"I'll light a fire," Elijah said. "It gets chilly in the autumn, once the sun goes down. And damp. It looks like rain."

Paxton stood in the center of the room, trying to remember.

Grandma was a painter and Nelson was a naturalist, but what about old Granther?

"The old gentleman," said the robot, stooping at the fireplace, "will send you up a drink. He'll insist on brandy, but if you wish it, sir, I could get you something else."

"No, thank you. Brandy will be fine."

"The old gentleman's in great fettle. He'll have a lot to tell you. He's just finished his sonata, sir, after working at it for almost seven years, and he's very proud of it. There were times, I don't mind telling you, when it was going badly, that he wasn't fit to live with. If you'd just look here at my bottom, sir, you can see a dent . . ."

"So I see," said Paxton uncomfortably.

The robot rose from before the fireplace and the flames began to crackle, crawling up the wood.

"I'll go for your drink," Elijah said. "If it takes a little longer than seems necessary, do not become alarmed. The old gentleman undoubtedly will take this opportunity to lecture me about hewing to civility, now that we have a guest."

Paxton walked to the bed, took off his cloak and hung it on a bedpost. He walked back to the fire and sat down in a chair, stretching out his legs toward the warming blaze.

It had been wrong of him to come here, he thought. These people should not be involved in his problems and his dangers. Theirs was the quiet world, the easygoing, thoughtful world, while his world of Politics was all clamor and excitement and sometimes agony and fear.

He'd not tell them, he decided. And he'd stay just the night and be off before the dawn. Somehow or other he would work out a way to get in contact with his party. Somewhere else he'd find people who would help him.

There was a knock at the door. Apparently it had not taken Elijah as long as it had thought.

"Come in," Paxton called.

It was not Elijah; it was Nelson Moore.

He still wore a rough walking jacket and his boots had mud upon them and there was a streak of dirt across his face where he'd brushed back his hair with a grimy hand.

"Grandma told me you were here," he said, shaking Paxton by the hand.

"I had two weeks off," said Paxton, lying like a gentleman.

"We just finished with an exercise. It might interest you to know that I was elected President."

"Why, that is fine," said Nelson enthusiastically.

"Yes, I suppose it is."

"Let's sit down."

"I'm afraid I may be holding up the dinner. The robot said—"

Nelson laughed. "Elijah always rushes us to eat. He wants to get the day all done and buttoned up. We've come to expect it of him and we pay him no attention."

"I'm looking forward to meeting Anastasia," Paxton said. "I remember that you wrote of her often and—"

"She's not here," said Nelson. "She—well, she left me. Almost five years ago. She missed Outside too much. None of us should marry outside Continuation."

"I'm sorry. I shouldn't have—"

"It's all right, Stan. It's all done with now. There are some who simply do not fit into the project. I've wondered many times, since Anastasia left, what kind of folks we are. I've wondered if it all is worth it."

"All of us think that way at times," said Paxton. "There have been times when I've been forced to fall back on history to find some shred of justification for what we're doing here. There's a parallel in the monks of the so-called Middle Ages. They managed to preserve at least part of the knowledge of the Hellenic world. For their own selfish reasons, of course, as Continuation has its selfish reasons, but the human race was the real beneficiary."

"I go back to history, too," said Nelson. "The one that I come up with is a Stone Age savage, hidden off in some dark corner, busily flaking arrows while the first spaceships are being launched. It all seems so useless, Stan . . ."

"On the face of it, I suppose it is. It doesn't matter in the least that I was elected President in our just-finished exercise. But there may be a day when that knowledge and technique of politics may come in very handy. And when it does, all the human race will have to do is come back here to Earth and they have the living art. This campaign that I waged was a dirty one, Nelson. I'm not proud of it."

"There's a good deal of dirty things in the human culture," Nelson said, "but if we commit ourselves at all, it must be all the way—the vicious with the noble, the dirty with the splendid."

A door opened quietly and Elijah glided in. It had two glasses on a tray.

"I heard you come in," it said to Nelson, "so I brought you something, too."

"Thank you," Nelson said. "That was kind of you."

Elijah shuffled in some embarrassment. "If you don't mind, could you hurry just a little? The old gentleman has almost killed the bottle. I'm afraid of what might happen to him if I don't get back to the table."

II

Dinner had been finished and young Graham hustled off to bed. Granther unearthed, with great solemnity, another bottle of good brandy.

"That boy is a caution," he declared. "I don't know what's to become of him. Imagine him out there all day long, fighting those fool battles. If he was going to take up something, I should think he'd want it to be useful. There's nothing more useless than a general when there are no wars."

Grandma clacked her teeth together with impatience. "It isn't as if we hadn't tried. We gave him every chance there was. But he wasn't interested in anything until he took up warring."

"He's got guts," said Granther proudly. "That much I'll say for him. He up and asked me the other day would I write him some battle music. Me!" yelled Granther, thumping his chest.

"Me write battle music!"

"He's got the seeds of destruction in him," declared Grandma righteously. "He doesn't want to build. He just wants to bust."

"Don't look at me," Nelson said to Paxton. "I gave up long ago. Granther and Grandma took him over from me right after Anastasia left. To hear them talk, you'd think they hated him. But let me lift a finger to him and the both of them—"

"We did the best we could," said Grandma. "We gave him every chance. We bought him all the testing kits. You remember?"

"Sure," said Granther, busy with the bottle. "I remember well. We bought him that ecology kit and you should have seen the planet he turned out. It was the most pitiful, down-at-heels, hungover planet you ever saw. And then we tried robotry—"

"He did right well at that," said Grandma tartly.

"Sure, he built them. He enjoyed building them. Recall the time he geared the two of them to hate each other and they fought until they were just two piles of scrap? I never saw anyone have such a splendid time as Graham during the seven days they fought."

"We could scarcely get him in to meals," said Grandma.

Granther handed out the brandy.

"But the worst of all," he decided, "was the time we tried religion. He dreamed up a cult that was positively gummy. We made short work of that . . ."

"And the hospital," said Grandma. "That was your idea, Nels . . ."

"Let's not talk about it," pleaded Nelson grimly. "I am sure Stanley isn't interested."

Paxton picked up the cue Nelson was offering him. "I was going to ask you, Grandma, what kind of painting you are doing. I don't recall that Nelson ever told me."

"Landscapes," the sweet-faced old lady said. "I've been doing some experimenting."

"And I tell her she is wrong," protested Granther. "To experiment is wrong. Our job is to maintain tradition, not to let our work go wandering off in whatever direction it might choose."

"Our job," said Grandma bitterly, "is to guard the techniques. Which is not to say we cannot strive at progress, if it still is human progress. Young man," she appealed to Paxton, "isn't that the way you see it?"

"Well, in part," evaded Paxton, caught between two fires. "In Politics, we allow evolvement, naturally, but we make sure by periodic tests that we are developing logically and in the human manner. And we make very sure we do not drop any of the old techniques, no matter how outmoded they may seem. And the same is true in Diplomacy. I happen to know a bit about Diplomacy, because the two sections work very close together and—"

"There!" Grandma said.

"You know what I think?" said Nelson quietly. "We are a frightened race. For the first time in our history, the human race is a minority and it scares us half to death. We are afraid of losing our identity in the great galactic matrix. We're afraid of assimilation."

"That's wrong, son," Granther disagreed. "We are not afraid, my boy. We're just awful smart, that's all. We had a great culture at one time and why should we give it up? Sure, most humans nowadays have adopted the galactic way of life, but that is not to say that it is for the best. Some day we may want to turn back to the human culture or we may find that later on we can use parts of it. And this way, if we keep it alive here in Project Continuation, it will be available, all of it or any part, any time we need it. And I'm not speaking, mind you, from the human view alone, because some facet of our culture might sometime be badly needed, not by the human race as such, but by the Galaxy itself."

"Then why keep the project secret?"

"I don't think it's really secret," Granther said. "It's just that no one pays much attention to the human race and none at all to Earth. The human race is pretty small potatoes against all the rest of them and Earth is just a worn-out planet that doesn't amount to shucks."

He asked Paxton: "You ever hear it was secret, boy?"

"Why, I guess not," said Paxton. "All I ever understood was that we didn't go around shooting off our mouths about it. I've thought of Continuation as a sort of sacred trust. We're the guardians who watch over the tribal medicine bag while the rest of humanity is out among the stars getting civilized."

The old man chortled. "That's about the size of it. We're just a bunch of bushmen, but mark me well, intelligent and even dangerous bushmen."

"Dangerous?" asked Paxton.

"He means Graham," Nelson told him quietly.

"No, I don't," said Granther. "Not him especially. I mean the whole kit and caboodle of us. Because, don't you see, everybody who joins in this galactic culture that they are stewing up out there must contribute something and must likewise give up something—things that don't fit in with the new ideas. And the human race has done just like the rest of them, except we haven't given up a thing. Oh, on the surface, certainly. But everything we've given up is still back here, being kept alive by a bunch of subsidized barbarians on an old and gutted planet that a member of this fine galactic culture wouldn't give a second look."

"He's horrible," said Grandma. "Don't pay attention to him. He's got a mean and ornery soul inside that withered carcass."

"And what is Man?" yelled Granther. "He's mean and ornery, too, when he has to be. How could we have gone so far if we weren't mean and ornery?"

And there was some truth in that, thought Paxton. For what humanity was doing here was deliberate doublecrossing. Although, come to think of it, he wondered, how many other races might be doing the very selfsame thing or its equivalent?

And, if you were going to do it, you had to do it right. You couldn't take the human culture and enshrine it prettily within a museum, for then it would become no more than a shiny showpiece. A fine display of arrowheads was a pretty thing to look at, but a man would never learn to chip a flint into an arrowhead by merely looking at a bunch of them laid out on a velvet-covered board. To retain the technique of chipping arrows, you'd have to keep on chipping arrows, generation after generation, long after the need of them was gone. Fail by one generation and the art was lost.

And the same necessarily must be true of other human techniques and other human arts. And not the purely human arts alone, but the unique human flavor of other techniques which in themselves were common to many other races.

Elijah brought in an armload of wood and dumped it down upon the hearth, heaped an extra log or two upon the fire, then brushed itself off carefully.

"You're wet," said Grandma.

"It's raining, madam," said Elijah, going out the door.

And so, thought Paxton, Project Continuation kept on practicing the old arts, retaining within a living body of the race the knowledge of their manipulation and their use.

So the section on politics practiced politics and the section on diplomacy set up seemingly impossible problems in diplomacy and wrestled with those problems. And in the project factories, teams of industrialists carried on in the old tradition and fought a never-ending feud with the trade unionism teams. And, scattered throughout the land, quiet men and women painted and composed and wrote and sculpted so that the culture that had been wholly human would not perish in the face of the new and wonderful galactic culture that was evolving from the fusion of many intelligences out in the farther stars.

And against what day, wondered Paxton, do we carry on this work? Is it pure and simple, and perhaps even silly, pride? Is it no more than a further expression of human skepticism and human arrogance? Or does it make the solid sense that old Granther thinks it does?

"You're in Politics, you say," Granther said to Paxton. "Now that is what I'd call a worthwhile thing to save. From what I hear, this new culture doesn't pay too much attention to what we call politics. There's administration, naturally, and a sense of civic duty and all that sort of nonsense—but no real politics. Politics can be a powerful thing when you need to win a point."

"Politics is a dirty business far too often," Paxton answered. "It's a fight for power, an effort to override and overrule the principles and policies of an opposing body. In even its best phase, it brought about the fiction of the minority, with the connotation that the mere fact of being a minority carries with it the penalty of being to a large extent ignored."

"Still, it could be fun. I suppose it is exciting."

"Yes, you could call it that," said Paxton. "This last exercise we carried out was one with no holds barred. We had it planned that way. It was described somewhat delicately as a vicious battle."

"And you were elected President," said Nelson.

"That I was, but you didn't hear me say I was proud of it."

"But you should be," Grandma insisted. "In the ancient days, it was a proud thing to be elected President."

"Perhaps," Paxton admitted, "but not the way my party did it."

It would be so easy, he thought, to go ahead and tell them, for they would understand. To say: I carried it too far. I blackened my opponent's name and character beyond any urgent need. I used all the dirty tricks. I bribed and lied and compromised and traded. And I did it all so well that I even fooled the logic that was the referee, which stood in lieu of populace and voter. And now my opponent has dug up another trick and is using it on me.

For assassination was political, even as diplomacy and war were political. After all, politics was little more than the short-circuiting of violence; an election was held rather than a revolution. But at all times the partition between politics and violence was a thin and flimsy thing.

He finished off his brandy and put the glass down on the table.

Granther picked up the bottle, but Paxton shook his head.

"Thank you," he said. "If you don't mind, I shall go to bed soon. I must get an early start."

He never should have stopped here. It would be unforgivable to embroil these people in the aftermath of the exercise.

Although, he told himself, it probably was unfair to call it the aftermath—what was happening would have to be a part and parcel of the exercise itself.

The doorbell tinkled faintly and they could hear Elijah stirring in the hall.

"Sakes alive," said Grandma, "who can it be this time of night? And raining outdoors, too!"

It was a churchman.

He stood in the hall, brushing water from his cloak. He took off his broad-brimmed hat and swished it to shake off the raindrops.

He came into the room with a slow and stately tread.

All of them arose.

"Good evening, Bishop," said old Granther. "You were fortunate to find the house in this kind of weather and we're glad to have Your Worship."

The bishop beamed in fine, fast fellowship.

"Not of the church," he said. "Of the project merely. But you may use the proper terms, if you have a mind. It helps me stay in character."

Elijah, trailing in his wake, took his cloak and hat. The bishop was arrayed in rich and handsome garments.

Granther introduced them all around and found a glass and filled it from the bottle.

The bishop took it and smacked his lips. He sat down in a chair next to the fire.

"You have not dined, I take it," Grandma said. "Of course you haven't—there's no place out there to dine. Elijah, get the bishop a plate of food, and hurry."

"I thank you, madam," said the bishop. "I've had a long, hard day. I appreciate all you're doing for me. I appreciate it more than you can ever know."

"This is our day," Granther said merrily, refilling his own glass for the umpteenth time. "It is seldom that we have any guests at all and now, all of an evening, we have two of them."

"Two guests," said the bishop, looking straight at Paxton. "Now that is fine, indeed."

He smacked his lips again and emptied the glass.

III

In his room, Paxton closed the door and shot the bolt full home.

The fire had burned down to embers and cast a dull glow along the floor. The rain drummed faintly, half-heartedly, on the window pane.

And the question and the fear raced within his brain.

There was no question of it: The bishop was the assassin who had been set upon his trail.

No man without a purpose, and a deadly purpose, walked these hills at night, in an autumn rain. And what was more, the bishop had been scarcely wet. He'd shaken his hat and the drops had fallen off, and he'd brushed at his cloak and after that both the hat and cloak were dry.

The bishop had been brought here, more than likely, in a hovering flier and let down, as other assassins probably likewise had been let down this very night in all of half a dozen places where a fleeing man might have taken shelter.

The bishop had been taken to the room just across the hall and under other circumstances, Paxton told himself, he might have sought conclusions with him there. He walked over to the fireplace and picked up the heavy poker and weighed it in his hand. One stroke of that and it would be all over.

But he couldn't do it. Not in this house.

He put the poker back and walked over to the bed and picked up his cloak. Slowly he slid it on as he stood there, thinking, going over in his mind the happenings of the morning.

He had been at home, alone, and the phone had rung and Sullivan's face had filled the visor—a face all puffed up with fright.

"Hunter's out to get you," Sullivan had said. "He's sent men to get you."

"But he can't do that!" Paxton remembered protesting.

"Certainly he can," said Sullivan. "It comes within the framework of the exercise. Assassination has always been a possibility . . ."

"But the exercise is finished!"

"Not so far as Hunter is concerned. You went a little far. You should have stayed within the hypothesis of the problem; there was no need to go back into Hunter's personal affairs. You dug up things he thought no one ever knew. How did you do it, man?"

"I have my ways," said Paxton. "And in a deal like this, everything was fair. He didn't handle me exactly as if I were innocent."

"You better get going," Sullivan advised. "They must be almost there. I can't get anyone there soon enough to help you."

And it would have been all right, Paxton thought, if the flier had only held together.

He wondered momentarily if it had been sabotaged.

But be that as it may, he had flown it down and had been able to walk away from it and now, finally, here he was.

He stood irresolutely in the center of the room.

It went against his price to flee for a second time, but there was nothing else to do. He couldn't let this house become involved in the tag-end rough and tumble of his exercise.

And despite the poker, he was weaponless, for weapons on this now-peaceful planet were very few indeed—no longer household items such as once had been the case.

He went to the window and opened it and saw that the rain had stopped and that a ragged moon was showing through a scud of racing clouds.

Glancing down, he saw the roof of the porch beneath the window and he let his eye follow down the roof line. Not too hard, he thought, if a man were barefoot, and once he reached the edge there'd be a drop of not much more than seven feet.

He took off his sandals and stuffed them in the pocket of his cloak and started out the window. But, halfway out, he climbed back in again and walked to the door. Quietly he slid back the bolt. It wasn't exactly cricket to go running off and leave a room locked up.

The roof was slippery with the rain, but he managed it without any trouble, inching his way carefully down the incline. He dropped into a shrub that scratched him up a bit, but that, he told himself, was a minor matter.

He put on his sandals and straightened up and walked rapidly away. At the edge of the woods, he stopped and looked back at the house. It stood dark and silent.

Once he got back home and this affair was finished, he promised himself, he'd write Nelson a long apologetic letter and explain it all.

His feet found the path and he followed it through the sickly half-light of the cloudy moon.

"Sir," said a voice close beside him, "I see that you are out for a little stroll . . ."

Paxton jumped in fright.

"It's a nice night for it, sir," the voice went on quietly. "After a rain, everything seems so clean and cool."

"Who is there?" asked Paxton, with his hair standing quite on edge.

"Why, it's Pertwee, sir. Pertwee, the robot, sir."

Paxton laughed a little nervously. "Oh, yes, I remember now. You're Graham's enemy."

The robot stepped out of the woods into the path beside him.

"It's too much, I suppose," Pertwee said, "to imagine that you might be coming out to look at the battlefield."

"Why, no," said Paxton, grasping at a straw. "I don't know how you guessed it, but that's exactly what I'm doing. I've never heard of anything quite like it and I'm considerably intrigued."

"Sir," said the robot eagerly, "I'm entirely at your service. There is no one, I can assure you, who is better equipped to explain it to you. I've been in it from the very first with Master Graham and if you have any questions, I shall try to answer them."

"Yes, I think there is one question. What is the purpose of it all?"

"Why, at first, of course," said Pertwee, "it was simply an attempt to amuse a growing boy. But now, with your permission, sir. I would venture the opinion that it is a good deal more."

"You mean a part of Continuation?"

"Certainly, sir. I know there is a natural reluctance among humankind to admit the fact, or to even think about it, but for a great part of Man's history war played an important and many-sided role. Of all the arts that Man developed, there probably was none to which he devoted so much time and thought and money as he did to war."

The path sloped down and there before them in the pale and mottled moonlight lay the battle bowl. "That bowl," asked Paxton, "or whatever it might be that you have tipped over it? Sometimes you can just make it out and other times you miss it . . ."

"I suppose," said Pertwee, "you'd call it a force shield, sir. A couple of the other robots worked it out. As I understand it, sir, it is nothing new—just an adaptation. There's a time factor worked into it as an additional protection."

"But that sort of protection . . ."

"We use TC bombs, sir—total conversion bombs. Each side gets so many of them and uses his best judgment and . . ."

"But you couldn't use nuclear stuff in there!"

"As safe as a toy, sir," said Pertwee gaily. "They are very small, sir. Not much larger than a pea. Critical mass, as you well understand, no longer is much of a consideration. And the yield in radiation, while it is fairly high, is extremely short-lived, so that within an hour or so . . ."

"You gentlemen," said Paxton grimly, "certainly try to be entirely realistic."

"Why, yes, of course we do. Although the operators are entirely safe. We're in the same sort of position, you might say, as the general staff. And that is all right, of course, because the purpose of the entire business is to keep alive the art of waging war."

"But the art . . ." Paxton started to argue, then stopped.

What could he say? If the race persisted in its purpose of keeping the old culture workable and intact in Continuation, then it must perforce accept that culture in its entirety.

War, one must admit, was as much a part of the human culture as were all the other more or less uniquely human things that the race was conserving here as a sort of racial cushion against a future need or use.

"There is," confessed Pertwee, "a certain cruelty, but perhaps a cruelty that I, as a robot, am more alive to than would be the case with a human, sir. The rate of casualties among the robot troops is unbelievable. In a restricted space and with extremely high firepower, that would be the natural consequence."

"You mean that you use troops—that you send robots in there?"

"Why, yes. Who else would operate the weapons? And it would be just a little silly, don't you think, to work out a battle and then . . ."

"But robots . . ."

"They are very small ones, sir. They would have to be, to gain an illusion of the space which is normally covered by a full-scale battle. And the weapons likewise are scaled down, and that sort of evens things out. And the troops are very single-minded, completely obedient and dedicated to victory. We turn them out in mass production in our shops and there's little chance to give them varying individualities and anyhow . . ."

"Yes, I see," said Paxton, a little stunned. "But now I think that I . . ."

"But, sir, I have only got a start at telling you and I've not shown you anything at all. There are so many considerations and there were so many problems."

They were close to the towering, fully shimmering force field now and Pertwee pointed to a stairway that led from ground level down toward its base.

"I'd like to show you, sir," said Pertwee, ducking down the stairs.

It stopped before a door.

"This," it said, "is the only entrance to the battlefield. We use it to send new troops and munitions during periods of truce, and at other times we use it to polish up the place a bit."

Its thumb stabbed out and hit a button to one side of the door and the door moved upward silently.

"After several weeks of battle," the robot explained, "the terrain is bound to become a little cluttered."

Through the door, Paxton could see the churned-up ground and the evidence of dying, and it was as if someone had pushed him in the belly. He gulped in a stricken breath and couldn't let it out and he suddenly was giddy and nearly sick. He put out a hand to hold himself upright against the trenchlike wall beside him.

Pertwee pushed another button and the door slid down.

"It hits you hard the first time you see it," Pertwee apologized, "but given time, one gets used to it."

Paxton let his breath out slowly and looked around. The trench with the stairway came down to the door, and the door, he saw, was wider than the trench, so that at the foot of the steps the area had been widened into a sort of letter T, with narrow embrasures scooped out to face the door.

"You all right, sir?" asked Pertwee.

"Perfectly all right," Paxton told the robot stiffly.

"And now," said Pertwee happily, "I'll explain the fire and tactical control."

It trotted up the steps and Paxton trailed behind it.

"I'm afraid that would take too long," said Paxton.

But the robot brushed the words aside. "You must see it, sir," it pleaded plaintively. "Now that you are out here, you must not miss seeing it."

He'd have to get away somehow, Paxton told himself. He couldn't afford to waste much time. As soon as the house had settled down to sleep, the bishop would come hunting him, and by that time he must be gone.

Pertwee led the way around the curving base of the battle bowl to the observation tower which Paxton had come upon that evening.

The robot halted at the base of the ladder.

"After you," it said.

Paxton hesitated, then went swiftly up the ladder.

Maybe this wouldn't take too long, he thought, and then he could be off. It would be better, he realized, if he could get rid of Pertwee without being too abrupt about it.

The robot brushed past him in the darkness and bent above the bank of controls. There was a snick and lights came on in the panels.

"This, you see," it said, "is the groundglass—a representation of the battlefield. It is dead now, of course, because there is nothing going on, but when there is some action certain symbols are imposed upon the field so that one can see at all times just how things are going. And this is the fire control panel and this is the troop command panel and this . . ."

Pertwee went on and on with his explanations.

Finally it turned in triumph from the instruments.

"What do you think of it?" the robot asked, very clearly expecting praise.

"Why, it's wonderful," said Paxton, willing to say anything to make an end of his visit.

"If you are going to be around tomorrow," Pertwee said, "you may want to watch us."

And it was then that Paxton got his inspiration.

"As a matter of fact," Paxton said, "I'd like to try it out. In my youth, I did a bit of reading on military matters, and if you'll excuse my saying so, I have often fancied myself somewhat of an expert." Pertwee brightened almost visibly. "You mean, sir, that you'd like to go one round with me?"

"If you'd be so kind."

"You are sure you understand how to operate the board?"

"I watched you very closely."

"Give me fifteen minutes to reach my tower," said Pertwee. "When I arrive, I'll press the ready button. After that, either of us can start hostilities any time we wish."

"Fifteen minutes?"

"It may not take me that long, sir. I'll be quick about it."

"And I'm not imposing on you?"

"Sir," Pertwee said feelingly, "it will be a pleasure. I've fought against young Master Graham until the novelty has worn off. We know one another's tactics so well that there's little chance for surprise. As you can understand, sir, that makes for a rather humdrum war."

"Yes," said Paxton, "I suppose it would."

He watched Pertwee go down the ladder and listened to its footsteps hurrying away.

Then he went down the ladder and stood for a moment at the foot of it.

The clouds had thinned considerably and the moonlight was brighter now and it would be easier travelling, although it still would be dark in the denser forest.

He swung away from the tower and headed for the path, and, as he did so, he caught a flicker of motion in a patch of brush just off the trail.

Paxton slid into the denser shadow of a clump of trees and watched the patch of brush.

He crouched and waited. There was another cautious movement in the brush and he saw it was the bishop. Now suddenly it seemed that there was a chance to get the bishop off his neck for good—if his inspiration would only pay off.

The bishop had been let down by the flier in the dark of night, with the rain still pouring down and no moonlight at all. So it was unlikely that he knew about the battle bowl, although more than likely he must see it now, glittering faintly in the moonlight. But even if he saw it, there was a chance he'd not know what it was.

Paxton thought back along the conversation there had been after the bishop had arrived and no one, so far as he remembered, had mentioned a word of young Graham or the war project.

There was, Paxton thought, nothing lost by trying. Even if it didn't work, all he'd lose would be a little time.

He darted from the clump of trees to reach the base of the battle bowl. He crouched against the ground and watched, and the bishop came sliding out of his clump of brush and worked his way along, closing in upon him.

And that was fine, thought Paxton. It was working just the way he'd planned.

—

He moved a little to make absolutely sure his trailer would know exactly where he was and then he dived down the stairs that led to the door.

He reached it and thumbed the button and the door slid slowly upward without a single sound. Paxton crowded back into the embrasure and waited.

It took a little longer than he had thought it would and he was getting slightly nervous when he heard the step upon the stairs.

The bishop came down slowly, apparently very watchful, and then he reached the door and stood there for a moment, staring out into the churned-up battlefield. And in his hand he held an ugly gun.

Paxton held his breath and pressed his shoulders tight against the wall of earth, but the bishop didn't even look around. His eyes were busy taking in the ground that lay beyond the door.

Then finally he moved, quickly, like a leopard. His silken garments made a swishing noise as he stepped through the door and out into the battle area.

Paxton held himself motionless, watching the bishop advance cautiously out into the field, and when he was far enough, he reached out a finger and pressed the second button and the door came down, smoothly, silently.

Paxton leaned against the door and let out in a gasp the breath he had been holding.

It was over now, he thought.

Hunter hadn't been as clever as he had thought he was.

Paxton turned from the door and went slowly up the stairs.

Now he needn't run away. He could stay right here and Nelson would fly him, or arrange to have him flown, to some place of safety.

For Hunter wouldn't know that this particular assassin had hunted down his quarry. The bishop had had no chance to communicate and probably wouldn't have dared to even if he could.

On the top step, Paxton stubbed his toe and went down without a chance to catch himself, and there was a vast explosion that shook the universe and artillery fire was bursting in his brain.

Dazed, he got to his hands and knees and crawled painfully, hurling himself desperately down the stairs—and through the crashing uproar that filled the entire world ran an urgent thought and purpose.

I've got to get him out before it is too late! I can't let him die in there! I can't kill a man!

He slipped on the stairs and slid until his body jammed in the narrowness and stuck.

And there was no artillery fire, there was no crash of shells, no wicked little chitterings. The dome glittered softly in the moonlight and was as quiet as death.

Except, he thought, a little weirdly, death's not quiet in there. It is an inferno of destruction and a maddening place of sound and brightness and the quietness doesn't come until afterward.

He'd fallen and hit his head, he knew, and all he'd seen and heard had been within his brain. But Pertwee would be opening up any minute now and the quietness would be gone, and with it the opportunity to undo what he had so swiftly planned.

And somewhere in the shadow of the dome another self stood off and argued with him, jeering at his softness, quoting logic at him.

It was either he or you, said that other self. You fought for your life the best way you knew, the only way you knew, and whatever you may have done, no matter what you did, you were entirely justified.

"I can't do it!" yelled the Paxton on the stairs and yet even as he yelled he knew that he was wrong, that by logic he was wrong, that the jeering self who stood off in the shadows made more sense than he.

He staggered to his feet. Without his conscious mind made up, he went down the stairs. Driven by some as yet unrealized and undefined instinctive prompting that was past all understanding, he stumbled down the stairs, with the throb still in his head and a choking guilt and fear rising in his throat.

He reached the door and stabbed the button and the door slid up and he went out into the cluttered place of dying and stopped in horror at the awful loneliness and the vindictive desolation of this square mile of Earth that was shut off from all the other Earth as if it were a place of final judgment.

And perhaps it was, he thought—the final judgment of Man.

Of all of us, he thought, young Graham may be the only honest one; he's the true barbarian that old Granther thinks he is; he is the throwback who looks out upon Man's past and sees it as it is and lives it as it was.

Paxton took a quick look back and he saw the door was closed and out ahead of him, in the plowed and jumbled sea of tortured, battered earth, he saw a moving figure that could be no one but the bishop.

Paxton ran forward, shouting, and the bishop turned around and stood there, waiting, with the gun half lifted.

Paxton stopped and waved his arms in frantic signaling. The bishop's gun came up and there was a stinging slash across the side of Paxton's neck and a sudden, gushing wetness. A small, blue puff of smoke hung on the muzzle of the distant gun.

Paxton flung himself aside and dived for the ground. He hit and skidded on his belly and tumbled most ingloriously into a dusty crater. He lay there, at the bottom of the crater, huddled against the fear of a bullet's impact while the rage and fury built up into white heat.

He had come here to save a man and the man had tried to kill him!

I should have left him here, he thought.

I should have let him die.

I'd kill him if I could.

And the fact of the matter now was that he had to kill the bishop. There was no choice but to kill him or be killed himself.

Not only did he have to kill the bishop, but he had to kill him soon. Pertwee's fifteen minutes must be almost at an end and the bishop had to be killed and he had to be out the door before Pertwee opened fire.

Out the door, he thought—did he have a chance? If he ran low and dodged, perhaps, would he have a chance to escape the bishop's bullets?

That was it, he thought. Waste no time on killing if he didn't have to; let Pertwee do the killing. Just get out of here himself.

He put his hand up to his neck, and when he lifted it, his fingers were covered with a sticky wetness. It was funny, he thought, that it didn't hurt, although the hurt, no doubt, would come later.

He crawled up the crater's side and rolled across its lip and found himself lying in a small, massed junkyard of smashed and broken robots, sprawled grotesquely where the barrage had caught them.

And lying there in front of him, without a scratch upon it, where it had fallen from a dying robot's grasp, was a rifle that shone dully in the moonlight.

He snatched it up and rose into a crouch and as he did he saw the bishop, almost on top of him; the bishop coming in to make sure that he was finished!

There was no time to run, as he had planned to—and, curiously, no desire to run. Paxton had never known actual hate before, never had a chance to know it, but now it came and filled him full of rage and a wild and exultant will and capacity to kill without pity or remorse.

He tilted up the rifle and his finger closed upon the trigger and the weapon danced and flashed and made a deadly chatter.

But the bishop still came on, not rushing now, but plodding

ahead with a deadly stride, leaning forward as if his body were absorbing the murderous rifle fire, absorbing it and keeping on by will power alone, holding off death until that moment when it might snuff out the thing that was killing it.

The bishop's gun came up and something smashed into Paxton's chest, and smashed again and yet again, and there was a flood of wetness and a spattering and the edge of Paxton's brain caught at the hint of something wrong.

For two men do not—could not—stand a dozen feet apart and pour at one another a deadly blast and both stay on their feet. No matter how poor might be their aim, it simply couldn't happen.

He rose out of his crouch and stood at his full height and let the gun hang uselessly in his hand. Six feet away, the bishop stopped as well and flung his gun away.

They stood looking at one another in the pale moonlight and the anger melted and ran out of them and Paxton wished that he were almost anywhere but there.

"Paxton," asked the bishop plaintively, "who did this to us?"

And it was a funny thing to say, almost as if he'd said: "Who stopped us from killing one another?"

For a fleeting moment, it almost seemed to Paxton as though it might have been a kinder thing if they had been allowed to kill. For killing was a brave thing in the annals of the race, an art of strength and a certain proof of manhood—perhaps of human-hood.

A kinder thing to be allowed to kill. And that was it, exactly. They had not been allowed to kill.

For you couldn't kill with a pop-gun that shot out plastic pellets of liquid that burst on contact, with the liquid running down like blood for the sake of realism. And you couldn't kill with a gun that went most admirably through all the motions of chattering and smoking and flashing out red fire, but with nothing lethal in it.

And was this entire battle bowl no more than a toy set with

robots that came apart at the right and most dramatic moments and then could be put back together at a later time? Were the artillery and the total-conversion bombs toy things as well, with a lot of flash and noise and perhaps a few well-placed items to plow up the battlefield, but without the power to really hurt a robot?

The bishop said, "Paxton, I feel like an utter fool." And he added other words which a real bishop could never bring himself to say, making very clear just what kind of obscene fool he was.

"Let's get out of here," said Paxton shortly, feeling like that same kind of fool himself.

"I wonder . . ." said the bishop.

"Forget about it," Paxton growled. "Let's just get out of here. Pertwee will be opening up . . ."

But he didn't finish what he was about to say, for he realized that even if Pertwee did open up, there'd be little danger. And there wasn't any chance that Pertwee would open up, for it would know that they were here.

Like a metal monitor watching over a group of rebellious children—rebellious because they weren't adult yet. Watching them and letting them go ahead and play so long as they were in no danger of drowning or of falling off a roof or some other reckless thing. And then interfering only just enough to save their silly necks. Perhaps even encouraging them to play so they'd work off their rebelliousness—joining in the game in the typically human tradition of let's pretend.

Like monitors watching over children, letting them develop, allowing them to express their foolish little selves, not standing in the way of whatever childish importance they could muster up, encouraging them to think they were sufficient to themselves.

Paxton started for the door, plodding along, the bishop in his bedraggled robes stumbling along behind him.

When they were a hundred feet away, the door started sliding up and Pertwee stood there, waiting for them, not looking any different than it had before, but somehow seeming to have a new measure of importance.

They reached the door and sheepishly trailed through it, not looking right or left, casually and elaborately pretending that Pertwee was not there.

"Gentlemen," said Pertwee, "don't you want to play?"

"No," Paxton said. "No, thank you. I can't speak for both of us—"

"Yes, you can, friend," the bishop put in. "Go right ahead."

"My friend and I have done all the playing we care to do," said Paxton. "It was good of you to make sure we didn't get hurt."

Pertwee managed to look puzzled. "But why should anybody be allowed to get hurt? It was only a game."

"So we've discovered. Which way is out?"

"Why," said the robot, "any way but back."

CRYING JAG

Originally sold as "All the Sad Stories," this story first appeared in the February 1960 issue of Galaxy Magazine. Horace Gold accepted the story for publication just eight days after Cliff Simak mailed it to him. It fits tidily into that species of Simak story that portrays an alien coming to a small town (a town, as is common in Cliff's stories, named Millville).

Worse than a case of the blind leading the blind is the case of the drunk leading the drunk.

—dww

It was Saturday evening and I was sitting on the stoop, working up a jag. I had my jug beside me, handy, and I was feeling good and fixing to feel better, when this alien and his robot came tramping up the driveway.

I knew right off it was an alien. It looked something like a man, but there weren't any humans got robots trailing at their heels.

If I had been stone sober, I might have gagged a bit at the idea there was an alien coming up the driveway and done some arguing with myself. But I wasn't sober—not entirely, that is.

So I said good evening and asked him to sit down and he thanked me and sat.

"You, too," I said to the robot, moving over to make room

"Let him stand," the alien said. "He cannot sit. He is a mere machine."

The robot clanked a gear at him, but that was all it said.

"Have a snort," I said, picking up the jug, but the alien shook his head.

"I wouldn't dare," he said. "My metabolism."

That was one of the double-jointed words I had acquaintance with. From working at Doc Abel's sanitorium, I had picked up some of the medic lingo.

"That's a dirty shame," I said. "You don't mind if I do?"

"Not at all," the alien said.

So I had a long one. I felt the need of it.

I put down the jug and wiped my mouth and asked him if there was something I could get him. It seemed plain inhospitable for me to be sitting there, lapping up that liquor, and him not having any.

"You can tell me about this town," the alien said. "I think you call it Millville."

"That's the name, all right. What you want to know about it?"

"All the sad stories," said the robot, finally speaking up.

"He is correct," the alien said, settling down in an attitude of pleasurable anticipation. "Tell me about the troubles and the tribulations."

"Starting where?" I asked.

"How about yourself?"

"Me? I never have no troubles. I janitor all week at the sanitorium and I get drunk on Saturday. Then I sober up on Sunday so I can janitor another week. Believe me, mister," I told him, "I haven't got no troubles. I am sitting pretty. I have got it made."

"But there must be people . . ."

"Oh, there are. You never saw so much complaining as there is in Millville. There ain't nobody here except myself but has got a load of trouble. And it wouldn't be so bad if they didn't talk about it."

"Tell me," said the alien.

So I had another snort and then I told him about the Widow Frye, who lives just up the street. I told him how her life had been just one long suffering, with her husband running out on her when their boy was only three years old, and how she took in washing and worked her fingers to the bone to support the two of them, and the kid ain't more than thirteen or fourteen when he steals this car and gets sent up for two years to the boys' school over at Glen Lake.

"And that is all of it?" asked the alien.

"Well, in rough outline," I said. "I didn't put in none of the flourishes nor the grimy details, the way the widow would. You should hear her tell it."

"Could you arrange it?"

"Arrange what?"

"To have her tell it to me."

"I wouldn't promise you," I told him honestly. "The widow has a low opinion of me. She never speaks to me."

"But I can't understand."

"She is a decent, church-going woman," I explained, "and I am just a crummy bum. And I drink."

"She doesn't like drinking?"

"She thinks it is a sin."

The alien sort of shivered. "I know. I guess all places are pretty much alike."

"You have people like the Widow Frye?"

"Not exactly, but the attitude's the same."

"Well," I said, after another snort, "I figure there is nothing else to do but bear up under it."

"Would it be too much bother," asked the alien, "to tell me another one?"

"None at all," I said.

So I told him about Elmer Trotter, who worked his way through law school up at Madison, doing all kinds of odd jobs to earn his way, since he had no folks, and how he finally got through and passed the bar examination, then came back to Millville to set up an office.

I couldn't tell him how it happened or why, although I had always figured that Elmer had got a belly full of poverty and grabbed this chance to earn a lot of money fast. No one should have known better than he did that it was dishonest, being he was a lawyer. But he went ahead and did it and he got caught.

"And what happened then?" asked the alien breathlessly. "Was he punished?"

I told him how Elmer got disbarred and how Eliza Jenkins gave him back his ring and how Elmer went into insurance and just scraped along in a hand-to-mouth existence, eating out his heart to be a lawyer once again, but he never could.

"You got all this down?" the alien asked the robot.

"All down," the robot said.

"What fine nuances!" exclaimed the alien, who seemed to be much pleased. "What stark, overpowering reality!"

I didn't know what he was talking about, so I had another drink instead.

Then I went ahead, without being asked, and I told him about Amanda Robinson and her unhappy love affair and how she turned into Millville's most genteel and sorriest old maid. And about Abner Jones and his endless disappointments, but his refusal to give up the idea that he was a great inventor, and how his family went in rags and hungry while he spent all his time inventing.

"Such sadness!" said the alien. "What a lovely planet!"

"You better taper off," the robot warned him. "You know what happens to you."

"Just one more," the alien begged. "I'm all right. Just one more."

"Now, look here," I told him, "I don't mind telling them, if that is what you want. But maybe first you better tell me a bit about yourself. I take it you're an alien."

"Naturally," said the alien.

"And you came here in a spaceship."

"Well, not exactly a spaceship."

"Then, if you're an alien, how come you talk so good?"

"Now, that," the alien said, "is something that still is tender to me."

The robot said scornfully: "They took him good and proper."

"You mean you paid for it."

"Too much," the robot said. "They saw that he was eager, so they hiked the price on him."

"But I'll get even with them," the alien cut in. "If I don't turn a profit on it, my name isn't ———."

And he said a word that was long and twisted and didn't make no sense.

"That your name?" I asked.

"Yeah, sure. But you can call me Wilbur. And the robot, you may call him Lester."

"Well, boys," I said, "I'm mighty glad to know you. You can call me Sam."

And I had another drink.

We sat there on the stoop and the moon was coming up and the fireflies were flickering in the lilac hedge and the world had an edge on it. I'd never felt so good.

"Just one more," said Wilbur pleadingly.

So I told him about some of the mental cases up at the sanitorium and I picked the bad ones and alongside of me Wilbur started blubbering and the robot said: "Now see what you've done. He's got a crying jag."

But Wilbur wiped his eyes and said it was all right and that if I'd just keep on he'd do the best he could to get a grip on himself.

"What is going on here?" I asked in some astonishment. "You sound like you get drunk from hearing these sad stories."

"That's what he does," said Lester, the robot. "Why else do you think he'd sit and listen to your blabber."

"And you?" I asked of Lester.

"Of course not," Wilbur said. "He had no emotions. He is a mere machine."

I had another drink and I thought it over and it was as clear as day. So I told Wilbur my philosophy: "This is Saturday night and that's the time to howl. So let's you and I together—"

"I am with you," Wilbur cried, "as long as you can talk."

Lester clanked a gear in what must have been disgust, but that was all he did.

"Get down every word of it," Wilbur told the robot. "We'll make ourselves a million. We'll need it to get back all overpayment for our indoctrination." He sighed. "Not that it wasn't worth it. What a lovely, melancholy planet."

So I got cranked up and kept myself well lubricated and the night kept getting better every blessed minute.

Along about midnight, I got falling-down drunk and Wilbur maudlin drink and we gave up by a sort of mutual consent. We got up off the stoop and by bracing one another we got inside the door and I lost Wilbur somewhere, but made it to my bed and that was the last I knew.

When I woke up, I knew it was Sunday morning. The sun was streaming through the window and it was bright and sanctimonious, like Sunday always is around here.

Sundays usually are quiet, and that's one thing wrong with them. But this one wasn't quiet. There was an awful din going on outside. It sounded like someone was throwing rocks and hitting a tin can.

I rolled out of bed and my mouth tasted just as bad as I knew it would be. I rubbed some of the sand out of my eyes and started for the living room and just outside the bedroom door I almost stepped on Wilbur.

He gave me quite a start and then I remembered who he was and I stood there looking at him, not quite believing it. I thought at first that he might be dead, but I saw he wasn't. He was lying flat upon his back and his catfish mouth was open and every time he breathed the feathery whiskers on his lips stood straight out and fluttered.

I stepped over him and went to the door to find out what all the racket was. And there stood Lester, the robot, exactly where we'd left him the night before, and out in the driveway a bunch of kids were pegging rocks at him. Those kids were pretty good. They hit Lester almost every time.

I yelled at them and they scattered down the road. They knew I'd tan their hides.

I was just turning around to go back into the house when a car swung into the drive. Joe Fletcher, our constable, jumped out and came striding toward me and I could see that he was in his best fire-eating mood.

Joe stopped in front of the stoop and put both hands on his hips and starred first at Lester and then at me.

"Sam," he asked with a nasty leer, "what is going on here? Some of your pink elephants move in to live with you?"

"Joe," I said solemn, passing up the insult, "I'd like you to meet Lester."

Joe had opened up his mouth to yell at me when Wilbur showed up at the door.

"And this is Wilbur," I said. "Wilbur is an alien and Lester is a . . ."

"Wilbur is a *what!*" roared Joe.

Wilbur stepped out on the stoop and said: "What a sorrowful face. And so noble, too!"

"He means you," I said to Joe.

"If you guys keep this up," Joe bellowed, "I'll run in the bunch of you."

"I meant no harm," said Wilbur. "I apologize if I have bruised your sensitivities."

That was a hot one—Joe's sensitivities!

"I can see at a glance," said Wilbur, "that life's not been easy for you."

"I'll tell the world it ain't," Joe said.

"Nor for me," said Wilbur, sitting down upon the stoop. "It seems that there are days a man can't lay away a dime."

"Mister, you are right," said Joe. "Just like I was telling the missus this morning when she up and told me that the kids needed some new shoes . . ."

"It does beat hell how a man can't get ahead."

"Listen, you ain't heard nothing yet . . ."

And so help me Hannah, Joe sat down beside him and before you could count to three started telling his life story.

"Lester," Wilbur said, "be sure you get this down."

I beat it back into the house and had a quick one to settle my stomach before I tackled breakfast.

I didn't feel like eating, but I knew I had to. I got out some eggs and bacon and wondered what I would feed Wilbur. For I suddenly remembered how his metabolism couldn't stand liquor, and if it couldn't take good whisky, there seemed very little chance that it would take eggs and bacon.

As I was finishing my breakfast, Higman Morris came busting through the back door and straight into the kitchen. Higgy is our mayor, a pillar of the church, a member of the school board and a director of the bank, and he is a big stuffed shirt.

"Sam," he yelled at me, "this town has taken a lot from you. We have put up with your drinking and your general shiftlessness and your lack of public spirit. But this is too much!"

I wiped some egg off my chin. "What is too much?"

Higgy almost strangled, he was so irritated. "This public exhibition. This three-ring circus! This nuisance! And on a Sunday, too!"

"Oh," I said, "you mean Wilbur and his robot."

"There's a crowd collecting out in front and I've had a dozen calls, and Joe is sitting out there with this—this—"

"Alien," I supplied.

"And they're bawling on one another's shoulders like a pair of three-year-olds and . . . *Alien!*"

"Sure," I said. "What did you think he was?"

Higgy reached out a shaky hand and pulled out a chair and fell weakly into it. "Samuel," he said slowly, "give it to me once again. I don't think I heard you right."

"Wilbur is an alien," I told him, "from some other world. He and his robot came here to listen to sad stories."

"Sad stories?"

"Sure. He likes sad stories. Some people like them happy and others like them dirty. He just likes them sad."

"If he is an alien," said Higgy, talking to himself.

"He's one, sure enough," I said.

"Sam, you're sure of this?"

"I am."

Higgy got excited. "Don't you appreciate what this means to Millville? This little town of ours—the first place on all of Earth that an alien visited!"

I wished he would shut up and get out so I could have an after-breakfast drink. Higgy didn't drink, especially on Sundays. He'd have been horrified.

"The world will beat a pathway to our door!" he shouted. He got out of the chair and started for the living room. "I must extend my official welcome."

I trotted along behind him, for this was one I didn't want to miss.

—

Joe had left and Wilbur was sitting alone on the stoop and I could see that he already had on a sort of edge.

Higgy stood in front of him and thrust out his chest and held out his hand and said, in his best official manner: "I am the mayor of Millville and I take great pleasure in extending to you our sincerest welcome."

Wilbur shook hands with him and then he said: "Being the mayor of a city must be something of a burden and a great responsibility. I wonder that you bear up under it."

"Well, there are times . . ." said Higgy.

"But I can see that you are the kind of man whose main concern is the welfare of his fellow creatures and as such, quite naturally, you become the unfortunate target of outrageous and ungrateful actions."

Higgy sat down ponderously on the stoop. "Sir," he said to Wilbur, "you would not believe all I must put up with."

"Lester," said Wilbur, "see that you get this down."

I went back into the house. I couldn't stomach it.

There was quite a crowd standing out there in the road—Jake Ellis, the junkman, and Don Myers, who ran the Jolly Miller, and a lot of others. And there, shoved into the background and sort of peering out, was the Widow Frye. People were on their way to church and they'd stop and look and then go on again, but others would come and take their place, and the crowd was getting bigger instead of thinning out.

I went out to the kitchen and had my after-breakfast drink and did the dishes and wondered once again what I would feed Wilbur. Although, at the moment, he didn't seem to be too interested in food.

Then I went into the living room and sat down in the rocking chair and kicked off my shoes. I sat there wiggling my toes and thinking about what a screwy thing it was that Wilbur should get drunk on sadness instead of good red liquor.

The day was warm and I was wore out and the rocking must have helped to put me fast asleep, for suddenly I woke up and there was someone in the room. I didn't see who it was right off, but I knew someone was there.

It was the Widow Frye. She was all dressed up for Sunday, and after all those years of passing my house on the opposite side of the street and never looking at it, as if the sight of it or me might contaminate her—after all these years, there she was all dressed up and smiling. And me sitting there with all my whiskers on and my shoes off.

"Samuel," said the Widow Frye, "I couldn't help but tell you. I think your Mr. Wilbur is simply wonderful."

"He's an alien," I said. I had just woke up and was considerable befuddled.

"I don't care what he is," said the Widow Frye. "He is such a gentleman and so sympathetic. Not in the least like a lot of people in this horrid town."

I got to my feet and I didn't know exactly what to do. She'd caught me off my guard and at a terrible disadvantage. Of all people in the world, she was the last I would have expected to come into my house.

I almost offered her a drink, but caught myself just in time.

"You been talking to him?" I asked lamely.

"Me and everybody else," said the Widow Frye. "And he has a way with him. You tell him your troubles and they seem to go away. There's a lot of people waiting for their turn."

"Well," I told her, "I am glad to hear you say that. How's he standing up under all this?"

The Widow Frye moved closer and dropped her voice to a whisper. "I think he's getting tired. I would say—well, I'd say he was intoxicated if I didn't know better."

I took a quick look at the clock.

"Holy smoke!" I yelled.

It was almost four o'clock. Wilbur had been out there six or seven hours, lapping up all the sadness this village could dish out. By now he should be stiff clear up to his eyebrows.

I busted out the door and he was sitting on the stoop and tears were running down his face and he was listening to Jack Ritter—and Old Jack was the biggest liar in all of seven counties. He was just making up this stuff he was telling Wilbur.

"Sorry, Jack," I said, pulling Wilbur to his feet.

"But I was just telling him . . ."

"Go on home," I hollered, "you and the others. You got him all tired out."

"Mr. Sam," said Lester, "I am glad you came. He wouldn't listen to me."

The Widow Frye held the door open and I got Wilbur in and put him in my bed, where he could sleep it off.

When I came back, the Widow Frye was waiting. "I was just thinking, Samuel," she said. "I am having chicken for supper and there is more than I can eat. I wonder if you'd like to come on over."

I couldn't say nothing for a moment. Then I shook my head.

"Thanks just the same," I said, "but I have to stay and watch over Wilbur. He won't pay attention to the robot."

The Widow Frye was disappointed. "Some other time?"

"Yeah, some other time."

I went out after she was gone and invited Lester in.

"Can you sit down," I asked, "or do you have to stand?"

"I have to stand," said Lester.

So I left him standing there and sat down in the rocker.

"What does Wilbur eat?" I asked. "He must be getting hungry."

The robot opened a door in the middle of his chest and took out a funny-looking bottle. He shook it and I could hear something rattling around inside of it.

"This is his nourishment," said Lester. "He takes one every day."

He went to put the bottle back and a big fat roll fell out. He stooped and picked it up.

"Money," he explained.

"You folks have money, too?"

"We got this when we were indoctrinated. Hundred-dollar bills."

"Hundred-dollar bills!"

"Too bulky otherwise." said Lester blandly. He put the money and the bottle back into his chest and slapped shut the door.

I sat there in a fog. Hundred-dollar bills!

"Lester," I suggested, "maybe you hadn't ought to show anyone else that money. They might try to take it from you."

"I know," said Lester. "I keep it next to me." And he slapped his chest. His slap would take the head right off a man.

I sat rocking in the chair and there was so much to think about that my mind went rocking back and forth with the chair. There was Wilbur first of all and the crazy way he got drunk, and the way the Widow Frye had acted, and all those hundred-dollar bills.

Especially those hundred-dollar bills.

"This indoctrination business?" I asked. "You said it was bootleg."

"It is, most definitely," said Lester. "Acquired by some misguided individual who sneaked in and taped it to sell to addicts."

"But why sneak in?"

"Off limits," Lester said. "Outside the reservation. Beyond the pale. Is the meaning clear?"

"And this misguided adventurer figured he could sell the information he had taped, the—the—"

"The culture pattern," said Lester. "Your logic trends in the correct direction, but it is not as simple as you make it sound."

"I suppose not," I said. "And this same misguided adventurer picked up the money, too."

"Yes, he did. Quite a lot of it."

I sat there for a while longer, then went in for a look at Wilbur. He was fast asleep, his catfish mouth blowing the whiskers in and out. So I went into the kitchen and got myself some supper.

I had just finished eating when a knock came at the door.

It was old Doc Abel from the sanitorium.

"Good evening, Doc," I said. "I'll rustle up a drink."

"Skip the drink," said Doc. "Just trot out your alien."

He stepped into the living room and stopped short at the sight of Lester.

Lester must have seen that he was astonished for he tried immediately to put him at ease. "I am the so-called alien's robot. Yet despite the fact that I am a mere machine, I am a faithful servant. If you wish to tell your sadness, you may relate it to me with perfect confidence. I shall relay it to my master."

Doc sort of rocked back on his heels, but it didn't floor him.

"Just any kind of sadness?" he asked, "or do you hanker for a special kind?"

"The master," Lester said, "prefers the deep-down sadness, although he will not pass up any other kind."

"Wilbur gets drunk on it," I said. "He's in the bedroom now sleeping off a jag."

"Likewise," Lester said, "confidentially, we can sell the stuff. There are people back home with their tongues hanging to their knees for this planet's brand of sadness."

Doc looked at me and his eyebrows were so high that they almost hit his hairline.

"It's on the level, Doc," I assured him. "It isn't any joke. You want to have a look at Wilbur?"

Doc nodded and I led the way into the bedroom and we stood there looking down at Wilbur. Sleeping all stretched out, he was a most unlovely sight.

Doc put his hand up to his forehead and dragged it down across his face, pulling down his chops so he looked like a bloodhound. His big, thick, loose lips made a blubbering sound as he pulled his palm across them.

"I'll be damned!" said Doc.

Then he turned around and walked out of the bedroom and I trailed along behind him. He walked straight to the door and went out. He walked a ways down the driveway, then stopped and waited for me. Then he reached out and grabbed me by the shirt front and pulled it tight around me.

"Sam," he said, "you've been working for me for a long time now and you are getting sort of old. Most other men would fire a man as old as you are and get a younger one. I could fire you any time I want to."

"I suppose you could," I said and it was an awful feeling, for I had never thought of being fired. I did a good job of janitoring up at the sanitorium and I didn't mind the work. And I thought how terrible it would be if a Saturday came and I had no drinking money.

"You been a loyal and faithful worker," said old Doc, still hanging onto my shirt, "and I been a good employer. I always give you a Christmas bottle and another one at Easter."

"Right," I said. "True, every word of it."

"So you wouldn't fool old Doc," said Doc. "Maybe the rest of the people in this stupid town, but not your old friend Doc."

"But, Doc," I protested, "I ain't fooling no one."

Doc let loose of my shirt. "By God, I don't believe you are. It's like the way they tell me? He sits and listens to their troubles, and they feel better once they're through?"

"That's what the Widow Frye said. She said she told him her troubles and they seemed to go away."

"That's the honest truth, Sam?"

"The honest truth," I swore.

Doc Abel got excited. He grabbed me by the shirt again.

"Don't you see what we have?" he almost shouted at me.

"*We?*" I asked.

But he paid no attention. "The greatest psychiatrist," said Doc, "this world has ever known. The greatest aid to psychiatry anyone ever has dredged up. You get what I am aiming at?"

"I guess I do," I said, not having the least idea.

"The most urgent need of the human race," said Doc, "is someone or something they can shift their troubles to—someone who by seeming magic can banish their anxieties. Confession is the core of it, of course—a symbolic shifting of one's burden to someone else's shoulders. The principle is operative in the church confessional, in the profession of psychiatry, in those deep, abiding friendships offering a shoulder that one can cry upon."

"Doc, you're right," I said, beginning to catch on.

"The trouble always is that the agent of confession must be human, too. He has certain human limitations of which the confessor is aware. He can give no certain promise that he can assume the trouble and anxiety. But here we have something different. Here we have an alien—a being from the stars—unhampered by human limitations. By very definition, he can take anxieties and mother them in the depths of his own non-humanity . . ."

"Doc," I yelled, "if you could only get Wilbur up at the sanitorium!"

Doc rubbed mental hands together. "The very thing that I had been thinking."

I could have kicked myself for my enthusiasm. I did the best I could to gain back the ground I'd lost.

"I don't know, Doc. Wilbur might be hard to handle."

"Well, let's go back in and have a talk with him."

"I don't know," I stalled.

"We got to get him fast. By tomorrow, the word will be out and the place will be overrun with newspapermen and TV trucks and God knows what. The scientific boys will be swarming in, and the government, and we'll lose control."

"I'd better talk to him alone," I said. "He might freeze up solid if you were around. He knows me and he might listen to me."

Doc hemmed and hawed, but finally he agreed.

"I'll wait in the car," he said. "You call me if you need me."

He went crunching on down the driveway to where he had the car parked, and I went inside the house.

"Lester," I said to the robot, "I've got to talk to Wilbur. It's important."

"No more sad stories," Lester warned. "He's had enough today."

"No. I got a proposition."

"Proposition?"

"A deal. A business arrangement."

"All right," said Lester. "I will get him up."

It took quite a bit of getting up, but finally we had him fought awake and sitting on the bed.

"Wilbur, listen carefully," I told him. "I have something right down your alley. A place where all the people have big and terrible troubles and an awful sadness. Not just some of them, but every one of them. They are so sad and troubled they can't live with other people . . ."

Wilbur struggled off the bed, stood swaying on his feet.

"Lead me to 'em, pal," he said.

I pushed him down on the bed again. "It isn't as easy as all that. It's a hard place to get into."

"I thought you said—"

"Look, I have a friend who can arrange it for you. But it might take some money—"

"Pal," said Wilbur, "we got a roll of cash. How much would you need?"

"It's hard to say."

"Lester, hand it over to him so he can make this deal."

"Boss," protested Lester, "I don't know if we should."

"We can trust Sam," said Wilbur. "He is not the grasping sort. He won't spend a cent more than is necessary."

"Not a cent," I promised.

Lester opened the door in his chest and handed me the roll of hundred-dollar bills and I stuffed it in my pocket.

"Now you will wait right here," I told them, "and I'll see this friend of mine. I'll be back soon."

And I was doing some fast arithmetic, wondering how much I could dare gouge out of Doc. It wouldn't hurt to start a little high so I could come down when Doc would roar and howl and scream and say what good friends we were and how he always had given me a bottle at Christmas and at Easter.

I turned to go out into the living room and stopped dead in my tracks.

For standing in the doorway was another Wilbur, although when I looked at him more closely I saw the differences. And before he said a single word or did a single thing, I had a sinking feeling that something had gone wrong.

"Good evening, sir," I said. "It's nice of you to drop in."

He never turned a hair. "I see you have guests. It shall desolate me to tear them away from you."

Behind me, Lester was making noises as if his gears were stripping, and out of the corner of my eye I saw that Wilbur sat stiff and stricken and whiter than a fish.

"But you can't do that," I said. "They only just showed up."

"You do not comprehend," said the alien in the doorway. "They are breakers of the law. I have come to get them."

"Pal," said Wilbur, speaking to me, "I am truly sorry. I knew all along it would not work out."

"By this time," the other alien said to Wilbur, "you should be convinced of it and give up trying."

And it was plain as paint, once you came to think of it, and I wondered why I hadn't thought of it before. For if Earth was closed to the adventurers who'd gathered the indoctrination data . . .

"Mister," I said to the alien in the doorway, "there are factors here of which I know you ain't aware. Couldn't you and me talk the whole thing over alone?"

"I should be happy," said the alien, so polite it hurt, "but please understand that I must carry out a duty."

"Why, certainly," I said.

The alien stepped out of the doorway and made a sign behind him and two robots that had been standing in the living room just out of my line of vision came in.

"Now all is secure," said the alien, "and we can depart to talk. I will listen most attentively."

So I went out into the kitchen and he followed me. I sat down at the table and he sat across from me.

"I must apologize," he told me gravely. "This miscreant imposes upon you and your planet."

"Mister," I told him back, "you have got it all wrong. I like this renegade of yours."

"Like him?" he asked, horrified. "That is impossible. He is a drunken lout and furthermore than that—"

"And furthermore than that," I said, grabbing the words right from his mouth, "he is doing us an awful lot of good."

The alien looked flabbergasted. "You do not know that which you say! He drags from you your anxieties and feasts upon them most disgustingly, and he puts them down on record so he can pull them forth again and yet again to your eternal shame, and furthermore than that—"

"It's not that way at all," I shouted. "It does us a lot of good to pull out our anxieties and show them—."

"Disgusting! More than that, indecent!" He stopped. "What was that?"

"Telling our anxieties does us good," I said as solemnly as I could. "It's a matter of confession."

The alien banged an open palm against his forehead and the feathers on his catfish mouth stood straight out and quivered.

"It could be true," he said in horror. "Given a culture so primitive and so besodden and so shameless . . ."

"Ain't we, though?" I agreed.

"In our world," said the alien, "there are no anxieties—well, not many. We are most perfectly adjusted."

"Except for folks like Wilbur?"

"Wilbur?"

"Your pal in there," I said. "I couldn't say his name, so I call him Wilbur. By the way . . ."

He rubbed his hand across his face, and no matter what he said, it was plain to see that at that moment he was loaded with anxiety. "Call me Jake. Call me anything. Just so we get this mess resolved."

"Nothing easier," I said. "Let's just keep Wilbur here. You don't really want him, do you?"

"Want him?" wailed Jake. "He and all the others like him are nothing but a headache. But they are our problem and our responsibility. We can't saddle you."

"You mean there are more like Wilbur?"

Jake nodded sadly.

"We'll take them all," I said. "We would love to have them. Every one of them."

"You're crazy!"

"Sure we are," I said. "That is why we need them."

"You are certain, without any shadow of your doubt?"

"Absolutely certain."

"Pal," said Jake, "you have made a deal."

I stuck out my hand to shake on it, but I don't think he even saw my hand. He rose out of the chair and you could see a vast relief lighting up his face.

Then he turned and stalked out of the kitchen.

"Hey, wait a minute!" I yelled. For there were details that I felt we should work out. But he didn't seem to hear me.

I jumped out of the chair and raced for the living room, but by the time I got there, there was no sign of Jake. I ran into the bedroom and the two robots were gone, too. Wilbur and Lester were in there all alone.

"I told you," Lester said to Wilbur, "that Mr. Sam would fix it."

"I don't believe it, pal," said Wilbur. "Have they really gone? Have they gone for good? Is there any chance they will be coming back?"

I raised my arm and wiped off my forehead with my sleeve. "They won't bother you again. You are finally shut of them."

"That is excellent," said Wilbur. "And now about this deal."

"Sure," I said. "Give me just a minute. I'll go out and see the man."

I stepped out on the stoop and stood there for a while to get over shaking. Jake and his two robots had come very close to spoiling everything. I needed a drink worse than I had ever needed one, but I didn't dare take the time. I had to get Doc on the dotted line before something else turned up.

I went out to the car.

"It took you long enough," Doc said irritably.

"It took a lot of talking for Wilbur to agree," I said.

"But he did agree?"

"Yeah, he agreed."

"Well, then," said Doc, "what are we waiting for?"

"Ten thousand bucks," I said.

"Ten thousand . . ."

"That's the price for Wilbur. I'm selling you my alien."

"*Your* alien! He is not your alien!"

"Maybe not," I said, "but he's the next best thing. All I have to do is say the word and he won't go with you."

"Two thousand," declared Doc. "That's every cent I'll pay."

We got down to haggling and we would up at seven thousand dollars. If I'd been willing to spend all night at it, I would have got eighty-five hundred. But I was all fagged out and I needed a drink much worse than I needed fifteen hundred extra dollars. So we settled on the seven.

We went back into the house and Doc wrote out a check.

"You know you're fired, of course," he said, handing it to me.

"I hadn't thought about it," I told him, and I hadn't. The check for seven thousand in my hand and that roll of hundred-dollar bills bulging out my pocket added up to a lot of drinking money.

I went to the bedroom door and called out Wilbur and Lester and I said to them: "Old Doc here has made up his mind to take you."

And Wilbur said, "I am so happy and so thankful. Was it hard, perhaps, to get him to agree to take us?"

"Not too hard," I said. "He was reasonable."

"Hey," yelled Doc, with murder in his eyes, "what is going on here?"

"Not a thing," I said.

"Well, it sounds to me . . ."

"There's your boy," I said. "Take him if you want him. If it should happen you don't want him, I'll be glad to keep him. There'll be someone else along."

And I held out the check to give it back to him. It was a risky thing to do, but I was in a spot where I had to bluff.

Doc waved the check away, but he was still suspicious that he was being taken, although he wasn't sure exactly how. But he couldn't take the chance of losing out on Wilbur. I could see that he had it all figured out—how he'd become world famous with the only alien psychiatrist in captivity.

Except there was one thing that he didn't know. He had no idea that in just a little while there would be other Wilburs. And I stood there, laughing at him without showing it, while he herded Wilbur and Lester out the door.

Before he left, he turned back to me.

"There is something going on," he said, "and when I find out about it, I am going to come back and take you apart for it."

I never said a word, but just stood there listening to the three of them crunching down the driveway. When I heard the car leave, I went out into the kitchen and took down the bottle.

I had a half a dozen fast ones. Then I sat down in a chair at the kitchen table and practiced some restraint. I had a half a dozen slow ones.

I got to wondering about the other Wilburs that Jake had agreed to send to Earth and I wished I'd been able to pin him down a bit. But I had had no chance, for he had jumped up and disappeared just when I was ready to get down to business.

All I could do was hope he'd deliver them to me—either in the front yard or out in the driveway—but he'd never said he would. A fat lot of good it would do me if he just dropped them anywhere.

And I wondered when he would deliver them and how many there might be. It might take a bit of time, for more than likely he would indoctrinate them before they were dropped on Earth, and as to number, I had not the least idea. From the way he talked, there might even be a couple of dozen of them. With that many, a man could make a roll of cash if he handled the situation right.

Although, it seemed to me, I had a right smart amount of money now.

I dug the roll of hundred-dollar bills out of my pocket and made a stab at counting them, but for the life of me I couldn't keep the figures straight.

Here I was drunk and it wasn't even Saturday, but Sunday. I didn't have a job and now I could get drunk any time I wanted.

So I sat there working on the jug and finally passed out.

—

There was an awful racket and I came awake and wondered where I was. In a little while I got it figured out that I'd been sleeping at the kitchen table and I had a terrible crick in my neck and a hangover that was even worse.

I stumbled to my feet and looked at the clock. It was ten minutes after nine.

The racket kept right on.

I made it out to the living room and opened the front door. The Widow Frye almost fell into the room, she had been hammering on the door so hard.

"Samuel," she gasped, "have you heard about it?"

"I ain't heard a thing," I told her, "except you pounding on the door."

"It's on the radio."

"You know darn well I ain't got no radio nor no telephone nor no TV set. I ain't got no time for modern trash like that."

"It's about the aliens," she said. "Like the one you have. The nice, kind, understanding alien people. They are everywhere. Everywhere on Earth. There are a lot of them all over. Thousands of them. Maybe millions . . ."

I pushed past her out the door.

They were sitting on front steps all up and down the street, and they were walking up and down the road, and there were a bunch of them playing, chasing one another, in a vacant lot.

"It's like that everywhere!" cried the Widow Frye. "The radio just said so. There are enough of them so that everyone on Earth can have one of their very own. Isn't it wonderful?"

That dirty, doublecrossing Jake, I told myself. Talking like there weren't many of them, pretending that his culture was so civilized and so well adjusted that there were almost no psychopaths.

Although, to be fair about it, he hadn't said how many there might be of them—not in numbers, that is. And even all he had dumped on Earth might be a few in relation to the total population of his particular culture.

And then, suddenly, I thought of something else.

I hauled out my watch and looked at it. It was only a quarter after nine.

"Widow Frye," I said, "excuse me. I got an errand to run."

I legged it down the street as fast as I could.

One of the Wilburs detached himself from a group of them and loped along with me.

"Mister," he said, "have you got some troubles to tell me?"

"Naw," I said. "I never have no troubles."

"Not even any worries?"

"No worries, either."

Then it occurred to me that there was a worry—not for me alone, but for the entire world.

For with all the Wilburs that Jake had dumped on Earth, there would in a little while be no human psychopaths. There wouldn't be a human with a worry or a trouble. God, would it be dull!

But I didn't worry none.

I just loped along as fast as I could go.

I had to get to the bank before Doc had time to stop payment on that check for seven thousand dollars.

HUNGER DEATH

Street & Smith Publications paid Clifford Simak $120 for "Hunger Death." It appeared in the October 1938 issue of Astounding Science Fiction. The story continues several themes of the author's earliest fiction, including a Mars inhabited by more than one race of intelligent beings, the Earthian newspaper known as the Evening Rocket, its editor, and its sports editor. But those veins were playing out. . . .

—dww

Old Doc Trowbridge was napping in his office, with his feet on the desk and an empty *bocca* bottle on the floor beside him. Angus MacDonald, New Chicago's marshal, shook him gently. Doc opened one eye and stared at Angus in mild reproach.

"Radium City wants to talk to the health officer," announced Angus. "I guess that's you."

Doc pulled his feet off the desk and slowly rose. He rubbed his eyes and glanced at the marshal's dripping raincoat.

"Still raining," he remarked.

"Hell, it always rains on Venus," said Angus.

Doc stretched his arms over his head and yawned.

"Better hurry along, Doc," urged Angus. "Maybe some of the big doctors over at Radium City want to call you into consultation."

Doc snorted. Once he might have been insulted by so thinly veiled sarcasm. But Doc now was past the possibility of being insulted. Ten years on Venus, a hand-to-mouth existence and rotten liquor had taken their toll.

Doc puffed into his raincoat and followed Angus down the rickety stairs. Rain beat at them as they stepped from the building and sloshed up the red mud slough that was the main street of New Chicago.

At the radio station on the edge of the landing field, the town's only contact with the outside world, they were greeted by Angus' son, Sandy.

"I'll get Radium City for you," said Sandy. "It sounded as if it might be important."

"Nothing important ever happens in New Chicago," Doc grumbled. "Nothing since old Jake Hansler died. And they blamed that on me."

Sandy was speaking into the transmitter. "New Chicago calling Radium City. Answer please. New Chicago calling Radium City. Answer please."

Out of the amplifier came the voice of the Radium City operator. "Radium City answering New Chicago. Have you located Dr. Trowbridge?"

"Just a second," said Sandy.

He switched off the amplifier and handed Doc a set of headphones. Doc clamped them over his ears and lowered his rolypoly body into the operator's chair. He hiccoughed slightly and spoke into the transmitter.

"This is Dr. Trowbridge," he said.

"Dr. Trowbridge," said the voice in Radium City, "my name is Tony Paulson. I am a reporter for the Inter-World Press Service. I'm just checking up on this new disease—the Hunger Disease. Have you any cases in New Chicago?"

"Hunger Disease," snapped Doc. "What are you talking about? I never heard of such a disease."

"This is something different," said the voice. "A new disease. It has broken out all over Venus. Quite a few cases on Earth, too.

Patient can't seem to get enough to eat. That's why we call it the Hunger Disease."

"Never heard of it," declared Doc.

"Are there any other doctors in New Chicago?" asked the reporter.

"No," said Doc. "I'm the only one and they could get along without me. Practically starving me to death. Never saw a healthier place in all my life."

"You're sure there's nobody sick in New Chicago," persisted the newspaperman.

"Sure I'm sure," protested Doc. "Last time anybody was sick here was when Steve Donagan's kid, Susan, had the measles. And that was three months ago."

"O.K.," said the voice. "Thank you, doctor. Any other news out in New Chicago?"

"Not a damn thing ever happens here," Doc declared.

"O.K.—good-by then, and thanks again."

"Good-by," said Doc, slipping the headphones from his ears.

He heaved himself to his feet.

"That's what comes of being buried in a mud-hole like this," he announced to Angus and Sandy. "Here I am, not knowing a thing about this new disease. Why, once I was regarded as an authority on diagnosis. That was before I came to New Chicago. Fellow in Radium City says there is a new disease breaking out there. Acute hunger is one symptom. He didn't tell me anything more about it. Never heard anything like that before."

He shook his head dolefully and headed for the door.

"Thanks for calling me," he said and plunged out into the rain.

The marshal and his son saw him waddle rapidly down the street, heading for the Venus Flower saloon.

"He'll tell the boys about this new disease," said Angus, "and they'll buy him drinks. Before night he'll be a disgrace to humanity."

—

Arthur Hart, editor of the *Evening Rocket*, tapped his finger against a paragraph in a news story appearing on the front page of the early afternoon edition.

"Something funny here," he told Bob Jackson.

He shook his head. "Mighty funny," he mused.

Bob Jackson said nothing. He scented trouble in the air. Whenever the chief took to shaking his head and muttering to himself it meant trouble for someone. Bob had the feeling he was the victim this time.

"Listen to this," commanded Hart.

He read the paragraph: "The only community on Venus reporting no cases of the Hunger Disease is New Chicago. Dr. Anderson Trowbridge, health officer, told the Inter-World Press Service today there was no sickness of any sort in that city."

"Healthy place," said Bob, wondering if he was saying the right thing.

"Too damn healthy," snapped Hart. "That's what makes it funny. With this Hunger Disease rampant over the whole face of the planet, why does New Chicago escape? People dying like flies everywhere else and the folks in New Chicago not bothered a bit."

Hart fixed the reporter with a steely glare.

"That's where you come in," he announced.

"Listen," Bob bristled, "if you think you're going to pack me off to some God-forsaken trading post on Venus to find out why nobody ever gets sick there, you better start looking for someone to take my place. I was on Venus once and I don't like it. It gives me the creeps. Rains all the time. Never see the sun. Sticky-hot. Why, the rain is even lukewarm. And bugs—man, there's millions of them. All shapes and all sizes. I hate the damn things."

Hart laid down the paper, carefully smoothed it out on his desk.

"Now, Bob," he said softly, "I'm asking you to do this because you are the one man I can depend on. If there's anything to be found in New Chicago, you are the man to find it. And I think there is something to find. Something mighty important.

"Right now the Earth is faced by one of the gravest threats it has known in years. The Hunger Disease. You know what it is. Speeds up metabolism. Speeds it up to a point that a man must eat almost continuously to provide the body with fuel to keep going. And all the time the victim ages visibly. His skin wrinkles, his hair turns gray, his teeth fall out. In only a few days he lives the equivalent of years, and in a week or ten days he dies of what amounts to old age."

Hart's eyes narrowed and his voice was sharper now.

"Our medical authorities haven't a single clue. They haven't been able to isolate the germ or bacteria or whatever it is that causes the disease. They know it is contagious and that just about sums up their knowledge. They don't know what causes it. They don't know how to prevent it or cure it. So far, every single person who has contracted the disease has died—or is going to die."

Hart fixed Jackson with a frigid stare.

"I am offering you a chance," he said, "to do a great service to humanity. There must be some reason New Chicago has not been hit by the disease. If you could find this reason—Don't you see, Bob, it's a chance to save the Earth!"

"It's a chance for the *Evening Rocket* to pull down a billion bucks of gilt-edge promotion," snarled Bob. "Big headlines *Rocket* Reporter Finds Cure for Hunger Disease."

Hart sighed.

"There's only one thing that appeals to your sordid soul," he said. "There isn't a fleck of human kindness in you. You have a heart of zero steel. How much does the *Rocket* have to pay you to get you to go out to Venus?"

Bob pondered.

"I hate that place, Hart," he said. "I don't like it at all. There's too many bugs there. Too damn many bugs. Let's say a bonus of—well—of about five thousand."

"All right," snarled Hart. "Now you get out of my sight before I lose control of myself. You get out to Venus just as soon as a space eater can get you there—and so help me Hannah, if you flunk out on this assignment I'll put you on the obituary desk and what's more, by the Lord Harry, I'll see that you stay there."

Outside the door, Bob gave himself a mental kicking.

"You damn fool," he told himself, "you should have made it ten thousand. He'd have paid it just as quick."

II

Zeke Brown sat disconsolately on the chopping block in front of his weather-beaten cabin and watched his neighbor, Luther Bidwell, come down the road.

Luther was a nondescript figure. Clad in blue denim overalls, he bore an unshaven and unwashed look. His ragged hat sagged over a shock of disordered hair, hanging halfway to his shoulders. His gait was a half slouch, half gallop, as if he might be in a hurry, but didn't want anyone to think he was.

Zeke hailed him from a distance.

"Howdy, Luther."

"Howdy, Zeke," Luther called back.

Zeke waited, smoking his pipe, his eyes sweeping the pitiful failure and delusion of his Venusian farm. The fields covered by huge patches of polka-dot weeds, the encroaching jungle, the rusting machinery, the steaming pools of water drowning out the last of his stand of corn. From the jungle came the high-pitched chirping of the dingbats, insects which in their own proper time would come forth to devour whatever might be left in the fields.

Something rustled in a clump of polka-dot weeds near the

wood pile and Zeke, turning swiftly, saw a pair of pointed ears
and two gleaming eyes staring at him. With a swift motion he
whipped out the gun which dangled from the belt at his hip.
But before he could clear the weapon the evil face had disappeared.

"Dang you," said Zeke without emphasis, "just stick your
head out again. I'll get you."

But the skink was gone. Zeke grumbled and holstered his gun.

Turning his eyes back to the road, he watched Luther continue
down the trail, raising little spurts of mud as his feet clopped on
the ground. Luther turned in at the sagging gate and took a seat
beside Zeke.

"Just saw you pull your gun," he commented. "See something?"

"A skink," said Zeke. "Dang things overrunning the place.
Just about cleaned out the chickens. Just a few old hens left now."

"They cleaned me out the other night," Luther said. "Killed
every hen on the place and then got into the hog pen. Tackled the
hogs, I guess, but them porkers was too much for them. Must of
been quite a herd of them at that, for they chawed some of them
pigs up right handsome. The hogs killed a couple of them and I
ain't been able to go into that hog house since then. They sure
carry a powerful scent, them fellers. Worse than the polecats back
in Iowa. Hogs don't mind, seems. They ate 'em."

"They give me the creeps," said Zeke. "Almost like human
beings running around on all four legs. Naked, not a single hair
on them and meaner than poison. If you get them mad, they'll go
around stinking up a place just out of pure orneriness, like they
was trying to get even. But I cleared quite a few of them out of
this neck of the woods lately."

He patted the gun at his side.

"But you know what I'd like best of all, Luther?" Zeke asked.

"Nope," said Luther.

"I'd like to catch up with that slick land agent. I would sure burn his hide full of fancy holes. He's the feller I'd really like to get in front of this gun. But he's still back on Earth. He knew dang well that after he got us out here on Venus we couldn't ever get back to Earth.

"Remember the things he told us? He talked slick as all get out when he came to our little place back in Iowa. Told us about all the advantages there were on Venus for a progressive farmer. He sure painted a pretty picture. He said there wasn't no winter here and that a feller could grow four or five crops a year. He said there was always plenty of rainfall. He was plumb full of talk about the virgin soil of Venus, how it had never been plowed and was just waiting to grow bumper crops and make us all rich. And how there'd always be a big market for everything we grew because the farms were right on the edge of New Chicago. Remember how he told us New Chicago was going to be a big city and the folks there would be willing to pay high prices for the stuff we grew?"

"Sure I remember it," said Luther. "He told me the same thing. So me and Ma talked it over and we decided to come out here. After all, we figured Venus had been colonized for over 300 years and was getting pretty civilized. Sounded pretty good to me, I admit. Matter of fact, soil was getting mighty puny back on Earth. Even good old Iowa soil. Just about all the good drained out of it and all cut up by ditches. You can't farm the same land for over five thousand years without taking proper care of it and still expect the crops to grow the way they ought to."

The skink stuck its head out of the clump of weeds beside the wood pile again and Zeke swore sulphurously as it disappeared before he could clear his gun.

"Dang you, I'll get you yet," he shouted, waving the gun. From the wood pile came the sneering chittering of the animal.

Zeke holstered his gun and stuffed his pipe with a fresh load of Venusian tobacco.

"But there was a lot of things that feller didn't tell us, Luther," he said. "He didn't tell us that this planet was full of all sorts of wild animals and birds and that it had reptiles ten times as poisonous as rattlers. And that it had a billion different kinds of bugs, all ornery as hell. He said there was plenty of rainfall—but he didn't tell us there was so much that it would drown out our crops. He didn't say a dang thing about the dingbats that eat up every green thing in sight when the hunger comes on them and he plumb forgot to mention the elephant-lizards that can tramp down a field of corn quicker than you can blink your eye. He didn't tell us it was so damp all our machinery would rust and not make even good scrap iron."

Luther spat disgustedly and added his words to the indictment.

"And not a word did that slicker tell us of what kind of a city New Chicago was. He told us it was a growing city, which was stretching the truth a dang sight farther than the law allows. A stinking little trading post with just a few stores and saloons and a couple of hell-joints for the hunters and prospectors and traders who come to town once or twice a year. He said there'd be a market for our stuff. Of course, that doesn't matter much, because we ain't had nothing to sell. We been here five years and ain't had a thing to sell all that time. We're lucky if we have eating for ourselves."

"Been eating on wild game and jungle fruit and greens ourselves for the past month," said Zeke.

"We got a little flour and some sugar over at our house," offered Luther. "Not much, but be glad to divvy up with you."

Zeke shook his head.

"No," he said. "You keep it. You got young ones and they need it. There's just the old woman and me. We'll get along. We been a pack of fools, Luther, and I lay awake nights trying to figure out what to do about it. But there don't seem no way. We couldn't raise money enough among the whole fifty families of us to buy even one ticket back to Earth. If we could do that, one of us might go back and see if somebody couldn't help us. But I guess we just been a bunch of suckers, that's all."

Luther sighed.

"Wish I was back in Iowa," he said.

III

"Nope," rumbled Doc, "I can't tell you a thing about it. Don't even know what this Hunger Disease is, except for what you told me just now. First I ever heard of it was when that newspaperman from Radium City called me up about it."

Doc tilted a bottle of *bocca* and drank. He waved the bottle at Bob.

"Want a snort?" he invited.

Bob shook his head. "Too early in the morning to start drinking," he explained.

"Listen," said Doc, "any time of the day or night is the proper time to drink in New Chicago. Hell, drink is the only excitement we have around this dump. Only fun I ever had since I been here was when old Jake Hansler died. Interesting case. Something he caught on Mars. Bug bit him or something. Wish he had lived longer so I could have studied it better. People blamed me for him dying. Said I was drunk. Wouldn't have made any difference, though, because it was a funny disease."

He helped himself to another long one.

"Jake Hansler," said Bob. "That name sounds familiar. I've heard it somewhere before."

"Sure you have," said Doc. "Dr. Jacob Hansler, the great botanist."

"That's it," said Bob. "I remember that he died on Venus."

"He came here to do some experimental work and to study some of our plant life," Doc rumbled. "Queer old fellow. Folks here didn't like him any too well, because he wouldn't pay much attention to them. But he talked to me. Got to be good friends. He told me a lot about what he was doing, but I can't remember much about it now. He brought a bunch of seeds here that he found on Mars. Found them in the ruins of an old laboratory dating back to the Genzik dynasty. The seeds were all dried up and most of them wouldn't grow, but some of them did and he nursed them along. Claimed those seeds were thousands of years old. He brought them here, because he figured the soil and climate on Venus were just right for plant life. Said if a plant wouldn't grow on Venus it wouldn't grow anywhere."

"What happened to the plants after Dr. Hansler died?" Bob asked.

Doc snorted.

"You ought to see the damn things now," he said. "They're regular pests. Growing all over town. Just weeds now. One of them is a sort of rose, with big purple blooms. Real pretty flower and the women around town sort of coddle them along for the bouquets. Not that they need much coddling. Then there's another one that's sort of a wild pea. Pretty good eating. Then there's the polka-dot weed. Makes a right good dish of greens. Got spinach beat all hollow."

"Dr. Hansler sounds like an interesting person," said Bob.

"Mighty funny old duck," said Doc, wagging his head. "Had all sorts of funny notions. Obstinate old cuss. Other botanists told him the seeds he got on Mars wouldn't grow. They must of been over 5,000 years old. But he thought they would and he tried them and they did. That's him all over.

"He had another idea, too, that everybody laughed at, but he died believing that it was the truth. It wasn't exactly in his line of work and so he never said a great deal about it. He told me, though. You know about the Genzik dynasty, don't you?"

Bob nodded. "Took a course in Martian history in school," he said.

"Well," said Doc, "you'll remember, then, that the Genzik dynasty was composed of a group of scientists that practically ruled Mars. They must have been old hell-cats for a fact, because the Martians rose up and rebelled against them and, history tells you, wiped out every last one of them. They destroyed all the laboratories the Genziks had set up and did everything possible to erase any memory of them. As a result there isn't much known about them now."

"Martian history suggests they were only a higher Martian race," said Bob. "I know there's all sorts of myths about them."

"Well, sir," said Doc, "Jake had a myth about them that would knock your hat off. He claims that a few of them escaped the general massacre and fled to the deserts and that their descendants are still there. Got it from desert tribes who claimed to know all about it. And Jake thought the Genziks were Earth people, maybe folks from Atlantis, who had reached Mars thousands of years ago, long before the present Terrestrial race sent a spaceship there."

"That's a new one," said Bob. "Never heard that before. Have you got any of Jake's notes around here? Did he leave any books or anything?"

Doc chuckled. "Looking for a story, I see," he said.

"The chief will sure give me hell if I don't get something on this trip," Bob told him, "and you certainly haven't helped me any with this Hunger Disease business."

Doc finished off the bottle with gusto, then held it up to the light and sighed. "There's one story you could write," said Doc, setting the bottle on the window ledge, along with several others. "A story that should be written. It's about those farmers here. The Venus Land Company brought them out. Knew they couldn't grow a thing, but that didn't stop those sharks. Took everything those poor devils had and dumped them in the jungle here. It does beat hell how the new land racket will get the suckers. Venus Land cooked up this farm scheme and sold it to a bunch of poor

Iowa farmers. The worst of it is that the farmers don't even own the land they've built their homes on. Some of them came up to see me about getting their money back. You know how it is—they figure a doctor knows everything, not ever dreaming how damn little some doctors do know. I looked over their contracts. Far as I can see they're airtight. But I found the farmers settled on the wrong tract of land. I asked them how they knew what land they had bought and they told me a company representative staked it out for them. They settled on the east side of town and the land they bought is on the west side."

"Do they know about this?" Bob asked.

Doc shook his head. "No, I didn't tell them," he said. "Don't suppose it makes much difference. Venus Land won't bother them any more. They got all the boys had and the land is worthless anyhow."

Boots clumped on the stairs and in a moment Angus MacDonald loomed in the doorway. "Doc," he said, "Steve Donagan's kid is sick again."

Doc heaved out of his chair.

"If some of the rest of the people in New Chicago were like Susan," he said, "maybe I could gain back some of my self-respect. She's the only one who ever gets sick around here."

"Doc," said Angus and one could sense stark terror in his voice.

"Yes, yes, go on," snapped Doc. Angus swallowed and started over again. "Doc," he said, "Steve thinks she's got that Hunger Disease."

Johnny Mason, wire editor, laid a slip of yellow paper on Editor Hart's desk. "A special just out of New Chicago," he explained.

Hart snapped up the paper and read:

"NEW CHICAGO, VENUS—THE HUNGER DISEASE, TO WHICH IT WAS BELIEVED THIS REMOTE TRADING POST WAS IMMUNE, STRUCK HERE TODAY. THE VIC-

TIM IS SUSAN DONAGAN, NINE-YEAR-OLD DAUGH-
TER OF MR. AND MRS. STEPHEN DONAGAN.

DR. ANDERSON TROWBRIDGE, THE TOWN'S ONLY
DOCTOR, A FRIEND OF THE FAMILY WHO BROUGHT
SUSAN INTO THE WORLD AND HAS ATTENDED HER
THROUGH A LONG SERIES OF CHILDHOOD DIS-
EASES, SAID THAT—"

Hart flung the paper down on the desk.

"Johnny," he said, "right now, you're looking at the biggest
damn fool in the newspaper business. I got a hunch and sent Bob
out there after a big story. He isn't there more than ten hours and
the story is all shot to hell."

Zeke Brown and his wife, Mary, sat on the doorstep of their cabin
and gazed out over their farm.

Night was closing down over the land and in the jungle night-
things were awakening. Howls, roars, bellows and yelps mingled
to make the night hideous. Zeke shivered as he listened and his
hand crept to the butt of his gun. For five years he had heard this
nightly chorus of hate and murder, but it always brought tremors
of terror with each coming of darkness.

"We'd ought to have some 'taters pretty soon, Mary," he said,
striving to keep a tremble out of his voice. "I was looking at them
today. Planted them in that sandy patch and the water drained off
pretty good. They'll taste fine."

He heard soft sobs and saw that his wife was weeping.

"What's the matter, Mary?" he asked. "Dog-gone, what are
you crying for?"

"It's the chickens, Zeke," she told him. "I set such stock by
them hens of mine. And now they're all gone. We won't have no
more eggs."

Zeke cursed.

"Next time I see a skink," he said, "I'm going to catch him alive
and dunk him into one of them acid pools over there by the river."

Roughly he patted his wife's shoulder.

"I'll sure fix them for what they done to our chickens," he said.

A thrumming roar sounded over the horizon and Zeke looked up quickly. The roar became louder and louder. With tubes red-hot, a flier swept over the edge of the jungle, dipped toward the ground with forward rockets blasting.

Zeke leaped to his feet, waving his arms, cursing.

"Keep out of my 'tater patch, damn you!" he screamed. "I'll sure for certain take the hide off you if you bust up my 'tater patch."

The ship plunged downward, too fast for a safe landing. Its nose struck the potato patch, ripping into the soft soil, throwing it aside in great furrows like the mold-board of a giant plow.

"Now you done it, damn it, now you done it," shrieked Zeke. "You ruined my 'tater crop!"

He raced swiftly through the waist-high patches of polka-dot weeds that lay between the cabin and the potato patch.

The ship's nose was buried deep in the cushioning earth, but it did not appear to be damaged. As Zeke approached, the cabin door opened and a man staggered out.

At the sight of Zeke he cried out, a piteous, animal-like cry. "Food, for the love of Heaven—food!" he cried. "I'm starving!"

In the light which flooded from the cabin door Zeke saw the man's face and his anger turned swiftly to pity. He saw an old man, his form emaciated, his face pinched, eyes staring out of deep hollows, his cheeks sunken—a living skeleton.

The man took a step forward, staggered and fell. Zeke scooped him up and galloped for the house.

"Mary," he yelled. "Get some food. This man is nearly starved."

A voice sounded out of the gloom. It was Luther, on his way over to spend a few hours with his friend.

"What's the matter, Zeke?"

"Plane crashed," Zeke yelled. "Better run to town and get Doc. There's some other fellers in there. They look bad hurt."

"Be back in a minute with Doc if he's sober," Luther yelled back.

Zeke heard his feet pounding rapidly down the road.

"Zeke," Mary's voice was on the verge of despair, "I ain't got nothing but a mess of greens. That ain't fitten food for a sick man."

"It's better than nothing," said Zeke. "Give me a dish of it. This feller's starved, I tell you."

IV

"About all you can say for New Chicago is that nobody bothers you much here," Doc told Bob. "Right good place for a man to hide out if he's got something he don't want known.

"Take the feller who runs the Venus Flower saloon. He was a big racketeer back in Old Chicago on Earth. Came here three or four years ago. Then Angus MacDonald, you seen him this afternoon. His real name isn't Angus MacDonald. Folks say he was one of the pirates that raised so much hell on the Earth-Mars run years ago. Then there's old Hank Smith. Nice old feller. But he's the head of a utility company that went haywire back on Earth. Lots of investors would like to get their fingers on him."

"How about yourself, Doc?" asked Bob. "No skeletons rattling around in your closet, is there?"

"Hell, no," said Doc. "I was just a damn fool who came out here to grow up with the country."

Doc patted the bottle that stood on the desk.

"You certainly are a proper judge of liquor," he said. "First time I had anything like this for years."

He tilted the bottle and it gurgled pleasantly.

A rattle of footsteps sounded on the stairs.

Luther Bidwell stormed into the room. "Doc," he shouted, "a

plane just crashed out in Zeke Brown's potato patch. Some of the fellers are in bad shape."

Doc reached for his raincoat. "Business picking up today," he commented. "Two calls in a few hours."

He slipped the bottle into his coat pocket.

With Luther in the lead, the three men raced down the stairs and out into the street. The weather had cleared to some extent, but the street was one vast mud-hole.

Running, they took the road to Zeke's house, a little over a mile distant.

Zeke greeted them at the doorway. "Hated to bother you, Doc," he said, "but didn't know how bad it was. Starving man and four dead men in the plane. Looks like they died from starvation. Old men, white hair and every one of them just skin and bones. The feller I brought here was pretty bad off when I picked him up, but Mary fed him up and he seems all right now."

"Starving," asked Doc. "Do you mean they look like they died because of lack of food?"

"Sure do," Zeke affirmed.

Bob shoved the farmer to one side and ducked into the cabin. He made out the figure of a man lying on the bed. With one stride he was across the room and bending over the man.

"Were you the man in the plane?" he asked.

"Yes, I was," the flier replied. "This farmer tells me all the others died."

"Did you have the Hunger Disease?" demanded Bob.

"I guess so," the man answered weakly. "We were at a post on the Pearl River. Heard about it over the radio and figured we were lucky to be out of touch with everyone. Thought we were safe. But it hit us day before yesterday. We started for Radium City, thinking we might find help there."

"How do you feel now?" asked Bob.

The man ran a skeletonlike hand over his stomach, pressed and punched his midriff.

"Pain's all gone," he announced. "Feel fine. Not hungry any more. First time I haven't been hungry for two days. Before this it didn't matter how much I ate, I was always hungry."

"Did you eat much here?"

"No, just a dish of greens of some sort. Seemed to fill me up right away and gave me a lot of strength. Still pretty weak, but I feel different. Feel like myself again. Not sick any longer. Feel like I'm going to get well."

Bob rose and turned around. "Zeke," he asked, "what did you feed this man?"

Mary Brown answered the question. "All I had was some greens. I was so ashamed, but Zeke said they was better than nothing."

"Mrs. Brown," asked Bob, "what were those greens made out of?"

"Why," she said, "polka-dot weeds. They make fine greens."

"Doc," Bob shouted.

Doc waddled across the room.

"Listen to me," said Bob, taking hold of the slack at the throat of Doc's raincoat. "Does everyone in New Chicago eat greens made out of the polka-dot weed?"

Doc squirmed. "Why, I guess so," he said. "Everybody likes it. Me, I eat all I can get of them."

"Does Susan Donagan eat it? Does she like it?"

"No," said Doc, "come to think of it, she doesn't. Doesn't like anything green. Her mother frets a lot because she won't touch spinach."

"Doc," said Bob, "listen to me and do what I tell you. Try to get that old alcohol-fogged brain of yours to working. You get down to Donagan's as fast as you can. Feed Susan polka-dot greens. Hold her and cram them down her throat if you have to. And then watch. If she gets well, I'll make you famous. I'll write your name in 72 point type and put your mug on every front page in the System."

Doc cracked his fist in the palm of his hand.

"I see what you are getting at, Bob," he shouted.

Quickly he spun about and made for the door.

Bob shouted after him. "Remember, Doc, keep sober. You'll need all the sense you have."

"Sure will," said Doc.

Half a mile down the road he took the bottle from his pocket and flipped it into the underbrush. A few quick steps and he turned back. On hands and knees he fumbled beside the road. His questing hand touched something smooth. He lifted the bottle, pulled the cork with his teeth. The liquor gurgled down his throat.

On the road again, trudging toward town, Doc wiped his mouth with his coat sleeve.

"It wasn't like it was just plain rotgut," he told himself. "Been all right to throw that kind of stuff away. But it would have been downright sinful to waste good Scotch."

Arthur Hart paced the floor of his office.

Hap Folsworth, sports editor, sat with his feet on Hart's desk and smoked a Venus-weed cigar.

"What in hell do you suppose Bob's run into out there?" Hart demanded of Hap. "He sends me word to wait for a real story. No hint of what it is. Nothing to go on."

"He's sitting down in a Venusian saloon laughing up his sleeve at you," said Hap. "He's getting even with you for sending him out there."

Hart smoothed out the piece of paper that had come over the interworld teletype three hours before.

It read:

HOLD PRESSES READY FOR EXTRA. HAVE MOST IMPORTANT IMPORTANT IMPORTANT STORY. CAN'T BE SURE YET. WILL KNOW IN FOUR HOURS, MAYBE LESS. BOB.

Hart raged.

"Here I've held a secret wave length open for him ever since the last edition. The theatres will be closed pretty soon and we'll lose all our street sales. If he's running a sandy on me I'll bust him wide open when he gets back."

A boy stuck his head in the door. "Receiving signal on the New Chicago machine," he shouted.

Hart spun about and raced after the boy. In his wake lumbered the sports editor. The city room was tense with excitement.

"Receiving signal just came over," said Johnny Mason. "Ought to be along anytime now."

The machine chattered and chittered, but the keys still remained motionless.

Then the machine lurched to a start.

Methodically the keys tapped out:

THE QUICK BROWN FOX JUMPED OVER THE LAZY DOG'S BACK. THE QUICK BROWN FOX JUMPED—"

"A test," said Johnny. "The operator at New Chicago is running a test."

Then the machine stood motionless for a moment.

"Get going," yelled Hart, pounding the machine cover with a clenched fist.

Again the keys moved, slowly, maddeningly methodical—: NEW CHICAGO, VENUS—DR. ANDERSON TROWBRIDGE, HEALTH OFFICER AND ONLY PHYSICIAN IN THIS TINY TRADING POST, ANNOUNCED TODAY HE HAD DISCOVERED A CURE FOR THE HUNGER DISEASE. THE CURE IS OBTAINED FROM AN HERB, KNOWN LOCALLY AS THE POLKA-DOT WEED. AN ANCIENT PLANT FROM THE PLANET MARS, BROUGHT HERE SIX YEARS AGO BY DR. JACOB HANSLER, WHO FOUND THE SEEDS IN A RUINED LABORATORY DATING BACK TO THE GENZIK DYNASTY, THE POLKA-DOT WEED IS—"

Hart rushed from the tiny cubbyhole housing the machine.

"Herb," he shouted to his assistant editor, "get pictures of Dr. Jacob Hansler. Pictures of Bob Jackson. Pictures of Dr. Anderson Trowbridge—"

"Who in hell," asked Herb, "is Dr. Anderson Trowbridge?"

"How in hell should I know?" roared. Hart. "Phone the International Medical Society. They'll tell you. But get pictures! He's the biggest news in ten years. Write headlines a foot high in three shades blacker than night. We roll in half an hour."

He turned to Hap Folsworth.

"We'll have them fighting to get this one," he exulted. "We'll get out the biggest damn extra and score the biggest scoop this city has ever seen."

V

Bob Jackson sat on a log with Zeke Brown in front of Zeke's cabin.

"Zeke," said Bob, "you'll have to realize that you and all the rest of the farmers here are rich. You're just plain filthy rich. You couldn't grow corn and you couldn't keep chickens—but all the time you were growing the polka-dot weed. And for that you can ask your own price. This is the only place in the universe today where the polka-dot weed can be obtained. Even now ships are on their way from Earth and from Radium City to get a supply. And you boys can ask whatever you please."

Zeke pushed back his hat and scratched his head.

"Well, you see," he said, "it's this way. Me and the rest of the boys ain't hankering to hold nobody up. We understand that other people need this weed dang bad and that we can ask our own price. But all we want is a fair price. The past five years have been mighty hard years and we ought to make something out of it, but we ain't aiming to profiteer on the misery of other folks."

"Sure, I know about that," said Bob. "But you fellows don't want to be damn fools. This is your big chance. Here's a chance to cash in on your five years and get paid well for every hour of them."

Zeke shuffled to his feet.

"Somebody coming up the road," he announced. "Heard a ship come in awhile ago. Maybe it's somebody wanting the weed."

"They haven't had time to get here yet," Bob pointed out.

Angus MacDonald led the party that plodded up the road through the everlasting red mud. There were five of them.

They halted outside the gate and Angus stepped forward.

"Zeke," he said, "I got a paper to serve on you. Don't like to do this, but it's my duty."

"Paper?" asked Zeke.

"Yes, a paper." Angus reached into his inside coat pocket and drew forth a sheaf of documents.

"One of these for you," he announced, thumbing through them.

"What's the paper for?" asked Zeke, suspicion creeping into his voice.

"Claims you don't own this land," replied Angus. "Must be some mistake. You boys been living here for a good many years now. Seems if you didn't own it, you could have found out before this."

Cold anger dripped from Zeke's words.

"Who claims they own it? If we don't own it, who does own it?"

"The Venus Land Company says they own it," declared Angus. "I sure hate to do this, Zeke."

Zeke looked past Angus, to the other four who stood behind him.

"I suppose you snakes are the representatives for the Venus Land Company," he stated bluntly.

One of the four stepped forward. "You're right," he said, "we are. And if I were you I wouldn't try to start anything. We know how to handle smart guys when they try to make trouble."

Bob saw that Zeke's thumbs were hitched over his gun belt, his fingers poised over the butt of the flame at his hip.

And in that moment, Zeke was no longer a farmer dressed in dirty overalls and ragged shirt. He was something else, something that thrilled a man to see—a man ready to fight for his land.

Zeke's words came slowly, unlike his usual drawl—and each was a danger warning, plain for all to see.

"If any of you polecats think you're horning in on me now," he said, "you are mistaken. And that goes for the rest of us around here, too. If you try to get rough, we'll just naturally strew your guts all over a forty-acre pasture."

"Don't talk to me about the due process of law," roared Arthur Hart. "Babble like that might impress some folks, but it leaves me cold. What I want to know is are you going to stand by and let a set of racketeers like Venus Land rob a bunch of poor Iowa farmers a second time—? Yes, I know that's libelous, but it isn't on paper and you can't prove a thing. And let me tell you, mister, if you don't act damn soon I'll give you something you can bring a libel suit for. I'll fix it so that you won't get one single cock-eyed vote for any public office again. Before I get through with you you'll think you've been hit by a windmill. I got three or four stories filed away that the public will fight to read. The Universal Power Trust case, just for one example. I'll tell the people just what sort of a grafting old buzzard you are—and what's more I'll make it stick."

The face in the visi-plate was purple with rage, but Interplanetary Chief Justice Elmer Phillips knew when he was beaten.

"Mr. Hart," he said, "I don't like your attitude. I deny every insinuation you have made. But I do see some merit in what you propose. I will do it."

"You're damn right you'll do it," snarled Hart, "and what's more, you'll do it right away. If you don't give me a story saying that you have issued an injunction stopping Venus Land or anyone else from monkeying around with the polka-dot weed farms by the time we put our last edition to bed, I'll have another story in its place that will blast you and your Interplanetary Justice commission right out of the water."

"You can rest assured I will do it," Justice Phillips told him. "I'm a man of my word."

"And so am I," said Hart.

The editor thrust the visa-phone receiver back in its cradle and swung around in his chair.

Hap Folsworth chased his cigar from one corner of his mouth to the other.

"I'll say this for you," he remarked, "when you get your tail up you don't let a little thing like blackmail stop you."

"That wasn't blackmail," Hart snapped. "The Justice and I understand one another. He knows well enough I could rip him wide open for some of the stunts the justice commission has pulled and he's ready to play ball. That's all."

Hart's collar was open, his necktie was twisted under one ear, his hair was rumpled.

"You look like you been in a street fight," Hap observed.

"Listen, Hap," said Hart, "I am in a fight. I'm fighting red tape and governmental stupidity and bureaucratic inefficiency. Fighting for the rights of some poor, simple-minded farmers who let a racketeering land company sell them worthless land on Venus. And now that the land has something on it that is valuable the land company wants to take it away from them again. I'm going to have the government declare the polka-dot weed a public utility and take control of it. That will keep out the rats and the slickers and will insure a fair price."

Hap changed his cigar to the other corner of his mouth.

"You've still got ideals, Hart," he mocked. "Ideals after 18 years in a newspaper office. That's something."

"Look here," snarled Hart, "you get back to your silly prize fights and your asinine baseball games and leave me alone. I got a man's job to do."

Johnny Mason, a sheet of yellow paper gripped in his hand, stuck his head in the door.

"Got a load of bad news," he said. "Funny news."

"What is it?" asked Hart.

Johnny laid the paper in front of him.

"Three ships took off from Radium City for New Chicago," Johnny said, "to get a shipment of polka-dot weed. They've disappeared. No radio contact. No reports. Nothing."

Hart hummed under his breath. "Something funny here," he said.

"And that's not all," Johnny told him. "The freighter that was sent out from New York to Venus for the weed is coming back. Got out just beyond the orbit of the moon and blew three tubes. Improper fuel mixture."

Bob found Doc at a table in the Venus Flower saloon. "How's Susan?" Bob asked.

"Getting along all right," said Doc dolefully. "She'll be up and around in a few days."

Doc fondled his bottle, gazed mournfully at it and shoved it across the table to the reporter. Bob tilted it and the living fire of Martian *bocca* slashed down his throat. He set the bottle back on the table and coughed.

"Bob," said Doc, "I feel lower than a snake's belly. I have been sitting off to one side talking to myself and I am downright astounded at what I found out."

"That's a fine way for the man who discovered a cure for the Hunger Disease to be talking," Bob remarked.

"That's just it," explained Doc. "You see, I didn't discover that cure. I would never have guessed it in a hundred years. But you told the people I was the one who did it. And now the International Medical Society wants me to come to New York and be the guest of honor at a big banquet. They are going to decorate me. Just talked to the Society president over the radio."

"That's fine," said Bob.

Doc shook his head.

"It isn't fine," he protested. "Long as I am out here, buried in this mud-hole, I'm a world hero because you've made me one. But it won't take those doctors in New York five minutes to find I am a phony. I am just an old booze-hound. I haven't got too much brain left any more. Liked liquor too well. About all I'm fit to be is a doctor out here. I can patch up a busted leg and I can pull an aching tooth and I can doctor colds, but that's about all I'm good for any more."

"You're drunk," Bob accused. "You'll feel differently when you sober up. I made you a hero and I'm going to keep you a hero if I kill you doing it."

"Maybe you're right," Doc mumbled. "Anyhow, I'm not looking forward to that trip to New York."

In silence they sat and watched the rain pour down, making a river of the street.

"How's everything out at the farms?" Doc asked.

"Still peaceful," Bob said. "I hope I can keep it that way until Hart gets the court to issue that injunction. There were about a dozen Venus Land men came over from Radium City in the ship. When Zeke showed some fight and Angus refused to serve any more papers, the ones who went out with Angus went back to the ship for reinforcements. Then the whole mob went back to Zeke's place and found it deserted. Zeke and his wife had skinned out to warn their friends. So the Venus Land bunch moved in, figuring, I suppose, that they should establish some sort of possession rights. Zeke roused up his boys and that place is an armed camp. They have every path guarded and a ring thrown around Zeke's cabin. They're hoping the Venus Land boys make just one false move, so they can have an excuse to start shooting. But I got Zeke to promise he'd keep peaceable as long as possible."

"If something don't happen pretty soon," said Doc, "we'll have a posse from town going out there. Nobody around here has much love for Venus Land."

"All we can do is wait," Bob said. "Hart will move heaven and hell to get that injunction through. Those ships that were sent out to get the weed should be here pretty soon. Should have been here before now, in fact."

VI

"What's that?" Hart yelled into the phone. "I know what you have to say is important, but wait just a second. Get your breath. Talk slowly, so I can understand you."

In the visi-plate Hart saw the reporter gulp and draw in a deep breath.

"It's like this," the reporter said, talking slowly, with clipped precise speech, as if he had applied an actual physical brake to his tongue. "The boys down here at Interplanetary Police headquarters have been working for the past several months on a tip some big plot was underway, aimed against the system government.

"That plot broke today when the police captured one of the men in the ring. They did some persuading and he talked. He said that the gang he was working with was responsible for the Hunger Disease. They had spread the bacteria that caused it all over both Venus and Earth. They had planned to spread it on Mars, too."

"Edwards," snarled Hart, "are you sure you got the right dope?"

"You bet I am," said the reporter. "The chief down here just released the story."

"Herb," Hart roared to his assistant, "get on the extension and listen to this."

"Now," he said to the reporter, "go ahead."

"It's a screwy story, but it's the straight dope," the reporter cautioned.

"I don't give a damn how screwy it is" yelled Hart. "If it's news we print it."

"The police didn't give us the name of this fellow who confessed, but I saw him. He is a big man, a good deal larger than the average man, and his skin is a deep tan, almost black, as if he had been out in the sun a lot."

"Say," said Hart, "are you going to tell us what happened or are you going to spend the afternoon just blabbering around? I want facts and the quicker I get them the better it will be for you."

"All right," said Edwards, "here they are.

"The man the police rounded up told them that he was not really a Terrestrial. Said he came from Mars and was the member of some secret organization. I got that spelled out. Had the chief spell for me. G-e-n-z-i-k, Genzik. At one time he claimed his people ruled Mars. That was thousands of years ago. But the Martians rose up and ousted them, chased them out. Since then the tribe, or whatever it is, has been living out in the desert."

"Edwards," snarled Hart, "that's all a matter of history. There was a Genzik dynasty on Mars thousands of years ago."

"Oh, so that's it," said Edwards. "I couldn't figure out that part of the story very well. Anyhow, this fellow told the police that for years and years the Genziks have planned to take over the three worlds of Mars, Earth and Venus. There weren't enough of them to do any real fighting, so they developed this Hunger Disease bacteria. Seems that it was the bacteria of a disease that at one time almost wiped out all of Mars' population. They sent their men all over Venus and Mars and spread the bacteria where it would do the most good. The police have sent out warnings to all police stations all over and they are trying to round up the rest of the gang. Far as I could make out, there are several thousand Genziks loose on Venus and Earth."

"Say," snapped Hart, "did the chief tell you that the Genziks were responsible for the disappearance of the three ships that left Radium city?"

"Yes," said Edwards, "I was just getting around to that. And he said they were responsible for the wrecking of the Earth freighter that started out for Venus to get this polka-dot weed. You see, they knew about the polka-dot weed. That was what saved Mars when the Hunger Disease threatened to wipe it out years ago. But they didn't know there was any polka-dot weed growing any more until they read the New Chicago story in the papers late last night. This fellow claimed that after the Genziks were chased out by the Martians there wasn't much science or knowledge left on Mars. The Genziks, he said, were the intellectual boys on that planet and had done a lot to help the Martians and that's what made them so mad when the Martians turned against them. He said that the Genziks came from Earth a long time ago, thousands of years ago. From some place like Atlantic—"

"Atlantis?" asked Hart.

"Yeah, that's it," said Edwards, joyfully.

"Listen," said Hart, "do you mean to tell me you don't even know the old story of Atlantis? You don't know enough Martian history to know who the Genziks were. You thought they were some kind of a gang. You figured maybe this was a big story, but you haven't got any idea how damn big it is. Now, I want you to go back to police headquarters and try not to act too damn dumb. I'll be sending some of the other boys down and when they get there you come back here. I'm going to try you out as a copy boy and if you don't make good there, I'm going to bounce you right out on your ear."

Hart slammed up the phone and switched around to face his assistant.

"You got that, Herb?" he asked, tensely.

Herb nodded.

"All right then," said Hart, "get to work. Send one of the photographers down to try to get a shot of this bird the police caught. Send somebody down to replace Edwards. He's too dumb to breathe. Have someone look up the history of the old Genziks and write a feature yarn. Use the revenge angle. Those boys have been hiding out somewhere up on Mars for centuries, frothing at the mouth and planning revenge ever since they were turned out by the Martians. Play up the Atlantis angle. Somebody once advanced the theory that the Genziks were either from Atlantis or Mu. Said they had built spaceships when our forefathers were still swinging around in trees and went out to Mars to establish the dynasty. Can't remember who it was—but whoever it was got laughed at plenty."

"I know who it was," said Herb quietly. "It was our old friend, Dr. Jacob Hansler. Everybody thought he was teched in the head."

Hart smote the desk with his fist.

"Herb," he said, "that's the angle. Old Jake again. Go to town on that story. It ties right up with the polka-dot weed yarn—how Jake found it and everything."

The editor switched back to his desk.

"I'm going to call the IP chief and find out if he's taking any measures to protect New Chicago. Hell's liable to pop there any minute. The Genziks will try to destroy the weed fields or I'm a dirty space-rat."

But as he lifted the receiver the buzzer rang softly.

Snapping on the visi-plate connection, Hart saw the face of Justice Phillips.

"Oh, it's you," he said.

"Yes, Mr. Hart," said the Justice. "I'm just calling you to tell you that I acted as you suggested. The New Chicago authorities already have been notified of the injunction and instructed to act accordingly."

VII

Angus MacDonald hitched up his trousers and shifted his chew to the other side of his mouth. "In all my years as marshal of this town," he announced, "I never enjoyed anything like I'm going to enjoy this job. I sure am going to have a lot of fun kicking those Venus Land babies out of Zeke's place."

He doubled up one powerful fist and looked at it admiringly.

"I sure hope they resist," he remarked wistfully.

He stuffed into his pocket the yellow slip of paper on which his instructions from the Radium City court were typed.

"Going with me, Bob?" he asked.

"No," said Bob, "I'm going to stay here and wait for the police ships from Radium City. They ought to be here any minute now. From what Hart told me just now we're sitting right on top of a keg of dynol and I'll feel a lot safer when the police get here."

"You want to go, Doc?" asked Angus.

"Nope," said Doc. "This has been an exciting day and I feel all tuckered out. But I'm a happy man. This news about the Genziks has justified my faith in old Jake. They laughed at him back on Earth when he said the Genziks were the old Atlanteans. And now it sure looks like they were."

"All right, then," said Angus. "But you boys are missing a lot of fun."

Plodding through the ankle-deep red mud Angus started down the road.

"Still a regular old war-horse," observed Doc. "From what I have heard he sure was an old hell-hound in his day. He damn near stopped all traffic between Mars and Earth thirty years ago. Had the whole Interplanetary Police force on his trail at times. But he had a good ship and he always showed them a clean pair of heels. Old-timers claim he could make a spaceship turn on a dime."

"Let's go back to the station," suggested Bob. "You and Sandy can finish that game of checkers while we're waiting for the police ships."

"O. K.," said Doc.

From far up the road came a hail from Angus.

"Ship coming in," he yelled.

They stood stock-still, waiting. From the east, faintly, they heard the roar of rocket tubes.

"Right close down," Angus yelled to them.

Again came the blasting of the tubes, nearer this time.

"That isn't any police ship," said Bob.

"And it isn't a transport, either," declared Doc.

The tubes roared again, and over the eastern horizon the watchers saw the reddish glare of the explosion through the blanketing clouds.

Then the blast seemed to be almost over them and, far up, dimmed by the heavy cloud layer, they saw the angry belching of the rockets.

The ship circled to the west, turned back, stabbing away with short blasts.

"They're coming in," said Bob.

The ship dropped down, heading for the landing field. It was a beautiful ship, gleaming, silvery even in the dimness of approaching twilight.

"Never saw one like that before," said Doc.

Only a few hundred feet up it rushed over the town, swung in for the field.

Suddenly a tongue of red flame leaped out from the bow of the ship, a flame that smashed against the radio station and wiped it out in a furnace blast of terrific heat.

A scorching wave of heat swept over Bob and Doc, heat that stifled them, seemed to sear their eyeballs. As if someone had suddenly opened the door of a white-hot fire box.

The ship swooped over the field, swung in a wide arc, heading back toward the town.

"Run," Bob shouted to Doc. "Into the jungle! It's the Genziks! They're going to blast the town!"

But Doc did not run. Instead he caught Bob by the sleeve and pointed out on the field.

"Look at Angus," he shouted. "What's the damn fool up to now?"

Angus was running across the field, jerking out his flame pistol as he ran, straight toward the Venus Land ship.

"My Lord," breathed Bob. "He's going to fight them single-handed."

"Angus," shouted Doc, "come back here. You can't do that. You haven't a chance. That ship's not armed."

But Angus apparently did not hear.

They saw him reach the ship and blast the door lock with a single shot from the pistol. With bare hands he wrenched the red-hot door open and disappeared within the ship.

"The old fool's crazy mad," said Doc. "Sandy was in the station and he's dead now. Angus thought the world of that boy. Had a right to."

The Genzik ship was coming back, bearing down on the town. It swept over the landing field and once again from its bow reached out the tongue of flame. A building went up in a puff of flashing fire. Another and another. As the ship zoomed up it left behind it a line of death and destruction, the entire east side of the street burned to the ground, a blackened ruin, with a few steel girders still glowing.

The street was alive with screaming humanity. Running, terrified human beings, some seeking shelter in the jungle, others running aimlessly, a few standing as if paralyzed, gazing up into the clouds.

From the landing field came a roar and the Venus Land ship shot upward with terrific speed to disappear in the heavy clouds.

The Genzik ship was circling, blasting away with short explosions, jockeying into position to strike at the row of buildings on the west side of the street.

"Maybe we better take to the jungle," suggested Doc.

Bob nodded. "There won't be much left of New Chicago after those fellows get through," he said. "They'll blast the town and then they'll sweep the farms. They'll turn this one little section into a desert. After they are through there won't be any polka-dot weed or anything else left."

"Angus is up there," said Doc.

"But he won't be able to do a thing. He has nothing to fight with," protested Bob.

The Genzik ship was headed back toward the town. Through the clouds the two in the road could see its silvery bulk.

Swiftly Doc and Bob sprinted toward the jungle, but at its edge they halted and looked back as a series of deafening explosions seemed to shake the ground beneath their feet.

The Genzik ship was nearing the edge of the town, but above it, bearing down upon it, with tubes wide open, came a black ship—the Venus Land ship guided by the hand of an old daredevil of space, a man old-timers said could turn a spaceship on a dime.

Like a flaming meteor the black ship speared downward, the world a-tremble with the roaring of its tubes.

Then the rocket blast was drowned out as the sky was lighted with a mushrooming blaze of white light and the very jungle rocked to the detonations of a violent explosion.

For a split second Bob saw the two ships locked together, surrounded by a corona of eye-searing blue-white flame as the fuel tanks exploded at the impact.

Trailing a column of fire, the ships dropped like a plummet and thudded into the jungle.

"By Heaven," said Doc, "he did it. And he died the way he always wanted to, with his hands on space controls."

—

"You know," said Doc, "I've regained my confidence. I'm not going to let any of those high-powered New York medics high-hat me. I got what I'm going to say all figured out. I am going to say, 'Gentlemen: I am very pleased to be here—'"

"Sure," said Bob, "you got that much figured out, but what are you going to say after that?"

"Say," said Doc, "I got that all figured out, too."

"Listen, Doc," warned Bob, "you pipe down. It's time for us to get on board. There's a rule against letting drunks aboard and if you don't straighten up they'll make you wait until the next ship."

Together the two moved toward the huge ship that rested, ready for the takeoff, on the New Chicago field.

Bob, with one foot on the gangplank, turned when he heard his name shouted.

Across the field ran Zeke, his arms waving, the flame pistol holster flapping against his thigh.

"Wait a minute," he shouted. "Wait a minute, Bob."

Bob waited.

At the foot of the gangplank Zeke gripped his hand.

"Remember that skink I was telling you about?" he asked. "The one that took to living in my wood pile?"

Bob nodded.

"He dang near tantalized me to death for months," Zeke said. "I laid for him, but I never could get him."

"So I suppose you finally did get him," Bob said.

"Hell, no," said Zeke. "This morning he had pups!"

MUTINY ON MERCURY

As far as I can tell from the author's journals, Clifford Simak wrote this story in 1930, making it perhaps his very first. But since it was initially rejected by Astounding Science Fiction, *and then by* Wonder Stories, Miracle Science and Fantasy Stories, *and* Argosy All-Story Weekly, *it was not the first of his stories to appear in print. (Wonder Stories ultimately accepted and published it in 1932.)*

As might be expected, "Mutiny on Mercury" is a crude first attempt at writing. It is also, as might be expected from its era, violent and displays elements clearly derivative of Edgar Rice Burroughs's John Carter of Mars *series. And there's plenty of room for argument about its implications. . . .*

—dww

Tom Clark stared at the sword he held in his hand. It should have been in a museum, for it was a rare specimen. The steel was bright and the hilt was an example of workmanship in which the ancients had excelled.

It had been centuries since a sword had been used in battle. But on this day, in the atmosphere plant which supplied oxygen to the great quartz dome on the twilight belt of the planet Mercury, a naked blade had leaped and flashed, a weapon again. It was no longer a relic doomed to be regarded with curiosity by a race that had forgotten its use.

The blade had belonged to Ben Jacobs, an heirloom which had been handed down, in the name of sentiment, from father to son, for many generations. Undoubtedly it was worth a small fortune, for the museums of the Earth held only a few such weapons. But now Ben Jacobs lay in a heap on the floor of the plant, struck down by a burly Selenite.

To Jacobs the sword had been a symbol. He had carried it from the Earth to this forsaken planet, where the only evidence of life was ten huge domes of quartz set over as many mines, owned and operated completely by the Universal Ore Mining Company.

Only twenty-four hours ago he had told Tom the story of the sword. Now Jacobs lay motionless on the floor and the ancient blade was dyed with the blood of vanquished foemen.

Gently Tom lowered the point of the sword to the floor and gazed upon his handiwork. Before him lay three bodies. One was that of a Martian, a yellow-skinned, eight-limbed body, the skin covered with hideous warts. The grinning head, almost severed from the trunk, boasted three eyes, two in the same position as those of a Terrestrial, the other on the top of the hairless head. The mouth was large, as was also the nose, with the ears almost twice as large as those of an Earth man.

The other two bodies were those of Selenites, the gigantic Moon men with their small heads, their abnormally developed torsos and correspondingly large, powerful arms and their small, but singularly powerful legs, built on the same lines as those of a kangaroo.

Tom lifted the sword again and ran his fingers along its edge. They came away red and sticky.

He laughed grimly. The sword, ancient weapon as it may have been, had another tale added to the long list which had started, said legends, in the year 1815, in the Napoleonic Wars. For century upon century the blade had been regarded as a heirloom, a thing of sentiment. On this day, however, it had come again into its own. It had leaped and flashed, bitten deeply into flesh and bone, drunk blood.

Stepping over the body of one of the Selenites, Tom made his way to the side of the prostrate figure of Ben Jacobs. He had seen Jacobs felled like an ox by the huge fist of one of the now dead Selenites, but there was a chance the man still lived.

Kneeling on the floor, he placed his ear to the breast of the prone body. There was not so much as a flutter of the heart. Tom turned his attention to Jacobs' head and what he found there convinced him the brilliant young scientist, who had been in charge of the atmosphere plant, was no longer alive.

Tom stood up and gazed about the death-ridden room. It presented a spectacle of ordered complexity with its many dials, tubes, pipes, valve controls, motors and the huge central control board. A silence, which was only accentuated by the steady hum of the machinery, assailed him and he suddenly realized he was the only Terrestrial alive at Shaft Number Nine.

Outside there might still lurk a few of the Selenites and possibly a few Martians, but they would be few. The only machine gun at the station, spitting out over 150 atomic pellets every minute, had wrought havoc among the mutineers before a stone, thrown by one of the Selenites, had bowled over McGregor, the radio operator. The latter, who had been taken unawares by the outbreak, had been unable to reach his post to send out an S.O.S.; and had philosophically, and entirely in keeping with his Scotch blood, done the next best thing by unlimbering the gun and turning it against the mob of howling miners who were destroying the radio station.

If McGregor had been at his desk, as his duty required him to be, instead of playing a few hands of cards with old Andy Schwartz, the head engineer, word of the uprising and an appeal for help would have been sent out at once. Failing in this, he had at least saved the mine and costly apparatus from immediate destruction, by the simple process of reducing the number of hands for the performance of the pending destruction.

The uprising had been a complete surprise, coming just as the second shift was coming out of the shaft and the third shift ready to go down. The miners in Shift Number One, evidently by a pre-arranged signal, had come storming forth from their quarters as soon as the attack was launched.

Evidently the captains underground had been neatly disposed of, for there had been no warning anything was amiss. The first indication of trouble came when the men had come up without the captains. Even before questions could be asked concerning the absent Terrestrials, the blow had been struck.

"It's those damn Martians," Hal Eaton, young time keeper, only six weeks from the Earth, had screamed as a huge Selenite struck him down with a blow of his mighty pick.

Tom, jerking his atomic pistol from its holster, knew that what young Eaton had just screamed was true. The Martians were the trouble-makers and the traitors of the solar system. Once an insolent people, who had regarded themselves as the most advanced in culture and erudition in the universe, they still, even after hundreds of years, resented the bondage in which it had been necessary to place them to curb their diabolic cunning and haughty egotism. They were forever forming secret societies, always cooking up local revolutions. Where there was trouble, one would usually find a scheming Martian.

Tom leveled the pistol at the mob of Selenites rushing at him and pressed the trigger. There was a sharp, spiteful spat. The leading Moon man disappeared in a puff of white dust, his upraised shovel clattering to the ground.

Rapidly the pistol spat and the charge broke. Even the ape-brained Selenites, who seldom knew fear, could not stand in front of that pistol which caused one of their number to evaporate into thin air every time it spoke.

From all over the compound came the sound of firing and the pounding of many feet on the hard packed earth. There were no other sounds. It was uncanny, the way these dumb, ox-like Selenites attacked, silently, ponderously, armed only with their mining tools, or lacking these, with bare hands.

From somewhere near the atmosphere plant came a rapid "pit-pat," a sound not unlike the tramp of rain across a tin roof. Someone had unlimbered the machine gun. Lucky thing! Lulled into a false sense of security by the apparent orderliness of the station, the former superintendent, a soft fool who had no business holding such a position, had ordered the gun stored away as a thing for which there would be no further need. He had lasted six months and had been transferred back to Earth, at his own request. Too bad he couldn't have stayed to taste the fruits of his asinine management.

A stone whizzed past Tom's head. The Moon men were returning. They had retreated as far as the rock pile. From around the corner of the pile they came, each carrying an armful of missiles, heaving them as they ran.

Tom jerked up his arm, leveling his gun. Before he could press the trigger a rock, flung with considerable strength, caught him flush on the elbow. The gun clattered to the baked earth.

As he dived to retrieve it, another stone struck him in the ribs and toppled him sidewise. Stones pattered all about him and as he struggled to his knees he was again bowled over.

The Moon men were almost upon him. They were rotten throwers, or they would have bagged him for good and all. They couldn't keep on making only casual hits, however. Eventually one would connect with his head and it would be lights out. For a fleeting moment, he hoped one would finish him before the lousy beggars reached him.

"Lie low, I'll clean the devils out."

Tom twisted his head as the spiteful rattle of the machine gun broke loose.

In front of the atmosphere plant, old McGregor, his white hair looking like a lion's mane, his shirt ripped to shreds, his teeth working savagely on an oversized quid of tobacco, squatted behind the gun. It seemed to quiver with the excitement of the moment as it spat out blasting death.

Over Tom's head the pellets whispered their death song and behind him he knew the charging Selenites were being blown into clouds of white ash.

Slowly he started to worm his way toward McGregor, keeping his head low, for he did not wish to intercept one of the lethal pellets.

The patter of the gun and the whisper of the speeding bullets ceased.

"All right, lad," cried old McGregor and Tom, leaping to his feet, rushed forward, forgetting his pistol, which lay where it had fallen.

When he was only a matter of a few feet from the old man, who was disengaging a magazine preparatory to slipping another into place, a Martian, followed by two Selenites rushed around the corner of the atmosphere plant.

Before Tom could warn his friend, one of the Selenites hurled a stone, which caught McGregor flush on the temple.

The old man slowly slid from his seat on the gun. The Martian and the two Selenites raced for the door of the atmosphere plant.

Tom leaped after them, forgetful for the moment that he was unarmed. As he sped past old McGregor he noted that the white leonine head rested in a pool of blood and that a death pallor stamped the features.

Cursing under his breath, Tom rushed the three mutineers who were trying by brute force and awkwardness to force the locked door of the plant.

Seeing the Earth-man almost upon them, the two Selenites, trained for years to look upon the Terrestrials as their superiors and masters, momentarily forgot their rebellion and crying out in terror, threw their combined weight against the door. It splintered inward under the impact.

Tom arrived at the doorway just in time to see one of the huge brutes crush young Jacobs to the floor with a savage blow of his fist.

—

At Tom's cry of rage the three whirled to face him. The faces of the two Moon men were expressionless except for their beady eyes, which shone with a wild light; the features of the Martian were distorted into the snarl of a cornered beast.

It was then Tom realized he was unarmed. His eyes lighted upon the sword lying on the table to his left. It had been only a few hours ago he had listened to the tale of that very sword from the lips of Jacobs. It was a thrilling tale, a story of the days when men fought hand to hand.

His left hand reached out to clutch the scabbard and as he jerked the steel from its resting place, the three leaped to meet him.

With his back to the table he jabbed at the leading Selenite, to send him reeling backwards, howling with pain and clutching his belly. The point off the blade was red.

The second Moon man momentarily checked his rush and, seizing this opportunity, Tom leaped at him with the sword raised high. The brute tried to dodge, but the steel, fairly whistling through the air, caught him at the juncture of the neck and shoulder, cleaving deep. The Moon man slumped to the floor and the blade came free.

A heavy wrench, thrown by the Martian, missed Tom's head by a fraction of an inch and crashed into an array of bottles on a shelf against the wall.

"I'm coming to get you," said Tom, addressing the Martian, and the fellow snarled in hate as he backed across the room before the advance of the Terrestrial.

The remaining Selenite, still clutching his belly, staggered forward to place himself between the Earthman and the Martian. Without ado Tom methodically cut him down with a thrust to the throat.

Stepping over the prostrate body, he advanced on the Martian, who was crouched in a corner of the room.

Then, with his six arms outstretched, fingers hooked like talons about to strike, his fang-rimmed mouth opened wide, the Martian sprang to the attack.

Tom, taken by surprise, sprang back and stumbled over the dead Selenite, sprawling backwards, flat on his back, with the Martian almost on top of him.

He looked straight into the red eyes of his assailant, felt the talon-like fingers on his throat. The fanged mouth poised over his face drooled saliva on his cheek.

With all his strength, Tom brought his clenched left fist up, striking the Martian on the temple. As the grip of the fingers momentarily loosened under the impact of the blow, he threw himself sideways and rolled free of the man above him.

Both men sprang to their feet at the same instant and faced one another.

Tom lifted the sword.

"I surrender, I surrender," mouthed the Martian, fear in his eyes at the sight of the glistening blade poised to strike.

With a crooked smile on his lips, Tom brought the sword down. The Martian, his eight limbs sprawling grotesquely, sagged to the floor, his head almost severed from his body.

Tom wiped the sword and returned it to the scabbard.

Jacobs was dead. So was McGregor. There was no doubt all of the other Terrestrials, except himself, had likewise been killed.

Standing in the center of the room, he tried to determine his next course.

There were likely a few dozen Moon men and Martians still at the station. They were probably already at their work of destruction, wreaking their foolish vengeance upon the dominant Earth race that forced them to labor in the mines and forests on the several far-flung planets.

He cold-bloodedly considered the situation. First he would arm himself and routing out the last of the mutineers, slay them. Then he would remain until assistance came. Headquarters at

Shaft Number One, failing to get messages through, would suspect something amiss and investigate. In a very few hours his plight would be discovered.

The atmosphere plant, even unattended, would function for a few hours, long enough, at least, for the investigating party to arrive.

In a cabinet drawer Tom found a pistol and assuring himself it was loaded, slipped it into his holster.

As he started for the door his attention was arrested by a dial. The needle was swinging crazily. He stared in amazement, then in despair. One of the fools had evidently managed to open one of the air locks in the dome and the atmosphere was rushing out into the almost airless desert. Soon the two atmospheres would be equalized and every man caught without some sort of artificial protection and oxygen generator would be killed.

There was only one thing to do. He must reach one of the cars and escape to Shaft Number Eight, ten miles distant.

As he reached the door he realized he still clutched the sword and was about to drop it, when he made a sudden decision to take it with him. Why, he didn't know. Perhaps, he told himself with a grin, Jacobs' family might like it returned if and when he got back to Earth.

Outside, a violent wind, something unknown under the great dome, caught and almost swept him off his feet. It was caused by the air rushing for the open lock.

A World of Chaos

Bucking the air currents, which buffeted him cruelly, Tom fought his way across the yard to the car shed.

Here he found everything in disorder. Three machines, smashed and dented by some heavy tool, possibly a sledge hammer, met his eye. There had been four cars. One was missing. Evidently a party of the mutineers had smashed the three cars and escaping in the remaining one, had left one of the air locks open. There must have been a Martian or two in the party. The cow-headed Selenites didn't have the necessary intelligence to open one of the doors, let alone operate a car.

Tom cursed bitterly. In an hour the dome would be atmospherically equal to the desert outside, in which no man could live. Why did those bone-headed officials insist that every mine employ a few Martians? It would have been better to have killed off the entire race.

There was the matter of the cars, too. Why didn't the company give them light rocket planes instead? Economy again! A car cost about half of what a rocket plane would. What did the square-heads who held down swivel chairs care for the men in these ungodly outposts? Nevertheless, cars or planes, either would have been smashed. His job was to get out of the mess.

The air currents, streaming out of the dome toward the open lock, rattled the loose sheets of galvanized steel on the roof of the shed.

For a moment Tom considered trying to reach and close the lock, but he knew, even as he thought of it, that it would prove an impossible feat. Evidently it was Lock Three, a good half mile to the east. It would take too much time to get there and even if he could reach it, he knew that the air currents would sweep him like a straw through the opening into the dread desert where the thin atmosphere made life impossible.

There remained one chance.

Stored in the cars were metal suits for both the Terrestrials and their underlings, the Martians and Moon men. The suits were equipped with a small oxygen generator. The air, as manufactured, was cooled by a miniature refrigerator, similar to the large refrigeration plant in connection with the atmosphere generators under the dome. The suit, supplied with cool air which somewhat offset the heat of the desert, served well enough for short excursions from the dome or a car, but it was doubtful if a man could cover even ten miles of burning desert sands in one of them.

While encased in one a man could neither eat nor drink. The thought of hours without water was appalling, but there was little that could be done about it. It was the one chance—if the mutineers had not thought to also destroy the suits. Luckily in a locker of one of the wrecked cars he discovered a number of the suits.

The atmosphere was already becoming rare and his heart was pounding savagely as he donned one of them and switched on the atmosphere generator.

About the suit he strapped his pistol and Jacobs' sword, and stumbled awkwardly forth, making his way to Lock Three.

Buffeted by the wind which carried with it a shower of fine stones and a cloud of dust, he proceeded through the yard, threaded his way along the streets of the location and found himself on the outskirts of the settlement, having covered about half the distance to the lock.

Behind him he heard a crash as one of the shaft houses, its guys loosened by the pressure of the wind against the tower, toppled to the ground.

Turning to watch he saw the second shaft house tumble, hurling broken boards and splinters far into the air. Sheets of corrugated iron, ripped from the roof of the buildings, gyrated across the yard.

He groaned. Working for many years with the Universal Ore Mining Company, it had become a part of his life, a very personal association. A blow at it was a blow at him. Station Number Nine would probably be completely wrecked by the terrific wind which milled in the great dome. It was wrecked as completely as it would have been by the victorious mutineers, had enough of them been left to effect the destruction.

Gallant men had died defending the station. Men he had known for years. Old McGregor, with his everlasting quid of tobacco and his lion heart. Young Jacobs, a brilliant scientist, a fine young fellow, with his old sword, the sword which now hung at Clark's side.

Eyes dimmed with tears, he faced about and plodded on.

The atmosphere machine was working well. He knew, however, that discomfort would be his in plenty before many miles had been covered. In the back of his mind lurked a persistent doubt of his ability to make those ten long miles of airless, scorching desert. But these thoughts he kept pushing back, realizing that any such doubts would only serve to minimize his chances of reaching Station Number Eight.

The wind was dying down now, but he walked slowly, knowing it would not be safe to approach the lock too soon, lest he be caught and dashed through the opening to his death.

Behind him the settlement was a mass of wreckage, only the stoutly built atmosphere plant standing.

The terrific air currents, in a few minutes, had decreased in ferocity, and Tom deemed it safe to make his way through the lock, which lay only a short distance ahead. He moved toward it. The air currents still tugged at him, but were steadily dying down.

Reaching the lock Tom noticed that the inner portal was intact, pressed tight against the air chamber, but the outer portal was ripped from its hinges and lay a hundred yards out in the desert, deeply embedded in the sand.

For a moment Tom stood in the air chamber, pondering. If he could close the inner door and the atmosphere plant was still working, he could again bring about a suitable atmospheric condition. He suspected it would take some time to restock the huge dome with life-sustaining air. Just how long, he did not know. He was a geologist, not an engineer. While the plant manufactured the air, he could live in the suit and await the coming of a rescue party.

He grasped the door and slowly pulled it back into its proper position. It came to with a hollow sound, but there was no resounding click as the automatic bolts shot home.

Inside the helmet, Tom's face paled. The lock was broken, smashed in the course of a diabolic plot on the part of the mutineers to destroy the station. The last chance was gone. The desert was the only remaining hope.

Tom squared his shoulders. If only the desert remained, the desert it would be.

Stepping out of the air chamber, his eyes opened wide. To his left, several hundred yards distant, lying on its side, was the car which had apparently been stolen by the Martians and Selenites.

His heart thumping with excitement Tom hurried forward. Evidently something had happened. Ten to one the poor fools had forgotten that opening the two doors at the same time would be as disastrous to themselves as to those in the dome. The first blast had hurled the car and its occupants to destruction.

Upon reaching the machine he found that three of the ports had been smashed. Looking inside he saw the corpses of six Moon men and two Martians, their eyes wide with terror, their mouths stained with blood.

The hope which had risen in him at the sight of the car vanished as he noted the extent of the damage. Besides the three smashed ports, he saw that some of the machinery was also broken. A slight damage he might have repaired, and righting the car by means of jacks, used it in his enforced trip across the desert.

That hope also was now gone.

For a moment he considered remaining near or in the dome to await the coming of a rescue ship.

Little thought was needed, however, to convince him that it would be a foolhardy thing to do. If the rescue ship did not arrive in three hours they would find his corpse inside the suit, for it was beyond human endurance to remain in one longer. If nothing else, a man would go stark, raving mad from the discomfort and the heat, which, after a time, the miniature refrigerator could not mitigate.

He must tackle the desert. There was no alternative. Perhaps he would reach Shaft Number Eight—perhaps not.

With the sand sliding under his feet and the sun, forever hanging like a huge ball of fire over the eastern horizon, beating pitilessly upon his left side, he started the long trek.

He walked in a world where no living thing existed. On every hand was white and yellow sand as dry as dust, drained long ago of any moisture the surface of the planet may once have held. Here and there lay grotesque piles of boulders. There was no life, not a single tree, or a blade of grass. There was no appreciable atmosphere, no water. It was a dead planet, chained forever to its tyrant master, the sun, its rotation on its own axis slowed down so that one heat-tortured hemisphere eternally faced the sun, while the other, frozen solid and night-ridden forever, stared out into infinite space.

Here, on the twilight belt was the only spot on the planet where man, even with the aid of all the artificial protection at his beck and call, could exist at all. Here, on the rim of the planet, where the rays of the sun were always nearly horizontal, man could live if he had at hand means of creating oxygen and a protection from the semi-vacuum of the desert.

To the left lay a seething furnace of a world, to the right, a frigid ice box of a world.

For what seemed ages, Tom tramped, stumbling, across the scorching desert. The treacherous, sliding sand, time after time, brought him to his knees. Despite the slight attraction of gravity, his progress was slow, for the suit was heavy. On earth its weight would have crushed a man flat to the ground.

He had covered approximately four miles when he saw looming a short distance ahead of him a gigantic ridge of tumbled gray rock. It was one of those occasional outcroppings which occurred on the surface of the planet.

—

Tom noted it with relief. It would offer shade, momentary respite from the burning rays of the sun. Fagged, he headed for the outcropping.

It seemed an interminable distance, but finally he reached it and slumped down in the shade, leaning against a huge boulder. With a sigh of thankfulness, he closed his eyes. He could not remain there long, but he meant to make the most of it.

Opening his eyes he saw two shadows moving across the sand beyond the limit of the shade. Evidently some living thing was on the ridge of rock behind him.

Getting swiftly to his feet, he faced two Martians, equipped with shining air suits.

For a split second Tom stared in surprise at the two, then his hand snapped to his holster. But his steel gloved fingers found it empty. His face blanched. Somewhere on the back trail the pistol had dropped out and now lay in the sands of the trackless desert.

The Martians had watched as his hand went back to his side. Now as he gazed at them he saw a slow, crooked smile come over their ugly faces behind the glass helmets. They knew his pistol was gone; that he was easy prey.

They carried huge clubs fashioned of wood, probably with a good chunk of lead weighing the business end, and these they now shifted to obtain a better grip as they moved toward him.

As his hand came away from the holster it struck the hilt of the sword and his fingers closed about it.

As he retreated slowly before the deliberate advance of the Martians, he jerked the blade from the scabbard.

Seeing the flash of steel and realizing that their foe was armed with some sort of a strange weapon, the two Martians leaped silently forward, five hands outstretched in the usual manner of attack, the sixth member clutching the upraised club.

Tom knew the greatest danger lay in the clubs of his opponents breaking the steel of his suit or smashing his helmet, thus robbing him of his artificial atmosphere and exposing him to the horrible vacuum of the planet.

Hampered by his awkward suit, he knew he would be unable to sidestep the blows of the club, so he resorted to different tactics.

The point of the sword flicked out, aimed straight at the wrist of the Martian who was closing in, with the club already descending. There was no sound of steel on steel, for in that atmosphereless place no sound was possible. But the aim of the Martian was deflected and the club missed its target, Tom's helmet, by a wide margin.

Tom now turned his attention to the other Martian. If he could slash the armored suit of the second attacker, he would have only one foe.

The Martian raised his club, but as the sword drove at him point first, he stepped quickly backward, out of reach of the threatening point. Following this advantage Tom lunged again and the point struck hard against the armored breast, the force of the blow knocking the Martian off balance, so that he fell sprawling to the sands.

Almost feeling his other foe close behind him ready to strike, Tom swung on his heel, but his apprehension was unfounded, for the other lay, a heap of glistening armor, in the shade of the ridge.

In some unaccountable manner the sword point, in striking the wrist to ward off the blow, had penetrated the steel. Just a small hole, perhaps, but the Martian had died as the air rushed out of the suit.

He turned quickly to the second Martian, who was struggling to his feet. With a powerful and well directed kick Tom sent him reeling, to sprawl again on his back. With sword raised high, both fists clutching the hilt, ready to put every ounce of strength into a blow calculated to smash its way through heavy steel, Tom straddled the prostrate foeman.

The Martian raised clasped hands in signal of surrender and a plea for mercy, for all the world like a dog groveling to ward off a well-deserved kick. Tom stared straight down into the warted, yellow face, upon which terror was stamped. Well might terror be there, for it was a tradition that any lesser man who raised a hand against a Terrestrial was automatically doomed to death. Seldom had mercy ever been shown.

As Tom stared down into the mottled face behind the helmet, something akin to sympathy touched his heart.

He slowly lowered the sword, touched the point gently on the Martian's helmet and then raised it and with a questioning look, pointed with it in several directions.

A flash of understanding came into the eyes of the prostrate figure and his lips moved slowly. He pointed toward the outcropping of rock.

Watching his lips, Tom read the word, "Ship."

"It Is Not Only Mercury"

The Martian had come from a ship. But how had he obtained a ship? For ages no Martian had been anything other than a slave, a troublesome slave, but a slave, of a greater race.

Tom pointed to the body of the dead Martian and then to his captive.

"How many more?" he formed the words with his lips.

The Martian shook his head. He pointed to himself and his dead companion and again made the sign of negation. There were apparently no others.

Tom stepped back, sword still in hand, and motioned the other to rise.

Slowly Tom followed his captive, sword held ready for instant use, across the sand and up the rocky outcropping. At the top of the ridge the Martian halted and pointed with one of his six arms.

Looking in the direction of the pointing arm, Tom saw a small rocket plane resting on the sand. Upon its silver nose was painted the ancient emblem of Mars, a red equilateral triangle inside a blue circle which, in turn, was surrounded by a yellow square.

He marveled, for that emblem had not been seen, except in the museums of the worlds, for many years.

Inside the flyer, and with the air locks closed, Tom snapped back his helmet and gulped in great breaths of the pure air.

The Martian had also removed his helmet and now the two men faced one another.

"I don't know why I let you live," said Tom, "but I did. However, one false move and it's taps for you."

"Yes, master," said the Martian in a voice humble and subservient.

"Where did you get this plane?" asked Tom.

"I and others took it and ten others from Station Number One a few hours ago."

"Station One," screamed Tom, clutching the sword. "Was there an uprising there, too?"

"At the same hour today, master, there was an uprising in every station on Mercury."

Tom took a step forward.

"Were all successful?"

"I do not know, master. All should have been. They were carefully planned."

"And the emblem of Mars?"

"Tars Kors and I painted it while we were waiting here for the arrival of our men from Station Number Nine. They should be arriving at any time now. If they do not arrive in a half hour, I am supposed to make an observation flight around the dome."

Tom smiled grimly.

"Put on your helmet," he said. "You are going to paint out your damned emblem and paint in the correct one. You needn't expect your friends from Number Nine. They are all dead. Also, if there is any flying to be done, I do it. Understand?"

The Martian nodded and donned his helmet. Under the directions of the Terrestrial he painted out the emblem of Mars and painted in its stead an emblazoned golden sun, insignia of the Earth.

Back in the flyer, always keeping a watchful eye on his captive, Tom checked over the machine. It was one of the police craft maintained by the government at Station Number One for emergency calls and was built for speed and intricate maneuvers, a fighting ship.

It was equipped with four guns, one a projector of the Allison heat ray, and the other three rapid fire guns.

Everything seemed in perfect condition.

"How did you capture these machines?" asked Tom. The police were not often caught napping and they were fighters of renown.

"Our plans were well laid, master," said the Martian blandly.

Tom snorted. They must have been well laid, he thought. According to this fellow's story, Mercury had at one stroke fallen into the hands of the Martians, who had used the stupid Moon men as mere pawns to crush the Terrestrial rule.

"What about firearms?" he asked. "How does it happen you tackled me with clubs? Are there no pistols on board?"

"It was all very confusing," explained the Martian, "Tars Kors and I were only to capture the flyer and bring it here to meet the men from Station Number Nine. Undoubtedly, if they had come. they would have brought firearms."

"And what do you fellows plan to do now that you have momentarily conquered Mercury?"

The Martian spread six claw-like hands.

"A start, master, just a start. We plan to establish independence.'

"A hell of a fat chance you have," Tom informed him. "Don't you know that only a few hours will bring a flight of fighters that will wipe out every one of you."

The Martian smiled crookedly.

"But, master," he used the word with faint sarcasm, "it is not only Mercury."

Tom started.

"You scum! Do you mean—"

"Everywhere, at the same hour, the Martian struck, aided by the other races you have enslaved. On Mars, on Earth, on Venus, on every planet and satellite—"

"Enough," screamed Tom. "Another word out of you and I'll wring your filthy neck. You poor fools! You would try to conquer the masters!"

"Yes, master," said the Martian.

Tom leaped at the man and his fist, lashing out like a whip, smashed squarely into the leering, yellow, wart-covered face. The Martian spun like a top, slipping and sliding across the metal floor, to crash with a thud into a corner.

With feet spread far apart, Tom glared at the Martian.

"Get into that seat," he snarled, pointing to the pilot's chair, "and do exactly what I tell you. If you pull one boner I'll chop you to bits with this sword."

The terrified Martian scrambled out of the corner and scuttled for the seat.

"Now, listen to me," said Tom, "there are at least ten other machines that you rats have stolen. We are out to get them. We are going to wipe out as many Martians and Moon men as we can before it's all over with us. You and I are going to do that—you and I—do you understand? We are going to be avengers—"

The Martian half rose out of his seat, but Tom struck him with his open palm and he again collapsed into it.

"If we get out of this," Tom told him, "I'll swear that you stuck by me, that you still were faithful. I'll recommend you for special privileges. Do you understand?"

The Martian nodded.

"If you fail me, however, I'll finish you myself. Now start her up and get out of here. Fly straight ahead until I tell you to do something else. Remember I am right behind you at the gun controls and your life isn't worth a plugged nickel to me."

The Martian kicked the starter and the rocket motors came to life. With a roar the machine shot forward, taking off easily and smoothly.

In a few minutes the shining dome of Station Number Eight loomed on the horizon.

As the flyer swept down over the dome, Tom saw a plane resting before one of the locks. Close beside it stood a car, which was disgorging figures clad in metal suits. Another car lumbered out of the air locks and made for the plane, upon which was emblazoned the Martian symbol. The victors were transporting their forces to the stolen plane.

Swiftly he spun a wheel and through the range finders saw the plane outlined against the cross-hairs. But before he could touch the lever which released the heat ray, the floor tilted sickeningly beneath his feet.

Whirling from the gun controls he leaped at the Martian.

"Put her up," he shouted. When his command was not obeyed he struck a single blow, knocking the pilot out of the seat.

Through the observation window he glimpsed the ground rushing up at him. The sturdy little ship groaned in every joint as he put it up sharply, missing the ground by only a few feet. The rocket exhausts roared louder as the ship charged upward at a tremendous speed.

The Martian lay huddled at the foot of a locker, dead to the world. Tom had not pulled the punch which had spun the helpless one out of the pilot's chair.

At a mile altitude Tom leveled off the ship and nosed it slightly downward. Far below him the Martian ship was taking off. Just above the horizon he glimpsed the dome of Station Nine, which he had quitted a few hours before.

Tom again put the ship up. There was no sense in attempting to fight. He could not pilot the machine and handle the guns at the same time.

He cursed the silent figure on the floor. If the blasted fool had only stuck to his job. Nevertheless, one could hardly blame the fellow. It wasn't natural to fight your own. Probably, under similar circumstances, he would have done the same.

Through a port he saw the Martian plane far behind, following rapidly. The emblem of the Earth on the nose of his machine must have been sighted.

He went back to the controls and advanced the little plane to top speed. With his lighter load he might be able to outdistance the Martian machine.

Over the horizon loomed the dome of Station Seven and a few minutes later Station Six swung into view. Stations Five and Four were past and the Martian plane was falling far behind.

Another dome appeared ahead of the racing flyer. Above it hung a huge silver ship, which Tom recognized as the transport from Station One.

As he watched, the dome, lying directly beneath the transport, crumbled, falling in upon itself, a cloud of dust rising slowly.

The Martians, having captured the transport, were using the huge heat ray machine aboard to destroy the domes. It seemed their purpose to destroy every work of man on the planet.

Red rage rising in him, Tom leaped to the gun controls, moved the ray nozzle to point straight down, shoved the release lever over and locked it in position.

Back at the pilot controls he threw the ship down in a long dive, straight over the transport. Passing directly over the ship the ray would slice it in two—halt further destruction of the domes. The ray machines on the smaller planes, he knew, were not large enough to touch the huge quartz structures.

With the speed indicator pressed against the pin, the machine flashed down, the ray streaming beneath it.

Tom brought the plane to an even keel and almost as the transport disappeared beneath the machine, he heard a faint click.

Beside the gun controls stood the Martian, his hand still upon the ray lever. He supported himself by gripping the iron railing which ran around the control board. The effects of the blow had not totally left him. He was evidently still dizzy, but the half smile on his repulsive features told Tom he had reached the controls in time to save the transport.

For a moment the two stood eye to eye, then Tom's hand went back to the hilt of the sword and jerked the blade free. There was not a word spoken.

At the sight of the blade in Tom's hand, the Martian seemed to come to life. He leaped away from the gun control and ran toward the end of the ship. The Terrestrial dived after him.

The ship tilted far to one side and both of the men lost their balance on the sloping floor. Tom, still clutching the sword crashed solidly against the side of the hull.

One of the locker doors on the opposite side swung open and with a clatter a varied assortment of tools hit and slid across the floor.

Struggling to his feet, Tom worked his way up the slanting floor to the controls. Out of the corner of his eye he caught sight of the Martian huddled in one corner of the cabin.

With his outstretched fingers almost touching the control lever, Tom turned again to look at the Martian.

What he saw brought a scream from his lips. On his knees before one of the ports, the Martian was aiming a heavy wrench at the quartz. If that quartz were broken it meant death for both of them. With a rush the air would leave the flier and both of them would fall in their tracks.

At the sound of the scream, the Martian turned his head and his aim was deflected. The wrench brought up with a metallic crash against the hull, missing the port by a scant inch.

Quickly the Martian poised the wrench again and as he did so Tom hurled the sword at him. End over end the weapon flew. Its point caught the man of Mars at the base of the skull and drove deep. The Martian rolled to one end and the wrench clattered to the plates of the floor.

Tom stared. He had not thought he would kill the man by merely throwing the weapon. It had been his intention to thwart the other in his act and then to settle with him in a hand-to-hand encounter. After all, it didn't matter. Sooner or later one of them would have had to die. There was not room on the ship for both of them.

He fought his way up the inclining floor to the controls. The ship, he saw, had nosed upward and was tearing spaceward. He brought it on even keel and turned it down.

Far below him, he saw the surface of Mercury. He could plainly see the nine domed stations, but only six of the domes remained intact. To his right he could see the edge of the hot side of the planet, where molten ores bubbled eternally and lakes of melted lead sent up fumes that mingled with the low-lying gases that hung over the entire Sunward half of the planet.

Between the twilight belt and this seething cauldron ran a low lava ridge, which rose at varying heights over the level of the molten sea. At places, Tom could see, unusual activity in the sluggish liquid metal had sent streams of it coursing out into the twilight belt, where it ran slowly for several miles before congealing. He suspected that here lay the secret of the rocky ridges, beside which he had met the two Martians.

To his left he saw the stark frigidness of the cold side of the planet. There, chained forever as ice and frost, was the last vestige of the atmosphere and water of Mercury.

He glanced down toward the region where the domes lay and saw that ships were rapidly taking off from Station Three. The huge transport, slower in motion than the smaller planes, was far below him and to the right.

He grinned grimly. The planes were too low to attack him, and the transport, much too valuable for the Martians and Selenites to lose, was moving out of the way of chance rays.

He would see about that. It was plainly up to him to destroy the transport. It was too dangerous to leave it in the hands of the mutineers. With it, they could leave Mercury. It was the only space-going ship on the planet. It had arrived only a few hours before with supplies for the stations, consisting largely of explosives to be used in the mines. He wondered if it had been unloaded.

The planes were climbing swiftly toward him. He could see the Martian symbol, painted on the bow of the foremost, flashing in the sunlight. Behind the first plane trailed at least a dozen others.

They had gained too great an altitude for him now to attack the transport. He would have to fight his way through. He realized he must be cautious. He was fairly familiar with the operation of a ship, and in that one thing he had an advantage over the Martians and Selenites, who were rank amateurs. In all other things the enemy had the advantage. They were greater in number and each ship carried a gunner.

Sharply he swung the ship up and locked the controls. Leaving the pilot's chair, he moved to the gun controls. Here he moved the ray nozzle to point slightly forward and down. The three rapid fire guns he aimed straight ahead and to each control lever tied a length of copper wire. He shoved the ray control clear over and locked it in position, and trailing the copper wires in his hand went back to the pilot's seat.

Carefully he arranged the wires where he could grasp them at a second's notice and then in a long loop turned the plane over and plunged down.

To the thirteen planes pursuing him had been added several others. Only then did Tom realize the true odds against him.

With the vicious heat ray streaming from the nozzle under the machine he dived with reckless speed at the attackers. Like a plummet he dropped toward the lead plane. He could plainly see one of the rapid fire guns mounted on it quivering and knew that he was under fire. So far, however, none of the atomic pellets had found their mark and he doubted if they would at that distance. The distance was great even for an experienced gunner and the Martians were far from that.

Half a mile above the lead plane, he leveled off and went up in a great zoom to gain altitude. On altitude everything depended. So long as he could keep above his attackers, all was well; once he fell below them he was at their mercy.

Beneath him the lead plane, caught in the Allison ray, split in two and plunged toward the surface, a mass of smoking wreckage. Another plane, its right wing seared by the ray, tottered for a moment in midair and then side-slipped, falling faster and faster, defying all the frantic efforts of its pilot to right it.

With the rocket exhaust roaring like mad, Tom's plane swung over on its back and nosed down again. Almost directly beneath him the Terrestrial saw three of the mutineers' planes and jerked one of the copper wires. One of the rapid fire guns clattered viciously and one of the planes disappeared in a puff of white smoke. Tom's hand jerked at a control and the plane protested with a groan of metal at a slight change in direction. Another plane, however, brought directly beneath the nose of the Terrestrial's ship, also disappeared in a white cloud that slowly sifted downward.

As Tom leveled off, one of the Martian planes turned over on its back and from its underside a ray sliced upward, but missed the Terrestrial ship by a wide margin.

Off to the right and just over the edge of the ridge which separated the twilight belt from the hot side of the planet, Tom saw the transport hanging in all its silver bulkiness. There was not a single ship between it and him! With a catch in his breath he flung his ship down in a long dive. His heart sang exultantly as the machine screamed down on the transport.

Those on the great ship must have noticed his maneuver, for the huge transport stirred, swinging slowly around in an attempt to escape. It was not built, however, for quick getaway. It had not a single chance to elude the lightning flier.

Not more than a hundred feet above it, Tom drove his plane, and as he screamed over it, he swung back hard on the control lever and the little ship shrieked upward. Beneath him the transport, cleanly rayed, split in two, dropped toward the molten sea.

Tilting the machine, Tom stared down through a side observation port. He gasped in amazement and then held his breath.

Where the transport had fallen rose a great geyser of molten ore and rock. Slowly a part of the great ridge toppled and fell. Like a monstrous tongue of flame the molten geyser curled over and poured downward, while the mighty sea of sluggish liquid rushed for the hole blown in the ridge which separated the twilight belt from the hot side of the planet. Great clouds of heavy gases rolled upward, blotting out the scene below. The planes driven by the Martians, caught in the terrible blast, were tossed about like leaves in an autumn gale and out of control, were falling back to the surface. The only thing that had saved him from a similar fate, Tom knew, was his hasty break for altitude after raying the transport.

The transport had carried a consignment of explosives, he remembered, and had arrived only a few hours before the general mutiny. Evidently it had not been unloaded and had exploded when the disabled ship struck the bubbling sea.

At three miles he leveled off and stared down at the surface of the twilight belt. Like a great river the molten metal was pouring through the break in the wall and was rapidly spreading over the unprotected region. Not a single plane was in the air.

As he watched, the advancing flood struck Station Number Three and seemed to rear up to surge over it. Even from his great height he saw pitifully small figures running for their lives before the great wave. He knew that, hampered by space suits, they could not run far before being overtaken.

Part of the wave seemed to be congealing, but even as it did so, more of the molten stream poured over it and rushed on. One tongue gradually pushed its way across the belt and stopped only a few miles short of the cold side of the planet, frozen into a solid mass by the frigid conditions on that side of Mercury.

Tom noticed that the congealing of the metal stream was slowly backing up the outpouring of the liquid through the break in the wall. In a few hours a vast new barrier would be thrown up between the twilight belt and the bubbling ocean, but buried beneath that new barrier would be the failure of a rebellion on Mercury. The Terrestrial had proven himself master again.

A blue light flashed on the instrument board. He reached over and plugged in a connection. He spoke into a small microphone.

"Tom Clark, geologist of the Universal Ore Mining Company, stationed on Mercury, ready to receive," he said.

"Commander James Smith, of the Earth vessel, *Star Ogre*, speaking," replied a faint voice, "now running near orbit of Venus. Have five ships to put down uprising on Mercury. Hold on!"

"Send back four of your ships," said Tom. "Only one is needed to take off survivors. The mutiny is suppressed."

"How many survivors?" the voice asked laconically.

"Only one," said Tom, "and that's me."

JACKPOT

"Jackpot" is another of those stories in which Clifford D. Simak portrayed Earthlings out among the stars as rapacious explorers, roaming the galaxy in search of things that could be taken, grabbed, or exploited. Among others in the same vein are "Beachhead," "Junkyard," "Installment Plan," and "Retrograde Evolution." This story originally appeared in the October 1956 issue of Galaxy Science Fiction.

At least in this case, some of the Earthlings are better students.

—duw

I found Doc in the dispensary. He had on quite a load. I worked him over some to bring him half awake.

"Get sobered up," I ordered curtly. "We made planetfall. We've got work to do."

I took the bottle and corked it and set it high up on the shelf, where it wasn't right at hand.

Doc managed to achieve some dignity. "You needn't worry, Captain. As medic of this tub—"

"I want all hands up and moving. We may have something out there."

"I know," Doc said mournfully. "When you talk like that, it's bound to be a tough one. An off-beat climate and atmosphere pure poison."

"It's Earth-type, oxygen, and the climate's fine so far. Nothing to be afraid of. The analyzers gave it almost perfect rating."

Doc groaned and held his head between his hands. "Those analyzers of ours do very well if they tell us whether it is hot or cold or if the air is fit to breathe. We're a haywire outfit, Captain."

"We do all right," I said.

"We're scavengers and sometimes birds of prey. We scour the Galaxy for anything that's loose."

I paid no attention to him. That was the way he always talked when he had a skin full.

"You get up to the galley," I told him, "and let Pancake pour some coffee into you. I want you on your feet and able to do your fumbling best."

But Doc wasn't ready to go just yet. "What is it this time?"

"A silo. The biggest thing you ever saw. It's ten or fifteen miles across and goes up clear out of sight."

"A silo is a building to store winter forage. Is this a farming planet?"

"No," I said, "it's desert. And it isn't a silo. It just looks like one."

"Warehouse?" asked Doc. "City? Fortress? Temple—but that doesn't make any difference to us, does it, Captain? We loot temples, too."

"Get up!" I yelled at him. "Get going."

He made it to his feet. "I imagine the populace has come out to greet us. Appropriately, I hope."

"There's no populace," I said. "The silo's just standing there alone."

"Well, well," said Doc. "A second-story job."

He started staggering up the catwalk and I knew he'd be all right. Pancake knew exactly how to get him sobered up.

I went back to the port and found that Frost had everything all set. He had the guns ready and the axes and the sledges, the coils of rope and the canteens of water and all the stuff we'd need. As second in command, Frost was invaluable. He knew what to do and did it. I don't know what I'd have done without him.

I stood in the port and looked out at the silo. We were a mile or so away from it, but it was so big that it seemed to be much closer. This near to it, it seemed to be a wall. It was just God-awful big.

"A place like that," said Frost, "could hold a lot of loot."

"If it isn't empty," I answered. "If there isn't someone or something there to stop us taking it. If we can get into it."

"There are openings along the base. They look like entrances."

"With doors ten feet thick."

I wasn't being pessimistic. I was being logical—I'd seen so many things that looked like billions turn into complicated headaches that I never allowed myself much hope until I had my hands on something I knew would bring us cash.

Hutch Murdock, the engineer, came climbing up the catwalk. As usual, he had troubles. He didn't even stop to catch his breath.

"I tell you," he said to me, "one of these days those engines will just simply fall apart and leave us hanging out in space light-years from nowhere. We work all the blessed time to keep them turning over."

I clapped him on the shoulder. "Maybe this is it. Maybe after this we can buy a brand-new ship."

But it didn't cheer him up. He knew as well as I did that I was talking to keep up my spirit as well as his.

"Someday," he said, "we'll have bad trouble on our hands. Those boys of mine will drive a soap bubble across three hundred light-years if it's got an engine in it. But it's got to have an engine. And this wreck we got . . ."

He would have kept right on, but Pancake blew the horn for breakfast.

—

Doc was already at the table and he seemed to be functioning. He had a moderate case of shudders and he seemed a little pale. He was a little bitter, too, and somewhat poetic.

"So we gather glory," he told us. "We go out and lap it up. We haunt the ruins and we track the dream and we come up dripping cash."

"Doc," I said, "shut up."

He shut up. There was no one on the ship I had to speak to twice.

We didn't dally with the food. We crammed it down and left. Pancake left the dishes standing on the table and came along with us.

We got into the silo without any trouble. There were entrances all around the base and there weren't any doors. There was not a thing or anyone to stop us walking in.

It was quiet and solemn inside—and unspectacular. It reminded me of a monstrous office building.

It was all cut up with corridors, with openings off the corridors leading into rooms. The rooms were lined with what looked like filing cases.

We walked for quite a while, leaving paint markers along the walls to lead us back to the entrance. Get lost inside a place like that and one could wander maybe half a lifetime finding his way out.

We were looking for something—almost anything—but we didn't find a thing except those filing cases.

So we went into one of the rooms to have a look inside the files.

Pancake was disgusted. "There won't be nothing but records in those files. Probably in a lingo we can't even read."

"There could be anything inside those files," said Frost. "They don't have to be records."

Pancake had a sledge and he lifted it to smash one of the files, but I stopped him. There wasn't any use doing it messy if there was a better way.

We fooled around a while and we found the place where you had to wave your hand to make a drawer roll out.

The drawer was packed with what looked like sticks of dynamite. They were about two inches in diameter and a foot, or maybe a little more, in length, and they were heavy.

"Gold," said Hutch.

"I never saw black gold," Pancake said.

"It isn't gold," I told them.

I was just as glad it wasn't. If it had been, we'd have broken our backs hauling it away. Gold's all right, but you can't get rich on it. It doesn't much more than pay wages.

We dumped out a pile of the sticks and squatted on the floor, looking them over.

"Maybe it's valuable," said Frost, "but I wouldn't know. What do you think it is?"

None of us had the least idea.

We found some sort of symbols on each end of the sticks and the symbols on each stick seemed to be different, but it didn't help us any because the symbols made no sense.

We kicked the sticks out of the way and opened some more drawers. Every single drawer was filled with the sticks.

We went into some other rooms and we waved our hands some more and the drawers came popping out and we didn't find anything except more sticks.

When we came out of the silo, the day had turned into a scorcher. Pancake climbed the ladder to stack us up some grub and the rest of us sat down in the shade of the ship and laid several of the sticks out in front of us and sat there looking at them, wondering what we had.

"That's where we're at a big disadvantage," said Hutch. "If a regular survey crew stumbled onto this, they'd have all sorts of experts to figure out the stuff. They'd test it a dozen different ways and they'd skin it alive almost and they'd have all sorts of ideas and they'd come up with some educated guesses. And pretty soon, one way or another, they'd know just what it was and if it was any use."

"Someday," I told them, "if we ever strike it rich, we'll have to hire us some experts. The kind of loot we're always turning up, we could make good use of them."

"You won't find any," said Doc, "that would team up with a bunch like us."

"Where do you get 'bunch-like-us' stuff?" I asked him, a little sore. "Sure, we ain't got much education and the ship is just sort of glued together and we don't use any fancy words to cover up the fact that we're in this for all we can get out of it. But we're doing an honest job."

"I wouldn't call it exactly honest. Sometimes we're inside the law and sometimes outside it."

That was nonsense and Doc knew it. Mostly where we went, there wasn't any law.

"Back on Earth, in the early days," I snapped back, "it was folks like us who went into new lands and blazed the trails and found the rivers and climbed the mountains and brought back word to those who stayed at home. And they went because they were looking for beaver or for gold or slaves or for anything else that wasn't nailed down tight. They didn't worry much about the law or the ethics of it and no one blamed them for it. They found it and they took it and that was the end of it. If they killed a native or two or burned a village or some other minor thing like that, why, it was just too bad."

Hutch said to Doc: "There ain't no sense in you going holy on us. Anything we done, you're in as deep as we are."

"Gentlemen," said Doc, in that hammy way of his, "I wasn't trying to stir up any ruckus. I was just pointing out that you needn't set your heart on getting any experts."

"We could get them," I said, "if we offered them enough. They got to live, just like anybody else."

"They have professional pride, too. That's something you've forgotten."

"We got you."

"Well, now," said Hutch, "I'm not too sure Doc is professional. That time he pulled the tooth for me—"

"Cut it out," I said. "The both of you."

This wasn't any time to bring up the matter of the tooth. Just a couple of months ago, I'd got it quieted down and I didn't want it breaking out again.

Frost picked up one of the sticks and turned it over and over, looking at it.

"Maybe we could rig up some tests," he suggested.

"And take the chance of getting blown up?" asked Hutch.

"It might not go off. You have a better than fifty-fifty chance that it's not explosive."

"Not me," said Doc. "I'd rather just sit here and guess. It's less tiring and a good deal safer."

"You don't get anywhere by guessing," protested Frost. "We might have a fortune right inside our mitts if we could only find out what these sticks are for. There must be tons of them stored in the building. And there's nothing in the world to stop us from taking them."

"The first thing", I said, "is to find out if it's explosive. I don't think it is. It looks like dynamite, but it could be almost anything. For instance, it might be food."

"We'll have Pancake cook us up a mess," said Doc.

I paid no attention to him. He was just needling me.

"Or it might be fuel," I said. "Pop a stick into a ship engine that was built to use it and it would keep it going for a year or two."

Pancake blew the chow horn and we all went in.

After we had eaten, we got to work.

We found a flat rock that looked like granite and above it we set up a tripod made out of poles that we had to walk a mile to cut and then had to carry back. We rigged up a pulley on the tripod and found another rock and tied it to the rope that went up to the pulley. Then we paid out the rope as far as it would go and there we dug a foxhole.

By this time, the sun was setting and we were tuckered out, but we decided to go ahead and make the test and set our minds at rest.

So I took one of the sticks that looked like dynamite and while the others back in the foxhole hauled up the rock tied to the rope, I put the stick on the first rock underneath the second and then I ran like hell. I tumbled into the foxhole and the others let go of the rope and the rock dropped down on the stick.

Nothing happened.

Just to make sure, we pulled up and dropped the rock two or three times more and there was no explosion.

We climbed out of the foxhole and went over to the tripod and rolled the rock off the stick, which wasn't even dented.

By this time, we were fairly well convinced that the stick couldn't be set off by concussion, although the test didn't rule out a dozen other ways it might blow us all up.

That night, we gave the sticks the works. We poured acid on them and the acid just ran off. We tried a cold chisel on them and we ruined two good chisels. We tried a saw and they stripped the teeth clean off.

We wanted Pancake to try to cook one of them, but Pancake refused.

"You aren't bringing that stuff into my galley," he said. "You do, you can cook for yourselves from now on. I keep a good clean galley and I try to keep you guys well fed and I ain't having you mess up the place . . ."

"All right, Pancake," I said. "Even with you cooking it, it probably wouldn't be fit to eat."

We wound up sitting at a table, looking at the sticks piled the center of it. Doc brought out a bottle and we all had a drink or two. Doc must have been considerably upset to share his liquor with us.

"It stands to reason," said Frost, "that the sticks are good for something. If the cost of that building is any indication of their value, they're worth a fortune."

"Maybe the sticks aren't the only things in there," Hutch pointed out. "We just covered part of the first floor. The might be a lot of other stuff in there. And there are all those other floors. How many would you say there were?"

"Lord knows," said Frost. "When you're on the ground, you can't be sure you see to the top of it. It just sort of fades away when you look up at it."

"You notice what it was built of?" asked Doc.

"Stone," said Hutch.

"I thought so, too," said Doc. "But it isn't. You remember those big apartment mounds we ran into in that insect culture out on Suud?"

We all remembered them, of course. We'd spent days trying to break into them because we had found a handful of beautifully carved jade scattered around the entrance of one of them and we figured there might be a lot of it inside. Stuff like that brings money. Folks back in civilization are nuts about any kind of alien art and that jade sure enough was alien. We'd tried every trick that we could think of and we got nowhere. Breaking into those mounds was like punching a feather pillow. You could dent the surface plenty, but you couldn't break it because the strength of the material built up as pressure compressed the atoms. The harder you hit, the tougher it became. It was the kind of building material that would last forever and never need repair and those insects must have known they were safe from us, for they went about their business and never noticed us. That's what made it so infuriating.

And material like that, I realized, would be just the ticket for a structure like the silo. You could build as big or as high as you had a mind to; the more pressure you put on the lower structure, the stronger it would be.

"It means," I said, "that the building out there could be much older than it seems to be. It could be a million years or older."

"If it's that old," said Hutch, "it could really be packed. You can store away a lot of loot in a million years."

Doc and Frost drifted off to bed and Hutch and I sat there alone, looking at the sticks.

I got to thinking about some of the things that Doc was always saying, about how we were just a bunch of cut-throats, and I wondered if he might be right. But think on it as hard and as honest as I could, I couldn't buy it.

On every expanding frontier, in all of history, there had been three kinds of men who went ahead and marked out the trails for other men to follow—the traders and the missionaries and the hunters.

We were the hunters in this case, hunting not for gold or slaves or furs, but for whatever we could find. Sometimes we came back with empty hands and sometimes we made a haul. Usually, in the long run, we evened out so we made nothing more than wages. But we kept on going out, hoping for that lucky break that would make us billionaires.

It hadn't happened yet, and perhaps it never would. But some-day it might. We touched the ghostly edge of hope just often enough to keep us thinking that it would. Although, I admitted to myself, perhaps we'd have kept going out even if there'd been no hope at all. Seeking for the unknown gets into your blood.

When you came right down to it, we probably didn't do a bit more harm than the traders or the missionaries. What we took, we took; we didn't settle down and change or destroy the civiliza-tions of people we pretended we were helping.

I said as much to Hutch. He agreed with me.

The missionaries are the worst," he said. "I wouldn't be a mis-sionary no matter what they paid me."

We weren't doing any good just sitting there, so I got up to start for bed.

"Maybe tomorrow we'll find something else," I said.

Hutch yawned. "I sure hope we do. We been wasting our time on these sticks of dynamite."

He picked them up and on our way up to bed, he heaved them out the port.

The next day, we did find something else.

We went much deeper into the silo than we had been before following the corridors for what must have been two miles or more.

We came to a big room that probably covered ten or fifteen acres and it was filled from wall to wall with rows of machines, all of them alike.

They weren't much to look at. They resembled to some extent a rather ornate washing machine, with a bucket seat attached and a dome on top. They weren't bolted down and you could push them around and when we tipped one of them up to look for hidden wheels, we found instead a pair of runners fixed on a swivel so they'd track in any direction that one pushed. The runners were made of metal that was greasy to the touch, but when you rubbed your fingers on them, no grease came off them.

There was no power connection.

"Maybe it's a self-powered unit," said Frost. "Come to think of it, I haven't noticed any power outlets in the entire building."

We hunted for some place where we could turn on the power and there wasn't any place. That whole machine was the smoothest, slickest hunk of metal you ever saw. We looked for a way to get into its innards, so we could have a look at them, but there wasn't any way. The jacket that covered the works seemed to be one solid piece without an apparent seam or a sign of a bolt or rivet.

The dome looked as though it ought to come off and we tried to get it off, but it remained stubbornly in place.

The bucket seat, however, was something else again. It was lousy with all sorts of attachments to accommodate the sitting surface of almost any conceivable kind of being. We had a lot of fun adjusting it in different ways and trying to figure out what kind of animal could have a seat like that. We got a bit obscene about it, I remember, and Hutch was doubled up laughing.

But we weren't getting anywhere and we were fairly sure we wouldn't until we could get a cutting tool and open up one of the machines to find out what made it tick.

We picked out one of them and we skidded it down the corridors. When we got to the entrance, we figured we would have to carry it, but we were mistaken. It skidded along over the ground and even loose sand almost as well as it did in the corridors.

After supper, Hutch went down to the engine room and came back with a cutting tool. The metal was tough, but we finally got at least some of the jacket peeled away.

The innards of that machine were enough to drive you crazy. It was a solid mass of tiny parts all hooked together in the damnedest jumble. There was no beginning and no end. It was like one of those puzzle mazes that go on and on forever and get no place.

Hutch got into it with both hands and tried to figure out how to start taking it apart.

After a while, he sat back on his heels and growled a little at it. "There's nothing holding them together. Not a bolt or rivet, not even so much as a cotter pin. But they hang together somehow."

"Just pure cussedness," I said.

He looked at me kind of funny. "You might be right, at that."

He went at it again and bashed a couple of knuckles and sat there sucking at them.

"If I didn't know that I was wrong," he said, "I'd say that it was friction."

"Magnetism," Doc offered.

"I tell you what, Doc," said Hutch. "You stick to what little medicine you know and let me handle the mechanics."

Frost dived in quick to head off an argument. "That frictional idea might not be a bad one. But it would call for perfect machining and surface polish. Theoretically, if you place two perfectly polished surfaces together, the molecules will attract one another and you'll have permanent cohesion."

I don't know where Frost got all that stuff. Mostly he seemed to be just like the rest of us, but occasionally he'd come out with something that would catch you by surprise. I never asked him anything about himself; questions like that were just plain bad manners.

We messed around some more and Hutch bashed another knuckle and I sat there thinking how we'd found two items in the silo and both of them had stopped us in our tracks. But that's the way it is. Some days you can't make a dime.

Frost moved around and pushed Hutch out of the way. "Let me see what I can do."

Hutch didn't protest any. He was licked.

Frost started pushing and pulling and twisting and fiddling away at that mess of parts and all at once there was a kind of whooshing sound, like someone had let out their breath sort of slow and easy, and all the parts fell in upon themselves. They came unstuck, in a kind of slow-motion manner, and they made a metallic thump along with tinkling sounds and they were just a heap inside the jacket that had protected them.

"Now see what you done!" howled Hutch.

"I didn't do a thing," said Frost. "I was just seeing if I could bust one loose and one did and the whole shebang caved in."

He held up his fingers to show us the piece that had come loose.

"You know what I think?" asked Pancake. "I think whoever made that machine made it so it would fall apart if anyone tried to tinker with it. They didn't want no one to find out how it was put together."

"That makes sense," said Doc. "No use getting peeved at it. After all, it was their machine."

"Doc," I said, "you got a funny attitude. I never noticed you turning down your share of anything we find."

"I don't mind when we confine ourselves to what you might call, in all politeness, natural resources. I can even stomach the pillaging of art-forms. But when it comes to stealing brains—and this machine is brains—"

Frost let out a whoop.

He was hunkered down, with his head inside the jacket of the machine, and I thought at first he'd got caught and that we'd have to cut him out, but he could get out, all right.

"I see now how to get that dome off the top," he said. It was a complicated business, almost like a combination on a safe. The dome was locked in place by a lot of grooves and you had to know just how to turn it to lift it out of place.

Frost kept his head inside the jacket and called out directions to Hutch, who twisted the dome first this way and then that, sometimes having to pull up on it and other times press down to engage the slotted mechanism that held it locked in place. Pancake wrote down the combinations as Frost called them off and finally the dome came loose in Hutch's hands.

Once it was off, there was no mystery to it. It was a helmet, all rigged out with adjustable features so it could be made to fit any type of head, just as the seat was adjustable to fit any sitting apparatus.

The helmet was attached to the machine with a retractable cable that reeled out far enough to reach someone sitting in the seat.

And that was fine, of course. But what was it? A portable electric chair? A permanent-wave machine? Or what?

So Frost and Hutch poked around some more and in the top of the machine, just under where the dome had nested, they found a swivel trap door and underneath it a hollow tube extending down into the mass of innards—only the innards weren't a mass any more, but just a basket of loose parts.

It didn't take any imagination to figure what that hollow tube was for. It was just the size to take one of the sticks of dynamite.

Doc went and got a bottle and passed it around as a sort of celebration and after a drink or two, he and Hutch shook hands and said there were no hard feelings. But I didn't pay much attention to that. They'd done it many times before and then been at one another's throat before the night was over.

Just why we were celebrating was hard to figure. Sure, we knew the machine fitted heads and that the dynamite fitted the machine—but we still had no idea what it was all about.

We were, to tell the truth, just a little scared, although you couldn't have gotten one of us to admit it.

We did some guessing, naturally.

"It might be a mechanical doctor," said Hutch. "Just sit in that seat and put the helmet on your head and feed in the proper stick and you come out cured of whatever is wrong with you. It would be a blessing, I can tell you. You wouldn't ever need to worry if your doctor knew his business or not."

I thought Doc was going to jump right down Hutch's throat, but he must have remembered how they had shaken hands and he didn't do it.

"As long as you're thinking along that line," said Doc, "let's think a little bigger. Let's say it is a rejuvenation machine and the stick is crammed with vitamins and hormones and such that turn you young again. Just take the treatment every twenty years or so and you stay young forever."

"It might be an educator," Frost put in. "Those sticks might be packed full of knowledge. Maybe a complete college subject inside of each of them."

"Or it might be just the opposite," said Pancake. "Those sticks might soak up everything you know. Each of those sticks might be the story of one man's whole life."

"Why record life stories?" asked Hutch. "There aren't many men or aliens or what-not that have life stories important enough to rate all that trouble."

"If you're thinking of it being some sort of communications

deal," I said, "it might be anything. It might be propaganda or religion or maps or it might be no more than a file of business records."

"And," said Hutch, "it might kill you deader than a mackerel."

"I don't think so," Doc replied. "There are easier ways to kill a person than to sit him in a chair and put a helmet on him. And it doesn't have to be a communicator."

"There's one way to find out," I said.

"I was afraid," said Doc, "we'd get around to that."

"It's too complicated," argued Hutch. "No telling what trouble it may get us into. Why not drop it cold? We can blast off and hunt for something simple."

"No!" shouted Frost. "We can't do that!"

"I'd like to know why not," said Hutch.

"Because we'd always wonder if we passed up the jackpot. We'd figure that maybe we gave up too quick—a day or two too quick. That we got scared out. That if we'd gone ahead, we'd be rolling in money."

We knew Frost was right, but we batted it around some more before we would admit he was. All of us knew what we had to do, but there were no volunteers.

Finally we drew straws and Pancake was unlucky.

"Okay," I said. "First thing in the morning . . ."

"Morning, nothing!" wailed Pancake. "I want to get it over with. I wouldn't sleep a wink."

He was scared, all right, and he had a right to be. He felt just the way I would have if I'd drawn the shortest straw.

I didn't like barging around on an alien planet after dark, but we had to do it. It wouldn't have been fair to Pancake to have done otherwise. And, besides, we were all wrought up and we'd have no rest until we'd found out what we had.

So we got some flashes and went out to the silo. We tramped down the corridors for what seemed an endless time and came to the room where the machines were stored.

There didn't seem to be any difference in the machines, so we picked one at random. While Hutch got the helmet off, I adjusted the seat for Pancake and Doc went into an adjoining room to get a stick.

When we were all ready, Pancake sat down in the seat.

I had a sudden rush of imbecility.

"Look," I said to Pancake, "you don't need to do this."

"Someone has to," said Pancake. "We got to find out somehow and this is the quickest way."

"I'll take your place."

Pancake called me a dirty name and he had no right to do that, for I was only being helpful. But I called him another and we were back to normal.

Hutch put the helmet on Pancake's head and it came down so far you couldn't see his face. Doc popped the stick into the tube and the machine purred a little, starting up, then settled into silence. Not exactly silence, either—when you laid your ear against the jacket, you could hear it running.

Nothing seemed to happen to Pancake. He sat there cool and relaxed and Doc got to work on him at once, checking him over.

"His pulse has slowed a little," Doc reported, "and his heart action's sort of feeble, but he seems to be in no danger. His breathing is a little shallow, but not enough to worry about."

It might not have meant a thing to Doc, but it made the rest of us uneasy. We stood around and watched and nothing happened. I don't know what we thought might happen. Funny as it sounds, I had thought that something would.

Doc kept close watch, but Pancake got no worse.

We waited and we waited. The machine kept running and Pancake sat slumped in the seat. He was as limp as a dog asleep and when you picked up his hand, you'd think his bones had melted plumb away. All the time we got more nervous. Hutch wanted to jerk the helmet off Pancake, but I wouldn't let him.

No telling what might happen if we stopped the business in the middle.

It was about an hour after dawn that the machine stopped running. Pancake began to stir and we removed the helmet.

He yawned and rubbed his eyes and sat up straight. He looked a bit surprised when he saw us and it seemed to take a moment for him to recognize us.

"What happened?" Hutch asked him.

Pancake didn't answer. You could see him pulling himself together, as if he were remembering and getting his bearings once again.

"I went on a trip," he said.

"A travelogue!" said Doc, disgusted.

"Not a travelogue. I was there. It was a planet, way out at the rim of the Galaxy, I think. There weren't many stars at night because it was so far out—way out where the stars get thin and there aren't many of them. There was just a thin strip of light that moved overhead."

"Looking at the Galaxy edge on," said Frost, nodding. "Like you were looking at a buzz-saw's cutting edge."

"How long was I under?" asked Pancake.

"Long enough," I told him. "Six or seven hours. We were getting nervous."

"That's funny," said Pancake. "I'll swear I was there for a year or more."

"Now let's get this straight," Hutch said. "You say you were there. You mean you saw this place."

"I mean I was there!" yelled Pancake. "I lived with those people and I slept in their burrows and I talked with them and I worked with them. I got a blood blister on my hand from hoeing in a garden. I traveled from one place to another and I saw a lot of things and it was just as real as sitting here."

We bundled him out of there and went back to the ship. Hutch wouldn't let Pancake get the breakfast. He threw it together himself and since Hutch is a lousy cook, it was a miserable meal. Doc dug up a bottle and gave Pancake a drink, but he wouldn't let any of the rest of us have any of it. Said it was medicinal, not social.

That's the way he is at times. Downright hog-selfish.

Pancake told us about this place he had been to. It didn't seem to have much, if any, government, mostly because it didn't seem to need one, but was a humble sort of planet where rather dim-witted people lived in a primitive agricultural state, They looked, he said, like a cross between a human and a groundhog, and he drew a picture of them, but it didn't help a lot, for Pancake is no artist.

He told us the kind of crops they raised, and there were some screwy kinds, and what kind of food they ate, and we gagged at some of it, and he even had some of the place names down pat and he remembered shreds of the language and it was outlandish-sounding.

We asked him all sorts of questions and he had the answers to every one of them and some were the kind he could not have made up from his head. Even Doc, who had been skeptical to start with, was ready to admit that Pancake had visited the planet.

After we ate, we hustled Pancake off to bed and Doc checked him over and he was all right.

When Pancake and Doc had left, Hutch said to me and Frost: "I can feel those dollars clinking in my pocket right this minute."

We both agreed with him.

We'd found an entertainment gadget that had anything yet known backed clear off the map.

The sticks were recordings that packed in not only sight and sound, but stimuli for all the other senses. They did the job so well that anyone subjected to their influence felt that he was part of the environment they presented. He stepped into the picture and became a part of it. He was really there.

Frost already was planning exactly how we'd work it.

"We could sell the stuff," he said, "but that would be rather foolish. We want to keep control of it. We'll lease out the machines and we'll rent the sticks and since we'll have the sole supply, we can charge anything we wish."

"We can advertise year-long vacations that take less than half a day," said Hutch. "They'll be just the thing for executives and other busy people. Why, in a single weekend you could spend four or five years' time on several different planets."

"Maybe it's not only planets," Frost went on. "There might be concerts or art galleries and museums. Maybe lectures on history and literature and such."

We were feeling pretty good, but we were tuckered out, so we trailed off to bed.

I didn't get into bed right away, however, but hauled out the log. I don't know why I ever bothered with it. It was a hit-and-miss affair at best. There would be months I'd not even think about it and then all at once I'd get all neat and orderly and keep a faithful record for several weeks or so. There was no real reason to make an entry in it now, but I was somewhat excited and had a feeling that perhaps what had just happened should be put down in black and white.

So I crawled under the bunk and pulled out the tin box I kept it and the other papers in, and while I was lifting it to the bunk, it slipped out of my hands. The lid flew open. The log and all the papers and the other odds and ends I kept there scattered on the floor.

I cussed a bit and got down on my hands and knees to pick up the mess. There was an awful lot of it and most of it was junk. Someday, I told myself, I'd have to throw a lot of it away. There were clearance papers from a hundred different ports and medical certificates and other papers that were long outdated. But among it I found also the title to the ship.

I sat there thinking back almost twenty years to the day I'd bought the ship for next to nothing and towed it from the junkyard and I recalled how I'd spent a couple of years spare time and all I could earn getting it patched up so it could take to space again. No wonder, I told myself, that it was a haywire ship. It had been junk to start with, and during all those years, we'd just managed to keep it glued together. There had been many times when the only thing that got it past inspection had been a fast bribe slipped quietly to the man. No one in the Galaxy but Hutch could have kept it flying.

I went on picking up the papers, thinking about Hutch and all the rest of them. I got a little sentimental and thought a lot of things I'd have clobbered anyone for if they had dared to say them to me. About how we had stuck together and how any one of them would have died for me and I for any one of them.

There had been a time, of course, when it had not been that way, back in the days when they'd first signed on and had been nothing but a crew. But that day was long past; now they were more than just a crew. There had been no signing on for years, but just staying on as men who had a right to stay. And I sat there, flat on the floor, and thought how we'd finally done the thing we'd always hoped to do, how we'd caught up with the dream—us, the ragamuffin crew in the glued-together ship—and I felt proud and happy, not for myself alone, but for Hutch and Pancake and Doc and Frost and all the rest.

Finally I got the papers all picked up and back in the box again and tried to write up the log, but was too tired to write, so I went to bed, as I should have done in the first place.

But tired as I was, I lay there and thought of how big the silo was and tried to estimate how many sticks might be cached away there. I got up into the trillions and I saw it was no use; there was no way to keep the figures straight.

The whole deal was big—bigger than anything we'd ever found before. It would take a group of men like us at least five lifetimes of steady hauling to empty the silo. We'd have to set up a corporation and get a legal staff (preferably one with the lowest kind of ethics) and file a claim on this planet and go through a lot of other red tape to be sure we had it all sewed up.

We couldn't take a chance of letting it slip through our fingers because of any lack of foresight. We'd have to get it all doped out before we went ahead.

I don't know about the rest of them, but I dreamed that night of wading knee-deep through a sea of crisp, crinkly banknotes.

When morning came, Doc failed to show up for breakfast. I went hunting him and found he hadn't even gone to bed. He was sprawled in his rickety old chair in the dispensary and there was one empty bottle on the floor and he trailed another, almost empty, alongside the chair, keeping a rather flimsy hold upon its neck. He still was conscious, which was about the most that could be said of him.

I was plenty sore. Doc knew the rules. He could get paralyzed as soon or as often or as long as he wanted to when we were in space, but when we were grounded and there was work to do and planet ailments to keep an eye out for, he was expected to stay sober.

I kicked the bottle out of his fist and I took him by the collar with one hand and by the seat of his britches with the other and frog-walked him to the galley.

Plunking him down in a chair, I yelled for Pancake to get another pot of coffee going.

"I want you sobered up," I told Doc, "so you can go out with us on the second trip. We need all the manpower we have."

Hutch had rounded up his gang and Frost had got the crew together and had rigged up a block and tackle so we could start loading. Everyone was ready to begin bringing in the cargo except Doc and I swore to myself that, before the day was over, I'd work the tail right off him.

As soon as we had breakfast, we started out. We planned to get aboard as many of the machines as we could handle and to fill in the space between them with all the sticks we could find room for.

We went down the corridors to the room that held the machines and we paired off, two men to the machine and started out. Everything went fine until we were more than half-way across the stretch of ground between the building and the ship.

Hutch and I were in the lead and suddenly there was an explosion in the ground about fifty feet ahead of us.

We skidded to a halt.

"It's Doc!" yelled Hutch, grabbing for his belt-gun.

I stopped him just in time. "Take it easy, Hutch."

Doc stood up in the port and waved a rifle at us.

"I could pick him off," Hutch said.

"Put back that gun," I ordered.

I walked out alone to where Doc had placed his bullet.

He lifted his rifle and I stopped dead still. He'd probably miss, but even so, the kind of explosive charge he was firing could cut a man in two if it struck ten feet away.

"I'm going to throw away my gun," I called out to him. "I want to talk with you."

Doc hesitated for a moment. "All right. Tell the rest of them to pull back a way."

I spoke to Hutch over my shoulder. "Get out of here. Take the others with you."

"He's crazy drunk," said Hutch. "No telling what he'll do."

"I can handle him," I said, sounding surer than I felt.

Doc let loose another bullet off to one side of us.

"Get moving, Hutch." I didn't dare look back. I had to keep an eye on Doc.

"All right," Doc finally yelled at me. "They're back. Throw away your gun."

Moving slow so he wouldn't think I was trying to draw on him, I unfastened the buckle of the gunbelt and let it fall to the ground. I walked forward, keeping my eyes on Doc, and all the time my skin kept trying to crawl up my back.

"That's far enough," Doc said when I'd almost reached the ship. "We can talk from here."

"You're drunk," I told him. "I don't know what this is all about, but I know you're drunk."

"Not nearly drunk enough. Not drunk enough by half. If I were drunk enough, I simply wouldn't care."

"What's eating you?"

"Decency," said Doc, in that hammy way of his. "I've told you many times that I can stomach looting when it involves no more than uranium and gems and other trash like that. I can even shut my eyes when you gut a culture, because you can't steal a culture—even when you get through looting it, the culture still is there and can build back again. But I balk at robbing knowledge. I will not let you do it, Captain."

"I still say you're drunk."

"You don't even know what you've found. You are so blind and greedy that you don't recognize it."

"Okay, Doc," I said, trying to smooth his feathers, "tell me what we've found."

"A library. Perhaps the greatest, most comprehensive library in all the Galaxy. Some race spent untold years compiling the knowledge that is in that building and you plan to take it and sell it and scatter it. If that happens, in time it will be lost and what little of it may be left will be so out of context that half its meaning will be lost. It doesn't belong to us. It doesn't even belong to the human race alone. A library like that can belong only to all the peoples of the Galaxy."

"Look, Doc," I pleaded, "we've worked for years, you and I and all the rest of them. We've bled and sweated and been disappointed time and time again. This is our chance to make a killing. And that means you as well as the rest of us. Think of it, Doc—more money than you can ever spend—enough to keep you drunk the rest of your life!"

Doc swung the rifle around at me and I thought my goose was cooked. But I never moved a muscle.

I stood and bluffed it out.

—

At last he lowered the gun. "We're barbarians. History is full of the likes of us. Back on Earth, the barbarians stalled human progress for a thousand years when they burned and scattered the libraries and the learning of the Greeks and Romans. To them, books were just something to start a fire with or wipe their weapons on. To you, this great cache of accumulated knowledge means nothing more than something to make a quick buck on. You'll take a scholarly study of a vital social problem and retail it as a year's vacation that can be experienced in six hours' time and you'll take—"

"Spare me the lecture, Doc," I said wearily. "Tell me what you want."

"Go back and report this find to the Galactic Commission. It will help wipe out a lot of things we've done."

"So help me, Doc, you've gone religious on us."

"Not religious. Just decent."

"And if we don't?"

"I've got the ship," said Doc. "I have the food and water."

"You'll have to sleep."

"I'll close the port. Just try getting in." He had us and he knew he did. Unless we could figure out a way to grab him, he had us good and proper.

I was scared, but mostly I was burned. For years, we'd listened to him run off at the mouth and never for a moment had any of us thought he meant a word of it. And now suddenly he did—he meant every word of it.

I knew there was no way to talk him out of it. And there was no compromise. When it came right down to it, there was no agreement possible, for any agreement or compromise would have to be based on honor and we had no honor—not a one of us, not even among ourselves. It was stalemate, but Doc didn't know that yet. He'd realize it once he got a little sober and thought about it some. What he had done had been done on alcoholic impulse, but that didn't mean he wouldn't see it through.

One thing was certain: As it stood, he could outlast us.

"Let me go back," I said. "I'll have to talk this over with the others."

I think that Doc right then began to suspect how deeply he had become committed, began to see for the first time the impossibility of us trusting one another.

"When you come back," he told me, "have it all thought out. I'll want some guarantees."

"Sure, Doc," I said.

"I mean this, Captain. I'm in deadly earnest. I'm not just fooling."

"I know you aren't, Doc."

I went back to where the others were clustered just a short distance from the building. I explained what was up.

"We'll have to spread out and charge him," Hutch decided. "He may get one or two of us, but we can pick him off."

"He'll simply close the port," I said. "He can starve us out. In a pinch, he could try to take the ship up. If he ever managed to get sober, he could probably do it."

"He's crazy," said Pancake. "Just plain drunken crazy."

"Sure he is," I said, "and that makes him twice as deadly. He's been brooding on this business for a long, long time. He built up a guilt complex that is three miles high. And worst of all, he's got himself out on a limb and he can't back down."

"We haven't got much time," said Frost. "We've got to think of something. A man can die of thirst. You can get awfully hungry in just a little while."

The three of them got to squabbling about what was best to do and I sat down on the sand and leaned back against one of the machines and tried to figure Doc.

Doc was a failure as a medic; otherwise he'd not have tied up with us. More than likely, he had joined us as a gesture of defiance or despair—perhaps a bit of both. And besides being a failure, he was an idealist. He was out of place with us, but there'd been nowhere else to go, nothing else to do. For years, it had eaten at him and his values got all warped and there's no place better than deep space to get your values warped.

He was crazy as a coot, of course, but a special kind of crazy. If it hadn't been so ghastly, you might have called it glorious crazy.

You wanted to laugh him off or brush him to one side, for that was the kind of jerk he was, but he wouldn't laugh or brush.

I don't know if I heard a sound—a footstep, maybe—or if I just sensed another presence, but all at once I knew we'd been joined by someone. I half got up and swung around toward the building and there, just outside the entrance, stood what looked at first to be a kind of moth made up in human size.

I don't mean it was an insect—it just had the look of one. Its face was muffled up in a cloak it wore and it was not a human face and there was a ruff rising from its head like those crests you see on the helmets in the ancient plays.

Then I saw that the cloak was not a cloak at all, but a part of the creature and it looked like it might be folded wings, but it wasn't wings.

"Gentlemen," I said as quietly as I could, "we have a visitor."

I walked toward the creature soft and easy and alert, not wanting to frighten it, but all set to take evasive action if it tried to put the finger on me.

"Be ready, Hutch," I said.

"I'm covering you," Hutch assured me and it was a comfort to know that he was there. A man couldn't get into too much trouble with Hutch backing him.

I stopped about six feet from the creature and he didn't look as bad close up as he did at a distance. His eyes seemed to be kind and gentle and his funny face, alien as it was, had a sort of peacefulness about it. But even so, you can't always tell with aliens.

We stood there looking at one another. The both of us under-stood there was no use in talking. We just stood and sized one another up.

Then the creature took a couple of steps and reached out a hand that was more like a claw than hand. He took my hand in his and tugged for me to come.

There were just two things to do—either snatch my hand away or go.

I went.

I didn't stop to get it figured out, but there were several factors that helped make up my mind. First off, the creature seemed to be friendly and intelligent. And Hutch and all the others were there, just behind me. And over and above all, you don't get too far with aliens if you act stand-offish.

So I went.

We walked into the silo and behind me I heard the tramping feet of the others and it was a sound that was good to hear.

I didn't waste any time wondering where the creature might have come from. I admitted to myself, as I walked along, that I had been half-expecting something just like this. The silo was so big that it could hold many things, even people or creatures, we could not know about. After all, we'd explored only one small corner of the first floor of it. The creature, I figured, must have come from somewhere on the upper floors as soon as he learned about us. It might have taken quite a while, one way or another, for the news to reach him.

He led me up three ramps to the fourth floor of the build-ing and went down a corridor for a little way, then went into a room.

It was not a large room. It held just one machine, but this one was a double model; it had two bucket seats and two helmets. There was another creature in the room.

The first one led me over to the machine and motioned for me to take one of the seats.

I stood there for a while, watching Hutch and Pancake and Frost and all the others crowd into the place and line up against the wall.

Frost said: "A couple of you boys better stay outside and watch the corridor."

Hutch asked me: "You going to sit down in that contraption, Captain?"

"Why not?" I said. "They seem to be all right. There's more of us than them. They don't mean us any harm."

"It's taking a chance," said Hutch.

"Since when have we stopped taking chances?"

The creature I had met outside had sat down in one of the seats, so I made a few adjustments in the other. While I was doing this, the second creature went to a file and got out two sticks, but these sticks were transparent instead of being black. He lifted off the helmets and inserted the two sticks. Then he fitted one of the helmets on his fellow-creature's head and held out the other to me.

I sat down and let him put it on and suddenly I was squatting on the floor across a sort of big coffee-table from the gent I had met outside.

"Now we can talk," said the creature, "which we couldn't do before."

I wasn't scared or flustered. It seemed just as natural as if it had been Hutch across the table.

"There will be a record made of everything we say," said the creature. "When we are finished, you will get one copy and I will get the other for our files. You might call it a pact or a contract or whatever term seems to be most applicable."

"I'm not much at contracts," I told him. "There's too much legal flypaper tied up with most of them."

"An agreement, then," the creature suggested. "A gentlemen's agreement."

"Good enough," I said.

Agreements are convenient things. You can break them any time you want. Especially gentlemen's agreements.

"I suppose you have figured out what this place is," he said.

"Well, not for sure," I replied. "Library is the closest that we have come."

"It's a university, a galactic university. We specialize in extension or home-study courses."

I'm afraid I gulped a bit. "Why, that's just fine."

"Our courses are open to all who wish to take them. There are no entrance fees and there is no tuition. Neither are there any scholastic requirements for enrollment. You yourself can see how difficult it would be to set up such requirements in a galaxy where there are many races of varying viewpoints and abilities."

"You bet I can."

"The courses are free to all who can make use of them," he said. "We do expect, of course, that they make proper use of them and that they display some diligence in study."

"You mean anyone at all can enroll?" I asked. "And it don't cost anything?"

After the first disappointment, I was beginning to see the possibilities. With bona fide university educations for the taking, it would be possible to set up one of the sweetest rackets that anyone could ask for.

"There's one restriction," the creature explained. "We cannot, obviously, concern ourselves with individuals. The paperwork would get completely out of hand. We enroll cultures. You, as a representative of your culture—what is it you call yourselves?"

"The human race, originally of the planet Earth, now covering some half million cubic light-years. I'd have to see your chart . . ."

"That's not necessary at the moment. We would be quite happy to accept your application for the entrance of the human race."

It took the wind out of me for a minute. I wasn't any representative of the human race. And if I could be, I wouldn't. This was my deal, not the human race's. But I couldn't let him know that, of course. He wouldn't have done business with me.

"Now not so fast," I pleaded. "There's a question or two I'd like to have you answer. What kind of courses do you offer? What kind of electives do you have?"

"First there is the basic course," the creature said. "It is more or less a familiarization course, a sort of orientation. It includes those subjects which we believe can be of the most use to the race in question. It is, quite naturally, tailored specifically for each student culture. After that, there is a wide field of electives, hundreds of thousands of them."

"How about final exams and tests and things like that?" I wanted to know.

"Oh, surely," said the creature. "Such tests are conducted every—tell me about your time system." I told him the best I could and he seemed to understand.

"I'd say," he finally said, "that about every thousand years of your time would come fairly close. It is a long-range program and to conduct tests any oftener would put some strain upon our resources and might be of little value."

That decided me. What happened a thousand years from now was no concern of mine.

I asked a few more questions to throw him off the track—just in case he might have been suspicious—about the history of the university and such.

I still can't believe it. It's hard to conceive of any race working a million years to set up a university aimed at the eventual education of an entire galaxy, travelling to all the planets to assemble data, compiling the records of countless cultures, correlating and classifying and sorting out that mass of information to set up the study courses.

It was just too big for a man to grasp.

—

For a while, he had me reeling on the ropes and faintly starry-eyed about the whole affair. But then I managed to snap back to normal.

"All right, Professor," I said, "you can sign us up. What am I supposed to do?"

"Not a thing," he said. "The recording of our discussion will supply the data. We'll outline the course of basic study and you then may take such electives as you wish."

"If we can't haul it all in one trip, we can come back again?" I asked.

"Oh, definitely. I anticipate you may wish to send a fleet to carry all you need. We'll supply sufficient machines and as many copies of the study recordings as you think you will need."

"It'll take a lot," I said bluntly, figuring I'd start high and haggle my way down. "An awful lot."

"I am aware of that," he told me. "Education for an entire culture is no simple matter. But we are geared for it."

So there we had it—all legal and airtight. We could get anything we wanted and as much as we wanted and we'd have a right to it. No one could say we stole it. Not even Doc could say that.

The creature explained to me the system of notation they used on the recording cylinders and how the courses would be boxed and numbered so they could be used in context. He promised to supply me with recordings of the electives so I could pick out what we wanted.

He was real happy about finding another customer and he proudly told me of all the others that they had and he held forth at length on the satisfaction that an educator feels at the opportunity to pass on the torch of knowledge.

He had me feeling like a heel.

Then we were through and I was sitting in the seat again and the second creature was taking the helmet off my head.

I got up and the first creature rose to his feet and faced me. We couldn't talk any more than we could to start with. It was a weird feeling, to face a being you've just made a deal with and not be able to say a single word that he can understand.

But he held out both his hands and I took them in mine and he gave my hands a friendly squeeze.

"Why don't you go ahead and kiss him?" asked Hutch. "Me and the boys will look the other way."

Ordinarily, I'd have slugged Hutch for a crack like that, but I didn't even get sore.

The second creature took the two sticks out of the machine and handed one to me. They'd gone in transparent, but they came out black.

"Let's get out of here," I said.

We got out as fast as we could and still keep our dignity—If you could call it that.

Outside the silo, I got Hutch and Pancake and Frost together and told them what had happened.

"We got the Universe by the tail," I said, "with a downhill pull."

"What about Doc?" asked Frost.

"Don't you see? It's just the kind of deal that would appeal to him. We can let on we're noble and big-hearted and acting in good faith. All I need to do is get close enough to grab him."

"He won't even listen to you," said Pancake. "He won't believe a word you say."

"You guys stay right here," I said. "I'll handle Doc."

I walked back across the stretch of ground between the building and the ship. There was no sign of Doc. I was all set to holler for him, then thought better of it. I took a chance and started up the ladder. I reached the port and there was still no sign of him.

I moved warily into the ship. I thought I knew what had become of him, but there was no need to take more chances than I had to.

I found him in his chair in the dispensary. He was stiffer than a goat. The gun lay on the floor. There were two empty bottles beside the chair.

I stood and looked at him and knew what had happened. After I had left, he had got to thinking about the situation and had run into the problem of how he'd climb down off that limb and he had solved it the way he'd solved most of his problems all his life.

I got a blanket and covered him. Then I rummaged around and found another bottle. I uncorked it and put it beside the chair, where he could reach it easy. Then I picked up the gun and went to call the others in.

I lay in bed that night and thought about it and it was beautiful. There were so many angles that a man didn't know quite where to start.

There was the university racket which, queerly enough, was entirely legitimate, except that the professor out in the silo never meant it to be sold.

And there was the quickie vacation deal, offering a year or two on an alien planet in six hours of actual time. All we'd need to do was pick a number of electives in geography or social science or whatever they might call it.

There could be an information bureau or a research agency, charging fancy prices to run down facts on any and all subjects.

Without a doubt, there'd be some on-the-spot historical recordings and with those in hand, we could retail adventure, perfectly safe adventure, to the stay-at-homes who might hanker for it.

I thought about that and a lot of other things which were not quite so sure, but at least probable and worth investigating, and I thought, too, about how the professors had finally arrived at what seemed to me a sure-fire effective medium for education.

You wanted to know about a thing, so you up and lived it; you learned it on the ground. You didn't read about it or hear about it or even see it in plain three-dimension—you experienced it. You walked the soil of the planet you wanted to know about; you lived with the beings that you wished to study; you saw as an eye-witness, and perhaps as a participant, the history that you sought to learn.

And it could be used in other ways as well. You could learn to build anything, even a spaceship, by actually building one. You could learn how an alien machine might operate by putting it together, step by simple step. There was no field of knowledge in which it would not work—and work far better than standard educational methods.

Right then and there, I made up my mind we'd not release a single stick until one of us had previewed it. No telling what a man might find in one of them that could be put to practical use.

I fell asleep dreaming about chemical miracles and new engineering principles, of better business methods and new philosophic concepts. And I even figured out how a man could make a mint of money out of a philosophic concept.

We were on top of the Universe for sure. We'd set up a corporation with more angles than you could shake a stick at. We would be big time. In a thousand years or so, of course, there'd be a reckoning, but none of us would be around to take part in it.

Doc sobered up by morning and I had Frost heave him in the brig. He wasn't dangerous any longer, but I figured that a spell in pokey might do him a world of good. After a while, I intended to talk to him, but right at the moment I was much too busy to be bothered with him.

I went over to the silo with Hutch and Pancake and had another session with the professor on the double-seat machine and picked out a batch of electives and settled various matters.

Other professors began supplying us with the courses, all boxed and labeled, and we set the crew and the engine gang to work hauling them and the machines aboard and stowing them away.

Hutch and I stood outside the silo and watched the work go on.

"I never thought," said Hutch, "that we'd hit the jackpot this way. To be downright honest with you, I never thought we'd hit it. I always thought we'd just go on looking. It goes to show how wrong a man can be."

"Those professors are soft in the head," I said. "They never asked me any questions. I can think of a lot they could have asked that I couldn't answer."

"They're honest and think everyone's the same. That's what comes of getting so wrapped up in something you have time for nothing else."

And that was true enough. The professor race has been busy for a million years doing a job it took a million years to do—and another million and a million after that—and that never would be finished.

"I can't figure why they did it," I said. "There's no profit in it."

"Not for them," said Hutch, "but there is for us. I tell you, Captain, it takes brains to work out the angles."

I told him what I had figured out about previewing everything before we gave it out, so we would be sure we let nothing slip away from us.

Hutch was impressed. "I'll say this for you, Captain—you don't miss a bet. And that's the way it should be. We might as well milk this deal for every cent it's worth."

"I think we should be methodical about this previewing business," I said. "We should start at the beginning and go straight through to the end."

Hutch said he thought so, too. "But it will take a lot of time," he warned me.

"That's why we should start right now. The orientation course is on board already and we could start with that. All we'd have to do is set up a machine and Pancake could help you with it."

"Help me!" yelled Hutch. "Who said anything about me doing it? I ain't cut out for that stuff. You know yourself I never do any reading—"

"It isn't reading. You just live it. You'll be having fun while we're out here slaving."

"I won't do it."

"Now look," I said, "let's use a little sense. I should be out here at the silo seeing everything goes all right and close at hand so I can hold a pow-wow with the professor if there's any need of it. We need Frost to superintend the loading. And Doc is in the clink. That leaves you and Pancake. I can't trust Pancake with that previewing job. He's too scatterbrained. He'd let a fortune glide right past him without recognizing it. Now you're a fast man with a buck and the way I see it—"

"Since you put it that way," said Hutch, all puffed up, "I suppose I am the one who should be doing it."

That evening, we were all dog-tired, but we felt fine. We had made a good start with the loading and in a few more days would be heading home. Hutch seemed to be preoccupied at supper. He fiddled with his food. He didn't talk at all and he seemed like a man with something on his mind.

As soon as I could, I cornered him.

"How's it going, Hutch?"

"Okay," he said. "Just a lot of gab. Explaining what it's all about. Gab."

"Like what?"

"Some of it is hard to tell. Takes a lot of explaining I haven't got the words for. Maybe one of these days you'll find the time to run through it yourself."

"You can bet your life I will," I said, somewhat sore at him.

"There's nothing worth a dime in it so far," said Hutch.

I believed him on that score. Hutch could spot a dollar twenty miles away.

I went down to the brig to see Doc. He was sober. Also unrepentant.

"You outreached yourself this time," he said. "That stuff isn't yours to sell. There's knowledge in that building that belongs to the Galaxy—for free."

I explained to him what had happened, how we'd found the silo was a university and how we were taking the courses on board for the human race after signing up for them all regular and proper. I tried to make it sound as if we were being big, but Doc wouldn't buy a word of it.

"You wouldn't give your dying grandma a drink of water unless she paid you in advance," he said. "Don't give me any of that guff about service to humanity."

So I left him to stew in the brig a while and went up to my cabin. I was sore at Hutch and all burned up at Doc and my tail was dragging. I fell asleep in no time.

The work went on for several days and we were almost finished.

I felt pretty good about it. After supper, I climbed down the ladder and sat on the ground beside the ship and looked across at the silo. It still looked big and awesome, but not as big as that first day—because now it had lost some of its strangeness and even the purpose of it had lost some of its strangeness, too.

Just as soon as we got back to civilization, I promised myself, we'd seal the deal as tight as possible. Probably we couldn't legally claim the planet because the professors were intelligent and you can't claim a planet that has intelligence, but there were plenty of other ways we could get our hooks into it for keeps.

I sat there and wondered why no one came down to sit with me, but no one did, so finally I clambered up the ladder.

I went down to the brig to have a word with Doc. He was still unrepentant, but he didn't seem too hostile.

"You know, Captain," he said, "there have been times when I've not seen eye to eye with you, but despite that I've respected you and sometimes even liked you."

"What are you getting at?" I asked him. "You can't soft-talk yourself out of the spot you're in."

"There's something going on and maybe I should tell you. You are a forthright rascal. You don't even take the trouble to deny you are. You have no scruples and probably no morals, and that's all right, because you don't pretend to have. You are—"

"Spit it out! If you don't tell me what is going on, I'll come in there and wring it out of you."

"Hutch has been down here several times," said Doc, "inviting me to come up and listen to one of those recordings he is fooling with. Said it was right down my alley. Said I'd not be sorry. But there was something wrong about it. Something sneaky." He stared round-eyed through the bars at me. "You know, Captain, Hutch was never sneaky."

"Well, go on!"

"Hutch has found out something, Captain. If I were you, I'd be finding out myself."

I didn't even wait to answer him. I remembered how Hutch had been acting, fiddling with his food and preoccupied, not talking very much. And come to think of it, some of the others had been acting strangely, too. I'd just been too busy to give it much attention.

Running up the catwalks, I cussed with every step I took. A captain of a ship should never get so busy that he loses touch—he has to stay in touch all the blessed time. It had all come of being in a hurry, of wanting to get loaded up and out of there before something happened.

And now something had happened. No one had come down to sit with me. There'd not been a dozen words spoken at the supper table. Everything felt deadly wrong.

Pancake and Hutch had rigged up the chart room for the previewing chore and I busted into it and slammed the door and stood with my back against it. Not only Hutch was there, but Pancake and Frost as well and, in the machine's bucket seat, a man I recognized as one of the engine gang.

I stood for a moment without saying anything, and the three of them stared back at me. The man with the helmet on his head didn't notice—he wasn't even there.

"All right, Hutch," I said, "come clean. What is this all about? Why is that man previewing? I thought just you and—"

"Captain," said Frost, "we were about to tell you."

"You shut up! I am asking Hutch."

"Frost is right," said Hutch. "We were all set to tell you. But you were so busy and it came a little hard . . ."

"What is hard about it?"

"Well, you had your heart all set to make yourself a fortune. We were trying to find a way to break it to you gentle."

I left the door and walked over to him.

"I don't know what you're talking about," I said, "but we still make ourselves a killing. There never was a time of day or night, Hutch, that I couldn't beat your head in and if you don't want me to start, you better talk real fast."

"We'll make no killing, Captain," Frost said quietly. "We're taking this stuff back and we'll turn it over to the authorities."

"All of you are nuts!" I roared. "For years, we've slaved and sweated, hunting for the jackpot. And now that we have it in our mitts, now that we can walk barefooted through a pile of thousand-dollar bills, you are going chicken on me. What's—"

"It's not right for us to do it, sir," said Pancake.

And that "sir" scared me more than anything that had happened so far. Pancake had never called me that before.

I looked from one to the other of them and what I saw in their faces chilled me to the bone. Every single one of them thought just the same as Pancake.

"That orientation course!" I shouted.

Hutch nodded. "It explained about honesty and honor."

"What do you scamps know about honesty and honor?" I raged. "There ain't a one of you that ever drew an honest breath."

"We never knew about it before," said Pancake, "but we know about it now."

"It's just propaganda! It's just a dirty trick the professors played on us!"

And it was a dirty trick. Although you have to admit the professors knew their onions. I don't know if they figured us humans for a race of heels or if the orientation course was just normal routine. But no wonder they hadn't questioned me. No wonder they'd made no investigation before handing us their knowledge. They had us stopped before we could even make a move.

"We felt that since we had learned about honesty," said Frost, "it was only right the rest of the crew should know. It's an awful kind of life we've been living, Captain."

"So," said Hutch, "we been bringing in the men, one by one, and orienting them. We figured it was the least that we could do. This man is about the last of them."

"A missionary," I said to Hutch. "So that is what you are. Remember what you told me one night? You said you wouldn't be a missionary no matter what they paid you."

"There's no need of that," Frost replied coldly. "You can't shame us and you can't bully us. We know we are right."

"But the money! What about the corporation? We had it all planned out!"

Frost said: "You might as well forget it, Captain. When you take the course—"

"I'm not taking any course." My voice must have been as deadly as I felt, for not a one of them made a move toward me. "If any of you mealy-mouthed missionaries feel an urge to make me, you can start trying right now."

They still didn't move. I had them bluffed. But there was no point in arguing with them. There was nothing I could do against that stone wall of honesty and honor.

I turned my back on them and walked to the door. At the door, I stopped. I said to Frost: "You better turn Doc loose and give him the cure. Tell him it's all right with me. He has it coming to him. It will serve him right."

Then I shut the door behind me and went up the catwalk to my cabin. I locked the door, a thing I'd never done before.

I sat down on the edge of the bunk and stared at the wall and thought.

There was just one thing they had forgotten. This was my ship, not theirs. They were just the crew and their papers had run out long ago and never been renewed.

I got down on my hands and knees and hauled out the tin box I kept the papers in. I went through it systematically and sorted out the papers that I needed—the title to the ship and the registry and the last papers they had signed.

I laid the papers on the bunk and shoved the box out of the way and sat down again.

I picked up the papers and shuffled them from one hand to the other.

I could throw them off the ship any time I wished. I could take off without them and there was nothing, absolutely nothing, they could do about it.

And what was more, I could get away with it. It was legal, of course, but it was a rotten thing to do. Now that they were honest men and honorable, though, they'd bow to the legality and let me get away with it. And in such a case, they had no one but themselves to thank.

I sat there for a long time thinking, but my thoughts went round and round and mostly had to do with things out of the past—how Pancake had gotten tangled up in the nettle patch out in the Coonskin System and how Doc had fallen in love with (of all things) a tri-sexual being that time we touched at Siro and how Hutch had cornered the liquor supply at Munko, then lost it in a game that was akin to craps except the dice were queer little living entities that you had no control of, which made it tough on Hutch.

A rap came at the door.

It was Doc.

"You all full of honesty?" I asked him.

He shuddered. "Not me. I turned down the offer."

"It's the same kind of swill you were preaching at me just a couple of days ago."

"Can't you see," asked Doc, "what it would do to the human race?"

"Sure. It'll make them honorable and honest. No one will ever cheat or steal again and it will be cozy . . ."

"They'll die of complicated boredom," said Doc. "Life will become a sort of cross between a Boy Scout jamboree and a ladies sewing circle. There'll be no loud and unseemly argument and they'll be polite and proper to the point of stupefaction."

"So you have changed your mind."

"Not really, Captain. But this is the wrong way to go about it. Whatever progress the race has ever made has been achieved by the due process of social evolution. In any human advance, the villains and the rascals are as important as the forward-looking idealist. They are Man's consciences and Man can't get along without them."

"If I were you, Doc," I said, "I wouldn't worry so much about the human race. It's a pretty big thing and it can take a lot of bumps. Even an overdose of honesty won't hurt it permanently."

Actually, I didn't give a damn. I had other things on my mind right then.

Doc crossed the room and sat down on the bunk beside me. He leaned over and tapped the papers I still held in my hand.

"You got it all doped out," he said.

I nodded bleakly. "Yeah."

"I thought you would."

I shot a quick glance at him. "You were way ahead of me. That's why you switched over."

Doc shook his head emphatically. "No. Please believe me, Captain, I feel as bad as you do."

"It won't work either way." I shuffled the papers. "They acted in good faith. They didn't sign aboard, sure. But there was no reason that they should have. It was all understood. Share and share alike. And that's the way it's been for too long to repudiate it now. And we can't keep on. Even if we agreed to dump the stuff right here and blast off and never think of it again, we'd not get rid of it. It would always be there. The past is dead, Doc. It's spoiled. It's smashed and it can't be put back together."

I felt like bawling. It had been a long time since I had felt that full of grief.

"They are different kind of men now," I said. "They went and changed themselves and they'll never be the same. Even if they could change back, it wouldn't be the same."

Doc mocked me a little. "The race will build a monument to you. Maybe actually on Earth itself, with all the other famous humans, for bringing back this stuff. They'd be just blind enough to do it."

I got up and paced the floor. "I don't want any monument. I'm not bringing it in. I'm not having anything more to do with it."

I stood there, wishing we had never found the silo, for what had it done for me except to lose me the best crew and the best friends a man had ever had?

"The ship is mine," I said. "That is all I want. I'll take the cargo to the nearest point and dump it there. Hutch and the rest of them can carry on from there, any way they can. They can have the honesty and honor. I'll get another crew."

Maybe, I thought, some day it would be almost the way it had been. Almost, but not quite.

"We'll go on hunting," I said. "We'll dream about the jackpot.

We'll do our best to find it. We'll do anything to find it. We'll break all the laws of God or Man to find it. But you know something, Doc?"

"No, I don't," said Doc.

"I hope we never find it. I don't want to find another. I just want to go on hunting." We stood there in the silence, listening to the fading echoes of those days we hunted for the jackpot.

"Captain," said Doc, "will you take me along?"

I nodded. What was the difference? He might just as well.

"Captain, you remember those insect mounds on Suud?"

"Of course. How could I forget them?"

"You know, I've figured out a way we might break into them. Maybe we should try it. There should be a billion . . ."

I almost clobbered him.

I'm glad now that I didn't.

Suud is where we're headed.

If Doc's plan works out, we may hit that jackpot yet!

DAY OF TRUCE

Although "Day of Truce" originally appeared in the February 1963 issue of Galaxy Magazine, *it is intriguing to note that a cryptic entry in one of the author's journals, dated October of 1957, says, simply: "Did a lot of work on Kid War story." It would be four and a half years before "Day of Truce" would be mailed out—so is this the story that cryptic notes references? If so, it would have been an extraordinary delay; getting the copy out was ground into old newspapermen like Clifford Simak.*

This is a disturbing story in many ways, and I find myself wondering if this is a sort of counterpoint to stories like "Neighbor."

—du·w

I

The evening was quiet. There was no sign of the Punks. Silence lay heavily across the barren and eroded acres of the subdivision and there was nothing moving—not even one of the roving and always troublesome dog packs.

It was too quiet, Max Hale decided.

There should have been some motion and some noise. It was as if everyone had taken cover against some known and coming violence—another raid, perhaps. Although there was only one place against which a raid could possibly be aimed. Why should others care, Max wondered; why should they cower indoors, when they had long since surrendered?

Max stood upon the flat lookout-rooftop of the Crawford stronghold and watched the streets to north and west. It was by one of these that Mr. Crawford would be coming home. No one could guess which one, for he seldom used the same road. It was the only way one could cut down the likelihood of ambush or of barricade. Although ambush was less frequent now. There were fewer fences, fewer trees and shrubs; there was almost nothing behind which one could hide. In this barren area it called for real ingenuity to effect an ambuscade. But, Max reminded himself, no one had ever charged the Punks with lack of ingenuity.

Mr. Crawford had phoned that he would be late and Max was getting nervous. In another quarter hour, darkness would be closing in. It was bad business to be abroad in Oak Manor after dark had fallen. Or, for that matter, in any of the subdivisions. For while Oak Manor might be a bit more vicious than some of the others of them, it still was typical.

He lifted his glasses again and swept the terrain slowly. There was no sign of patrols or hidden skulkers. There must be watchers somewhere, he knew. There were always watchers, alert to the slightest relaxation of the vigilance maintained at Crawford stronghold.

Street by street he studied the sorry houses, with their broken window panes and their peeling paint, still marked by the soap streaks and the gouges and the red-paint splashes inflicted years before. Here and there dead trees stood stark, denuded of their branches. Browned evergreens, long dead, stood rooted in the dusty yards—yards long since robbed of the grass that once had made them lawns.

And on the hilltop, up on Circle Drive, stood the ruins of Thompson stronghold, which had fallen almost five years before.

There was no structure standing. It had been leveled stone by stone and board by board. Only the smashed and dying trees, only the twisted steel fence posts marked where it had been.

Now Crawford stronghold stood alone in Oak Manor. Max thought of it with a glow of pride and a surge of painful memory. It stood because of him, he thought, and he would keep it standing.

In this desert it was the last oasis, with its trees and grass, with its summer houses and trellises, with the massive shrubbery and the wondrous sun dial beside the patio, with its goldfish-and-lily pond and the splashing fountain.

"Max," said the walkie-talkie strapped across his chest.

"Yes, Mr. Crawford."

"Where are you located, Max?"

"Up on the lookout, sir."

"I'll come in on Seymour Drive," said Mr. Crawford's voice. "I'm about a mile beyond the hilltop. I'll be coming fast."

"The coast seems to be quite clear, sir."

"Good. But take no chances with the gates."

"I have the control box with me, sir. I can operate from here. I will keep a sharp lookout."

"Be seeing you," said Crawford.

Max picked up the remote control box and waited for his returning master.

The car came over the hill and streaked down Seymour Drive, made its right-hand turn on Dawn, roared toward the gates.

When it was no more than a dozen feet away, Max pushed the button that unlocked the gates. The heavy bumper slammed into them and pushed them open. The buffers that ran along each side of the car held them aside as the machine rushed through. When the car had cleared them, heavy springs snapped them shut and they were locked again.

Max slung the control-box strap over his shoulder and went along the rooftop catwalk to the ladder leading to the ground.

Mr. Crawford had put away the car and was closing the garage door as Max came around the corner of the house.

"It does seem quiet," said Mr. Crawford. "Much quieter, it would seem to me, than usual."

"I don't like it, sir. There is something brewing."

"Not very likely," said Mr. Crawford. "Not on the eve of Truce Day."

"I wouldn't put nothing past them dirty Punks," said Max.

"I quite agree," said Mr. Crawford, "but they'll be coming here tomorrow for their day of fun. We must treat them well for, after all, they're neighbors and it is a custom. I would hate to have you carried beyond the bounds of propriety by overzealousness."

"You know well and good," protested Max, "I would never do a thing. I am a fighter, sir, but I fight fair and honorable."

Mr. Crawford said, "I was thinking of the little gambit you had cooked up last year."

"It would not have hurt them, sir. Leastwise, not permanently. They might never have suspected. Just a drop or two of it in the fruit punch was all we would have needed. It wouldn't have taken effect until hours after they had left. Slow-acting stuff, it was."

"Even so," said Mr. Crawford sternly, "I am glad I found out in time. And I don't want a repeat performance, possibly more subtle, to be tried this year. I hope you understand me."

"Oh, certainly, sir," said Max. "You can rely upon it, sir."

"Well, good night, then. I'll see you in the morning."

It was all damn foolishness, thought Max—this business of a Day of Truce. It was an old holdover from the early days when some do-gooder had figured maybe there would be some benefit if the stronghold people and the Punks could meet under happy circumstance and spend a holiday together.

It worked, of course, but only for the day. For twenty-four hours there were no raids, no flaming arrows, no bombs across the fence. But at one second after midnight, the feud took up again, as bitter and relentless as if had ever been.

It had been going on for years. Max had no illusions about how it all would end. Some day Crawford stronghold would fall as had all the others in Oak Manor. But until that day, he pledged himself to do everything he could. He would never lower his guard nor relax his vigilance. Up to the very end he would make them smart for every move they made.

He watched as Mr. Crawford opened the front door and went across the splash of light that flowed out from the hall. Then the door shut and the house stood there, big and bleak and black, without a sliver of light showing anywhere. No light ever showed from the Crawford house. Well before the fall of night he always threw the lever on the big control board to slam steel shutters closed against all the windows in the place. Lighted windows made too good a nighttime target.

Now the raids always came at night. There had been a time when some had been made in daylight, but that was too chancy now. Year by year, the defenses had been built up to a point where an attack in daylight was plain foolhardiness.

Max turned and went down the driveway to the gates. He drew on rubber gloves and with a small flashlight examined the locking mechanism. It was locked. It had never failed, but there might come a time it would. He never failed to check it once the gates had closed.

He stood beside the gates and listened. Everything was quiet, although he imagined he could hear the faint singing of the electric current running through the fence. But that, he knew, was impossible, for the current was silent.

He reached out with a gloved hand and stroked the fence. Eight feet high, he told himself, with a foot of barbed wire along the top of it, and every inch of it alive with the surging current.

And inside of it, a standby, auxiliary fence into which current could be introduced if the forward fence should fail.

—

A clicking sound came padding down the driveway and Max turned from the gate.

"How you, boy," he said.

It was too dark for him to see the dog, but he could hear it snuffling and snorting with pleasure at his recognition.

It came bumbling out of the darkness and pushed against his legs. He squatted down and put his arms about it. It kissed him sloppily.

"Where are the others, boy?" he asked, and it wriggled in its pleasure.

Great dogs, he thought. They loved the people in the stronghold almost to adoration, but had an utter hatred for every other person. They had been trained to have.

The rest of the pack, he knew, was aprowl about the yard, alert to every sound, keyed to every presence. No one could approach the fence without their knowing it. Any stranger who got across the fence they would rip to bits.

He stripped off the rubber gloves and put them in his pocket.

"Come on, boy," he said.

He turned off the driveway and proceeded across the yard—cautiously, for it was uneven footing. There was no inch of it that lay upon the level. It was cleverly designed so that any thrown grenade or Molotov cocktail would roll into a deep and narrow bomb trap.

There had been a time, he recalled, when there had been a lot of these things coming over the fence. There were fewer now, for it was a waste of effort. There had been a time, as well, when there had been flaming arrows, but these had tapered off since the house had been fireproofed.

He reached the side yard and stopped for a moment, listening, with the dog standing quietly at his side. A slight wind had come up and the trees were rustling. He lifted his head and stared at the delicate darkness of them, outlined against the lighter sky.

Beautiful things, he thought. It was a pity there were not more of them. Once this area had been named Oak Manor for the stately trees that grew here. There, just ahead of him, was the last of them—a rugged old patriarch with its massive crown blotting out the early stars.

He looked at it with awe and appreciation—and with apprehension, too. It was a menace. It was old and brittle and it should be taken down, for it leaned toward the fence and some day a windstorm might topple it across the wire. He should have mentioned it long ago to Mr. Crawford, but he knew the owner held this tree in a sentimental regard that matched his own. Perhaps it could be made safe by guywires to hold it against the wind, or at least to turn its fall away from the fence should it be broken or uprooted. Although it seemed a sacrilege to anchor it with guywires, an insult to an ancient monarch.

He moved on slowly, threading through the bomb traps, with the dog close at his heels, until he reached the patio and here he stopped beside the sun dial. He ran his hand across its rough stone surface and wondered why Mr. Crawford should set such a store by it. Perhaps because it was a link to the olden days before the Punks and raids. It was an old piece that had been brought from a monastery garden somewhere in France. That in itself, of course, would make it valuable. But perhaps Mr. Crawford saw in it another value, far beyond the fact that it was hundreds of years old and had come across the water.

Perhaps it had grown to symbolize for him the day now past when any man might have a sun dial in his garden, when he might have trees and grass without fighting for them, when he might take conscious pride in the unfenced and unmolested land that lay about his house.

Bit by bit, through the running years, those rights had been eroded.

II

First it had been the little things—the casual, thoughtless tramp-pling of the shrubbery by the playing small fry, the killing of the evergreens by the rampaging packs of happy dogs that ran with the playing small fry. For each boy, the parents said, must have himself a dog.

The people in the first place had moved from the jam-packed cities to live in what they fondly called the country, so that they could keep a dog or two and where their children would have fresh air and sunlight and room in which to run.

But too often this country was, in reality, no more than another city, with its houses cheek by jowl—each set on acre or half-acre lots, but still existing cheek by jowl.

Of course, a place to run. The children had. But no more than a place to run. There was nothing more to do. Run was all they could do—up and down the streets, back and forth across the lawns, up and down the driveways, leaving havoc in their trail. And in time the toddlers grew up and in their teen-age years they still could only run. There was no place for them to go, nothing they might do. Their mothers foregathered every morning at the coffee klatches and their fathers sat each evening in the backyards drinking beer. The family car could not be used because gasoline cost money and the mortgages were heavy and the taxes terrible and the other costs were high.

So to find an outlet for their energies, to work off their unre-alized resentments against having nothing they could do, these older fry started out, for pure excitement only, on adventures in vandalism. There was a cutting of the backyard clotheslines, a chopping into bits of watering hoses left out overnight, a break-ing and ripping up of the patios, ringing of the doorbells, smash-ing of the windows, streaking of the siding with a cake of soap, splashing with red paint.

Resentments had been manufactured to justify this vandalism and now the resentments were given food to grow upon. Irate owners erected fences to keep out the children and the dogs, and this at once became an insult and a challenge.

And that first simple fence, Max told himself, had been the forerunner of the eight-foot barrier of electricity which formed the first line of defense in the Crawford stronghold. Likewise, those small-time soap-cake vandals, shrieking their delight at messing up a neighbor's house, had been the ancestors of the Punks.

He left the patio and went down the stretch of backyard, past the goldfish-and-lily pond and the tinkling of the fountain, past the clump of weeping willows, and so out to the fence.

"Psst!" said a voice just across the fence.

"That you, Billy?"

"It's me," said Billy Warner.

"All right. Tell me what you have."

"Tomorrow is Truce Day and we'll be visiting . . ."

"I know all that," said Max.

"They're bringing in a time bomb."

"They can't do that," said Max, disgusted. "The cops will frisk them at the gates. They would spot it on them."

"It'll be all broken down. Each one will have a piece. Stony Stafford hands out the parts tonight. He has a crew that has been practicing for weeks to put a bomb together fast—even in the dark, if need be."

"Yeah," said Max, "I guess they could do it that way. And once they get it put together?"

"The sun dial," Billy said. "Underneath the sun dial."

"Well, thanks," said Max. "I am glad to know. It would break the boss' heart should something happen to the sun dial."

"I figure," Billy said, "this might be worth a twenty."

"Yes," Max agreed. "Yes, I guess it would."

"If they ever knew I told, they'd take me out and kill me."

"They won't ever know," said Max. "I won't ever tell them."

He pulled his wallet from his pocket, turned on the flash and found a pair of tens.

He folded the bills together, lengthwise, twice. Then he shoved them through an opening in the fence.

"Careful, there," he cautioned. "Do not touch the wire."

Beyond the fence he could see the faint, white outline of the other's face. And a moment later, the hand that reached out carefully and grabbed the corner of the folded bills.

Max did not let loose of the money immediately. They stood, each of them, with their grip upon the bills.

"Billy," said Max, solemnly, "you would never kid me, would you? You would never sell me out. You would never feed me erroneous information."

"You know me, Max," said Billy. "I've played square with you. I'd never do a thing like that."

Max let go of the money and let the other have it.

"I am glad to hear you say that, Billy. Keep on playing square. For the day you don't, I'll come out of here and hunt you down and cut your throat myself."

But the informer did not answer. He was already moving off, out into the deeper darkness.

Max stood quietly, listening. The wind still blew in the leaves and the fountain kept on splashing, like gladsome silver bells.

"Hi, boy," Max said softly, but there was no snuffling answer. The dog had left him, was prowling with the others up and down the yard.

Max turned about and went up the yard toward the front again, completing his circuit of the house. As he rounded the corner of the garage, a police car was slowing to a halt before the gates.

He started down the drive, moving ponderously and deliberately.

"That you, Charley?" he called softly.

"Yes, Max," said Charley Pollard. "Is everything all right?"

"Right as rain," said Max.

He approached the gates and saw the bulky loom of the officer on the other side.

"Just dropping by," said Pollard. "The area is quiet tonight. We'll be coming by one of these days to inspect the place. It looks to me you're loaded."

"Not a thing illegal," Max declared. "All of it's defensive. That is still the rule."

"Yes, that is the rule," said Pollard, "but it seems to me that there are times you become a mite too enthusiastic. A full load in the fence, no doubt."

"Why, certainly," said Max. "Would you have it otherwise?"

"A kid grabs hold of it and he could be electrocuted, at full strength."

"Would you rather I had it set just to tickle them?"

"You're playing too rough, Max."

"I doubt it rather much," said Max. "I watched from here, five years ago, when they stormed Thompson stronghold. Did you happen to see that?"

"I wasn't here five years ago. My beat was Farview Acres."

"They took it apart," Max told him. "Stone by stone, brick by brick, timber by timber. They left nothing standing. They left nothing whole. They cut down all the trees and chopped them up. They uprooted all the shrubs. They hoed out all the flower beds. They made a desert of it. They reduced it to their level. And I'm not about to let it happen here, not if I can help it. A man has got the right to grow a tree and a patch of grass. If he wants a flower bed, he has a right to have a flower bed. You may not think so, but he's even got the right to keep other people out."

"Yes," said the officer, "all you say is true. But these are kids you are dealing with. There must be allowances. And this is a neighborhood. You folks and the others like you wouldn't have this trouble if you only tried to be a little neighborly."

"We don't dare be neighborly," said Max. "Not in a place like this. In Oak Manor, and in all the other manors and all the other acres and the other whatever-you-may-call-thems, neighborliness means that you let people overrun you. Neighborliness means you give up your right to live your life the way you want to live it. This kind of neighborliness is rooted way back in those days when the kids made a path across your lawn as a shortcut to the school bus and you couldn't say a thing for fear that they would sass you back and so create a scene. It started when your neighbor borrowed your lawn mower and forgot to bring it back and when you went to get it you found that he had broken it. But he pretended that he hadn't and, for the sake of neighborliness, you didn't have the guts to tell him that he had and to demand that he pay the bill for the repairing of it."

"Well, maybe so," said Pollard, "but it's gotten out of hand. It has been carried too far. You folks have got too high and mighty."

"There's a simple answer to everything," Max told him stoutly. "Get the Punks to lay off us and we'll take down the fence and all the other stuff."

Pollard shook his head. "It has gone too far," he said. "There is nothing anyone can do."

He started to go back to the car, then turned back.

"I forgot," he said. "Tomorrow is your Truce Day. Myself and a couple of the other men will be here early in the morning."

Max didn't answer. He stood in the driveway and watched the car pull off down the street. Then he went up the driveway and around the house to the back door.

Nora had a place laid at the table for him and he sat down heavily, glad to be off his feet. By this time of the evening he was always tired. Not as young, he thought, as he once had been.

"You're late tonight," said the cook, bringing him the food. "Is everything all right?"

"I guess so. Everything is quiet. But we may have trouble tomorrow. They're bringing in a bomb."

"A bomb!" cried Nora. "What will you do about it? Call in the police, perhaps."

Max shook his head. "No, I can't do that. The police aren't on our side. They'd take the attitude we'd egged on the Punks until they had no choice but to bring in the bomb. We are on our own. And, besides, I must protect the lad who told me. If I didn't, the Punks would know and he'd be worthless to me then. He'd never get to know another thing. But knowing they are bringing something in, I can watch for it."

He still felt uneasy about it all, he realized. Not about the bomb itself, perhaps, but something else, something that was connected with it. He wondered why he had this feeling. Knowing about the bomb, he all but had it made. All he'd have to do would be to locate it and dig it out from beneath the sun dial. He would have the time to do it. The day-long celebration would end at six in the evening and the Punks could not set the bomb to explode earlier than midnight. Any blast before midnight would be a violation of the truce.

He scooped fried potatoes from the dish onto his plate and speared a piece of meat. Nora poured his coffee and, pulling out a chair, sat down opposite him.

"You aren't eating?" he asked.

"I ate early, Max."

He ate hungrily and hurriedly, for there still were things to do. She sat and watched him eat. The clock on the kitchen wall ticked loudly in the silence.

Finally she said: "It is getting somewhat grim, Max."

He nodded, his mouth full of food and unable to speak.

"I don't see," said the cook, "why the Crawfords want to stay here. There can't be much pleasure in it for them. They could move into the city and it would be safer there. There are the juvenile gangs, of course, but they mostly fight among themselves. They don't make life unbearable for all the other people."

"It's pride," said Max. "They won't give up. They won't let Oak Manor beat them. Mr. and Mrs. Crawford are quality. They have some steel in them."

"They couldn't sell the place, of course," said Nora. "There would no one buy it. But they don't need the money. They could just walk away from it."

"You misjudge them, Nora. The Crawfords in all their lives have never walked away from anything. They went through a lot to live here. Sending Johnny off to boarding school when he was a lad, since it wouldn't have been safe for him to go to school with the Punks out there. I don't suppose they like it. I don't see how they could. But they won't be driven out. They realize someone must stand up to all that trash out there, or else there's no hope."

Nora sighed. "I suppose you're right. But it is a shame. They could live so safe and comfortable and normal if they just moved to the city."

He finished eating and got up.

"It was a good meal, Nora," he said. "But then you always fix good meals."

"Ah, go on with you," said Nora.

He went into the basement and sat down before the short-wave set. Systematically, he started putting in his calls to the other strongholds. Wilson stronghold, over in Fair Hills, had had a little trouble early in the evening—a few stink bombs heaved across the fence—but it had quieted down. Jackson stronghold did not answer. While he was trying to get through to Smith stronghold in Harmony Settlement, Curtis stronghold in Lakeside Heights began calling him. Everything was quiet, John Hennessey, the Curtis custodian told him. It had been quiet for several days.

He stayed at the radio for an hour and by that time had talked with all the nearby strongholds. There had been scattered trouble here and there, but nothing of any consequence. Generally it was peaceful.

He sat and thought about the time bomb and there was still that nagging worry. There was something wrong, he knew, but he could not put his finger on it.

Getting up, he prowled the cavernous basement, checking the defense material—extra sections of fencing, piles of posts, pointed stakes, rolls of barb wire, heavy flexible wire mesh and all the other items for which some day there might be a need. Tucked into one corner, hidden, he found the stacked carboys of acid he had secretly cached away. Mr. Crawford would not approve, he knew, but if the chips ever should be down, and there was need to use those carboys, he might be glad to have them.

He climbed the stairs and went outside to prowl restlessly about the yard, still upset by that nagging something about the bomb he could not yet pin down.

The moon had risen. The yard was a place of interlaced light and shadow, but beyond the fence the desert acres that held the other houses lay flat and bare and plain, without a shadow on them except the shadows of the houses.

Two of the dogs came up and passed the time of night with him and then went off into the shrubbery.

He moved into the backyard and stood beside the sun dial.

The wrongness still was there. Something about the sun dial and the bomb—some piece of thinking that didn't run quite true.

He wondered how they knew that the destruction of the sun dial would be a heavy blow to the owner of the stronghold. How could they possibly have known?

The answer seemed to be that they couldn't. They didn't. There was no way for them to know. And even if, in some manner, they had learned, a sun dial most certainly would be a fiddling thing to blow up when that single bomb could be used so much better somewhere else.

Stony Stafford, the leader of the Punks, was nobody's fool. He was a weasel—full of cunning, full of savvy. He'd not mess with any sun dial when there was so much else that a bomb could do so much more effectively.

And as he stood there beside the sun dial, Max knew where that bomb would go—knew where he would plant it were he in Stafford's place.

At the roots of that ancient oak which leaned toward the fence.

He stood and thought about it and knew that he was right.

Billy Warner, he wondered. Had Billy double-crossed him?

Very possibly he hadn't. Perhaps Stony Stafford might have suspected long ago that his gang harbored an informer and, for that reason, had given out the story of the sun dial rather than the oak tree. And that, of course, only to a select inner circle which would be personally involved with the placing of the bomb.

In such a case, he thought, Billy Warner had not done too badly.

Max turned around and went back to the house, walking heavily. He climbed the stairs to his attic room and went to bed. It had been, he thought just before he went to sleep, a fairly decent day.

III

The police showed up at eight o'clock. The carpenters came and put up the dance platform. The musicians appeared and began their tuning up. The caterers arrived and set up the tables, loading them with food and two huge punch bowls, standing by to serve.

Shortly after nine o'clock the Punks and their girls began to straggle in. The police frisked them at the gates and found no blackjacks, no brass knuckles, no bicycle chains on any one of them.

The band struck up. The Punks and their girls began to dance. They strolled through the yard and admired the flowers, without picking any of them. They sat on the grass and talked and laughed among themselves. They gathered at the overflowing boards and ate. They laughed and whooped and frolicked and everything was fine.

"You see?" Pollard said to Max. "There ain't nothing wrong with them. Give them a decent break and they're just a bunch of ordinary kids. A little hell in them, of course, but nothing really bad. It's your flaunting of this place in their very faces that makes them the way they are."

"Yeah," said Max.

He left Pollard and drifted down the yard, keeping as inconspicuous as he could. He wanted to watch the oak, but he knew he didn't dare to. He knew he had to keep away from it, should not even glance toward it. If he should scare them off, then God only knew where they would plant the bomb. He thought of being forced to hunt wildly for it after they were gone and shuddered at the thought.

There was no one near the bench at the back of the yard, near the flowering almond tree, and he stretched out on it. It wasn't particularly comfortable, but the day was warm and the air was drowsy. He dropped off to sleep.

When he woke he saw that a man was standing on the gravel path just beyond the bench.

He blinked hard and rubbed his eyes.

"Hello, Max," said Stony Stafford.

"You should be up there dancing, Stony."

"I was waiting for you to wake up," said Stony. "You are a heavy sleeper. I could of broke your neck."

Max sat up. He rubbed a hand across his face.

"Not on Truce Day, Stony. We all are friends on Truce Day."

Stony spat upon the gravel path.

"Some other day," he said.

"Look," said Max, "why don't you just run off and forget about it? You'll break your back if you try to crack this place. Pick up your marbles, Stony, and go find someone else who's not so rough to play with."

"Some day we'll make it," Stony said. "This place can't stand forever."

"You haven't got a chance," said Max.

"Maybe so," said Stony. "But I think we will. And before we do, there is just one thing I want you to know. You think nothing will happen to you even if we do. You think that all we'll do is just rip up the place, not harming anyone. But you're wrong, Max. We'll do it the way it is supposed to be with the Crawfords and with Nora. We won't hurt them none. But we'll get you, Max. Just because we can't carry knives or guns doesn't mean there aren't other ways. There'll be a stone fall on you or a timber hit you. Or maybe you'll stumble and fall into the fire. There are a lot of ways to do it and we plan to get you plenty."

"So," said Max, "you hate me. It makes me feel real bad."

"Two of my boys are dead," said Stony. "There are others who are crippled pretty bad."

"There wouldn't be nothing happen to them, Stony, if you didn't send them up against the fence."

He looked up and saw that hatred that lay in Stony Stafford's eyes, but washing across the hatred was a gleam of triumph.

"Good-by, dead man," said Stony.

He turned and stalked away.

Max sat quietly on the bench, remembering that gleam of triumph in Stony Stafford's eyes. And that meant he had been right. Stony had something up his sleeve and it could be nothing else but the bomb beneath the oak.

The day wore on. In the afternoon, Max went up to the house and into the kitchen. Nora fixed him a sandwich, grumbling.

"Why don't you go out and eat off the tables?" she demanded. "There is plenty there."

"Just as soon keep out of their way," said Max. "I have to fight them all the rest of the year. I don't see why I should pal up with them today."

"What about the bomb?"

"Shhh," said Max. "I know where it is."

Nora stood looking out the window. "They don't look like bad kids," she said. "Why can't we make a peace of some sort with them?"

Max grunted. "It's gone too far," he said.

Pollard had been right, he thought. It was out of hand. Neither side could back down now.

The police could have put a stop to it to start with, many years ago, if they had cracked down on the vandals instead of adopting a kids-will-be-kids attitude and shrugging it all off as just an aggravated case of quarreling in the neighborhood. The parents could have stopped it by paying some attention to the kids, by giving them something that would have stopped their running wild. The community could have put a stop to it by providing some sort of recreational facilities.

But no one had put a stop to it. No one had even tried.

And now it had grown to be a way of life and it must be fought out to the bitter end.

Max had no illusions as to who would be the winner.

Six o'clock came and the Punks started drifting off. By six thirty the last of them had gone. The musicians packed up their instruments and left. The caterers put away their dishes and scooped up the leftovers and the garbage and drove away. The carpenters came and got their lumber. Max went down to the gates and checked to see that they were locked.

"Not a bad day," said Pollard, speaking through the gates to Max. "They really aren't bad kids, if you'd just get to know them."

"I know them plenty now," said Max.

He watched the police car drive off, then turned back up the driveway.

—

He'd have to wait a while, he knew, until the dusk could grow a little deeper, before he started looking for the bomb. There would be watchers outside the fence. It would be just as well if they didn't know that he had found it. It might serve a better purpose if they could be left to wonder if it might have been a dud. For one thing, it would shake their confidence. For another, it would protect young Billy Warner. And while Max could feel no admiration for the kid, Billy had been useful in the past and still might be useful in the future.

He went down to the patio and crawled through the masking shrubbery until he was only a short distance from the oak.

He waited there, watching the area out beyond the fence. There was as yet no sign of life out there. But they would be out there watching. He was sure of that.

The dusk grew deeper and he knew he could wait no longer. Creeping cautiously, he made his way to the oak. Carefully, he brushed away the grass and leaves, face held close above the ground.

Halfway around the tree, he found it—the newly upturned earth, covered by a sprinkling of grass and leaves, and positioned neatly between two heavy roots.

He thrust his hand against the coolness of the dirt and his fingers touched the metal. Feeling it, he froze, then very slowly, very gently, pulled his hand away.

He sat back on his heels and drew in a measured breath.

The bomb was there, all right, just as he had suspected. But set above it, protecting it, was a contact bomb. Try to get the time bomb out and the contact bomb would be triggered off.

He brushed his hands together, wiping off the dirt.

There was, he knew, no way to get out the bombs. He had to let them stay. There was nothing he could do about it.

No wonder Stony's eyes had shown a gleam of triumph. For there was more involved than just a simple time bomb. This was a foolproof setup. There was nothing that could be done about it. If it had not been for the roots, Max thought, he might have taken a chance on working from one side and digging it all out. But with the heavy roots protecting it, that was impossible.

Stony might have known that he knew about it and then had gone ahead, working out a bomb set that no one would dare to mess around with.

It was exactly the sort of thing that would be up Stony's alley. More than likely, he was setting out there now, chuckling to himself.

Max stayed squatted, thinking.

He could string a line of mesh a few feet inside the tree, curving out to meet the auxiliary fence on either side. Juice could be fed into it and it might serve as a secondary defense. But it was not good insurance. A determined rush would carry it, for at best it would be flimsy. He'd not be able to install it as he should, working in the dark.

Or he could rig the tree with guywires to hold it off the fence when it came crashing down. And that, he told himself, might be the thing to do.

He got up and went around the house, heading for the basement to look up some wire that might serve to hold the tree.

He remembered, as he walked past the short wave set, that he should be sitting in on the regular evening check among the nearby strongholds. But it would have to wait tonight.

He walked on and then stopped suddenly as the thought came to him. He stood for a moment, undecided, then swung around and went back to the set.

He snapped on the power and turned it up.

He'd have to be careful what he said, he thought, for there was the chance the Punks might be monitoring the channels.

John Hennessey, custodian of the Curtis stronghold, came in a few seconds after Max had started calling.

"Something wrong, Max?"

"Nothing wrong, John. I was just wondering—do you remember telling me about those toys that you have?"

"Toys?"

"Yeah. The rattles."

He could hear the sound of Hennessey sucking in his breath. Finally he said: "Oh, those. Yes, I still have them."

"How many would you say?"

"A hundred, probably. Maybe more than that."

"Could I borrow them?"

"Sure," said Hennessey. "Would you want them right away?"

"If you could," said Max.

"Okay. You'll pick them up?"

"I'm a little busy."

"Watch for me," said Hennessey. "I'll box them up and be there in an hour."

"Thanks, John," said Max.

Was it wrong? he wondered. Was it too much of a chance?

Perhaps he didn't have the right to take any chance at all.

But you couldn't sit forever, simply fending off the Punks. For if that was all you did, they'd keep on coming back. But hit back hard at them and they might get a belly full. You might end it once for all. The trouble was, he thought, you could strike back so seldom. You could never act except defensively, for if you took any other kind of action, the police were down on you like a ton of bricks.

He licked his lips.

It was seldom one had a chance like this—a chance to strike back lustily and still be legally defensive.

IV

He got up quickly and walked to the rear of the basement, where he found the heavy flexible mesh. He carried out three rolls of it and a loop of heavy wire to hang it on. He'd have to use some trees to stretch out the wire. He really should use some padding to protect the trees against abrasion by the wire, but he didn't have the time.

Working swiftly, he strung the wire, hung the mesh upon it, pegged the bottom of the mesh tight against the ground, tied the ends of it in with the auxiliary fence.

He was waiting at the gates when the truck pulled up. He used the control box to open the gates and the truck came through. Hennessey got out.

"Outside is swarming with Punks," he told Max. "What is going on?"

"I got troubles," said Max.

Hennessey went around to the back of the truck and lowered the tail gate. Three large boxes, with mesh inserts, rested on the truck bed.

"They're in there?" asked Max.

Hennessey nodded. "I'll give you a hand with them."

Between them they lugged the boxes to the mesh curtain, rigged behind the oak.

"I left one place unpegged," said Max. "We can push the boxes under."

"I'll unlock the lids first," said Hennessey. "We can reach through with the pole and lift the lids if they are unlocked. Then use the pole again to tip the boxes over."

They slid the boxes underneath the curtain, one by one. Hennessey went back to the truck to get the pole. Max pegged down the gap.

"Can you give me a bit of light?" asked Hennessey. "I know the Punks are waiting out there. But probably they'd not notice just a squirt of it. They might think you were making just a regular inspection of the grounds."

Max flashed the light and Hennessey, working with the pole thrust through the mesh, flipped back the lids. Carefully, he tipped the boxes over. A dry slithering and frantic threshing sounds came out of the dark.

"They'll be nasty customers," said Hennessey. "They'll be stirred up and angry. They'll do a lot of circulating, trying to get settled for the night and that way, they'll get spread out. Most of them are big ones. Not many of the small kinds."

He put the pole over his shoulder and the two walked back to the truck.

Max put out his hand and the two men shook.

"Thanks a lot, John."

"Glad to do it, Max. Common cause, you know. Wish I could stay around . . ."

"You have a place of your own to watch."

They shook hands once again and Hennessey climbed into the cab.

"You better make it fast the first mile or so," said Max. "Our Punks may be laying for you. They might have recognized you."

"With the bumpers and the power I have," said Hennessey, "I can get through anything."

"And watch out for the cops. They'd raise hell if they knew we were helping back and forth."

"I'll keep an eye for them."

Max opened the gates and the truck backed out, straightened in the road and swiftly shot ahead.

Max listened until it was out of hearing, then checked to see that the gates were locked.

Back in the basement he threw the switch that fed current into the auxiliary fence—and now into the mesh as well.

He sighed with some contentment and climbed the stairs out to the yard.

—

A sudden flash of light lit up the grounds. He spun swiftly around, then cursed softly at himself. It was only a bird hitting the fence in flight. It happened all the time. He was getting jittery and there was no need of it. Everything was under control—reasonably so.

He climbed a piece of sloping ground and stood behind the oak. Staring into the darkness, it seemed to him that he could see shadowy forms out beyond the fence.

They were gathering out there and they would come swarming in as soon as the tree went down, smashing the fences. Undoubtedly they planned to use the tree as a bridge over the surging current that still would flow in the smashed-down fence.

Maybe it was taking too much of a chance, he thought. Maybe he should have used the guy-wires on the tree. That way there would have been no chance at all. But, likewise, there would have been no opportunity.

They might get through, he thought, but he'd almost bet against it.

He stood there, listening to the angry rustling of a hundred rattlesnakes, touchy and confused, in the area beyond the mesh.

The sound was a most satisfying thing.

He moved away, to be out of the line of blast when the bomb exploded, and waited for the day of truce to end.

UNSILENT SPRING

Clifford D. Simak and Richard S. Simak

Originally published in 1976 in the anthology Stellar Science Fiction Stories 2, *which was edited by Judy-Lynn del Rey, this is one of only two published stories in which Clifford Simak worked with a coauthor. This time, his coauthor was his son, a chemist who at one time worked for the U.S. government. The title of the story is, of course, a reference to* Silent Spring, *Rachel Carson's well-known book that controversially warned about environmental pollution and disinformation campaigns allegedly spread by certain industries, and ultimately led to the banning of the pesticide known as DDT (although Carson never actually called for that action), and the creation of the U.S. Environmental Protection Agency.*

—dww

1

Robert Abbott was a well-known man, so Dr. Arthur Benton had saved two hours for him in the middle of an afternoon of an ordinarily busy day. When Abbott had phoned ten days before, he had insisted that his visit was important.

Benton, watching the clock as the hour approached and trying to hurry Abby Clawson, who regarded a visit to a doctor's office as a social occasion, wondered once again what could be so important as to bring Abbott to this little Pennsylvania town. Abbott was a medical writer with two best sellers to his credit, one a book on cancer and the other an expose of faddy dieting. The doctors he consulted were important people, eminent medical researchers or lofty specialists; and Benton knew, with a twinge of honest envy, he was neither eminent nor lofty. He was just an old fuddy-duddy country doctor—a pusher of pills, a dispenser of liniments and salves, a setter of broken legs and arms, a wrapper-on of bandages, a deliverer of babies—who never had written a learned paper, conducted a research program, or been involved in medical studies, and who never would. He had not, in more than thirty years, done a single thing or uttered a single word that could be of the slightest interest to a man like Robert Abbott.

He had been wondering ever since the phone call why in the world Abbott should want to talk with him; and over the past few days he had evolved an elaborate theory that there were two Dr. Arthur Bentons and Abbott had confused him with the other Benton. He had been so haunted by the idea that he had looked through a medical directory in search of the other Arthur Benton. Although he had not found him, the idea still clung to his mind, for it seemed the only explanation.

He found himself glad that the hour of Abbott's visit had arrived, for once he knew what it was all about—if indeed Abbott really wanted *him*—he could quit his worrying and get down to business. The worry and the wonderment, he knew, had interfered with business—like that matter of Ted Brown's symptoms that had shouted diabetes but had turned out finally not to be diabetes. That had been damned embarrassing, even though Ted, an old and valued friend, had been nice about it. Nice, perhaps, because he was so relieved he was not diabetic.

That was the trouble, he told himself, sitting behind his desk and listening with only half an ear to Abby's departing chatter: all his patients were old and valued friends. He could no longer be objective; he bled for all of them. They came in, sick to death, and looked at him with trusting eyes because they knew in their secret hearts that good old Doc could help them. And when he couldn't help them, when there was no one on God's green earth who could help them, they died, forgiving him with the trust still in their eyes. That was the hell of family practice, that was the torture of being a country doctor in a little town—holding the trust of people who had no reason to trust you.

"I'll be coming in again," Abby said. "I been coming here for years and you always help me. I tell all my friends that I am lucky in my doctor."

"That's kind of you to say."

If they were all like Abby, it wouldn't be so bad. For with her, there was nothing wrong at all. She was a tough old woman who would outlive them all. The only thing wrong with her was a tendency to secrete an enormous amount of ear wax which required occasional irrigation. But the evident fact of sound, good health did not in the least deter the imaginary ills which brought her regularly to the office.

Rising to open the door for her, Benton wondered what she got from her regular visits, and thought he knew: fuel for conversation with her friends at the bridge table or with her neighbors across the backyard fence.

"Now you take care of yourself," he told her, putting into his voice a medical concern for which there was no need.

"I always do," she chirped in her bird-like old woman's voice. "If there's anything wrong, I'll come straight to you."

"Doctor," said Nurse Amy, hastening to guide Abby out, "Mr. Abbott has been waiting for you."

"Please send him in," said Benton.

Abbott was younger than Benton had expected him to be and not half as handsome. He was, in fact, a rather ugly-looking man—which explained, Benton thought, why the dust jackets of his books had not flaunted his photograph.

"I've looked forward to meeting you," Benton said, "and I don't mind telling you I've done some wondering at what brought you here. Surely there are other men."

"Very few," said Abbott, "like Dr. Arthur Benton. Surely you are aware that you are one of a dying breed. Not many medical men today are willing to devote their lives to a small community such as this."

"I've not regretted it," Benton replied. "The folks are good to me."

He waved Abbott to a chair and pulled another for himself from against the wall, not going back behind his desk.

"When I phoned you," Abbott said, "I couldn't very well explain. This is something that calls for face-to-face talk. Over the phone what I have to say would have made no sense at all. And I'm anxious that you understand what I am getting at because I'll be seeking your cooperation."

"Certainly. If I can help, I will."

"I came here for several reasons," Abbott explained. "You're in family practice and must work with a broad spectrum of the population. You must deal with a variety of illnesses and disabilities, unlike the specialist, who sees only certain cases and usually only those patients who can afford his fees. One other matter—at one time you were in epidemiology. And then there is a matter of geography, as well."

Benton smiled. "You have done a good workup on me. For several years, early on, I was an epidemiologist with the National Health people. But I came to realize the field was all too theoretical for me. I wanted to work with individuals."

"You came to the right place to do it," said Abbott.

"What's this business about geography?" Benton asked. "What's geography got to do with it?"

"I'm trying to track down an epidemic," Abbott said. "There may be a lot of factors involved."

"You can't be serious. There's no epidemic here or anywhere else I know of. Not even in India or the underdeveloped countries. Hunger, of course, but . . ."

"I'm fresh from months of burrowing through statistics," said Abbott, "and I can assure you there is an epidemic. A hidden epidemic. You've seen it yourself. I am sure you have. But it's been coming on so gradually and so undramatically that it has made no impression on you. A lot of little things that slipped by unnoticed. More people gaining weight—in some cases, very rapidly. That, by the way, may explain some of the faddish diets that are popping up. Wide variance in blood sugar levels—"

"Wait a minute," said Benton. "I had a patient just last week, and would have sworn he had diabetes."

Abbott nodded. "That's part of what I'm talking about. If you go back in your records, you'll probably find similar instances, perhaps not so dramatic as to suggest diabetes. But you'll find minor symptoms. I can tell you what else you'll find: More people feeling groggy, irritable, looking bleary-eyed. An increase in obesity. A lot of complaints about sore and aching muscles. People not feeling well—nothing specifically wrong with them, nothing you can put your finger on, but just not feeling well. A lot of people with no pep, a general tiredness, a loss of interest. Fifty years ago, you would have been prescribing tonic or sulfur and molasses to clear up the blood—thinning out the blood, I believe, was how they put it."

"Well, I don't know . . . the symptoms somehow sound familiar. But an epidemic?"

"If you'd seen the statistics I have seen," Abbott said, "you'd agree it's an epidemic. It's happening all over the country, perhaps all over the world."

"Okay, granting you are right—which I don't—why did you come here? You said you wanted my cooperation. How could I possibly help?"

"By keeping your eyes open. By thinking about what I've just told you. You're not the only one I'm seeing. I am talking to a number of other doctors, most of them in family practice. I will be asking them to do the same thing as I am asking you—observe, think about it, perhaps pick up a clue here and there."

"But why us? There are specialists."

"Look, Doctor," said Abbott, "how many people go to a specialist because they're feeling all beat out or have aching muscles or for most of the other things we have been talking about?"

"Not many, I would suppose."

"That's right. But they come running to good old Doc, belly-aching because they aren't up to par, figuring he'll pull a miracle out of his hat and fix them up."

"How about the disease-prevention people in Atlanta?" Benton asked.

"That's where I got some of my statistics," Abbott told him. "Some of the people there agree with me that there may be an epidemic, although I don't think any of them take it too seriously. Most of them think I'm trying to cook up another sensational book. Not that any of my books were sensational, but there are some doctors who think they are. The trouble with Atlanta is that they deal solely with data. What this job takes is field work. I need people like you, aware of the situation, looking at their patients and asking themselves questions, trying to see patterns. Not spending a lot of time at it, of course, for none of you will have the time, but keeping the problem there in the back of the mind. What I should like some months from now, if you are willing, are your impressions. Maybe then, with some input from a number of family doctors who see a lot of people representing a broad socio-economic range, it will be possible to pull together some sort of general picture of what is happening."

"I am afraid," said Benton, "that you contacted me because of my work in epidemiology. It is only fair to tell you I've forgotten most of what I ever knew in that particular field."

"Well, if it doesn't help, it certainly won't hurt. I might have come here anyhow. You may remember I said something about geography. Geography often is an epidemiological factor. Here you are located in a broad, fertile valley, while on either side of the valley lie rugged hills, an almost primitive area. I would assume that you have patients among both hill and valley people."

"That is true," Benton answered. "I guess most of the hill people figure I'm their doctor, although I don't see them often Either they don't get sick as often as the valley people, or when they do they manage to tough it out. Some of them may have an ingrained reluctance to submit to doctoring. A lot of them, I suspect, use folk medicine, old-time recipes handed down through the years. That is not to say there is anything wrong with that. Much as we may hate to admit it, some of those old cures work."

"Geography may have nothing to do with it," said Abbott, "but it's a factor we can't cancel out until we've had a look at it."

"And there's a possibility you are wrong. There may be nothing to look for."

Abbott shook his head. "I don't think so. Doctor, you *will* go along with me? You'll walk that extra mile?"

"Yes, of course," said Benton. "I'll keep it all in mind. I'll be seeing you again, you said, or hearing from you, a few months from now."

"I can't tell you exactly when. I have a lot of ground to cover. But I promise I'll be in touch again."

They talked a while longer, then Abbott left.

Benton followed him out to his car, thinking as he walked along with him that it had been a long time since he had met a man he liked so instinctively. Here was a man whose name in the last few years had become a household word and, yet, there was about him none of the self-importance that so many eminent men wore as a cloak wrapped about themselves. He found himself looking forward to that day, some months from now, when they would be in touch again. Here was a sincere man you did not brush off automatically, even if his ideas seemed a bit offbeat. Thinking of it, Benton had to admit that Abbott's idea did seem a bit offbeat.

His first patient after Abbott left was Helen Anderson.

Helen and Herb Anderson were old family friends, had been for many years. Herb owned a men's ready-to-wear store; he was one of the community's most successful businessmen. Helen was president of the Flower and Garden Club and, for years, her roses had been blue ribbon winners at the State Fair.

She showed him her right hand. The skin across the knuckles was rough and red. When he rubbed his thumb over it, it felt dry and scaly.

"Looks like eczema," he said. "We'll try some ointment on it."

"I worked in the garden after I noticed it," she said. "I don't suppose that did it any good."

"Probably no harm, either. How's the garden doing?"

"Couldn't be better. You should see my peas, and I am trying a new kind of tomato. You and Harriet drop over some evening and have a look at it. It's been a long time since the four of us have gotten together."

"That's part of being a doctor," Benton said. "You think you have an evening and then something happens. You never can be sure."

"You work too hard."

"All of us do," he told her. "We get involved. What we do assumes a great importance. Your garden, for example."

She said, seriously, "My garden goes me a lot of good. As you know, I'm not a fancy gardener. I'm a dirt gardener. I don't wear gloves. I get down in there with my hands. I like the feel of soil. It's so warm and it has such a nice texture. It has the feel of life to it. It plays hell with my hands, of course; but there's something so elemental in it that I can't resist. Herb, of course, thinks that I'm crazy."

Benton chuckled. "Herb's no gardener."

"He pokes gentle fun at me. He's a golfer at heart. But I don't make fun of his golf. I don't think it's fair."

"How's his golf this year? I remember he was bragging last year that he had improved."

Helen Anderson frowned. "He isn't playing as much this year. Not as much as he used to."

"Maybe he's busy. This is a bad year for business. Inflation and tight money and—"

"No, it isn't that," she said. "Doc, I'm worried about Herb. He seems to be tired all the time. He has to be really tired not to play golf. Does a lot of eating between meals. He's gaining weight. Grumpy, too. Some days he's so grumpy I'm glad to see him go to work. I've told him to come and see you."

"I wouldn't worry about him," said Benton. "Maybe he's working too hard. Why don't you try to get him to take a couple of weeks off and the two of you go on vacation? A rest would do him good."

"It's more than just tiredness," she continued. "I am sure of that. He's tired, of course, but there's something more than that. Doc, won't you talk with him?"

"I can't go out soliciting business. You know that."

"But as a friend . . ."

"I can tell him you're worried about him. I can lean on him a little."

"If you would," she suggested.

"Sure I will," said Benton. "But don't you go worrying yourself sick. It's probably nothing."

He wrote her a prescription and she left, extracting a promise he'd drop by soon to have a look at the garden.

The next patient was Ezra Pike. Ezra was a farmer south of town, seventy years old, still working his farm with only occasional help.

He had hand trouble, too. He had a nasty gash across the knuckles.

"The baler broke down," he explained, "and I was fixing it. The wrench slipped."

"We'll get that hand cleaned up," Benton said. "In a day or two it'll be like new. Don't see you often, Ezra. You *or* Mrs. Pike. I'd starve to death if everyone was like the two of you."

"Never did get sick much. Neither one of us. The boys, neither. We are a healthy family."

"How are the boys these days? I haven't seen them for ages."

"Dave, he's down in Pittsburgh. Working in a bank. Investments. Ernie is a teacher over in Ohio. School's out now, and he's running a boy's camp up in Michigan. We're real proud of our boys, both of them."

"How are the crops?" Benton asked.

"Good enough," said Pike. "Some trouble with bugs. Never used to have that kind of trouble, but it's different now. No DDT, you know. They up and banned the stuff. Was poisoning everything, they said. Maybe so, but it made farming easier."

Benton finished with the bandaging. "There, that's it," he said. "Keep watch of that hand. If it hurts a lot or gets red and puffy, come in to see me."

Pike got spryly from the chair. "Got a good crop of pheasants waiting for you. Soon as the season opens, we'll be looking for you."

"I'll be out," said Benton. "Always have, you know. It's been a long time, Ezra, I've been hunting on your land."

"You're welcome any time," Pike said. "But there ain't no need to tell you. I take it that you know."

Nurse Amy appeared as soon as Pike had left. "Mrs. Lewis is here," she said. "She has Danny with her. Someone bounced a rock off him. She is frothing mad."

Danny, who by all odds could be classified as the meanest kid in town, had a goose egg on his head. The rock had broken the skin and there was some blood, but an X-ray showed no fracture.

"Just wait," his mother raged, "until I get my hands on the kid who threw that rock. Here Danny was doing nothing, just walking down the street . . ."

She went on and on, but Benton got her quieted down and the two of them finally left.

After that came Mary Hansen, with her arthritis; Ben Lindsay, in for a post-coronary check; Betty Davidson, with a sore throat;

Joe Adams, with a lame back; Jenny Duncan, who was going to have twins and was twittery about it.

The last patient of the day was Burt Curtis, an insurance man.

"Goddamn it, Doc," he said, "I feel all beat out. Sure, a man expects to be tired after a long day's work, but I get tired in the middle of the morning. By ten o'clock, I am all pooped out."

"It's sitting at that desk," said Benton, kidding him, "lifting all those heavy pencils."

"I know, I know. You don't have to rub it in. I've never done an honest day's work in all my life. Selling insurance isn't something you can classify as labor. The funny thing is that I feel as if I were building roads. Muscles get sore and achy."

"Hungry, too?" Benton asked.

"Funny you should say that. I'm hungry all the time. Keep stuffing my gut. A lot of snacking. Never used to do that. Three squares were all I needed."

"Even-tempered, I suppose."

"What the hell, Doc! I come in to tell you I get tired and you ask about my temper."

"Well, are you? Even-tempered, I mean."

"Hell, no. I'm all out of sorts. No patience. Let one little thing go wrong and I start storming. No way for a businessman to act. Keep on like that, and you get a reputation. Adele says I get harder to live with every day."

"How about your weight?"

"Seems to me I'm getting heavier." Curtis patted his gut. "Had to let out my belt one notch."

"We'll get you on the scales and see," said Benton. "I'll tell you what I'd like to do: run some tests. Nothing fancy or expensive. We could do them here."

"You got something in mind, Doc? Something wrong with me. Something really wrong."

Benton shook his head. "Nothing at all. But I can't even make a guess until I see some tests. Blood sugar. Things like that."

"If you say so, Doc," said Curtis.

"Don't worry about it, Burt. But when a man comes in and says he's all tired out and gaining weight and getting downright mean, I have to look into it. That's my job. That's how I make my living and keep my patients well."

"Nothing serious, then?"

"Probably nothing much. Just some little thing that once we know about it, we can get it straightened out. Now, about those tests. When can you come in?"

"Tuesday be all right? Monday I'll be busy."

"Tuesday is just fine," Benton said. "Now get over on those scales."

When Burt had gone, Benton walked out into the empty waiting room. "I guess that's it for the day," he said to Amy. "Why don't you go home?"

Back in his office, he sat down at his desk and began filling in Burt Curtis' record. Tiredness, intermittent and persistent hunger, gaining weight, sore muscles, irritability—all the symptoms Abbott had talked about that very afternoon. And then there was Herb Anderson as well. From what Helen had said, his condition seemed much the same as Burt's. Both of them and Ted Brown, too.

What the hell, he wondered, could be going on? Abbott had said "epidemic." But did three people in one little town add up to an epidemic? He knew, however, that once he had gone through his records, he would probably find others.

The office was quiet. Amy had left and he was quite alone.

From some distance off came the wild and frantic snarling of a racing motorcycle. Young Taylor, more than likely, he thought. Someday the damn fool kid would break his neck. Twice he's needed patching up, and if he kept on there'd likely come a day when patching up would be superfluous—although, Benton told himself, that was no concern of his, or should be no concern of his. But the terrible thing about it was that he found himself concerned.

He was, he realized, concerned with everyone, too concerned with everyone in this silly little town. By what mysterious process, he wondered, did a man through the years manage to take an entire town to heart, shift its burdens to his back? Did the same thing happen to other aging doctors in other little towns?

He pushed Burt's record to one side and laid the pen beside it.

He gazed about the room, shifting his glance from one object to another as if he were seeing them for the first time and trying to fix them in his memory. They had been there all the time, but for the first time he was noticing them, becoming acquainted with this environment in which he had lived and functioned through the years. Too busy, he thought, too busy and concerned to have ever looked at them before. The framed diploma, hung proudly on the wall so many years ago and now becoming fly-specked; the fading and worn carpeting (some day, by God, when he found the money, he'd have new carpeting put in!); the battered scales shoved against the wall; the sink and basin; the cabinet where he kept all the samples sent out by pharmaceutical houses to be given patients (and there were many of them) who could not afford prescription drugs. Not the kind of office, he thought, that a big-city doctor would have, but the kind *he* had—a combination of office, examination room, treatment room—the hallmark of the family doctor always strapped for funds, hesitant to send out bills that would embarrass patients he knew were short of cash, trying to treat people who should go to specialists but who could not afford their fees.

He was getting old, he told himself—not too old yet, but getting there. There were lines upon his face and gray showing in his hair. There would come a time, perhaps, when he would have to take in a younger doctor who, hopefully, could carry on the practice when he would have to retire. But he shrank from doing so. He was jealous, he knew, of his position as the town's one doctor, even though he knew it was most unlikely the town would accept anyone that he brought in. Not for a long, long time would they accept anyone but him. Patients would refuse to see the new man, waiting for Old Doc. It would take years before he could shift any appreciable percentage of his patient load.

Over in Spring Valley, Dr. Herman Smith had a son who was in internship and who soon would join his father. Slowly, over the years, young Doc Smith would phase out old Doc Smith, father followed by the son, and there would be no hassle. Oh, some hassle, surely, but none that would be noticed. That, Benton told himself, was the ideal method of succession. But he and Harriet had never had a son—only the one daughter. He had hoped, for a time, he recalled, that April might want to be a doctor. But that would have posed problems, too, for it would be unlikely the town would accept a woman doctor. The problem, however, had never arisen, for April, it turned out, had been big on music and there was no stopping her. Not that he had ever wanted to. If music was what she wanted, then it would be music. She was in Vienna now. Christ, these kids! he thought. The world belongs to them. Off to London, Paris, Vienna, and God knows where else, with no thought that it was extraordinary. In his youth, he recalled, it had been a big adventure to get a hundred miles from home. And, come to think of it, even now he seldom got more than a hundred miles from town. He stuck close to his work.

I'm provincial, he thought, and what was wrong with that? A man could not encompass the world. If he tried, he would lose too much. Friends and familiarity of place, the warm sense of belonging . . . Since he had come to this town, many things had happened to him—good things—with quaint little privileges established. Like old Ezra Pike and his annual crop of pheasants reserved for good old Doc and a few others in the town, and for no one else.

He sat in the office and tried to peel the years away, back to the time when he had first come here; but the years refused to peel and the diploma still was fly-specked and the scales still battered and he remained an aging man who carried the town upon his back.

The phone rang and he picked it up. It was Harriet.

"When are you coming home?" she asked. "I have a leg of lamb and it will be ruined if you don't get here fairly soon."

"Right away," he said.

2

The next day was Saturday and office hours were from eight till noon. But, as was usually the case, the last patient was not gone until after one.

Once the waiting room was cleared and Amy had gone home, Benton got to work on the files. He went through them carefully, making notes as he went along. He didn't finish the work on Saturday, and came back Sunday morning.

Going back through ten years of records, he was able to isolate some trends. There had been, in those years, a substantial increase in the symptoms Abbott had outlined. The incidence of obesity had risen rapidly. In more instances that he had recalled, the high level of blood sugar had indicated diabetes, but further tests had inevitably failed to bear out his tentative diagnoses. There had been, increasingly, a spate of muscular soreness. There were an increasing number of patients who had complained of general malaise, with no apparent cause.

Most of the symptoms were found in townspeople. Among the farm families, only the members of one family, the Barrs, had experienced the symptoms. The Barrs, about three years before, had come from somewhere in Ohio, buying the farm of Abner Young, a recluse who finally had died of old age and general meanness. And not a single case with those symptoms showed up among the hill people.

Maybe, after all, Benton told himself, geography might be a factor in Abbott's epidemic—if there were an epidemic. But if some of the townspeople had the symptoms, why not all of them? If farmers were immune, as seemed to be the case, what about the Barrs? What was different about the Barrs? Recently arrived, of course, but what could that have to do with it? And what was so magic about the hills that in all the hill folk no symptom had turned up? Although, he reminded himself, he should not assign too much weight to the negative data from the hills. The people there, a hardy tribe, would not deign to visit a doctor for such minor reasons as being unaccountably tired or putting on some weight.

He pulled the sheets of notes together and, searching in his desk drawers, found some graph paper. The graphs, when he had them drawn, showed nothing more than he already knew; but they had a pretty look to them and he found himself imagining how they would look printed on the slick paper of a prestigious journal, illustrating a paper that might be entitled "The Epidemiology of Muscular Exhaustion" or "The Geographical Distribution of Obesity."

He went over the notes again, asking himself if he might not be looking at what amounted to medical constants—conditions persisting through the years, with only minor fluctuations from year to year. This did not seem to be the case. Ten years ago, there had been few of the symptoms—or at least few of his patients had shown up complaining of them. But, beginning seven or eight years ago, they had started to show up; and on the graph the curves showing their distribution over time rose sharply. There was no doubt the symptoms were a recent phenomenon. If this were so, there must be a cause, or perhaps several causes. He searched for a cause, but the few he could think of were too silly to consider.

Benton looked at his watch and saw it was after two o'clock. He had wasted most of the day and Harriet would be furious at his not showing up for lunch. Angrily, he shuffled the notes and graphs together and thrust them in a desk drawer.

He had wasted most of the weekend at it, and now he would wash his hands of the whole thing. Here was something that more properly belonged in a research center than in the office of a country doctor. His job was to keep his people well, not to tackle the problems of the world. After all, this was Abbott's baby and not his.

He wondered at the anger that he felt. It was not the wasted weekend, he was certain, for he had wasted many weekends. Rather, perhaps, it was anger at himself, at his own inadequacy at being able to recognize a problem, but be unable to do anything about it. It was no concern of his, he had insisted to himself. But now he had to admit, rather bitterly, that it was deeply important to him. Anything that affected the health and wellbeing of the town was his concern by automatic definition. He sat at the desk, his hands placed out before him, palms down on the wood. His *concern*, he thought. Most certainly. But nothing that for a time he should wrestle with. He had a job and that job came first. In the chinks of time left over, he could do some thinking on the problem. Perhaps by just letting it lie inside his mind an answer might be hatched, or at least the beginning of an answer. The thing to do, he decided, was forget it and give his subconscious a chance to work on it.

3

He tried to forget it, but over the weeks it nagged at him. Time and time again, he went back to the notes and graphs to convince himself that he was not imagining the evidence found in his records. Could it be, he wondered, a circumstance that prevailed only in this place? He wondered what the other physicians

Abbott had talked with were doing about it—if they were doing anything; if, in fact, they had even looked at their records; and if they had, what they might have found . . .

He spent hours going back through old issues of *The Journal of the American Medical Association* and other journals, digging into the dusty stacks down in the basement, where they were stored. He could easily have missed something bearing on the matter in the medical magazines, for up till now he had not been too conscientious in his reading of them. A man, he told himself—making excuses for himself—had so little time to read; and there was so damn much to read, so many medical eager beavers intent on making points that there was a continuous flood of papers and reports.

But he found nothing. Could it be possible, he wondered, that despite Abbott's work he, Benton, might be the only man who knew about the condition that he had come to characterize as the exhaustion syndrome?

A disease? he wondered. But he shied away from that. It was too selective to be a disease, its parameters too narrow. A metabolic disorder, more than likely. But for a metabolic disorder to come about, there must be an underlying cause.

Burt Curtis, it turned out, was no more diabetic than Ted Brown had been. His blood sugar was haywire, but he was not diabetic. After Helen had nagged at him for a time, Herb Anderson came in and his case was almost identical with Burt's and Ted's. An insurance salesman, a merchant, and a down-at-the-heels house painter—what in the name of God, he asked himself, could those three have in common? And then there was the Barr family! The Barr family bothered him a lot.

There were others now as well, not such classic examples as Burt and Ted and Herb; but each of them showed some of the symptoms of the exhaustion syndrome.

"You have to put it out of your mind," Harriet said one day at the breakfast table. "It's the 'good old Doc' complex again. You have allowed it to drive you all your life and here it's driving you again. You can't go on like this. You have other things to do, you have a full-time job. If this Abbott person had not shown up, you would not have noticed it."

He agreed with her. "No, I don't suppose I would have. Even if I had, I would not have paid too much attention to it. But when he talked to me, he made an uncommon lot of sense. As you've heard me say, I suppose far too often, medicine is not an exact science. There's an awful lot of it a man can't understand. A lot of problems he can't begin to understand."

"You've encountered those kind of problems before," Harriet pointed out, just a shade too sharply. "And you have always said—I have heard you say it often—that someday a researcher will come up with an answer. You didn't spend days fretting over those problems. Why can't you stop this fretting now?"

"Because, damn it," he told her, "here it is, right underneath my nose! There's Ted and Herb and Burt, and a lot of others— more of them every day. There is nothing I can do about it. It's nothing that I recognize: I'm completely in the dark. I'm tied hand and foot and I don't like the feeling."

"The trouble is, you are feeling guilty. You've got to cut that out."

"All right," he said. "I will cut it out."

But he didn't.

He did what, at the time, seemed rather silly things. He stopped at the Fanny Farmer candy shop and learned that in the last three years sales had increased by almost twenty-five percent. He phoned the two small factories at the edge of town and was told that sick leave and absenteeism had risen by almost ten percent in the last few months. At the drug store, he talked with his old friend the pharmacist, who told him that over-the-counter sales of analgesics were higher than at any time within memory.

That afternoon he phoned Dr. Herman Smith at Spring Valley. "You have a minute to talk with a competitor?" he asked.

Smith snorted. "You're no competition," he said. "We got that worked out years ago, remember? You work your side of the street and I work mine. We have our territories all laid out and fenced, and we have a gentleman's agreement to do no trespassing. But I won't let you in on any of my trade secrets, if that's what you're calling about."

"Nothing like that," said Benton. "I've been noticing some strange things. I've been wondering if you are noticing them as well."

Smith's voice became serious. "You sound worried, Art."

"Not worried. Puzzled, that's all." He went ahead and told Smith what he had been noticing, making no mention of Abbott.

"You think it's important?"

"I don't know about its importance, but it's a funny business. There seems to be no reason for it, no underlying cause. I've been wondering if it's only happening here or if—"

"If you want me to, I could have a look at my records."

"If you would," Benton said.

"No sweat. I'll let you know in a week or so. I'll even draw you up some graphs to match with yours. If I find anything, that is."

Dr. Smith didn't take his week. In four days' time there was a fat envelope. Opening it, Benton found not only the graphs, but statistical tables and a sheet of Xeroxed notes.

Benton had no need to take his own graphs out of the desk; he knew them now by heart. Staring at Smith's graphs laid out on the desk top, he knew immediately they were almost identical with his own.

He sat down weakly in his chair, grasping the arms so tightly that his fingers ached.

"I was right," he told himself. "God help us, I was right!"

4

When bird season opened, Benton drove out to the Ezra Pike farm for an afternoon of pheasant shooting, jotting down a mental note that before the day was over he would ask about the Barrs, who were Pike's next-door neighbors. But he never got around to it.

Pike had a lot to show him: the pen of shoats that were becoming sleek and plump for the late-fall market; the high-quality wheat from the little patch he had grown as a hobby and which he was intending to take in to Millville to an old-time water mill to be ground into flour by a genial, half-mad hermit who was unconvinced that he lived in the twentieth century; the ritual sampling of some cider Pike had run off, using the fruit from an ancient, withered tree, the only one remaining in the country that bore the famed snow apples of another day. There was politics to talk about and the rising prices of food; the gasoline-wasting propensities of the anti-pollution equipment which had been installed on cars; the latest, rather mild scandal of the neighborhood, involving a boy barely out of his teens and a widow who was old enough to be the lad's grandmother. They shot some pheasants, ate fresh apple pie—washing it down with milk—and talked of many things, the time passing pleasantly.

It was not until he was halfway home that Benton remembered he had not asked about the Barrs.

The following Saturday he skipped his morning office hours, loaded his gun into the car trunk, and took off for the hills, ostensibly to shoot quail. He made the quail trip several times each autumn, but when he thought about it he realized that it was not the quail he was looking for now, but the time that he could spend with the hill people.

If one had asked them what they were, they would have said that they were farmers; but precious few of them did any

actual farming. Their acreages mostly stood on end, with only
here and there a creek bottom or a hillside bench that was level
enough for a plow to turn the soil. They planted some corn to
fatten up the scrawny hogs that mostly ranged the woods for
acorns, a field of potatoes at times larger than the corn patch,
and a slightly smaller garden. They might at times plant other
crops as well, but mostly it was corn, potatoes, and the plants
in the garden. The women canned a lot of vegetables, for there
was no electricity to freeze them, and even if there had been, few
of the hill people could have scraped together the money for a
freezer. There were strawberry beds for eating and for canning
as well as wild fruits such as blackberries and raspberries. By
the end of autumn, the cellars of the hill farm homes were well
stocked with canned vegetables and fruits, with potatoes and
"winter keeper" apples from the scraggly trees of their haphaz-
ard orchards.

As he drove, Benton fell to wondering, as he had many times
before, just how the hill folk managed to live from year to year.
Each family ordinarily had a cow or two, as well as a few hogs and
a bedraggled flock of chickens. Most of the hogs were butchered
for meat rather than sold on market, and many of the farms had
smokehouses out in back in which hams and bacon were cured.
Game such as rabbits, squirrels, coons, and an occasional deer—
usually taken in a fine disregard of game laws—helped round out
their diet. Fish from the many streams, as well as ruffed grouse
and quail, were often on the table. Somehow or other they managed to eat rather well all the year round.

But they had little money. They were largely self-sufficient
and they had to be, raising and gathering most of their food. They
bought little at the grocery store: flour, sugar, coffee, salt . . . Living that way, Benton told himself, they didn't need much money.
What little they had they earned at odd jobs here and there. A
few of them worked at small industrial plants in the valley, but
not very many of them. He suspected that few had any taste for

such work. Occasionally some of them peddled firewood to the townspeople.

But, despite all the hardships which they probably did not regard as such, they were a relatively happy, reliable, proud, and independent people, filled with dignity and inborn courtesy.

Benton had a good day, dropping in at the homes of several families that he knew. He did a little hunting, but not a great deal, getting, in all, three quail. But he did a lot of talking, sitting on the steps of the sagging verandahs of houses so old that moss grew upon the clapboard and the brick—houses there so long that they were accepted even by the environment in which they sat as a part of that environment—or as he roosted on a split-rail fence that might have been erected a hundred years before or stood in the coolness of a springhouse after he had drunk a dipper full of ice-cold buttermilk.

They talked of many things, he and these scarecrow men with carefully sewn patches on their pants, their hair grown long not because long hair was in style but because no one in the family had as yet gotten around to cutting it. They talked of the weather, which bore heavily on their minds and was worthy of lengthy conversation; of someone having seen a panther, although wildlife biologists were agreed there had been no panthers in these hills for almost forty years; of times long gone and tales told by forebears now only dimly remembered.

In the course of these conversations Benton always got around to mentioning the exhaustion syndrome—although he did not use that term—explaining how patients for no apparent reason were gaining weight, were feeling all tired out in the middle of the morning, and had a seemingly never-satisfied longing for sweets. He didn't know what caused it, he told them; and he was somewhat upset about it and was wondering if there might be any such condition in the neighborhood.

They looked at him with ill-concealed laughter in their eyes and said, no, unless that was what might be wrong with Grandpa

Wilson or Gabby Whiteside or any one of another dozen people. They regaled him with stories of fabulously lazy men who, all their lives, had worked much harder to avoid work than the work would have been itself. But their tales all had the ring of folklore to them, so Benton accepted them as such. Most of the shiftless men who peopled the stories, he realized, did not exist and never had existed.

He came home convinced that no signs of Abbott's epidemic existed in the hills.

It could be body chemistry, he told himself—something in the hills, the way of life, the things they ate, the conveniences they could not afford—that made all the difference. Although maybe, he admitted, he had that turned around; not something that kept the syndrome from the hills, but something that afflicted the townspeople with the syndrome.

Nonetheless, Benton thought, this business of body chemistry might be the best bet yet. Figure what the townspeople had or did not have, did or did not do, and the answer *might* be there. But, he warned himself, the elusive factor that he sought must be unique to town life.

That evening he went to the office, pleading paperwork, and wrestled with himself. Sitting at the desk, doing nothing except sitting at the desk, with a single gooseneck lamp making a splash of light upon the desk top, he tried to think it through.

He had tried to forget all the silly business, but he could not forget it. Perhaps he was unable to forget it because it was not a silly business, because he knew all the time, deep down within that hidden core of medical awareness, that it was a greater threat than he had allowed himself to believe—and knew as well that if he were to keep faith with his community he must not go on ignoring it, or attempting to ignore it. Although, he asked himself, how, for my own peace of mind, can I do other than ignore it? I do not have the training . . . He was not a research man. For too long he had been a plodding country doctor, exerting all his energy and knowledge to fight disease and death in this tiny corner of the land. He had no tools for research; he did not have the brain for research; he did not have the time—and, he thought, he might as well admit it, he did not have the devoted objectivity and the narrowness of purpose to do a research job.

But, ill-equipped as he might be, he owed it to the town to have a go at it at least. That was the hell of it—he owed it to the town! All his life he had owed everything he was and ever hoped to be to the people of this little town in payment for the trust that they had in him. He had placed them in his debt, but they had placed him in even greater debt. Just walking in and talking with him cured half of what was wrong with them, and how did a man respond to a faith like that? They thought he had all the answers, so he could not tell them how few answers he did have. Their faith in his infallibility often was the one last resort they had going for them. They put their faith and trust in him, and in doing that they made him feel guilty when he was forced, through inadequacy, to betray that faith and trust. How, he wondered, was a man trapped? How had he allowed himself to be trapped into such a situation?

He dug into the desk drawer and brought out his notes and those of Dr. Smith. Carefully, he went through them, hoping that further study might give him a clue. But there seemed none.

Hormones? he wondered. Some sort of hormonal imbalance? If that were true, however, there would have to be something to have brought about such an imbalance. This was not the first time he had thought of hormones, for an imbalance of insulin would explain the diabetic symptoms; but the hell of it, he reminded himself, was that it had not been diabetes. Glucogen, perhaps? But the trouble there was that no one knew for certain what glucogen really did, although it was suspected that by elevating the glucose blood level it might kill appetite. The hypothalamus? he asked himself. Or the steroid hormones? No, it could be none of these.

Personality disturbances? Fine as far as obesity and irritability might be concerned, but certainly not for any of the other symptoms. And, anyhow, personality disturbances were slimy things to work with and psychiatric training was required to cope with them.

Enzymes? Vitamins? Trace elements?

He was going at it wrong, Benton told himself. He was going at it backward. The way to work out the syndrome was to find a common factor that might be the cause and then try to cipher out what effect the factor had. Although, still thinking of it backward, the enzymes might hold more promise than any of the others. Enzymes basically were catalysts that sped up biochemical reactions. Not that biochemical reactions could not occur without the enzymatic catalytic action, but the reactions would be so slow that the body could not function.

He sat quietly and ran through his mind what he could recall about enzymes. He was surprised to find that after all the years he had scarcely thought of enzymes, he could remember so much about them. The reason that he could recall so much was that instead of thinking directly about enzymes he found himself recalling Professor Walter Cox—old Stony Cox, eccentric and beloved in a rather ragged way—who had paced up and down when he lectured, bobbing like a ball, his head hunched forward between skinny lifted shoulders, punching the air with one clenched fist to emphasize his words. He wondered where Stony Cox might be this night. More than likely dead, he thought, for that had been more than thirty years ago and he had been an old man then.

Thirty years and all, the words came clearly to mind. "The enzymes," Cox had said, jabbing wildly at the air, "are made up of apoenzymes and coenzymes, the two forming a loose bond to make up an enzyme. The coenzyme normally is a vitamin plus another organic molecule, bonded together. And now, gentlemen, today I ask that you focus your attention on a single coenzyme, the coenzyme A, which is directly involved in two biochemical cycles, the fatty-acid cycle and the citric-acid cycle . . ."

Benton sat limp in his chair, shaken by what his mind had conjured up, dredging out of a past that measured more than thirty years an instant of almost complete recall—not of the man alone but of the words he had spoken, the slanted shine of sunlight through the slatted blinds, the smell of chalk dust in the air—hearing the words perhaps more distinctly than he had heard them at the time.

Was it a sign? he wondered. Had his subconscious mind reached back and laid a bony finger on this isolated incident to tell him what his conscious reasoning could not tell him?

The phone rang and it was not until the third ring that he realized what it was. Almost as if in a dream, he reached out for it.

"Hello," he said. "Dr. Benton here."

"Are you all right?" Harriet asked.

"Sure, I am all right."

"Do you know what time it is?"

"No. No, I hadn't noticed."

"It's two o'clock," Harriet said. "I became concerned about you."

"I'm sorry, dear," he said. "I'll be right home."

5

Late in the fall, Ezra Pike stopped by the office, not because he was sick, but because he had butchered one of his hogs and was bringing Benton a sack of sausages, Mrs. Pike being known throughout the valley as an expert sausage maker. Regularly, each fall at butchering time, Pike came by with a sack of sausages for old Doc.

It was one of the regional eccentricities that Benton had finally become accustomed to, although it had taken him a while. Over the course of any year, a lot of people would come by with something for old Doc—a bag of black walnuts, a basket of tomatoes, a clutch of fancy baking potatoes, a comb of honey fresh from the hive—free-will offerings that Benton had learned to accept with considerable grace.

Although patients were waiting, Benton had Pike step into his office and settled down for a chat with him. Toward the end of their talk he asked the question he had wanted to ask.

"What do you know about the Barr family?"

"You mean the ones that bought Abner Young's place?"

"Those are the ones," said Benton.

"Not really much," Pike answered. "They come from Ohio, I think. Were farmers there. Don't know why they moved here. I know Barr pretty well and have talked with him, but he never told me and I never asked. Maybe because they got Abner's place dirt cheap. When Abner died, the farm went to some shirttail relatives out in California—nephews, I gather. They didn't want to be bothered with it. They never came for the funeral or to settle the estate. They told Abner's lawyer to sell it for what he could get as soon as he could, and he offered it cheap."

"So that was the way of it. I never really got to know Abner. He was in a couple of times. A crusty old customer. Once he had a foot infection. Stepped on a nail, the way I remember it. The other time he was on the verge of pneumonia. I tried to get him to let me send him to a hospital, but he wouldn't do it. Wound up that I gave him some drugs and he went home and managed to live through it. Didn't see him after that, didn't really hear much about him until I heard he died. Found dead by one of the neighbors, wasn't he? Probably he got sick and figured he wanted no more to do with me. Afraid I might send him to a hospital. Likely neither myself nor a hospital could have helped him much. He was one of those characters who fought a doctor tooth and nail."

Pike chuckled, remembering his neighbor. "I know people said he was a mean man, and in some ways I suppose he was. Ran people off his place with a shotgun. The pheasants were knee-deep in his fields and he would allow no hunting. Wouldn't even shoot them himself. Never had much to do with his neighbors. Kept to himself. He'd gone sour on humanity. But he loved other things. He let his fence rows grow up to brush so that rabbits and woodchucks and birds would have a place to live. He always fed the birds in winter, and if English sparrows or blue jays came to feed he never tried to drive them off, or was put out about it the way a lot of people are. Said *they* got hungry, too."

"You sound as if you knew him fairly well, Ezra."

"Oh," said Pike, "we had our differences. He was a hard man to get along with. Unreasonable and had a bad temper. Had some funny ideas, too. He was an organic farmer. Never put a pound of commercial fertilizer on his land, refused to use pesticides. Said they were poison. Long before that lady wrote her book about a 'silent spring,' he said that they were poison."

Benton sat straight up. "You mean he never used any pesticides? No DDT at all?"

"That's what I mean," said Pike. "And the funny thing about it was that he grew as good a crop as any of the rest of us—that is, as long as he grew any crops. As he grew older, he farmed less and less. A good part of his land was idle. But what little he farmed, he farmed well. Abner was a first-class farmer."

Pike stayed a while longer and they talked of other things, but Benton scarcely heard him. His mind was buzzing with what Pike had said about Abner Young never using pesticides.

DDT! Benton thought. For the love of Christ, could it be DDT?

Here was the Barr family, farmers out of Ohio, where they probably had used DDT, then moving to a farm where not a grain of the chemical ever had been used. And among all the farmers in the valley, they were the only ones who had suffered from the exhaustion syndrome. Could it be that they had gotten used to DDT or something else in the pesticides, and now were sick because of the lack of it?

The other farmers were okay, he figured, because there still were traces of DDT in their soil, and by working in the soil they were picking up enough of it not to yet experience any ill effects from the lack of it.

And the folks out in the hills? That was simple enough, he told himself. They had never been exposed to it, had never developed whatever need for it the others had acquired. They had never been exposed to it because they were so bone poor they could not afford to buy it. Raising their own food, consuming what they grew, never eating commercially canned foods or buying foods that might have been grown on DDT-drenched land, they had never been exposed.

The next day was Saturday, and in the afternoon, after office hours were over, Benton went through his files once again and found what he had expected to find: that, with only two exceptions, townspeople who had gardens and who actually worked in them had never mentioned any of the symptoms of the exhaustion syndrome.

He phoned Helen Anderson. When she came on the line, he said, "This is your friendly family physician and I'm going to ask you a silly question. Please don't laugh at me, for maybe it's important."

"Ask away. You know I wouldn't laugh at you."

"All right, then. When DDT was still available, before it was banned, did you use it in your garden?"

"Sure I did," she said. "I think most gardeners did. I used it for years and years, and I tell you I miss it. This new stuff, the bugs positively like it. They lap it up and settle down to wait for more. It doesn't even faze them. Herb used to fuss at me for using DDT. He said he didn't want his vegetables salted with chemicals."

"And Herb? Herb never works in the garden, does he?"

"Doc, you know damn well he doesn't. He makes fun of me and my gardening. You have heard him do it."

"But he eats stuff from the garden?" Benton asked.

"Are you kidding? Of course he does."

"Fine," he said. "Thank you for not laughing."

"Doc, what is going on? Has this got something to do with Herb—with the way he feels?"

"Maybe. I don't know yet. Maybe I'll never know. I'm just scrabbling around."

"All right," she said. "I won't ask. When you know, you'll tell me?"

"You can count on that."

He made several other phone calls to people who had gardens and to those who didn't. The two exceptions said they had never used DDT because they didn't want to mess around with it. It was too much work, they said. No, they said, their gardens didn't do as well without it and through the summer they had always bought some garden stuff from others and, like most people, had always used a fair amount of canned goods.

All of them wanted to know why the doctor asked, and some of them laughed at him; but that was all right, he thought, it didn't mean a thing. Everyone knew that old Doc had some strange ideas, like the time when he had raised so much hell about the water from the old municipal well that a new one had to be drilled, or the time of his strict insistence, as the town's health officer, that all garbage cans must be covered. Old Doc, everyone agreed, was a fuddy-duddy; but they loved the man and went along with his craziness.

He hung up the phone after his last call and stared at the pad on which he had made notes as he made the calls.

This could be it, he thought; enzymes and DDT. Was it possible that a coenzyme, by forming a bond with a molecule of DDT, had become a super-catalyst? And now that DDT was no longer available, the super-catalytic action was no longer possible. That, he told himself, could account for the symptoms of the exhaustion syndrome.

Take coenzyme A, the one so intimately tied up with two bio-chemical cycles—the fatty-acid cycle, for example, which oper-ates to oxidize lipids. Deprived of the super-catalyst on which the people had come to depend, fewer lipids would be oxidized and more would be stored as fat. Thus, an increasing incidence of obesity. With fewer lipids being broken down, the body would have to depend almost totally on carbohydrates for energy. Thus, the need for between-meal snacks.

Carbohydrates are transformed into useful body energy by means of the citric-acid cycle and the glycolysis process. The citric-acid cycle also involved coenzyme A, while the glycolysis process did not. if the two processes should become irregular, a seesawing effect, where one effect took over when the other fal-tered, and vice versa, could have far-reaching consequences. The blood sugar level would become erratic, a great deal produced at one time, very little at another. Lactic acid production would rise when the citric-acid cycle slowed down, since one of the func-tions of the cycle was to break down lactic acid. One result of a rise in lactic acid would be sore and aching muscles. And, in addition to the variation in blood sugar levels, the production of insulin also would be erratic. As a result of both conditions, there would be times when the brain would starve for lack of glucose in the blood. The symptoms would vary from fainting spells, con-vulsions, and shock to grogginess, irritability, and bleary vision.

It fit! he realized. It all fit, perhaps too perfectly.

He felt a moment of panic and distrust. He was going at it wrong, he knew. He was working with deduction. There should be extensive laboratory testing. But he was not qualified for labo-ratory work of the caliber required. He was going on a hunch alone, with no real evidence. His conclusions were unscientific and medically unacceptable. But the pattern was there, all logi-cally laid out.

It was logical, he told himself, not only physiologically, but in other ways as well. It made sense evolutionally. Under the pressure of modern living, man was burning up more energy than he ever had before. Perhaps it was possible he had outrun the biochemical functioning of his body. Under such a circumstance, the body, as an evolutionary life system, would use anything available to permit it to function more efficiently. If DDT were something that would help it to do a better job, if DDT made the enzymes or even one enzyme into a super-catalyst that would do a better job, the body unhesitantly would latch onto DDT.

But now that the DDT was gone, the human body had gone back to where it was before. Among those people to whom DDT had not been available, the hill people for example, the old non-DDT system was still functioning, perhaps not as efficiently as if DDT had been available, but at least not disturbed by having become a new system which had operated successfully for a time but now was lost. Those whose bodies had become accustomed to the DDT system now were suffering a reaction—the old non-DDT system was sluggish in recovering, if it ever could recover, its old efficiency.

Someone other than himself, he knew, should look into the situation. But to look into it would take staff and money. Perhaps it was time that he got in touch with Abbott, not waiting for Abbott to get back to him. Then he realized he did not know how to get in touch with Abbott. The writer had left no address or phone number, probably because he had expected to be traveling and for a time would have no permanent base of operation.

The best approach, Benton decided, was to phone Abbott's publisher. Someone at the publishing house undoubtedly would know how to go about reaching him. But it was Saturday and publishing houses, he suspected, would be closed. He would do it the first thing Monday morning, recognizing even as he thought, that his urgency was motivated by his wish to shift the problem of the exhaustion syndrome off his back. He had done the thinking and had gone as far as he could go; now it was time for someone other than himself to take over.

Maybe research would prove that his deductions were wrong. Right or wrong, however, some effort, he was convinced, should be made to find the truth.

He phoned first thing Monday morning.

He identified himself and said, "I was hoping someone on your staff could tell me how to get in touch with Robert Abbott. He came to see me several months ago and it's rather important that I speak with him."

The woman who had answered hesitated for a moment; when she spoke, she sounded slightly flustered. "Just a moment, sir," she said.

A man came on the line. "You were asking about Abbott."

"Yes. It's important that I reach him."

"Doctor," the man asked, "don't you ever see a paper?"

"I'm ordinarily too busy," said Benton. "I simply glance at headlines. At times not even that."

"Then you don't know that Abbott's dead."

"Dead!"

"Yes, a couple of weeks ago. A highway crash somewhere in Colorado."

Benton said nothing.

"It was a shock to all of us," said the man in New York. "You say you knew him."

"I didn't really know him. He visited me a few months ago. We talked an hour or so. I assume you know what he was working on."

"No, we don't. We've often wondered. We knew he was onto something, but he was closemouthed about it. You may know a great deal more than we do."

"Not a great deal," Benton said. "Thank you very much. I hope I did not disturb you."

"Not at all. Thanks for calling. I'm sorry I had such bad news for you."

Benton hung up and stared blankly at the office wall, not seeing the fly-specked diploma that had hung there so long. What do I do now? he asked himself. Just what in hell do I do now?

6

The first hard frost had come the night before and there was a sharp chill in the air the day Lem Jackson came into the office. Jackson was one of the hill people, a tall, gangling man who appeared to be forty years or so of age. Benton knew who he was, but could not recall that he had ever been a patient.

Jackson sat down in a chair opposite the desk and dropped his shapeless, battered hat upon the carpeting.

"Maybe, Doc," he said, "I've done wrong in coming and taking up your time. But I feel all dragged out. I ain't worth a hoot. I am not myself. Seems like I'm tired all the time, and my muscles are sore. Most days I'm so ornery and feel so mean that I'm ashamed of myself, the way I treat the wife and kids."

"How about your appetite?" Benton asked. "You been eating well?"

"All the time. Can't seem to get filled up. I'm hungry all the time."

There it went, Benton thought—all the carefully worked out deductions, the elaborately constructed theory of the exhaustion syndrome. For Jackson was a hill man, and under Benton's theory the people of the hills had to be immune.

"What the trouble, Doc?" Jackson asked. "Did I say something I shouldn't?"

Benton shook himself mentally. "Not at all. I was just wondering. What have you been doing, Lem?"

"To tell the truth," said Jackson, "not much of anything. A little farming, that's all. An odd job now and then. I feel so beat out I'm not up to a day of honest work. I guess I'd have to say I don't do much of nothing."

Then he went on, "Some while ago I had a good job down in West Virginia, but I lost the job. If I could've stayed on, I'd be sitting pretty now. Short hours, work not too hard, and the pay was good. But they up and fired me. The foreman had it in for me. I tell you, Doc, there simply ain't no justice. I was as good on the job as any of the other men."

"What kind of work?" Benton asked, not really caring what kind of job it was, but just making conversation.

"Well, I suppose that even if I hadn't been fired the job wouldn't have lasted. They closed down after I left. It was a small chemical plant. They were making DDT, and I hear they banned the stuff."

Benton felt himself go limp as relief flowed through him. His theory still stood up, he thought triumphantly. Lem Jackson was the exception to the rule his theory had set up that helped to cinch that theory. But even as he felt elated at this evidence that his deductions had been right, he told himself that his reaction was wrong. He should have been glad, it seemed to him, when he first had thought Jackson's symptoms shot his theory down—for, come to think of it, this business of DDT and the human body was a ghastly thing. But, in a perverse way, he had become fond of his theory. After all the work and thought he had put into it, no one, not even the most humane person in the world, would have wanted to be proved wrong.

"Lem," he said, "I'm sorry, but there's not a thing I can do for you. Not yet. There are others like you. Perhaps there are a lot of others like you. It's a condition that has just come to be noticed and there is work being done on it. In time, there may be a cure. I am sorry I have to be this honest with you, but I think you're the kind of man who would want that kind of honesty."

"You mean," Jackson said, "that I'm going to die?"

"No, I don't mean that. I mean I can't make you feel any better. You probably won't get any worse. There'll be a time, I'm sure, when there'll be drugs or medicine."

And all that would be needed, he told himself rather bitterly, was a pill or a capsule with a requisite dosage of DDT incorporated with carrier ingredients.

Jackson picked up his battered hat and got slowly to his feet. "Doc, all the people in the hills say you're a square shooter. 'He don't feed you no crap,' they told me. 'He is a doctor it's safe to go to.' You say probably I won't get any worse."

"Probably not," said Benton.

"And maybe someday there'll be a medicine that'll do some good."

"I am hopeful."

Watching Jackson leave, he wondered why he had told him what he had. Why the brutal honesty? Why the giving of some hope? "There is work being done on it," he had said; but that had been a lie. Or had it? There was one person working on it and that one person, he grimly told himself, had better buckle down to business.

That evening he drafted a careful letter, setting forth in precise detail what he suspected. Then, as he found the time, working in the evening after office hours were over, he typed the letters and mailed them out. Then he sat back and waited.

The first reply came, in two weeks' time, from *JAMA*. His letter, it said, could not be considered for publication since it lacked research evidence. *JAMA* was kind enough, but final. It did not even suggest he institute further research. But that was only fair, he admitted to himself, since there had been no research to start with.

The second reply, from the National Institutes of Health, was barely civil in its officialese.

The third, from the Association for Biochemical Research, was curt.

On a Saturday afternoon, when the last patient had left, he sat at his desk with the three letters spread out before him. It had been unrealistic, he admitted, to think that any one of the three would have paid attention to his letter. After all, who was he? An unknown family physician in a town that was equally unknown, advancing a theory unsupported by any kind of research, relying only on observation and deduction. The reactions to what he had written could have been expected. Yet there was no question in his mind that he should have written the letters. If no more than a gesture, it was something that had needed to be done.

So now what did he do? Work through the medical association, starting with the county, going to the state? He knew that it was useless. Smith, he was certain, might give him support; but the others would laugh him off the floor. And even if this were not so, it would take years before there was any action.

A chemical company, perhaps. There would be millions of dollars' worth of business for a DDT capsule once what he now knew became general knowledge. But a chemical company, knowing the hassle of getting approval from the Food and Drug Administration, might shy away from it. Before a chemical company would even touch it, there would have to be years of laboratory work to provide supporting evidence to place before the FDA. On an idea so "far-out," he knew, no drug or chemical firm would put up the money that was necessary.

So he was licked. He had been licked before he even started. If Abbott had not died, there might have been an even chance. Abbott, writing about the syndrome, would have found a publisher, for he would have produced the kind of book publishers dream about—sensational, controversial, attention-grabbing. Published, the book would have created enough furor that someone would have worked on the theory, if for no other reason than to prove Abbott wrong.

But there was no use thinking about it. Abbott would not write the book. No one would write it. So this was the end of it, he thought. All the years he had left, he would carry the knowledge that he had found a truth the world would not accept.

The world! he thought. To hell with the world! The world was not his concern. His concern was for the people of this community, for Lem and Ted, for Burt and Herb, and for all the others. Maybe he couldn't help the world, but there might be a way, by God, he could help his people!

7

Lem Jackson lived on Coonskin Ridge, and Benton had to stop a couple of times to ask his way. But he finally found the farm, with its tilted acres and the little, falling-down house crouched against the wind that whipped across the ridges.

When he knocked, Jackson let him in.

"Come and sit by the fire. It's a nippy day and a fire feels good. Mary, how about pouring Doc a cup of coffee. What brings you out here, Doc?"

"A small matter of business," Benton said. "I thought maybe you'd be willing to do a job for me."

"If I can," Jackson answered. "If I'm up to it. I told you, remember, I'm not good for much."

"You have a truck outside. This would be a hauling job."

"I can manage a hauling job."

Mrs. Jackson brought the cup of coffee. She was a small, wispy woman with hair straggling down across her face, wearing a bedraggled dress. From a far corner of the room, faces of children, quiet as mice, stared intently out.

"Thank you, Mrs. Jackson," said Benton. "This will go good after the long drive out."

"I have a bottle of brandy with some left in it," said Jackson, "if you would like a splash in that there coffee."

"That would be splendid, if there's enough for both of us. I never drink good liquor by myself."

"There's plenty," said Jackson. "I always keep a little in the house."

Mrs. Jackson said, "Lem told me you would let him know if medicine ever came along that would do him good. I hope that's why you're here."

"Well, I'm not absolutely sure," Benton said, "but that's what I have in mind."

Jackson came back with the brandy and a cup of coffee for himself. He poured generous splashes and set the bottle on the floor.

"Now about this hauling job . . ." he said.

"When you were in to see me, you said you worked at a plant down in West Virginia, making DDT."

"That's right," said Jackson. "They fired me off the job, but the plant was closed not long after."

"It's abandoned now?"

"I suppose so. It was just a little plant. It only made DDT. No reason to keep it open."

"Would you be willing to drive down there and try to get into the plant?" Benton asked.

"Shouldn't be no trouble. They might have fenced it in, but there shouldn't be no guards. There's nothing there to guard. Probably just sitting empty there. I could get through a fence. Doc, what are you getting at?"

"I need some DDT."

Jackson shook his head. "There mightn't be any left. They might've destroyed any they had left."

"DDT would be nice to have," said Benton, "but I'd settle for some dirt that had DDT mixed in it. Would there be that kind of dirt?"

"Sure there'd be! I know a dozen places where I could find that kind of dirt. Is it dirt you want? I could bring back a truck-load. Even have a pal who would help—owes me a favor. Would a truckload be enough?"

"Plenty," Benton said. "I take it you will do it. There might be some danger."

"I don't think so," Jackson replied. "It's sort of isolated. No one nearby. If I picked the right time of day, there'd be no one to see me. But what do you want the dirt *for*, Doc? The damn stuff's poisonous."

"It also might be the drug I was telling you about. The drug that we don't have."

"You're spoofing me."

"No, I'm not."

"Well, I'll be damned!" said Jackson.

"You'll do it, then?"

"I'll start at sunup."

8

Late Monday afternoon, Nurse Amy stuck her head in the office door. "Lem Jackson's here to see you," she said. "He has a truck heaped full of dirt parked out in front."

"Fine. Please show him in."

Jackson was grinning when he came in. "I got the dirt," he said, "and better than that, I found three bags of DDT, tucked away in an old shed where someone had forgot them. Where do you want that dirt, Doc?"

"We'll put the bags of DDT down in the basement," said Benton. "Dump the dirt over in the northwest corner of my parking lot. And I wonder if you'd be willing to do something else for me?"

"Anything at all," said Jackson. "You just name it, Doc."

"Tomorrow I'd like you to come back and build a tight board fence around the dirt so no one can get at it. Then down in the basement I want a box built, a sort of sandbox, like the sandboxes kids play in."

Jackson scratched his head. "You sure do want the damnedest things. Maybe someday you'll tell me what it's all about."

"I'll tell you now," said Benton. "Old Doc's Dirt Box—that's the whole idea. After you get that box built, we'll fill it with some of the dirt you hauled and we'll seed it with a little extra DDT. Then I want you to sit down alongside that box and play in the dirt, just like a kid would play in sand. Make a dirt castle, build dirt roads, dig dirt wells—things like that, you know. You need DDT. Don't ask me to explain. Just do like I tell you."

Jackson grinned lopsidedly. "I'd feel like a goddamn fool," he said.

"Look," said Benton, "if I knew how much was safe, I'd put that DDT in capsules and you could swallow them. But I don't, and if I guessed wrong I could kill you off. But I do know that people like Helen Anderson, who works in a garden where there's still some DDT, are healthy as a hog—while Helen's husband, Herb, who won't dirty his hands in the garden, feels just the same way you do. All beat out, good for nothing, tired."

"Well," Jackson said reluctantly, "if I could do what you say by myself. If there was no one to see me . . ."

"I promise you no one will see you. I won't tell a soul."

Watching Jackson's retreating back, Benton stood for a time trying to figure out how he would convince Herb and Ted and Burt and all the others of them.

It might be a chore, he knew; but he would get it done. He would have them all down there in the basement, playing at that dirt box like a bunch of kids. After all, he was good old Doc and his people trusted him.

CLIFFORD D. SIMAK, during his fifty-five-year career, produced some of the most iconic science fiction stories ever written. Born in 1904 on a farm in southwestern Wisconsin, Simak got a job at a small-town newspaper in 1929 and eventually became news editor of the *Minneapolis Star-Tribune*, writing fiction in his spare time.

Simak was best known for the book *City*, a reaction to the horrors of World War II, and for his novel *Way Station*. In 1953 *City* was awarded the International Fantasy Award, and in following years, Simak won three Hugo Awards and a Nebula Award. In 1977 he became the third Grand Master of the Science Fiction and Fantasy Writers of America, and before his death in 1988, he was named one of three inaugural winners of the Horror Writers Association's Bram Stoker Award for Lifetime Achievement.

DAVID W. WIXON was a close friend of Clifford D. Simak's. As Simak's health declined, Wixon, already familiar with science fiction publishing, began more and more to handle such things as his friend's business correspondence and contract matters. Named literary executor of the estate after Simak's death, Wixon began a long-term project to secure the rights to all of Simak's stories and find a way to make them available to readers who, given the fifty-five-year span of Simak's writing career, might never have gotten the chance to enjoy all of his short fiction. Along the way, Wixon also read the author's surviving journals and rejected manuscripts, which made him uniquely able to provide Simak's readers with interesting and thought-provoking commentary that sheds new light on the work and thought of a great writer.

THE COMPLETE SHORT FICTION OF CLIFFORD D. SIMAK

FROM OPEN ROAD MEDIA

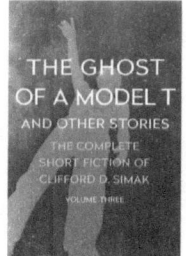

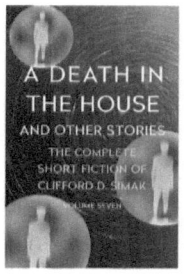

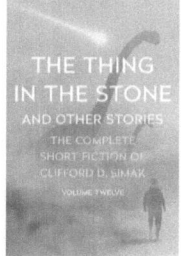

OPEN ROAD
INTEGRATED MEDIA

O P E N ROAD

INTEGRATED MEDIA

Find a full list of our authors and titles at www.openroadmedia.com

FOLLOW US
@OpenRoadMedia